Let Sleeping Secrets Lie

By

Geoff Stimson

To Bella

from

Geoff SC

ISBN: 9798861887083

Cover Illustration: Thabo Skhosana

PAT DEVEREAUX
PUBLISHING WORKS
patdevereaux@mac.com

For Kathy

CONTENTS

*I would like to thank **Kathy Stimson** for making good suggestions and just putting up with me generally, **Pam Kleinot** for persuading me to get it printed, **Pat Devereaux** for all her skill and patience making it happen, **Thabo Skhosana** for his inspired cover design, **the staff at the Family Records Office** for their help during my research into my own family tree that gave me the idea to write this in the first place, and **you** for reading it.*

CHAPTER 1

Secrets of the Big File

Clara knew just where to look. She had seen the battered old box file many times in Grandma's wardrobe when she and her cousin Sam used to come up here to the remote Scottish cottage on holiday as children for two glorious weeks every summer.

Sam's parents, Uncle Bernard and Aunt Alice, would bring them up to the wonderful Black Isle in the Highlands by train on the first Saturday morning, stay the weekend and then leave them with Grandma at her remote hillside cottage. Two weeks later, Clara's parents, Philip and Meg, arrived to collect them, stay the weekend in their turn and then head back south.

In between Grandma would lead the two of them around the Highland hills on three- and four-hour marches to see the ancient graves, the castles and battlefields, the ruined cottages and the ice-cold springs. And every one would have a story that Grandma would tell them as they rode on the buses or walked or sat outside the old cottage eating suppers of wonderful meat stew and oat or potato cakes that filled the night with delicious aromas.

Clara and Sam sat on the grass at her feet while the old lady weaved spells of magic so that the warriors and the country folk, the parsons and the fairies seemed to come alive again in the dusk – legends mixed with fact until they became indistinguishable.The wonderful, mystical names: *The Urquharts Of Cromarty, Stien Bheag o' Tarbat, The Gudewife Of Minitarf, Babble Hannah, The One-Eyed Stepmother, The Spectre Ships –* Grandma knew them all and told endless tales to her two unblinking listeners. Sam, even though nearly two years older than Clara, was just as susceptible and many nights the two cowered beneath their blankets in the narrow bedroom they shared beneath the eaves, giggling but unable to sleep for terror, expecting at any moment that The Green Lady would come and carry them off to be eaten by her children, leaving goblins in their place. When they were younger, they generally ended up in the same bed for extra security. Later, when they were bigger children of 8 and 10 and thought this was not somehow right, they would reach out and hold hands across the darkness for comfort.

But those were charmed summers and Clara grew to love the rolling countryside almost as much as Jane herself.

All that was a long time ago. Now Clara was alone in the creaking old cottage, on the hill just outside the village as the wind whistled around her in the dark night outside.

She was there because Grandma, after a lifetime of striding about the countryside and then 10 years of increasingly bedridden frailty, had finally died. And because Uncle Bernard – who would normally have handled such affairs on behalf of the family – was out of the country with Aunt Alice on a cruise, Clara had come north to take charge.

She could not actually remember ever hearing Grandma say the words, but it was well known in the family that Grandma's Big File was not to be opened until the old lady had died, and when it was opened, it would "take care of everything".

So now Clara, who had flown up that day, was sitting on Grandma's bed with the Big File on her knees.

She looked down at the old grey cardboard box, then stopped and realised where she was. This is the room where Grandma lay placidly for so long, and where the frail, old lady finally died. Here in this bed. Here, where she and Sam had sometimes brought her breakfast as a treat and sat planning the day's outing all those long years ago.

She looked around the room with its simple furniture. The large old bed with a plain wooden headboard, the upright walnut wardrobe in the corner, the dressing table with four drawers and a tilting mirror, the single padded chair – that was it. All Grandma's trinkets, many bought for her as presents by grateful grandchildren, lay where she had arranged them and Muriel, the housekeeper and nurse and companion, had dusted them for so long.

When Clara had opened the wardrobe door, a stench of mothballs mingled with Grandma's favoured lavender perfume wafted out at her. There was Grandma's row of cotton summer dresses and thicker winter skirts and jumpers. There on top were her hats – the straw summer bonnet, the woollen winter "tea cosy" as she called it. There in the bottom were her boots and shoes, simple and stout for walking. And there at the back was the Big File. Clara reached in and picked it up, carrying it back to the bed, where she sat, put it down on her knees and looked at it.

It was just a simple cardboard box file, slightly larger than A4, about three inches deep with a hinged top lid held in place by a brass clasp. Clara pushed back the clasp and opened the top. It was about three-quarters full of neatly-filed papers.

On the top of the papers was an unfolded letter that began: "Dearest Bernard…"

Clara closed the lid. Now what? She could hardly read someone else's mail, could she? A mother's final message to her son. But Bernard would not be here until Thursday at the earliest and the funeral was supposed to be on Friday. What if she took out the letter and just looked at what was underneath it? But that was no good. Obviously, the letter was Grandma's instructions to Bernard, the person she was expecting to open it. Those instructions needed to be followed. There was only one thing for it. She could always pretend later that she had not read it if it were too embarrassing.

Clara took a deep breath, opened the lid, took out the two-page letter and read the bold, rather shaky, but clear handwriting she recognised as Grandma's. It was dated November 1995 - some five years ago.

3

"*Dearest Bernard,*

I write this now as I begin to feel my mind and my body wasting away. Muriel tells me that you came to visit me last week and I am confounded if I remember a thing about it. She may just as well have said that Robert the Bruce brought a bunch of Martians in for tea for aught that I recall. I can scarcely tell you how it pains me that I missed such a pleasure as to see your face again, and I trust that I was in no way discourteous while you were here. I have my lucid moments such as I am enjoying now, but then long blanks for weeks together about which I recall little or nothing. Ah, well, at least I know that Muriel will not allow any harm to befall me during my hibernations. Enough of feeble lamentation. My only real grief is that I can no longer get out on the hills and feel the Black Isle wind howling up through my hair from the Moray Firth. But I still remember the sensation exactly and can lie abed and taste it all again at my leisure. What an Eden!

But to business. You and I both know the trials and traumas of the past 50 years and it is to your eternal credit that this family is in such fine shape as it is today. I know that I played a part in it, but the fortitude and perseverance and unending spirit that guided us through were yours and yours alone. Let others sleep easy while we bear the knowledge. I thank you from the bottom of my poor frail heart for your tireless endeavours, always thinking of others before yourself. Since I lost my dear, darling Thomas so many, many lonely nights ago, you have been my rock and my guide. Bless you, for that.

Now, you are reading this because I am at peace after so long (I wonder what the date is as you read? Strange quirk of time, this, don't you think? Did I last until 96 or 97 or even into the new century? I scarce think so, I feel so weak sometimes). In this file, as I always promised, are the necessary insurance papers to cover my funeral expenses together with details of the burial plot and my few last wishes, which I know you will honour. You will also find my will, such as it is. I leave everything to you in the absence of poor, foolish Susan. That girl broke my heart. What I would have given to see her again. But...

I want you to take care of the children. I still think of Philip as a child in spite of it all. I know that you will do what is best. You always did, dear Bernard.

I grow too weary to write anymore and wish nothing else but to sleep. I commend my body to the grave, my spirit to the Lord and my love, all my love, to you, Bernard. May God grant you the peace and happiness you so richly deserve, and may our secrets stay safely hidden forever.

Remember me to your darling, madcap Alice. Goodbye, Bernard, truly the most wonderful son a mother ever had,

Your Mother"

Clara sat stunned and read it over again. "... the trials and traumas of the past 50 years ... it is to your eternal credit that this family is in such fine shape as it is today ... Let others sleep easy while we bear the knowledge ... may our secrets stay safely hidden forever..."

What did it all mean? And why was everything left to Bernard and not shared between Grandma's two sons, Bernard and Philip? Did she really think that Clara's father Philip was such a child that he could not be trusted with money?

Clara shook her head slowly and turned back to the file. On top was an envelope with Bernard's name written on the front in Grandma's handwriting. It was not sealed, so Clara opened it. She pulled out three folded sheets, discoloured brown from age and many foldings. She carefully peeled open the first. It was a single long sheet with the crest of the Universal Scottish Amicable Society across the top. Underneath were details of an insurance policy taken out in 1947 to the value of £1,200 in the name of Jane Harvey, with details of payments and surrender value. The second was from the same company in 1927 and was to the value of £400. Clara turned to the third, mentally thinking that the funeral was already paid for as Grandma had always implied. It was dated 1920 and was from the Imperial Co-operative Mutual Society. This had a value of just £40. It was in the name of Jane Laker.

Odd, thought Clara. Grandma's maiden name was Jane Smeeton. She hadn't been married twice, had she? How old had she been when she married Thomas? Clara thought it was in her late twenties, but she remembered the wedding pictures and Grandma wore white, which meant a lot in those days. Surely she was not a widow.

Also in the envelope was a single sheet of paper, folded in half. This showed a sketch map of the local burial ground. On it was marked a plot at the top, with a signature next to it. Beside this was written in Grandma's hand: *"Dear Bernard, Our plot is on a slight incline, so if I am buried with my feet towards the sea, I will forever lie beside my darling Thomas and gaze at the Firth. Thank you, Mother."*

Clara turned back towards the file. Next came some photographs, most of which Clara had seen. Grandma as a girl and a young woman, pictures of her with Thomas on holiday and with the young Bernard and Susan, her daughter, who had run away from home to London as a teenager and was apparently never heard of again. Then some much later photos with Philip. Next, there was one that Clara had never seen. It was an old sepia print of a Victorian woman in a long black dress with ringlets tumbling down from beneath a straw hat, carrying a spray of three tulips. She was beautiful, with clear eyes and a lovely smile. She stood in a garden in bright sunshine with a row of bushes behind her. Clara turned the photo over and on the back was written in once-black, now brown ink at the top corner: "Rebecca Laker, Langton, May 1888".

Another Laker. Who on earth was she? Clara shook her head once again.

Next, she found an envelope marked: "Marriage and Birth Certificates" in Grandma's writing. It was empty.

Apart from that, there was the usual jumble of forms and papers and letters, many pictures of wild and rocky landscapes, details of school inoculations, passports, licences, mortgage papers and title deeds. And among them, all was an envelope printed with the words: "Last Will & Testament". Inside, apart from the customary flowery legalese was the simple sentence: "All my worldly goods I bequeath to my son Bernard to dispose of as he thinks best at the appropriate time."

Clara put everything carefully back in the file except for the letter to Bernard, which she read through once more, then lay it on top of the pile, closed the lid, pushed back the clasp and carefully replaced the file in the bottom of the wardrobe.

Outside, the wind was whistling and something screeched into the night. Clara shivered and went back down to the kitchen, pausing only to rummage in her bag and pull out a bottle of duty-free that she had picked up at the airport. She helped herself to a steaming plate piled with mincemeat in rich gravy, swede mashed with milk and cream, and an oatcake that Muriel had prepared and left quietly bubbling for her arrival. She poured herself a big glass of wine, sat at the kitchen table and attacked the food, wondering about Grandma's letter.

When she had finished and washed up, she went up to bed with another glass of wine, and as she lay awake gave no thought to the dark and the ghouls as she had feared she might. Instead, she went over and over in her mind what Grandma had written.

"Let others sleep easy while we bear the knowledge ... may our secrets stay safely hidden forever..."

When dawn began to break over the Mulbuie Ridge, Clara turned over and over in bed as her sleep was disturbed by vivid images of chasing Sam over the hills through thick clouds of fog. She looked around and Sam was gone, but a beautiful Victorian woman in ringlets and a straw hat was urging her to hide in a cottage. She found Sam inside and they spent the rest of the day roaming along the beach before having dinner with Grandma and the Victorian woman outside the cottage, Clara awoke with a smile, remembering those summers long past.

As soon as she was awake, she went straight to Grandma's Big File, read the letter to Bernard twice more, folded it in three in the same way as the rest of Grandma's papers were folded, took the insurance forms and the map of the churchyard out of the envelope with Bernard's name on it, put the letter inside in their place, licked and sealed it, put the forms and the map in her pocket, laid Bernard's letter in the envelope back on top of the pile in the Big File, closed the lid and put the file safely away in the wardrobe.

All sorted. And yet...

True, Grandma's story was now over. But this is not Grandma's story. This is Clara's story. And in Clara's story, the File had been opened and secrets that had been safely hidden, some for more than a century, had begun to emerge into the lives of those who had been peacefully unaware. Soon it would be impossible to know with certainty many of the truths that had until then been taken for granted. The solid earth itself was slowly beginning to move beneath Clara's feet and the backdrop to her world would soon start to change as she stared in disbelief. Murder, horror and deceit, along with mysteries and broken promises were all waiting to be discovered once more. Was this a good thing? Would anyone benefit from this new knowledge that was even now beginning to gather unseen just beyond the horizon like an impending sandstorm? That was no longer the issue. It was already too late to wonder or to ask it to stop. The door was now ajar. The box was open and it could never again be closed.

CHAPTER 2

George – The bell invites me

(August 1886)

George Harvey was twenty years old when he chanced upon Rebecca Laker and looked at the world around him for the first time. Until that August afternoon in Langton Market, he had always accepted his life and borne its troubles willingly, albeit with a vague sense of inevitable injustice. But in that moment when Rebecca and her friends approached a stall and Rebecca picked up a small bronze bell and shook it lightly, and George turned around at the noise, and saw her laughing in the bright sunshine, her dark hair falling in ringlets from under her straw bonnet – in that moment, George awoke.

In that simple instant, he understood the wrongs of the world, man's cruelty, the imprisonment of the spirit; he saw clearly his own station in life and what it meant, and he understood everyone he knew. He felt powerful, as though anything in the world were there for the taking. He refused to be bound by a set of unfair rules. He felt that there was a real point in a man holding aspirations, in daring to hope. He wanted to make those who needed his help happy. He knew that what he was doing was wrong.

And he wondered why he had never realised any of this before.

George was not a man of learning or even of especially great intelligence. He worked as a farm labourer in the vasty fields of Bedfordshire, playing off his puny might against the power of the earth and forcing it to yield up food. On Sundays, he went to Church and thanked the Lord that he mostly had bread enough to eat for him and his parents and brothers and sister. When decisions had to be made, which was rarely, he left them to his father. He enjoyed the satisfaction of being hardy enough to toil, of being one of the strongest men on the farm, even in the town and the surrounding villages. When he climbed into his bed at nights, he wore his weariness as a badge of pride for his achievements. He had done an honest day's work. He had lived a good life today. Not that he was vain, for he never bragged of his prowess. But, quietly, he was proud of his fortitude and endurance.

He knew what was expected of him, he was able to accomplish it, and his rewards were a full belly in this life and a promise of something better after he was dead. If he thought of heaven at all, it was a place like Langton with its fields and river and summer lanes, but with no work to be done, no freezing winters and no times of poverty and hunger. Beyond that, he had not known enough to wish.

But at that moment when he watched Rebecca laugh as she rang the tiny bell, he saw – without even enough understanding to explain it to himself – that just as he could move the soil in the fields, a man could move any obstacle, and that some men did so. And that some men did it for their own selfish ends and others did it so they could benefit the less well off.

Then, at the same second and as so often in such cases, George gave Rebecca all the credit not just for allowing him to see, but also for the visions themselves. It was far more than love, but it was certainly at first sight.

George continued watching Rebecca and followed her and her friends around the market from some distance away. He had simply never seen anyone more beautiful in his life. Her grace, her poise, her eyes and her smile. He felt that he had known and loved her for many long ages. He felt that they were meant to be together.

When it was finally time to go, he picked up his bundle, took a last, longing look at Rebecca and headed out of the market and onto the turnpike road towards London, feeling at once elated and disturbed. As the road began to come out of the town and sweep round to the right to head off southwards, George kept straight on between the rows of chestnut and oak trees down the twisting, shady lane that led to Stratton Farm, turned left at its outer hedges and walked around the back of a row of low cottages. He pushed open the back door of the first and went in.

Far behind him in the market, Rebecca's friends were still teasing her.

"He was looking only at you, Becky," laughed Molly.

"Why tis surely true. I saw it, too," agreed Mary.

"Oh, nonsense!" said Rebecca, slapping them both lightly on the arms and blushing shiny scarlet.

"I wonder who he was?" asked Mary.

"Some poor raving madman, I don't doubt," said Molly.

"Handsome, though, did you not think, Becky?" laughed Mary.

Rebecca brought the matter to a close.

"Come away, the both of you," she scolded. "We have a long road to walk before it grows dark and I am hungry already."

And they, too, left the market as the sun began to slip low over St Andrew's Church, and they walked along the riverbank, still laughing, and headed out over the fields to the south of Langton, as they spread out towards the village of Longford and beyond.

Rebecca hardly gave the handsome stranger another thought after those first five or six nights, and on her next visit to the market – which happened to be the very next weekend, even though it meant working hard to persuade her friends to go again so soon, saying that she needed to buy some buttons for a frock she was planning to sew – she barely looked out for him at all.

George, meanwhile, grew even more brooding than usual on that first night he returned from the market.

He sat in his usual place at the tea table and said nothing while his mother cut and handed around thick slices of bread to Dad, Joseph, Albert and Alice. Grandma was still too ill to come down.

"May the Lord bless us for what we receive of His bounty," said Dad and began spreading his bread with a think scrape of butter. He took a beetroot from the jar on the table, spearing it with his fork, and began cutting it in pieces.

"So how did the threshing go today, George?" he asked through a mouthful of bread and beetroot. "Have you got much left for Monday?"

"No, we've done it."

"What, all of it?"

"Yes."

"Hey!" shouted Dad suddenly, flicking out his arm and catching young Albert a clip around the ear that made him drop the big carving knife he was playing with. "You leave that be, you little devil!"

"Don't hurt him, Dad."

"He'll have his finger off with that, the young fool."

Albert began to cry and his mother hurried round the table to comfort him.

George sat in front of his untouched bread for a long time.

"What's the matter, George," said his mother at last. "Don't you want your tea?"

"What? Oh, no, Mum. I'm not that hungry. I had a big dinner. Here let Albert and Joe have it. I'm just going to take the dogs out round the top fields."

He got up, but the three shaggy black mongrels had heard his words and were already leaping around his throat. It was all he could do to get out of the back door without them knocking anything over.

When the four came back into the cottage, it was after bedtime and the dogs could barely walk from exhaustion. They *had* been round the top fields, twice in fact, but they had also spent a long time walking round and round the market place. George filled their water bowls, went up to bed, undressed and climbed in beside Joseph, who grunted and rolled over. Across the room, Albert and

Alice were breathing quietly in the other bed. It was a little after dawn when he finally closed his eyes and slept.

In the fields, George was always rather a loner, but now he hardly spoke to anyone, and began contriving jobs for himself that took him away into the outer reaches of the farm, labouring alone, still doing the work of three men, and returning wearily to the kitchen table and his early bed.

"I don't know whatever's up with George," his mother said to his father when they went to bed. "He shouldn't be like this. A young man and moping. I hope he isn't fevered."

"Now don't go on fretting so," replied his father. "There's nothing the matter with him as a good shaking wouldn't put right. And I'll give it to him an all if he don't buck hisself up."

"Oh, don't, Dad. Don't start on him."

She blew out the candle and turned over.

Perhaps he'll be better once the wedding's over and he's married to Marjory and settled, she thought, and tried to go to sleep.

CHAPTER 3

1-2-3, 1-2-3, 1-2-3, 10

Two days before she opened Grandma's Big File, Clara Harvey was sitting in her dressing gown at the kitchen table of her parents' house in Langton, amid the market-gardening flatness of Bedfordshire. She was enjoying both a plateful of scrambled egg on toast and generally being looked after for a week's mid-winter break from the bustle of London, where she lived and worked. Then the phone rang. She put down her newspaper.

"It's OK. I'll go."

She need not have worried about being beaten to it. Her mother Meg was out in the garden tidying some bushes and had not even heard the ring. Her father Philip was upstairs in the bath and generally avoided answering the phone anyway. There was no one else in the house.

Clara was 5 feet 11 and thought it was a little too tall. She had strong, wavy, shoulder-length dark brown hair that she wished was rather straighter and probably blonder. She had a figure that all her girlfriends envied but from which she always intended to ditch a stone to make it more svelte; high cheekbones that she was very fond of; brown eyes; a dazzling smile; good skin for a 29-year-old (she thought, as long as she did enough work on it); and a nose that she was convinced was too long. She tended to be hard on herself over her appearance, although two or three times a year she looked in the mirror as she was about to go out and thought: "Wow! Look at you. You got it right for once."

"Hello, Langton 637912, Clara speaking," she told the phone.

A few minutes later, Clara went out to the garden to tell her mother and by the time they got back to the kitchen, Philip was already sitting at the table, staring straight in front of him. Clara went and stood behind him and put her arms around his neck.

"Oh, Dad. It's Grandma. It's happened. She died this morning. Muriel rang while you were in the bath."

There was a pause. Philip generally thought before he spoke. Philip thought: "1-2-3, 1-2-3, 1-2-3, 10," as he always did, often silently tapping his leg so that he would not have to think the numbers, but could instead think his thoughts while he tapped. One tap for each of the ones and another for the 10. Four slow taps. Time to think. It was his little secret, and gave him time to make sure that he did not do or say anything that would hurt or offend. He had done that before and did not want to bear any more guilt. It was a habit deep within him.

Philip was 52, a couple of inches short of six foot, slightly stooping these days, with hair that had long since failed to cover his temples and was now losing the fight to be as black as it used to be. His eyes were piercing blue and always used to be smiling, but lately they looked more startled and suspicious. He still had his calm days when he was almost his old self if a little quieter and slower, but it was the other hours and days that concerned Meg and she tried everything she knew to keep him placid and "out of trouble".

As Philip took in this news, he counted. 1-2-3, 1-2-3, 1-2-3, 10. And while he counted, he thought: "It's been coming a long time after all. She was over a hundred and had been bedridden for years. She was not suffering at all. She's just slipped away. Meg and Clara won't be too devastated. They'll be most unhappy for me. I must appear upset and dignified, but calm and not distraught."

"Poor Mum," said Philip as he sat with his hands in his lap and Clara around his neck and stared straight ahead with glassy eyes.

"I always thought she'd die on a Friday. Not a Monday. Monday's not her sort of day really. Not after all she's been through."

That's about right, thought Philip. Calm and dignified.

Meg looked at Clara and then at Philip. "That's true enough, darling," Meg told him. "Now I'll put your eggs on. You must be hungry."

After breakfast Meg went off to the shops, thinking that they could have salmon for dinner. Philip liked that. Meg worried about Philip. There was no doubting that sometimes he said things and did things that were, well, odd. He had not always been like it. In his younger days he had been very witty and charming and they made each other laugh all the time. She could not say exactly when the change happened, but felt that he had a sadness deep inside him that put him under a pressure that he could not cope with. He was not senile by any means and could still be sharp when he needed to be. But always there was the shadow. She had tried speaking to him about it, but it was no use, he just talked about something else. Perhaps he did not even really know what it was himself any more.

Meg was in her early fifties and quite small and lean. Her hair was now greying with dark streaks and she still had the same quick mind although she seemed to have less chance to use it these days somehow.

Meg's goal in life now was just to get up in the morning, organise three meals for her and Philip, and go to bed. She did not understand why or how and there was no one who could or would tell her, but she knew that Philip was somehow battered and needed her help. If everyone brought happiness to those around them, she reasoned, there would be less trouble. Especially these days when Philip seemed... well... Meg left it there where it was still comfortable. She would put a bottle of Chablis in the fridge. Philip's favourite. And she would make a trifle for pudding. Clara always liked her trifles.

"You make great trifles, Mum," Clara would say.

What Clara actually did say was: "How will I ever lose my stone if you keep making me eat huge bowls of trifle, Mum?"

"Oh, you don't need to lose a stone. Would you like another helping?"

As the sun rose in a thin, pale, cold sky next morning, Philip's eyes were already open. He had hardly slept. He was worried about several of his projects at work and felt far from on top of at least three of them. This never used to happen. He was worried about Meg, who had a lot to do to manage the house and the garden, and he was constantly watching her for signs of the onset of fatal illnesses. He was worried about Clara. She had a good job, but she was still not settled with anyone. He and Meg had had high hopes of her old boyfriend William nearly five years ago, but nothing came of it. A nice boy. Philip was worried about young Sam, whose get-rich-quick schemes would surely one day bankrupt not only Sam, but his father Bernard as well. And now his own mother had died. So far away and so much to do to organise the funeral. If only Bernard were here. Bernard would handle it all and he would simply have to turn up. But Bernard was not due back in the country until Wednesday. He was on a cruise ship somewhere and there seemed little point in spoiling his holiday even if he could get off the ship while it was at sea. And it was not as if Bernard could do anything where he was, was it? No, he, Philip, would have to organise things. But he had so much on his plate.

Philip carried all his cares with him at all times as feelings. If he were worried about a report he had to write, he would feel the worry in his blood and his heart. It would make him breathe differently. It would be there when he went to sleep, and it would be there when he woke up, perhaps many times during the night, perhaps just once and for all. The feeling would be with him even before he realised what it signified, before the problem that caused the feeling came back to his consciousness.

And each emotion brought its own distinct feeling, so that if he were worried about his report and at the same time pleased that Clara was home for a while, the two would sit layered on top of each other, so that he could feel each separately when he thought about one or the other, but together they produced an amalgam that was something different, like a chord on a piano. And so he walked around with a medley of emotions playing inside him that gave him an aggregate feeling of happiness, equilibrium or fear as the case may be.

And underneath it all was the background wash of his permanent, unfathomable guilt.

It all meant that he had much to consider before speaking. Today, he had so many layers on his mind that he was close to being overwhelmed.

"Dad's taken all this very badly," Clara said to her mother in the kitchen a few hours later while Philip lay in his troubled bath.

"He'll be all right. He just has rather a lot on his mind. What with work and... well, more work. He seems to have so much to do."

"I've been thinking," said Clara slowly. "Uncle Bernard isn't back until Wednesday and someone needs to go up to Scotland and organise the funeral and things before then."

"Oh, yes. I don't suppose we can leave it all to Muriel. Can we..?"

"Perhaps we could, but we shouldn't really, should we? It ought to be family, didn't it?"

"I suppose so. But Philip is so busy. I could go with him, I suppose, couldn't I?"

"Yes... you could. Or... well, what if I went instead?"

"You? But you wouldn't know what to do, would you? There'd be undertakers and flowers and services and the wake and all sorts of things to arrange."

"I'm not a child, Mum. And I know where Grandma's Big File is – remember? Everything would be taken care of in her Big File, all the insurance and stuff, and Bernard would find everything sorted in there, but we were not to open it until after she died."

"Yes, but… Bernard really ought to be the one…"

"But he's in the middle of the Indian Ocean. He doesn't fly back until Wednesday, so he couldn't get to Scotland if he wanted to until Thursday. And what's the point in dragging him home from his holiday? I can open a file as well as he can. Look… If you and Dad pay for me to fly up to Inverness, I'll send a message to Muriel today, go tomorrow morning, arrange the funeral for Friday and you and Uncle Bernard and everyone can all come up for it on Thursday. You see, I've got it all planned in my head already."

"Oh, but you were going to be here and have a rest with us."

"But if I don't do it, who will? And few places are as restful as Grandma's Black Isle cottage."

"Well, I suppose…"

"Right, then. Who's going to tell Dad? I will if you like. Or… er… would it be better coming from you?"

"Tell me what?" asked Philip, appearing beside them at the kitchen door, holding his morning cup and saucer.

Clara took his arm and his cup and led him to the kitchen table.

"Sit down, Dad. You look tired. We'll get you some tea."

She settled him at the table and Meg began to pour. Clara looked at her mother then decided to go for it herself.

"You see," she said, "we've had an idea. Obviously with Uncle Bernard away, there's a lot falling onto you. And I wondered if you'd like me to help out as I'm free this week."

Philip looked at them both but said nothing, so Clara pushed on.

"I thought that I could fly up to Scotland tomorrow and sort everything out so that you and Mum and Uncle Bernard and Aunt Alice could just come up to the funeral on, say, Friday. Only I know how busy you are."

Philip thought: "1-2-3, 1-2-3, 1-2-3, 10."

Philip thought: "It would help a lot, but will they think that I'm being a bad son?"

Meg guessed his second worry.

"Grandma would have understood," she said.

"It makes sense while you're so busy," said Clara.

They waited.

Philip thought: "1-2-3, 1-2-3, 1-2-3, 10."

Philip thought: "Best seem practical and calm. Organise the details and then sort out the people."

"Well," he said. "We'd best find out about flights and things first, for whoever's going…"

"There's a British Airways flight from Gatwick direct to Inverness at 12.25 tomorrow," said Clara. "It gets there at 2.10 and costs £110 return."

"Heavens," laughed Meg. "Someone's been busy."

"I found it on the Internet this morning."

They waited.

Philip thought: "1-2-3, 1-2-3, 1-2-3, 10."

Philip thought: "Turn it around so that it looks positive for Clara – as though it is best for her."

Philip said: "Well I think that a few days in Scotland would be good for you, Clara. The air would be healthy. Why don't we let you go and we'll see you up there on Thursday or Friday or whenever. Of course, if you need any help, I'm only a phone call away…"

Clara gave him a hug.

"Dad, you're a sweetie," she said. "And you'll… er… pay for the flight..?"

"And we'll pay for the flight."

"Love you lots. Come on, Mum. You can help me pack while I book the flights and tell Muriel."

"You had this all planned, didn't you, minx?" said Meg as she hurried after her daughter.

Philip thought: "Good," and another set of feelings – relief tinged with guilt, blended with guilt at being relieved – were added to his orchestral mix.

When Clara had finished packing, it was time for a phone call.

"Sam, I'm sorry to have to break some bad news to you but I'm afraid you have to cancel all your plans for this weekend."

"That is bad news. Some of them are really spicy. What's all this about?"

"Sam, it's Grandma…"

"Oh that's OK then. That'll wait. You had me worried for a bit. You see I've just met this girl called…"

"Sam!" said Clara in the kind of voice that usually quiets small yappy dogs. It quieted Sam.

"Yes, Clara?"

"Sam, it's Grandma. I'm sorry to tell you that she died this morning. I'm flying up tomorrow to organise the funeral for Friday. Your Mum and Dad get back on Wednesday so you can come up with them on Thursday."

"Oooh, poor Grandma. Well that seems clear enough. But look…"

"Yes?"

"Well it really doesn't matter to Grandma now, does it? Couldn't we… sort of… push the funeral back until, say, Tuesday? Who's going to mind a few days? Only I've just met this girl called…"

"Sam, do you remember those wonderful holidays we had with Grandma? All the places she took us? All her stories? The walks? The glorious food?"

"Oh yes. Those were magical days, weren't they? Poor Grandma. But you see..."

"And, Sam, do you remember that time you annoyed me quite a lot? I can't even remember what you did now, but it made me really cross."

"I think I..."

"And do you remember what was hit – quite suddenly and violently I seem to remember – by Grandma's big old cast iron ladle a few days later when you weren't paying attention?"

"Ah, yes, I do remember that. I can still feel it when there's a vowel in the month."

"Well, Sam, I'd put money on a wager that Grandma's big old cast iron ladle is still there in her cottage. Wouldn't you think?"

"Well, I suppose it may be, but..."

"And, Sam, at some point you are going to go to the funeral and stay in Grandma's cottage. And I'd guess that there will be a moment during your stay when you won't be paying attention. Bound to be really, isn't there?"

"Well yes, there's every chance..."

"Sam, I think perhaps you are going to cancel your plans for the weekend, don't you?"

Sam sighed.

"Well how about if I bring someone with me?"

"Certainly. You can bring your Mum and Dad. This is a funeral, Sam, not a house party."

"Oh all right," he said grumpily.

"Cheer up, Sam. It means you get to see me again. It's been a while."

"I suppose. Well can we at least go for one of our walks along the beach?"

"Yes, we can. And have dinner in that place in Fortrose?"

"Definitely. And visit the standing stones we used to dance around?"

"And make up some more stories about the people who used to live there?"

"Oh yes. And play hide and seek in the garden? It'll be just like old times…"

"That's better, Sam. See you on Thursday."

"See you Thursday, Clara.

CHAPTER 4

Susan – City of dreams

(June 1946)

"**N**ow she," said Ron slowly, leaning forward over the table to get a better look past Charlie's shoulder, "is very, very lovely indeed."

"Which one?" asked Charlie, turning awkwardly around in his chair and scanning the dozen or so figures sitting at the coffee bar tables in the direction of Ron's gaze. "What, the blonde?"

Ron looked disgusted. He had indeed been looking at the blonde, but switched his affections immediately, as he often did, rather than be caught admiring the same woman as gawky, slow-witted Charlie. It really didn't matter and he could not be seen to have the same tastes as his companion.

"That, you see, Charles just shows the difference between you and I. The blonde is all lipstick and no class. She might leave dogs and small boys dribbling, but does nothing for the discerninger gentleman such as myself."

"Which one, then?" asked Charlie again, frowning and feeling the barb.

"Why the brunette in the white dress at the same table, of course. Elegant, beautiful and full of class."

Charlie looked once more and tried to see why the brunette should be a better class of woman to admire than the well-built blonde she was with. As far as he could see, the blonde was far more appealing. But Ron said the brunette had more class, and Charlie looked up to Ron. Charlie tried to make himself value the brunette more highly, in much the same way as he tried to like the jazz bands that Ron made him go along and listen to.

Ron leaned back and tipped his trilby forward over his eyes. He was 34 but seemed a little older. His birth certificate said that his name was Ronald Arthur Castle and that he was born in Gillingham, Kent, which would have surprised all of his acquaintances, who knew him as Ronaldo Castelli, a name he felt suited his persona rather better. His family, he let it be known, fled an undisclosed kind of persecution in Milan between the wars, and such was the hardship they endured that the only other member left alive was his aged and sick mother, for whom he cared without sharing accommodation, and who provided him with excuses to leave suddenly when situations became difficult or tiresome. No one had ever seen Mrs Castelli. Ron told them simply that it was: "Family." He would have had some difficulty in furnishing introductions in any case. His mother, it was true, was not in the best of health. In fact, she was so poorly that she was lying peacefully under six feet of Gillingham graveyard earth, where she had been these seven years. But Ron never let a little thing like death stand between him and a useful lie.

He would probably have looked like a typical East End spiv if he had just grown a thin moustache, cut his hair short, greased it back, and worn a sharp stripy suit. He was a little over medium height, with a slim waist and broad shoulders, giving the impression that he could look after himself. His hair was long for the time, long enough to show that it was wavy. It was also jet black and thick, as were his eyebrows over pale blue eyes. His complexion was on the healthy side of sallow, which just stopped him from looking gaunt and gave him an almost noble air with high cheekbones to go with his high forehead. His lips were full and his teeth perfect and white. His expression was intended to appear worldly, though it often came across as supercilious. The whole gave him the air of a dangerous, if somehow second division, Latin renegade, a semi-house-trained pirate, who would not have looked out of place in a big white shirt open to the waist and with huge, billowing sleeves, waving a small cutlass about.

Ron had left Gillingham as soon as he could get away and moved to London when he was 18 just before all the work dried up. He spent his time hanging around the docks, looking for an opportunity rather than for work like the others. He definitely had something about him and his newly-found origins and swarthy good looks picked him out from the crowd. He was quickly taken into the service of a small-time crook and would-be gangster called Mario, who liked him because they had so much in common. Mario's real name was Martin, but they never discussed their pasts. Mario first found Ron useful to fetch and carry, and then later on, when he grew to trust him, to send on those assignments in which there was a real risk of getting caught, a fact Mario knew perfectly well, but one which he was careful to keep from Ron. But somehow, with the luck of one who cannot even see the danger, Ron walked whistling right into it without knocking, took it unawares and was never caught, a fact that gradually grew his importance until, as a reward, he was allowed to manage certain aspects of the business on his own and largely for his own ends. Share options, as it were. The shiny wristwatch with the strap that looked like leather which he always wore, the powder-blue suit and the expensive shirt testified that business was going pretty well, thank you.

He looked at the watch now. One thirty. Now that he and Charlie had delivered their package safely onto the train, he had nothing to do today except meet Maude at eight, and if, meanwhile, the day threw something more interesting into his path, his mother could always be ill and his meeting with Maude delayed a day or two. Time to make a move.

"So, you like the blonde, eh, Charles?" he asked.

"Well… she's all right… the brunette's nicer, though… probably…" said Charlie uncertainly, suspecting a trap.

"Let's agree, Charles, that they are both prime examples of young femalehood, and as such should not be left unadmired and forlorn."

"Er... OK..." agreed Charlie, still waiting for the catch that would make him feel small.

"If beauty is in the eye of the beholder, Charles, then unseen beauty is no beauty at all," said Ron, quoting Mario faithfully as he often did. "Come, it is our duty as gallants to make the ladies beautiful again."

"Oh, yes, right," said Charlie, sensing that something was about to happen and emptying his cup hurriedly.

Across the coffee bar, all had not been sanguine with the objects of Ron and Charlie's evaluations.

"So now what, Susan?" asked the blonde for the fourth time, even more petulantly than the earlier three.

"I told you already," replied the brunette. "Something good will happen today. It just will. This is London. We're in London. We'll... we'll go for a walk... see some shops... look at the sights... I dunno. Something different at least. This is Lon-don, Annie, not Lang-ton."

She said the syllables slowly and reverently, almost religiously, in the capital's case.

"But what are we going to do?" repeated Annie, unconvinced.

"Look, aren't you enjoying just being in a city for a change? Look around you here. There are buildings and buses and people – hundreds of people – new people, different people. All we ever get at home is fields and vegetables and dull faces, and always the same fields and the same vegetables and the same dull faces. Just the same dull all the dull time, every dull day. This is exciting. Just being here is different and exciting. Oh, Annie, I can't explain it to you. I can't believe that you can't feel it, too. I don't know. Doesn't it just seem...better? There's a bit of magic here where people can do things they really want to instead of just looking at the sky all day and waiting until it's time to go to bed."

Annie looked around her. When Susan said it, Annie could feel it too, and she had wanted to come on the adventure. Somewhere inside her, though, she knew that if she had been here by herself, she would have got back on the next train home and held her breath until she reached Langton and everything was safe again. She felt like a rabbit that had strayed a little too far from its burrow. And she sensed that something bad was inevitably going to happen as a natural result.

"All right, Susan. Yes, it is exciting. But it's so big and noisy everywhere. Aren't you a little bit frightened of it all?"

The two friends had boarded the 8.12 fast train from Langton Station that morning with both their hearts beating faster than they usually did. Susan and Annie had been looking forward to their day out for weeks and it had finally come. They had saved their thrupenny bits and sixpences, run errands, done jobs and raided the Christmas boxes they had saved. Now, even after paying for their tickets, they had almost a pound left between them and a whole city to explore.

It was all Susan's idea. She was the one who suggested it, beat down the objections, organised the fund-raising and overcame the opposition of both her mother Jane and Annie's mother. In the end both the women gave up, shrugged their shoulders and realised that Susan was so wilful that if she were so minded she would go anyway, whatever they said and however hard they tried to stop her.

"Headstrong," Jane said by way of apology to Annie's mother when they met outside the butcher's one day.

"Ah, well. I suppose there's no holding them as wants to do things," agreed Annie's mother and they took comfort from having both done everything they could in the face of the impossible. Both thought it best to keep the outing from their husbands, however, and between them, they invented a trip to the next town to visit distant cousins as a way of covering the absences.

Susan was 19, six months older than Annie, but twice as grown up. She had shoulder-length shining brown hair, a clear, fresh country complexion, fierce brown eyes that glowed with defiance or delight depending on whether or not she was getting her own way, a strong, determined jaw and generous red lips. Few would have described her as a classic beauty, and yet she had a real, if oblique, almost intangible, attraction. Men often found that when she was in the same room, over to one side of them or viewed out of the corner of their eye, they sensed a presence and immediately looked round. Her beauty was more of an aura, an essence, than just a pretty face.

Susan's main characteristic was her absolute determination to have her own way, at all costs. Even occasionally when – during a lengthy battle – she had lost the desire for the original objective, she would still kill rather than give in. Have it she would. It would be easy to put this down to growing up as the younger sister of Bernard, a dominant and charismatic elder brother, and being forced to fight for her share of attention. Yet, as Jane remembered, she had such traits from the earliest weeks of her life and even then could not be crossed in her infant desires, having the ability to turn an alarming purple colour from rage if her feeding bottle were removed earlier than she would have wished or forced upon her longer than she cared. This continued through her schooldays when neither teachers nor fellow pupils were any match for her, and most of those who came into contact with her soon discovered what a charming and companionable person she could be just so long as everything around her was to her liking.

Perhaps it was because the world learned to acquiesce to her wishes and took away most of the obstacles from her day-to-day life that she gradually became oppressed with boredom at her environment and the lack of any challenges that it presented to her. Never made to do anything she did not wish, surrounded by girls and boys who never crossed her, she even grew tired of being unreasonable in the extreme to test her powers. She knew that she could make Albert Hancock wait two hours in the rain for her and that she could then berate him for being wet and he would apologise even though she was the one who was late without a reason. She knew that she could organise an outing for all of her acquaintances and then not turn up and leave them all standing in the street not knowing where they were meant to go, and that if she organised a subsequent outing the following week, they would all turn up again just the same. She knew that she could demand anything and everything of her circle and they would come back for more. She knew all of this because it had all happened. It was established. Even her gruff old father, who tried for longer than most to break her spirit, now shrugged his shoulders and said nothing. She knew. And she tired of it all.

Having the whole town under her sway, she began to wonder why it was so easy, and the answer she found was that she was bigger and better than these small people, that she was marked out for something grander than this little, little market garden town. An accident of birth, she reasoned, had set her down here, but her place was somewhere finer. In her secret fantasies, she saw herself being discovered, not exactly by a knight on a white charger, but by someone or something undefined and gloriously exciting. She was born to rule, but not just to rule Langton. She was born to rule... here she ran out of concepts to express what she knew was her destiny, and that was just what excited her even more and made her life in Langton so much harder to bear. One day, her future would appear in front of her and beckon her to her rightful place. She had but to wait.

Waiting in Langton, however, was proving a long and tiresome chore and so she had determined to give destiny a small nudge, a reminder not to overlook her. If destiny were in no hurry to come to find her, she would help it by putting herself in its way a little more prominently.

And so her outing with Annie was born. She had explained none of her reasoning to Annie, nor to anyone else, which made it harder to convince her friend that she knew what she was doing or what exactly would happen today. She did not know what would happen. She just knew that it would.

Her first small crisis, however, came when the two arrived at King's Cross Station and Susan did not have any idea where to go. In her dreams and plans, she had had a vague notion of going to the big shops, of walking in the parks, of being swept along by London's version of the Langton young people and of leaving the rest to them. If a young stranger had wandered into Langton Market this afternoon, perhaps visiting relatives, he or she would have become the centre of attention, would have been taken to the places where the young people went, shown the sights, invited into the circle and generally made much of. Susan wanted to go to the places where the young people of London would make much of her and to begin making her way along the path to enthronement. The trouble was, she did not know where to go. There were plenty of buses with place names on the front that she had never heard of – Aldgate, Hackney, Paddington, Holborn, Islington. They meant nothing at all to her. The one she liked the sound of was Marble Arch and she almost made the two of them get right on to it as they left the station. But then she hesitated, unsure for a moment. What if it were just a dull old church?

"I'm thirsty. Let's have a coffee before we move on," she lied brightly, to give herself time to think. "Look, there's a place."

She pointed to a small café opposite the station and, with some difficulty, the two crossed the busy, confusing road.

Annie followed meekly. A far less complex character, she was never bored with Langton. She loved the countryside and her life in it without ever giving it much thought, and would far rather have been spending the day taking little William, Mrs Hobbs's new baby from Number 31, for a walk around Langton Market in his pram and showing him off to her admiring friends. But she knew better than to cross Susan, so she swallowed her trepidation, told herself it was only one day and they would soon be back home, and went along.

Annie Wilkins was a big, well-built country girl with heavy limbs, a strong, curvy figure, straight, blonde hair, blue eyes and a fresh, blinking, constantly-startled expression. She was born in the house next to Susan, sat next to her all the way through school and was throughout their young lives her inseparable companion. Though theirs was a friendship that shared few deep intimacies, they had that comfortable understanding of each other born of much time spent together and of the complete lack of threat each posed to the other's ambitions.

As they ordered their coffee, Susan's self-belief began to return.

"Oh, Annie," she beamed as they sat at a table in the window and watched buses and trucks go rumbling past, "isn't this exciting?"

"Yes, ever so," agreed Annie, at least out loud.

"There are so many interesting people here. New faces. Interesting faces. Why look at that man over there on the pavement. Doesn't he look handsome? Doesn't he look as though he belongs here, as though he knows his way around the world?"

Annie looked, but could not see the man Susan meant.

"Yes," she said. "Yes, he does, Susan."

Susan turned back to Annie.

"I'll bet," she continued, "that anywhere you go in London the people are... 50 times more interesting than anyone in dull old Langton."

"Well, yes, but..."

"Why I'll bet that even in this one teashop there are interesting people."

She looked quickly around the entire place, scanning every face in the room, then, leaning forward towards Annie, she motioned over her shoulder and whispered conspiratorially.

"Look behind me. Those two men at the table in the corner. Why aren't they just the most handsome men in the place? Don't you feel that you would like to know who they are, how they came to be here and what they have done all their lives? They must be so interesting."

Annie began thinking about the people inside rather than buses and shops outside, and became more relaxed and interested herself. She looked over Susan's shoulder at the men indicated.

"They do look nice," she giggled in a whisper. "Especially the slim, dark one."

"What do you think he does for a living?"

"He must be quite well-off, I suppose," said Annie. "A bank manager, do you think?"

"Oh, no, no, no," laughed Susan. "He looks like an Army man to me. A Captain, probably, just got back from the Front Line in Italy. My, he must have some stories to tell."

"And what of his friend?" asked Annie, keen to continue the game.

"His friend, now," mused Susan, stealing another glance over her shoulder. "His friend is not so glamorous, and I rather suspect that he is a... a butcher, who escaped serving his country because he has flat feet."

Annie laughed again.

"He does have rather a nice smile, though," she added in the butcher's defence.

"So," said Susan decisively, "we must go over and talk to them."

Annie was shocked.

"But we don't know them... Whatever would they think of us..?"

"Lon-don, Annie. This is Lon-don, not Lang-ton. People are different here. And besides, there's no-one here as knows us. There's no mothers and gossips looking on."

She paused, then, seeing a double advantage, continued. "No, we'll just casually ask them directions, like strangers do in new cities."

She took another prolonged glance over her shoulder at the men and began trying to work out the best way to approach them without seeming to. She realised that when the men came to leave the coffee bar, they would have to pass by Susan and Annie's table. If the two friends were ready to go at the same time, they would naturally walk out together, the men would hold open the door and, once on the pavement, Susan could ask the way to Marble Arch. A conversation would begin and the day would be off to the start that Susan knew was waiting for her.

"They're looking at us," warned Annie.

"Good," said Susan, and laughed a high, tinkling laugh, throwing back her head and revealing her shapely neck as though enchanted by something Annie had said, as though she and Annie were having a highly amusing day and were great fun to be with.

Still looking sideways at the men, she was about to tell Annie to finish her coffee and be ready to go immediately the men got up to leave, when a voice in front of her said: "Why, Madame Trichot, how nice to see you again after so long. It is indeed a pleasure... Oh, my apologies, Madame..."

Susan started, turned around and was irritated to see an oldish, fairly tall, very dark and not overwhelmingly handsome man addressing her at just the wrong moment. What if the two objects of her attention were to leave the coffee bar now?

"I beg your pardon..?" she said, perplexed.

"My apologies, Madame, but this is quite extraordinary. I cannot tell you how much you resemble a French gentlewoman of my acquaintance. May I? Tell me, are you by any chance related to a Madame Augustine Trichot, from the Calais District of Paris? It can be the only explanation."

The "May I?" was to indicate that the man wished to join the ladies at their table, which he did in any case without waiting for a reply.

"Why, no, I do not believe I am," said Susan, in her polite voice, startled and not a little flattered, the other strangers in the corner completely forgotten.

"Extraordinary," repeated the man. "Oh, but how very rude of me. Whatever am I thinking of? Allow me to introduce myself. My name is Ronaldo Castelli – my family were forced to flee the persecution in Milan before the outbreak of war. This," he added, motioning Charlie to take the vacant chair at the table, "is Charles Sugden, a fine fellow."

Charlie nodded briefly and sat down rather uncomfortably, his eyes never leaving Ron.

"Pleased to meet you, Mr Castelli, Mr Sugden," murmured Susan, looking quickly at Annie with flashing eyes that said: 'Madame Augustine Trichot... Ronaldo Castelli... Calais... Paris... Milan... I told you that exciting things would happen once we stepped out of Langton.'

"Please, ladies, pardon my very rude interruption, I must leave you to your delights. But before I go, you must please tell me – if you are not Madame Trichot, then who shall I tell her is her very lovely mirror image?"

Susan was overcome by this sudden change in events. Just as she was working hard to effect an introduction to people who would make her day come alive, all by itself, destiny had brought forward a mysterious and very handsome stranger, who immediately sensed that she was different from the crowd, an exquisite bird caged in dowdy plumage, waiting to be freed, bedecked in glory and worshipped.

"Susan, Susan Harvey," she said with gravity. "And this," rather more reluctantly, but then fine ladies must show manners, "is Miss Anne Wilkins... my friend," she added, implying that that was sufficient introduction for anyone.

"Ah, la bellissimo senora Suzie," said Ron. "What a charming, charming name."

"Why, thank you, sir, but it's Susan, not Suzie."

"Exactly," said Ron. "Excuse my Italian. It comes back naturally sometimes when I feel a great emotion."

Susan flushed and felt hot. She had known all along.

"And so, ladies, what brings you to this part of London?"

"We're just up for the day," put in Annie quickly, unwilling to be left out of the conversation for too long.

Susan glared at her.

"Actually, we live just outside London and come in regularly," she said, then added casually: "We were planning to go to Marble Arch," and watched Ron's face carefully, hoping desperately that she had not said something stupid and was about to find out that Marble Arch was a prison.

Ron leaned back and opened his eyes wide.

"Well, if this isn't just a day of coincidences," he said. "Charles and I were just about to head that way ourselves, weren't we, Charles?"

"Oh... er... yes," said Charlie, catching on after a short pause. "Yes, we were. About to head that way ourselves. To Marble Arch. To... er, to..."

"Perhaps you know the times of the buses?" asked Susan, much relieved that Marble Arch was not only a satisfactory destination, but one to which society people travelled as well.

Ron raised his sleeve so everybody could see his wristwatch while he read the time.

"Oh, buses!" he said with contempt. "Can't rely on them at all. I much prefer taxicabs myself."

"Yes, so do I," agreed Susan.

"Well, then, that's settled, Suzie. Why don't we all share one?"

"What a good idea. Let's go at once." She stood up and motioned to Annie. "Oh, and the name is still Susan, not Suzie."

"Well, you said something would happen, and you were right, weren't you? Fancy us doing all those things and they wouldn't let us pay a ha'penny of it ourselves. Those boats on the lake were lovely, weren't they – even if I did get a bit splashed. It's nearly dry now. Whew! And those ice creams! Did you ever see anything so big? I just loved listening to the band as well. They were beautiful. What a day we've had! You were right all along, Susan. Didn't you say that things would happen if we went to London. Why I've never even seen a London taxicab that close up before, let alone go for three rides in them on the same afternoon. Golly, we really were toffs for the day, weren't we? Whew!"

Susan sat back in her seat on the train and gazed out of the window with a sublime and satisfied smile. Annie was gabbling on, but that was fine. It gave Susan time to think of how her life had changed. She had been right all along. She had known. Ronaldo Castelli, Ronaldo Castelli, she repeated to herself over and over again. The very name alone was wildly romantic and exciting.

Annie was leaning back as well now, eyes open wide and unblinking, mouth half open, too, in a soppy smile, a thousand thoughts and images crowding in on her. Susan wanted her to go on talking, a soothing background noise, so she prompted her to start again.

"And how was Charles? What was he like, Annie?" she asked, then turned back to the window again, safe with her own thoughts for a while.

"Charles? Oh, he was the perfect gentleman. Most of the time, that is." She giggled, blushed and flashed a small, guarded look at Susan, then went quickly on. "He was telling me in the park all about what it's like to live in London and all the madcap things they get up to. It does sound funny. I didn't like those whelk things he tried to make me eat, though. Like little slugs, they were – ugh! And he said he'd try to come and visit us in Langton one day in the summer and bring Ron with him as well. He said they can borrow a motorcar from one of their rich friends with no trouble at all. Have it for the whole weekend. They can drive up to Langton and take us out for a picnic. Can you imagine all their faces if Charlie and Ron came for us in a big motorcar? Can you imagine Ellen Reynold's face? And Mary Southern's? Oh what would they say? Charlie says his boss is very pleased with the work he's doing and that he'll soon be promoted – before Christmas easy…"

On and on went Annie, and Susan let her ramble. She did not know about Charlie's motorcars and picnics, and if they were genuine or just wild talk. But she did know about her dashing hero Ronaldo's promises. They were real enough, and she had tangible proof. She squeezed the two crisp banknotes inside her purse, banknotes that Ronaldo had put into her hand as they lay beside each other in the park in the shade of the chestnut tree, and she remembered her own promise to come back to London the very next weekend. Only this time alone.

CHAPTER 5

The Black Isle

When the slightly delayed flight from Gatwick made a bumpy landing at Inverness on the following afternoon, one of the 43 passengers who tottered down the steps, walked through the terminal and looked around for a taxi, was an excited Clara.

It was a great adventure to be back for the first time after what must be five or six years. It was her first visit to the airport, too, and the journey of an hour and three-quarters was certainly easier than the old rail trip of more than 12. She remembered those wonderful holidays, though. On the first day – which was always a Saturday – they would wake well before it was light in a frenzy of excitement, drag their cases downstairs for Bernard and Philip to carry on the short walk to the train that chugged into Langton Station before it had even woken up. She remembered the flasks of tea, the packets of bacon sandwiches and biscuits they had on the train, the endless miles of track, the station names they saw only once a year. She remembered how Bernard would tease her and Sam about what used to happen in each of the places they passed. Then there were the changes of trains at places like Peterborough and Edinburgh, the traditional games of cards they played through the afternoon on the bouncing table with bottles of orange and crisps and chocolate – games of rummy for which Sam always acted as scorer and always seemed to win – the thrill of crossing the border into Scotland accompanied by loud cheers, and finally the arrival at Inverness Station and the bumpy ride in Mr Moss's rattling taxi-cab to Grandma's cottage, where two tired children would still have enough energy left to run all over the garden and fields, into every room in the cottage and visit all their favourite places before Grandma's best supper of mince and tatties (another first night tradition) followed by slumping exhausted into the two little trestle beds in the eaves that would be home for the next two glorious weeks.

Those were magical summers, thought Clara, and felt a pang of sadness that they were in the past. A part of her life was over.

There was no Mr Moss to meet her today, so she took the first cab and it was a little after four o'clock when she climbed out of the taxi and was once more standing outside Grandma's cottage.

It was exactly as Clara remembered, with hardly a tree or a fence seeming to have changed. It was a solid, long, stone building with bright white-painted walls and four small square windows split into four square panes each, two on either side of a heavy, black-painted door set deep into the wall. The thatch was meticulously neat and curved four times along the bottom edge at the front to make way for the tiny upstairs windows of the little bedrooms Clara remembered so well. Swathes of honeysuckle covered most of the left-hand half of the front and arched over a trellis to form a canopy down the side of the house. The small front garden behind its low stone wall was as full of plants and flowers as Clara remembered it. Surely Gubby Robertson, the gardener who helped Grandma, was not still around after all this time?

Clara paid the taxi and carried her bag around under the honeysuckle, that still seemed to give off faint traces of its heady summer scents, and into the back garden. There was the little shed, the upturned wheelbarrow, the hedges and the ditches that enclosed Grandma's vegetable and herb garden – and had provided such grand hide-and-seek spots over the years. This garden did show some traces of neglect with many areas that once grew potatoes, beans and peas now replaced by scrubby grass. The herb garden was still there over on the far side in front of the large barns, where it could bask in the evening sun, but the plants were growing out of control and competing with less exotic varieties that had blown in uninvited.

The small paved area with its big terracotta flowerpots, its old wooden slatted table and the long wooden benches where they would take their evening meals when it was hot and listen to Grandma's legends and living history, was every inch intact but faded now with the scouring of many winters.

Clara lifted the third flower pot in the small back porch and was shocked to find that the big black key was missing. That's where Grandma always kept it. That key spent its life in one of only two places. When Grandma was at home, it sat in the lock, on the inside of the door. When she was not at home, it lived under the third flowerpot on the shelf in the porch. Always had.

Clara was puzzled. She tried the door. It opened and she was half-relieved and half-puzzled to see the key inside.

Then she sniffed the air. It couldn't be... It was. Mince and tatties. But...

"Clara – is it you?" called Muriel, coming out of the kitchen.

"Oh Muriel, it's good to see you," said Clara, running to give her a big hug. "I was just enjoying an old favourite smell of cooking," she said, then added: "Oh, I'm sorry, Muriel. All this has come as a bit of a shock and it is rather odd to be back here after so long. How was poor Grandma – that is, I know she died, but I mean, did she suffer at all at the end? I know how well you looked after her. You've been wonderful..."

"There, there, Miss Clara. Aren't you looking well, now? No, Mrs Harvey did not suffer. She hardly knew she was alive these past 12 months, poor soul, and so she could barely feel herself slipping away."

Muriel paused, then brightened suddenly as though with no effort.

"Now, settle yourself down, Miss Clara. You've had a long journey. Just let me pour you a cup of tea and you can tell me all about it. And yes, I thought I would continue the tradition of greeting your arrival with mince and tatties, just as Mrs Harvey would have wanted. It can cook on slow for as long as you like until you're ready to eat."

Clara accepted the cup of tea that was offered, let out a long sigh and sat by the stove watching Muriel bustle and chatter.

"Oh, but you come at a wonderful time of the year. The guillemots are active and the terns..."

Clara was not listening too carefully, but she felt comforted by the stream of Muriel's enthusiasm for all things natural on the Black Isle. Clara used to marvel at the contrast between Muriel and Grandma. If they both stood side by side and looked out from a hilltop over the Isle, Muriel would see and hear every tiny trace of the living beings in the fields below, their nests and burrows, the flit of a wing on the horizon, the call of a lost fledgling. Grandma would see the footprints of the people who lived there long ago, the remains of their buildings and earthworks, their cairns and dwelling places, and would almost watch them moving slowly across the hills. The two were so different it was almost impossible to imagine them getting on. Yet they did and would spend endless evenings sitting with their mugs of hot chocolate and talking of the villagers and the sand linnets and the stone age sites and the kites all around them.

Muriel was only an inch or two over five foot six tall and had the almost weightless frame of a bird or a small furry creature. Her movements matched so that she half flitted, half scurried around the kitchen. She had once been blonde but was now that curious straw-grey colour that yellow hair naturally becomes when allowed to.

"Oh, Muriel, that dinner smells fantastic," she said. "It makes me remember all those lovely, lovely summers. It smells every bit as good as Grandma used to make."

"So it should," laughed Muriel. "It was I who taught her how to cook it."

And so they sat in the kitchen in the late afternoon sun and talked over the old times and the days of Clara's visits, and of Sam – "that rascal" as Muriel remembered him – until the night outside was nearly dark. Muriel announced that she must be on her way.

"I've moved back into my old house now and I've to ride around by Munlochy Bay on my way home. Some guillemots have come in for the winter and I want to see if I can catch sight of them. As I say, the funeral arrangements are all in hand. You said in your message that Friday would be your preferred day and that is fine with the Minister and the undertakers, so I have set the wheels in motion. Anyhow, you must be tired. There's plenty of food in, everything is ready in your old room, I'm sure you'll be comfortable and I'll drop by about 11 in the morning to go over the rest of the details if that suits you."

"That's perfect, Muriel. Thanks a lot for everything."

"And don't get alarmed by any noises now. You know how the Black Isle can be. Well, I'll see you tomorrow."

And with a whirl of coats and baskets and a final hug, she was gone.

It was only then that Clara realised that this was the first time that she had ever been in Grandma's cottage on her own before. Every other time, there had been at least Grandma and Sam, and often her or Sam's parents as well. The house was always full of noise and lights and excitement, with plans for outings, picnics to make, Sam to play with, and wonderful, wonderful cooking smells from Grandma's kitchen.

Now it was eerily quiet.

Outside, apart from the wind in the trees at the back of the house, and the odd call of a bird or a fox, the whole world was silent. Clara determined to go straight away into Grandma's room and find the Big File before she ate. After all, that was why she was here.

On the way upstairs, she looked out of the window and saw a white cat in the garden. She quickly ran downstairs to make sure the door was shut and locked.

"Oh no you don't, matey," she thought, remembering a voice from long ago. Grandma's voice telling a story to two small children.

"It happened more than two hundred and fifty years ago, but some of the older ones in the village swear that it has been faithfully recorded and handed down generation by generation just as it happened. In the sandstone cottage at the top of the Rosebaugh Farm behind the dark oak trees lived old Mrs Macready, quite, quite alone. It was said that the townsfolk of Cromarty climbed up to that very spot at the top of Cromarty Hill on the fifteenth of April 1745 and looked across the Firth of Moray to Culloden Moor to the east of Inverness and saw the smoke from the very guns that wiped out Bonnie Prince Charlie's troops. Folk in the Black Isle then were strongly Presbyterian and the Isle was often savagely raided by Highlanders. They resented the Catholic and Gaelic and Highland army that was trying to overthrow their rightful King as they saw it and so these staunch Scots were actually cheering for the English that day.

"Some months later, a Highland chief was fleeing from Duke William's massacres in the glens that followed the English victory and he came to the Black Isle in search of a passage to Holland and safety. He had heard the story of the townsfolk on Cromarty Hill on the day of the battle and he paused his journey in mortal danger to himself to go and visit the place. Mrs Macready was already a little old lady. The chief put a curse on her that day and decreed that whenever she could she would steal a child from a Black Isle family and send it to the Devil until as many children had perished as brave Scots fell to the distant cheers from Cromarty Hill on that fateful day.

"About a week or two later, a fisherman from Cromarty and his young son were returning from some business at Rosemarkie and were journeying over the Cromarty Hill on their way home just as the darkness was falling. Lights shone in Mrs Macready's cottage, but they skirted it and hurried on, for no one knew Mrs Macready very well and they were secretly rather frightened of her.

" 'Come along now, Hugh,' said the father, pushing the lad ahead of him. 'It's not so far now. We'd best hurry.'

"But as the two passed the far end of Mrs Macready's cottage, a white cat jumped up onto the stone wall and mewed at them.

" 'Ah, look, Father,' said Hugh, a tall boy of about 12. 'Isn't it a fine wee cat?'

"Something made his father want to hurry on, but Hugh paused and leaned down to stroke the cat, which arched its back and purred under his touch.

" 'Come away now, Hugh. Come away...' said his father, more and more anxious, though he knew not why.

" 'Oh, but it's all right, Fath...' began Hugh, but he stopped as the cat's tail grew into a wreath of thick white smoke that curled and grew and hissed, denser and stronger until it swirled up and wrapped itself around both Hugh and the cat, covering them both from view. His father ran forward, but as he did so, the cascade of smoke became a roaring cyclone twice as tall as a man, turning ever faster round and round. Then it began to drill its way down into the very turf below, down and down until it grew shorter and shorter and finally disappeared, leaving but a small round smoking circle of scorched grass behind.

" 'No! No!' yelled Hugh's father and tried to dig at the turf with his bare hands, but was prevented by the searing heat coming from below.

"Hugh was never seen again and nor was Mrs Macready, and her cottage began to fall into the wreck it is now. But from that day to this, white cats have been feared in the Black Isle and no one will ever stroke one. And from that day to this children still vanish from time to time and it is said that plumes of smoke can be seen on a hill or down by the sea where they are last seen and that Mrs Macready has sent one more soul to the Devil."

Grandma's voice died away in Clara's memory and all was still again in the house. She told herself that she was being stupid.

The story did say children, she pointed out, and she hardly qualified as one of those.

Grandma Jane was born in this cottage on the Black Isle between the Firths of Moray and Cromarty when Queen Victoria still had nine years to reign. Her family had some money left over, originally from the proceeds of a little successful piracy business run in the seventeenth century by her ancestor William MacCludden, who was fond of raiding Spanish treasure ships off the coast of South America. This trove set up his three sons with the necessary trading sloops to take advantage of the cargoes to be carried from Edinburgh up the coast to Cromarty and beyond. Sadly, the winter tempests that also inhabited the same coastline foundered two of the sloops and dashed out the lives of two of the brothers on the jagged rocks. The remaining brother, John MacCludden, probably through grief, drank away a goodly part of the rest of the fortune until what was passed down to Jane as the last heir to the family was merely enough to keep her cushioned against circumstance and to save her from the need to sell the family cottage even when she moved away.

Jane first went to Cromarty and then to Edinburgh, where she became a nurse, which occupation she still followed when the Great War broke out and she found herself tending wounded soldiers shipped back from the front lines or brought in from the merchant fleet. One young soldier arrived in her care a year before the war ended. Thomas Harvey lost his left leg from the knee down when a sniper's bullet hit him as he crossed from one trench to another at Ypres, although he was lucky that he was not hit a little higher in the heart or head. He was lucky too that the leg was amputated before gangrene could set in and finish him off. Jane helped to bring him back from death and when the war was over, he brought her back to Langton as his bride and resumed work in the local fancy goods and household appliances shop. Thomas learned to walk again and went on to become an elder of the town council and an alderman.

All so very long ago now.

Ah well, thought Clara, Muriel seemed to have everything in hand, just as she had expected she would. So now Clara had the cottage all to herself for a couple of blissfully peaceful days. Oh, she had better go and take a look at the Big File, just so that she could say she had, she thought.

CHAPTER 6

Philip – An ally in the camp

(July 1965)

"**W**illoughby will set you on the right rails," Mr Thompson had said. "He's been around. Knows the ropes. Acquainted with the lie of the land."

He jabbed a finger into Philip's arm, drew closer and raised his grizzled eyebrows. "Don't listen to everything he says, mind. He can be a bit, well, temperamental... wayward, if you see what I mean."

He gave Philip a knowing look that Philip did not know what to do with.

"Let him guide you, but not slavishly if you take my drift. Don't let him rule you. Do you see? Oh, you'll soon pick it up and then you won't need him any more. I've every faith in you, Hardy..."

"Er... Harvey, Mr Thompson..."

"Yes, quite so... every faith. I think you will be a credit to the Company. In due course. A credit. Yes, that's what I think. Knew as soon as you walked in the door. You can tell after a while just by looking at them. A credit."

He paused and frowned.

"Just don't let Willoughby give you any of his bad habits. He's first-rate at what he's good at – and there you should follow him to the letter. But where he's weaker, well..."

Mr Thompson rubbed the side of his large red nose with a gnarled brown forefinger and grimaced.

"Well, where he's weaker, you mustn't listen to a word he says. Not a word."

"Yes, Mr Thompson," said Philip, convinced that he would surely take all the bad advice and ignore the good.

Mr Thompson picked up his telephone and began dialling. Philip waited, thinking perhaps that Mr Thompson was about to speak to Mr Willoughby and then give him further instructions. In fact, the interview was over and Mr Thompson had forgotten that Philip was still in the room.

"Hello, my love," said Mr Thompson. "No, I shall be a little late tonight. I have a dinner engagement with an important client over in Eastbourne. Bit of a bore, but nothing I can do, I'm afraid. Still, you'll be going to your bridge anyway, won't you? Where are you off to? Haywards Heath. And what time? Ah, good. Well, have a lovely evening and I'll see you later. Yes, you too, darling. Bye-bye."

Philip did not know how to get out of the room and waited helplessly for a sign from Mr Thompson.

Mr Thompson put down the phone, leaned forward and pressed one of the black buttons on a large silver box on his desk with wires coming out of the back.

"Eleanor," he said to it. "Could you book my usual table at the Astoria this evening, please. That's right, in the corner by the window. Yes, for two. What? No, I won't need to go to Eastbourne today. Sorted it out on the telephone."

Mr Thompson rose dreamily and walked to the window. He stood gazing out with his hands behind his back, chuckling quietly to himself and occasionally smoothing down his moustache with a thumb and finger.

Philip saw his chance and sidled quietly through the door.

It had all happened very quickly. Buying a new pair of shoes, packing his case while Mum fussed around him, listening carefully while his big brother Bernard took him into his bedroom and gave him a lot of advice, most of which he did not understand, having his last meal at home on the Saturday, being unable to sleep on a sweltering hot night, waking and dressing far too early for the train and being at the station 20 minutes before it was due, feeling his entrails clench and warp all the way down to Brighton, meeting Mr Willoughby for the first time on the platform and being taken to his guest house, the Bel Air just off the seafront, squirming as Mrs Hawkins, the wiry little guest house owner looked him up and down with a sneer, then shrugged and allowed him inside seemingly against her better instincts, putting his suitcase on the bed in the top-floor room with a view of a white-painted brick wall out of the window, sitting in a tea-shop eating an Eccles cake while Mr Willoughby explained for more than two hours how to sell encyclopedias, and wondering desperately which parts of this creed he should be following slavishly and which he should not listen to a word of, then being taken back to his room and told that Mr Willoughby would collect him at half past eight sharp the following morning and to try to get a good night's sleep. Then being on his own in his room.

It was half past four. He sat on his bed and looked around him. The room was narrow and the ceiling sloped down one side to about three feet off the ground. His iron-framed bed stood against this low wall. At one end of the white-painted room was a sash window that looked out at the brick wall of the next guest house. If you put your head out of this window and looked left, you could see a few yards of sea between the two guest houses on the opposite side of Narrow Road. At the other end of the room stood a single wooden wardrobe. Next to it was a plain wooden table, with a plain wooden chair. The only other furniture was a threadbare, brown armchair next to the window. A single picture hung in a light blue frame beside the door, a white cat with evil-looking yellow eyes glaring disconcertingly at him from a sofa. The dark-varnished floorboards were brightened only by a short piece of mangy, off-white carpet with raggy tassels beside the bed.

Dinner was at seven o'clock. Also sharp. He could see that he would have to get used to times coming with points around here.

He sat on his bed and looked around him. He was excited and scared. Mr Willoughby terrified him. He was a big man in an old tweed jacket with patched elbows and brown cord trousers. His hair was thick, black and wavy, but covered only the back and sides of his head, which otherwise stood aloof like a shiny pink beacon. Philip thought that he remembered about two sentences from his afternoon lesson. Always smile and be polite. Tell them how clever their children are. He couldn't remember exactly how the last bit helped. What if he was supposed to remember every word? He tried not to think about it until at least 8.30 in the morning. Sharp.

He opened his suitcase and hung up his shirts and his coat, put the rest of his clothes in the drawers and scattered his few books and his pen around the desk, then put his suitcase on top of the wardrobe.

Nearly quarter to five.

Philip felt lonely, small and afraid.

He had wanted to do this. Ever since he left school he had been looking for a chance to do something real. He had a few odd jobs. He worked behind the counter in Mr Huckle's grocery shop while Mr Huckle was recovering from his operation – a task that took Mr Huckle more than a year. He worked in Edward and Percy Bowles's lettuce and tomato greenhouses for almost another year until he could stand the smell of rotting tomatoes no longer. And he worked as a builder's labourer unloading bricks and timber and bags of cement from lorries as fast as his slight frame would allow, which he thoroughly enjoyed, especially the laughs with the workmen in the dinner hut. But none of it was what he wanted. He yearned to use his brains, to have a career, to MAKE something of himself.

So when he saw the advert in the paper offering a wonderful opportunity to learn the trade of a salesman and hinting at riches beyond belief for anyone who happened to apply, he wrote away immediately and two weeks later was taken on by Burridge, Thompson & Co Ltd, Publishers of Quality Literature, est 1896.

And here he was in a Brighton guest house, about to begin learning his new profession at the hands of Mr Willoughby.

Ten to five.

Philip sat on his bed.

If a stranger had walked through the door at that moment and told him that he could forget all about it, pack his suitcase and go home and no one at all would be cross with him, Philip would have run all the way to the station, pausing only to kiss the stranger's feet.

He had never felt so lost.

Soon he would have to go down to the Dining Room and eat his meal. He stopped himself from even thinking about it. He went over to the window and peered out again at the sliver of sea that looked deep blue in the afternoon sunlight. He yearned to go down and have a walk on the beach. Resolutely, he went to his door and opened it as slowly and silently as he could. He peeped out across at the other dark brown door on his dimly-lit floor. All was still. He went out onto the landing and carefully closed his door behind him, then tiptoed cautiously down the stairs and reached the landing, his heart thumping loudly. Very slowly, he peered over the wooden balustrade and down at the hallway beneath. He counted. Thirteen steps and five yards of carpet to the front door. The third from top step creaked as he stood on it and he paused, then continued to the next and the next. Then a door opened at the back of the house, a kitchen door leading into the hallway at the rear.

Philip was back in his room just before it had swung shut again.

Five to five

He sat on his bed.

A minute before half past seven.

He stood up, swallowed nervously and again went down the stairs, but this time purposefully, wishing only to be safely sharp.

He opened the door to the Dining Room at the front of the house and found that everyone else was already there and seven heads swivelled to look at him. There were six other rooms in the house and so six other guests, all men between the ages of 40 and 55. The most recent arrival other than Philip had moved in some eight years ago when Mr Willoughby himself had ceased to be a guest at the Bel Air "by mutual consent". Successful flattery since, however, meant that he was still held in high-enough esteem with Mrs Hawkins to allow him to install his new protégé on the death of the former inmate of Room 6, Mr Slough, the Assistant Surveyor, last month.

The rest of the seven rooms were occupied by Mr Lazenby, the architect, in Room 1; Mr Walters, who worked in the council offices, in Room 2; Mr Healey, the tailor's assistant, in Room 3; Mr Smith, the accounts clerk, in Room 4; Mr Stringer, the bank clerk, in Room 5; and Mr Humphreys, the undertaker, in Room 7. Mr Humphreys was the other occupant of the second floor, the rest residing on the first, where the rooms were slightly better appointed and consequently more expensive.

The Dining Room consisted of a large, round table in the bay window that seated five, and a smaller two-seater table against the back wall. Seniority was everything in the pecking order here, and Messrs Lazenby, Stringer, Walters, Smith and Healey occupied the large, round table with not a little pride and awareness of their own status, especially Mr Smith, who after 10 years' residence had been newly promoted to the top table only on the demise of Mr Slough after sharing the ignominy of the lesser table for all of his lengthy stay, most recently alongside Mr Humphreys, the undertaker. On his first night at the top table, the gentlemen performed a traditional ceremony. Smith was required to take his place at the smaller table and wait to be invited. Mr Lazenby, as the most senior member of the top table, then looked up and said: "Why there appears to be a spare place at the top

CHAPTER 7

Air pressure

On the following Thursday, Clara had a taxi waiting when Philip and Meg's flight from Gatwick touched down at Inverness Dalcross airport at 11.28 on a crisp, clear morning.

It was a little over eight hours later when Philip, Meg and Clara arrived back at Grandma's cottage at the end of a day that had seen waves of dark grey clouds build up from the west as the breeze freshened to a wind that sent sheets of relentless rain the length of the Black Isle.

Not that they had particularly noticed the weather. Nor was it the storms or even any road works that had turned a 15-mile trip from the airport into a day-long trek.

Clara had gone to the airport in a local taxi, which she ordered from Fortrose. The hold-up was to do with a police car and an ambulance which were also waiting for the flight.

Clara thought it was rather unusual when she saw them parked on the tarmac near the terminal building. Then she spotted the plane in the distance begin its long, slow descent from the east, over Nairn and Culloden. It touched down, bumped along the runway, vanished from sight around the side of the building, then reappeared and taxied up to where the steps were waiting. Once the engines had stopped, the police car and ambulance drove right up to the plane and uniformed men got out from both and stood in conversation with airport officials as they positioned the steps. After a long delay, the door finally swung open, the steps were wheeled up to it and two police officers climbed them and stood at the top, talking to a grey-jacketed stewardess who appeared inside the doorway.

Then one of the policemen went into the plane and reappeared a few minutes later, holding Philip by the arm. He led Clara's father down the steps and helped him into the back of the ambulance accompanied by one of the ambulance crew.

"Oh, my god," thought Clara. "He's had a heart attack."

Meanwhile, the other policeman went into the plane and came out leading Meg, helping her into the ambulance as well. The back doors were closed and the lone policeman remaining climbed back into his car.

Clara turned to a young woman member of the ground staff team, who had also been watching proceedings.

"What's happening?" she asked.

"Well, apparently there was an incident in the air. Someone tried to hijack the plane or something."

Clara thought better of saying: "That's my Dad," as she had intended, and settled simply for repeating: "Oh my god…"

Then she turned and sprinted back to her taxi, jumping in just as the ambulance and police car appeared in the distance from the road leading to the airfield itself, and sped past them on the road to Inverness.

"Um… follow that ambulance," she said, feeling foolish. "Please," she added, not at all like they do in films.

When Philip, Meg and Clara finally made it to the cottage, it was beginning to grow dark. They were expecting to find Bernard, Alice, Sam and Ian already waiting, but when they pushed the door open, only Bernard and Alice were to be seen, standing over a big cauldron that was filling the cottage kitchen with steam and fabulous smells.

"So here you are, you laggards," roared Bernard.

He and Alice put down their spoons and knives and came over towards the three bedraggled figures who just stood inside the doorway with their coats still on.

Clara reacted first and ran up to throw her arms around Bernard's neck and woodpecker him with kisses. She continued to laugh aloud and hug her uncle, but unseen by the others, she managed to hiss into his ear: "Pretend nothing has happened. I'll tell you later."

Then she rattled on aloud: "Uncle Bernard, it's so good to see you. How are you? How was the cruise? Where's my present? What did you bring me?"

"Well, I got you this wonderful secluded beach with pure, white sand and corals and palm trees and everything, but the nasty customs men made me leave it all bagged up at the airport. It would have been just the thing at the end of your garden."

Clara turned to Aunt Alice, and she hissed the same message to her aunt as they whirled each other around.

"It's so good to see you both," Clara continued as she went back to her parents at the door, raised her eyebrows at her mother as they both helped Philip off with his coat. "It's been such a long time since we were all together here. Well, nearly altogether."

"Ah mother's here," said Bernard. "She will always be here. This place is her. She's part of it. You can never look at her chair or use her saucepans or stoke her fire or walk in her garden without her seeing her, sensing her, feeling her presence."

There was silence for a moment, then Bernard added: "Speaking of spirits…"

"I was going to suggest a cup of tea," laughed Meg. "But you're probably right."

"Of course I am. And I brought my own, so let's have a toast to mother."

"Then you must be hungry," said Alice. "Don't worry, we've taken care of the victuals."

"So we can smell," said Clara. "And I'm up for a double helping."

Bernard had glasses of whisky poured in moments and the five of them clinked and drank "To Grandma...To Mother..."

"Where's Sam?" asked Clara, suddenly realising that he was missing.

"Oh he's coming up on an overnight train with Ian," said Alice. "They arrive with the dawn. Sam had something he couldn't rearrange apparently."

Clara narrowed her eyes.

Bernard sipped his drink and leaned against the fireplace again. He would have seemed a big man even if he had not been six foot four. His was an electric, magnetic personality. Bernard was also striking in appearance, it is true. Broad-shouldered, with massive arms and hands, his white-grey hair stood up high and fell down way past his ears in a wave that made him seem even taller. It had been grey since he was in his thirties, began going white when Clara first knew him and then stopped at an in-between, almost translucent shade that gave him the appearance of a ghost or a wizard. His beard, however, was pure white, long and straggly. His skin was like mid-brown leather from much time spent in all weathers, his nose somewhat long and broad-based, and his eyes flashing and so deep brown that they were almost black beneath shaggy white eyebrows. He could easily have looked fearsome, and yet those eyes never stopped laughing and his readiness to make all around him smile endeared him to all who met him. Children in particular loved to sit on his lap and feel safe, if tickled.

He had long worked in the academic world, writing papers, researching and providing course material for various universities and colleges on English literature, from Chaucer to Wordsworth mainly, as well as writing the odd book here and there. It gave him and Alice plenty of opportunity to do what they most loved, travel the world.

Bernard was a perfect benevolent dictator, who had been head of the family since his father died when Bernard was in his mid-twenties – and he liked his station. He was avuncular, kind, generous and huge fun, and no one thought to oppose him. And yet perhaps there was a side of him that few knew and even he had forgotten. He tended to play all games with a view to letting those around him win, especially the children. But if his concentration lapsed and he forgot himself, he would win the game in moments, automatically, then realise what he had done and turn it all back into a joke. And when it was not a game, Bernard would win every time.

Clara also brought them quickly up to date with the funeral arrangements for the morning. The undertakers were due to arrive at 11, and the service was at 11.30. Then back to the cottage where Muriel was arranging some food and drink.

"Well done, you," said Bernard.

Clara thought about admitting that Muriel had done it all, then just smiled. She would admit it later, but why not enjoy the moment?

"You did good," said Alice.

Alice would normally be thought of as tall, but as she spent most of her life near Bernard, and as she was two or three inches shorter than him, she seemed medium height. She was slim but powerful, muscular but feminine, her long black hair and shining blue eyes always twinkling with verve and mischief.

Dinner was jovial as they sat around the big dining table in the long open-plan ground floor of the cottage. At one end was the kitchen with the range, the tall cupboards and hanging saucepans. Then came the big oak table, acting as a barrier halfway down the room, and beyond that was the old red sofa, at one side of the big fireplace and Grandma's upright wooden chair at the other, then a couple of old armchairs and a table finished off the furnishings.

Bernard and Alice served them all with big platefuls of stew and mash as Meg and Clara opened the wine and the five had a jovial meal, ignoring the strange events of the day as Clara had requested. And it was just like old times. Even Philip relaxed, enjoyed a glass or two of wine and told some of his favourite stories.

When the washing up was done and as everybody was beginning to yawn, stretch and think of their beds, Bernard stood up and said: "I think I'll just walk up to the Crow's Nest and get a few lungfuls of this fine air to take to bed with me. I'll be up presently, Alice, darling."

He looked at Alice, then at Clara. Both nodded.

"Right, darling," said Alice. "I'll go up and make our nest."

"Don't mind if I join you, do you, Uncle?" said Clara. "It's a great place to sit under the stars."

"Put a coat on, darling," said Meg. "It is January, after all."

Bernard led the way out of the back door, through the garden and along the small pathway of bare earth worn by feet over the years. It turned around the rising ground behind the cottage, up the steep slope of the meadow and onto the brow of the hill, where a shallow ridge of rock cut just into the summit, about 20 yards long with a wall of rock some 10 feet high at the back and a ledge running the length of it like some grandiose piece of garden furniture. At one point, the ledge narrowed to a couple of feet so that it was possible to sit with your back to the wall and dangle your calves over the rock face, which dropped three or four feet onto the grassland meadow that fell slowly away towards the cottage. This was the Crow's Nest, a favourite place for Jane, and one that everyone who came to see her on the Black Isle soon discovered. Clara had spent whole afternoons here with Sam, just reading and playing cards and talking nonsense and gazing out across the deep, dark firth to the rising hills beyond.

Clara gave Meg, Philip and Alice a quick kiss each, grabbed her jacket and threw it over her shoulders as she ran out to catch up with the striding Bernard.

Tonight Bernard and Clara didn't say a word as they walked, Clara putting in a quick extra step every three or four paces to keep up so that by the time they reached the rocky height, she was almost out of breath. Clara made for her favourite spot and sat down, but Bernard walked slowly to the far end and looked out towards the east where on a clear day you could see the thin line of the North Sea in the distance, but tonight in the blackness only the dark shadows of the hills and the water of the firth could be made out.

It was a mild night for January, although the wind gusting from the north carried a reminder of the time of year, but the Crow's Nest itself was sheltered and pleasant enough for Clara to sit on the bare rock.

"Isn't it just as lovely as you remember it, Uncle?" said Clara, half-closing her eyes, tilting back her head and breathing in the clean air.

"It doesn't get any worse, does it?" he said. "No matter where you go on this whole planet, this spot takes a lot of beating. Mother knew a thing or two."

Then he came quickly back from the far end and sat down next to Clara. "OK, so what happened?" he asked. His voice was changed now. Some of the joviality had gone and he spoke quickly and with a purpose. This was Family Business.

Clara gave a long sigh.

"Well, I can tell you what happened, but as to why, well, you know as much as I do, Apparently from what I've been able to gather from Mum, after they'd had their breakfast and stuff on the plane, Dad went to sleep. They were sitting at the front in the first row and he was on the outside, on the aisle. Suddenly, he woke up, jumped up, rushed to the door and was trying to get it open, shouting something about having to stop her. 'Got to go... I said I'd visit her...' over and over, just that. Luckily, he was just pulling at the hinge so he had no chance of actually opening the door, but it took the co-pilot and the stewardess together to pull him off. They manhandled him into the galley and held him down on a chair, and he mumbled for a few minutes, then he went quiet for a bit and just stared, and then he started asking them what they were doing and where he was. Didn't even remember he was on a plane for a while, or why. He does sleep-walk occasionally – even gets dressed in the middle of the night and Mum sometimes catches him going out of the front door at four in the morning, but he hasn't done it for a while. Seems that that's what he was doing this time, though. And having some sort of nightmare. Of course, they radioed ahead so there were police and an ambulance waiting to take him off the plane. I followed them to the hospital and caught up with them there. Mum was worried about Dad but pretty calm. Then it was just endless questions. The same questions over and over again. Who was he? What was he doing? Did he have a history of mental illness? Had he ever tried to kill himself before? Did he have any strong religious convictions? Just on and on, over and over for hours. At one point they were going to keep him in for reports, but I managed to persuade them that it was just a nightmare, that he was sleep-walking and he wasn't a danger. They let us go in the end on police bail and they're still talking about charging him, but I think when they saw him just sitting on the chair and looking confused they realised that he wasn't much of a danger to anyone. So they let us go and here we are. He has to go back to the police station in Inverness on Sunday. And that's all I know. It's been a fairly horrible day really and one I would quite like to forget quite soon, please."

She stopped and gazed into the blackness, her knees pulled up against her chest.

Bernard was silent for a while, then said: "You did well."

He was silent again for a few moments, then added: "I think we can sort this out."

He paused again and the two sat under the brightness of a million stars as the wind drove wisps of thin, white clouds over their heads from the hilltop behind them.

Then suddenly Bernard looked round at Clara and asked: "And how are things with you, young Clara? Everything OK? Work? Love life?" The jovial voice was back.

Clara laughed. "Oh, work's fine and I don't actually HAVE a love life at the moment. I'm resting between boyfriends as they say."

Bernard looked at her and frowned.

"Problems at work, eh?" he said. "Hang on, we'd better get some central heating and then you can tell me about it."

He was wearing a green, sleeveless quilted waistcoat and out of one deep pocket, he pulled a respectable-sized hip flask.

"Old Boy Scout training," he said. "Wards off hypothermia."

"Mmm," approved Clara.

He delved into another other pocket and pulled out two small glasses. Then from his inside pocket came a small glass bottle.

"Here, hold these," he said, handing Clara the glasses, which he then half-filled with a pale, clear liquid that seemed to shimmer in the darkness.

"Nothing is finer," he added, replacing the cap on the hipflask and sliding it back into his pocket, then taking the top off the bottle and adding a mere splash of water into each.

He put away the water bottle, took a glass from Clara, clinked it against hers and said: "Here's to you, Clara."

"And to you, Uncle Bernard," she added, taking a sip and feeling the warmth rush into her.

He smacked his lips.

"Nothing like a single malt whisky, is there? Now. You were saying that you had problems at work. Anything I can help with?"

"I wasn't... I didn't... I said work was fine," said Clara, puzzled, looking at him quizzically in the darkness but seeing only the silhouette of his profile.

He turned towards her.

"Yes, those were the words you said. Now, what are the problems? Anything I can help with?"

She laughed and sighed.

"You are quite amazing, you know, Uncle."

"Not really," he said, wearily. "It's just practice." He paused. "You don't have to tell me if you don't want to. We can talk about the view or the funeral or Mother if you'd prefer."

"Oh I don't mind telling you, but it's nothing. I just have a boss who I can't seem to please. Whenever I do anything that I think is halfway decent, he always finds some glaring mistake in it and makes me feel stupid – often in front of other people. He's usually right, but he overlooks all the good things and I wonder if the bad ones really ARE so bad at all. I just don't know if it's because he doesn't like me personally or if I really am bad. If it's the first, then I should think about moving somewhere else, but if it's the second then I need to find another career or start doing better at the lottery."

"And this is on the magazine you write for?"

"That's right. *Allaire* – you know, the one I moved to last year. It's a sort of glorified European glossy, up-market what's on and lifestyle magazine. Oh, I'm getting interesting work to do and I can more or less pick my own interviews, but Peter – you know, Peter Denhartt, he's my boss and the chap who founded the magazine and then sold it to a French publishing company – Peter is still Editor and very much in charge and... well... can we talk about something else? I wanted to get away from all that up here, and it's so good to see you again and be back on the Black Isle. Tell me about Grandma or something."

"OK, but when it comes to bosses and jobs there is one rule – ALWAYS back your own judgement. If you're right you won't have to take any nonsense and you won't be held back. If you're wrong then at least you'll bring it to a head and you won't spend years suffering quietly."

He pulled out the hip flask and the water and gave them both another drink.

"What do you want to know about your Grandma?"

Clara wanted to say: "Why has she got an insurance policy in the name of Jane Laker? Was she married before? And who was Rebecca Laker, the woman in the picture? Is it her sister-in-law another fine type of wood. The thought of her own little cupboard with the squeaky door, and the nasty falling-apart box at the end of her bed where she kept her clothes filled her with shame.

Even the simple wooden chair beside the bed here was so much nicer than her old thing.

Susan sighed. Her head hurt quite a lot and she felt a little queasy, but she did not mind at all. Clearly, she would now need to get used to drinking more than a glass of sherry every Christmas. She laughed to herself and continued to look for things that were better now.

For one, sleeping naked was very enjoyable indeed. She wriggled a little to feel again the thrill of the sheets against her skin all over her body, the length of her warm thighs and across her tummy and brushing against her nipples, down her back and bottom. Mmm, what a wonderful feeling. She would never be able to do this in Langton. People would see her. She had no privacy at all, so she had to swaddle herself up in an awful nightgown. Well, she resolved, she would never, ever wear anything in bed again. Not if it felt this good to sleep with nothing on. Somehow it seemed right as well. Queenly, grown-up, exotic…

She would have liked a cup of tea or at least a glass of water to clear her parched mouth but she did not want to get up yet. She did not want to disturb the perfection of it all.

More light began to seep into the room and the pale grey finger across the ceiling grew crisper and almost white.

That was another thing. When she had had to share her bed in Langton with some cousin or other on account of an illness or horrible relatives coming to stay, it was so cramped and tiny that neither of them got any sleep at all. But here – she stretched out again, luxuriating in the amount of space she had – here there was plenty of room for her and Ronaldo without it feeling squashed in any way. She looked across at his slumbering figure, curled up with his back towards her, his dark hair on the pillow, breathing softly and rhythmically into the early morning gloom.

And she remembered once again the previous day as it all came tumbling back to her in a whirl of excitement and liberation.

Exactly a week after she and Annie had enjoyed their big adventure in London, Susan crept alone out of the house clutching her little bag of clothes and a few trinkets. This time she had not mentioned her trip to her parents or even to Annie. Softly she closed the door behind her and headed off to Langton station, her fingers reaching into her purse as she walked so that she could touch once again the two banknotes that Ronaldo had given her. She caught the same 8.12 train to London and sat in the same seat by the window, but saw nothing of the fields flying past her or even the billowing cloud of grey-white smoke from the engine that folded itself like a veil over her escape. If she had given any thought at all to the family and the mother that she was leaving behind in Langton, it would have been to expect them to forget her very quickly and go on with their dull little lives as though nothing had happened, as though she had not existed. Perhaps later she would have wanted them to remember her with affection and some awe, like a butterfly that lived briefly among them and that they were privileged to watch in the early stages of development before it swept up into the magnificent skies on its luxurious wings to soar far away from their little world.

But her thoughts were not on Langton or the past, they were all taken up with her arrival in the city again and with her new and glorious future. She went over in her mind everything that Ronaldo had said and done the week before and she was thrilled at the prospect of repeating their day, only this time without the encumbrance of Annie and Charlie.

She thought the train would never wheeze into the station and she almost ran to the coffee shop, where she took her place at the very same table as she had the previous Saturday. She looked at the clock on the wall. It was just after 10 o'clock. Ronaldo had said that he would meet her there at half past, so she ordered a cup of coffee as she had done seven days ago, although she was far too excited to drink it. She sat facing the door and tried to look up and down the street to see the approaching Ronaldo. The roads sweeping past King's Cross were full of the clatter of buses, trucks and cabs that gave Susan plenty to watch as she waited. She thrilled at the bustle and the noise and the smells as the whole of London seemed to jostle its way past the small windows. Her first cup of coffee went cold, but she ordered another and this time, by now feeling thirsty, she managed to sip some as she craned her neck to try to make out Ronaldo in the throng.

In her excitement, the time passed quickly and at a little after ten past eleven, Ronaldo appeared suddenly at the door, spotted her immediately even before she had waved her hand to attract him, and came across to the table.

"Well, well," he said, sliding into the empty chair beside her and taking both her hands in his, "I was about to ask if you had had a busy week since last we met, but now I see that you have spent the time growing even more lovely, and I would have sworn that such a thing was not possible."

Susan smiled and blushed at Mario's compliment that Ron had borrowed especially for the occasion. He too looked, she thought, even more dashing and handsome than the first time she had seen him, and she told him so.

Then they were off for a day in London. And what a day. If the weather was not as kind as last time, Susan minded not at all. Ronaldo had brought a large black umbrella with him and the two huddled closely together under its shelter against the driving, gusting rain as they wandered about, neither caring where they went. They did not take a boat out on the Serpentine this time but instead walked around and around it, he with an arm protectively on her shoulders to ensure that she stayed as fully as possible out of the rain. He gallantly carried her little bag, idly wondering what could be inside it.

Ron did most of the talking, telling her about his prospects and how his boss had praised his work again and again and had promised him increasing rewards, without specifying precisely the nature of business in which he was involved. Susan just let it wash over her as comforting background music to accompany her new life. Everything she saw and everything she smelled was fresh and exciting, and the reassuring words that Ronaldo spoke reached her like a helping hand, easing her into her future life. Ronaldo certainly seemed well-off with no shortage of taxi rides and banknotes about him. She would not be running away from any former meagre security into a life of uncertainty and poverty.

Even the rain stopped and Ronaldo shook the drips from his umbrella and furled it deftly, although he kept his arm around her shoulders to ward off any lingering chill as he led her towards Trafalgar Square, the size of which made her gasp with pleasure. Here was a stage that befitted her new stature. Here was an end to a life of tiptoeing through littleness and mediocrity. Once she had settled down and attracted the attention of the people of London as she had those in Langton, she would be able to grow tall in this rich new earth, swapping her cramped country flowerbed for the expanse of this vast and fertile future. She would be Queen of London Town.

On they wandered, along the Strand, into Fleet Street – the home of the nation's newspapers as Ronaldo explained – and he paused to pick up a copy of the *Daily Herald*. They turned right and Ronaldo led her down to the river at Blackfriars. They stood on the bridge and watched the boats sludging their way up and down the muddy water, as Susan compared its vast expanses with the reedy little brook of the River Ivel back at home. Then the two meandered back and took a stroll around St Paul's Cathedral, Ronaldo pointing out some of the windows that were fashioned by Italian craftsmen from his home city of Milan, and told her how the Germans had tried to bomb it during the Blitz but bungled every raid. When they stepped out of the gloom, they stopped for a pot of tea and some rhubarb jam sandwiches at a little tea shop in a

CHAPTER 9

The fixer

Clara sat across the table from Ian and Sam thinking how incredibly alike and different at the same time the brothers were. Ian spent a lot of his time abroad and she seldom saw them together. Ian in his mid-fifties, possibly taking more after Alice, but still with the unmistakable Harvey characteristics of deep forehead and square chin, shared by both Bernard and Philip. The front half of Ian's head was bald, but the hair he did have grew out of control, shaggy and unkempt, sweeping back into a long, grizzled ponytail held in place with rubber bands. His hair was now as much grey as the original black, and so was his shaggy beard, He was shortish and almost square with something of Alice's dark Latin looks. He might have been plump if he had led a more comfortable life, as his face had the beginnings of jowls. But since he graduated as a doctor, he had spent the last 30 years travelling the world helping refugees and sharing many of their hardships.

Sam, by contrast, was slighter, with quick, darting movements like a small rodent. He had dark hair and an all-year-round tan that came partly from jaunts to Ibiza and partly from the Tops'n'Tanners Hair And Grooming Salon in Battersea, near where he lived and from over which he ran his several business ventures. Sam, too, had Bernard and Philip's wide forehead, but with his thinner face, it made him look like some kind of good-looking and brainy puppet. His eyes were deep brown and he had a habit of tipping his head forwards and looking out at the world upwards through his raised eyebrows, making him at once arch and quizzical. It had taken much study in various mirrors to get the look just right, but now it came naturally and he was pleased with it. Sam's passport gave his occupation as "International Entrepreneur" and he spent his life trying for the main chance, the one deal that would bring him the lifestyle to which he yearned to become accustomed. In the early days, this was financed largely by his parents, but after two or three failures and a near disaster, he had tried other friends and even banks to fund his exploits. Nothing had hit the bull to date, but at 31 he seemed to have achieved the knack of breaking even so that as one venture folded, it just about raised enough cash to pay his debts, to live on and to fund most of the next project without ever giving him the sort of capital resources to play the game as hard as he would have wished. Not that he was about to give up.

It was late afternoon. Meg and Philip had retired upstairs for an afternoon nap. Bernard and Alice had gone with Muriel for a walk down to the bay to see the seals. The three "children" were sharing a peaceful afternoon together in the warm kitchen.

The funeral had been quiet and decorous. Bernard disappeared to collect Sam and Ian from the station early in the morning and only just got back in time. A dozen local people joined the family at the small church where the minister said some pretty things about Grandma and they sang *There Is A Green Hill Far Away*, *He Who Would Valiant Be* and *All Things Bright And Beautiful*. Then they gathered round the small grave on the slope overlooking the water and laid the coffin to rest with Grandma's feet pointing down towards the water as she had asked so that she would "forever gaze at the Firth". And they all wiped their eyes and remembered the happy times with the old lady. Then they all came back to the cottage, where Muriel had laid on sandwiches and cakes and tea, and everyone said what a wonderful woman Grandma was and how much she would be missed and how it was good to see the family again and how the children had grown and how they had come at a wonderful time of year and that it was an unusually mild winter which meant that they should be in for a good summer but the midges might be a problem. Then they drifted away in ones and twos until only the family remained.

Now the three sat around the table, sharing some cheap red wine that had become more drinkable by the second bottle.

Clara remembered the insurance certificates. She still wanted to find out the truth. Perhaps Ian might know.

"You've known Grandma longer than us, Ian," she said. "Have you ever heard her called Jane Laker before?"

"What by someone who was very bad at speaking and couldn't say Harvey?" asked Sam.

Ian said nothing, but sipped his drink and looked over the glass at Clara.

"What a strange question," he said, "but one which presumably has a modicum of reason behind it."

"Yes," said Clara, pouring them each another half-glass to finish the bottle. "You know I came up this week to sort things out? Well, when I was looking in Grandma's Big File like she told us, I found her insurance policies. Two were in the name of Jane Harvey but one was for Jane Laker. I thought her maiden name was Smeeton, wasn't it? She wasn't married before, was she? So I don't understand. Have you ever heard her called Laker before, Ian?"

Ian stood up wearily and smiled.

"You know," he said, "more and more when I come back to this country and see so many people running around inventing problems for themselves so that they have something to fret about to pass the time – more and more I feel like Gulliver, stumbling on a land where everyone is bonkers but too close to themselves to be able to see it. I'm going down the pub if anyone cares to join me. It's the one safe activity in this society of *sholomi*."

"You'd better not go out there alone," said Sam. "All those Picts and Celts and things. I'll come to look after you."

He stood up and pulled his jacket off the back of his chair.

"But..." said Clara, then shrugged and jumped up herself, running to get her coat and catch them up on the path.

The seven in the family stayed for the rest of the weekend, roaming over the Black Isle as in days gone by, and enjoying being together as a group, something that was unusual given that they were not often all in the country at the same time, let alone in the same place. The plan was to fly back on the Sunday afternoon and Clara was a little concerned about Philip on the flight – or even if the airline would LET him on the plane. He had to go to the police station first. She watched him closely the next day and he seemed back to his old self, even playing a round of golf with Bernard, Alice and Sam on the Saturday morning. Perhaps it *was* just a nightmare and it was over now. She asked Bernard what he thought as they walked along the shores of Avoch Bay on the Saturday afternoon. He would know. Perhaps if they all sat around him in the plane and kept him laughing. Perhaps if they kept him awake. She had not had a chance to talk to her mother about it properly – or to be truthful, she had avoided the subject. But Bernard would know.

Clara waited for her chance when Sam and Philip had gone on ahead as they walked, and while Alice and Ian were showing Meg how to skim stones and were lagging far behind.

Clara grabbed Bernard.

"How was the golf, Uncle Bernard?" she said.

"It's a fine course, is Chanonry," he said, then laughed. "Your father doesn't get better with age, though. He's a demon putter, but he couldn't hit a straight iron shot to save his life."

"He was all right, though?" she asked slowly. "I mean, he seems to have recovered after his little... incident on the plane."

"That? Oh yes, no problems. He's all right, is Philip, just a little scatty sometimes."

"It's just that I do worry about him," said Clara. "All this nightmare stuff. I suppose it comes to all of us in the end."

Bernard could remember when it started for Philip. To the day. After a lot of self-torment, he had decided that he no longer had the right to keep a secret from Philip. Philip had a right to know, so he told him. Not all of it, thank goodness, just the start. But he had misjudged terribly. Philip could not take it. Bernard remembered how he went pale and his hands shook, then went up to his head and he just kept saying: "No. No. No." Over and over again. It was a couple of years ago and the change was disturbing. From happy joker, telling gags all over the place, Philip turned into a worried, frightened, guilt-ridden shell. Not all at once, but gradually as it ate away at him. Bernard knew that Philip's latest exploit on the plane would not have happened but for that revelation. If only he had kept his mouth shut.

Luckily Meg was a genius at steering Philip through his life and not letting him dwell too much on it. Which was all the more remarkable given that Meg did not know what the secret was. There was no way that Bernard was going to tell her.

And once in a while, Philip went out of control. Like on the flight.

Bernard looked at Clara sideways as they walked.

"I wouldn't give it another thought," he said. "Let's cheer him up tonight and take him to that place in Fortrose – you know how much he loves their langoustine."

"Oh yes, that's a lovely idea."

"Excellent. I'm glad you approve. I booked the table this morning. Let it be a surprise for him, eh? Don't say anything until this evening. We don't want to get him too excited."

Then Clara let it all out in a rush.

"OK. Uncle Bernard... er, do you think he'll be OK on the plane back? I mean, what will the airline and the police do? He hasn't been charged, but they haven't said they won't yet, have they? Do you think they might take it further? Anything could happen when we get to the airport. It *is* worrying, isn't it? Even you must be worried, Uncle?"

Bernard laughed. He was enjoying knowing something that Clara did not and was in no hurry to waste it.

"Well, what's the worst thing that can happen?" he asked.

"The worst? That doesn't bear thinking about."

But now Bernard had said it, Clara *had* to think about it.

"The worst?" she went on. "I suppose it would be for him to be arrested and charged and for the newspapers to get hold of the story and have a huge picture of him on the front of *The Sun* looking dazed and confused as he gets off the plane home and suddenly finds a hundred flashlights going off in front of him. And for them to have some headline like: 'AIR THICKNESS' and 'Loony who tried to get out of a plane at 20,000ft' and for him to be a laughing stock and never allowed to fly again and to lose his job because they think he's crazy and… and…"

She tailed off.

Bernard laughed softly.

"A little bit unlikely, though, isn't it?"

"But that sort of thing happens all the time. If they dress it up like that, everyone will laugh at him and it will be read out by all the brain-dead DJs on every radio station. They don't give a flying fig for the people if they can have a funny headline and sell some papers or get some more listeners."

The more Clara thought about it, the more she was convinced that it was inevitable. Now she was really scaring herself.

"And what if we could keep it quiet?" he asked slowly.

"But what can we do? I don't see how…"

He laughed again.

"I can't tease you any more, young Clara," he said. "I popped into a few places on Friday morning on the way to picking up Ian and Sam. I don't think you need to worry. The police were very nice. They understand now. There will be no charges, no arrests, no newspaper stories. It's all sorted out."

She looked quickly at him.

"Really? You've managed it? But how? What?"

Bernard loved these moments. He felt like Sherlock Holmes on the last page of the last chapter. All powerful. the one with the knowledge, the keys to the mystery.

"Oh, you don't need to worry about the details. Let's just enjoy the scenery and help him to relax while he's up here."

Clara stared at him incredulously. then she had another thought.

"But what about the flight back? What if he does it again?"

"It seemed to me that it might be rather enjoyable if we had a pleasant train journey back on Sunday, just like in the old days. Takes a deal longer, but perhaps more relaxing, read the papers, spot of lunch – and not so far to fall if you accidentally open the door on the way."

He put his hand into his inside pocket and drew out a bulky brown envelope, which he handed to Clara.

"You'll find in there some rail tickets for the three of you together with a cheque for the refund on the plane tickets. Alice and I are on the same train, but Ian and Sam will be flying as they have to be back earlier. Sam has a lunch he has to go to and Ian is off to some swamp or other on Monday and has a midnight start."

Clara took the envelope and felt a thrill of relief sweep through her.

She threw herself at Bernard and gave him a huge hug.

"You really are amazing, Uncle," she said.

"Yes, I suppose I am," he laughed.

Uncle Bernard had long been able to conjure. It was like having a wizard in the family who went around making things better with very little fuss. When Sam got into trouble at school for not just smoking behind the bike sheds, but actually *selling* cigarettes, and seemed about to be expelled, Uncle Bernard went to see the Headmaster and everything was all right again. When Ian daubed some unkind thoughts about President Nixon on the wall of the nearby American Air Force base in a one-boy protest against the Vietnam War, there were threats of "tough action". But when Uncle Bernard came back from the base, none was taken. When Clara was being bullied at school, Uncle Bernard spoke to the bully's parents and the girl involved, and it stopped overnight. Uncle Bernard did not just right wrongs, he seemed to be able to undo the past in its entirety, as though it had never happened at all. He air-brushed history. No one knew exactly how he operated or what his methods were. No one in the family had ever seen him in action. Everything was done quietly to one side, behind closed doors, no fuss. All over before anyone realised that he had taken a hand in the matter. But he had a one hundred per cent record. He had never failed.

Even those he went to see could not tell you afterwards what had happened. They just knew that they had had a friendly chat with a very nice man and they found when he had gone that they had agreed to a change of mind without having a clear recollection of the conversation or why they felt the need to make the switch.

Everybody was in good spirits when they got back to Grandma's cottage and they enjoyed tea and cakes in front of the fire. Philip in particular was even more cheerful than usual. Now that he had settled down and completely forgotten the incident on the plane, now that he had spent some time with Bernard and Sam, and especially now that he was in this haven of serenity, he let all the good memories of the past wash back over him. This in turn brought smiles back to Meg, relieved and grateful to see him calm and happy again, and as Philip's major joy in life was to see Meg happy, each drove the other on, buoyed the other up in a spiral of self-sustaining contentment.

Ian sat in Grandma's chair sipping his tea and watching them all out of his dark brown eyes. He felt like the tribal elder who has seen too much and does not need to talk. They were not a bad crowd, and he would soon be back in his own world, barefoot in his tent. You needed a contrast to make what was real stand out in greater relief, he thought.

Sam had given up trying to get a signal on his mobile phone even at the top of the hill and came back in to share a game of backgammon with Philip on the kitchen table. He was rather regretting some of the things that he'd said to Suzie on Thursday evening, but she HAD asked for it. Now he couldn't make it up to her. Couldn't even get through to send her some flowers. And who would call first on Monday when he got back? Most times she called after a disagreement, so it would not disturb the balance overmuch if he rang her for once.

"Double six!" he yelled. "You're in trouble now, Philip."

"Oh no!" laughed Philip. "THREE off. You lucky bugger, Sam."

"Language!" scolded Meg at his elbow.

Perhaps he would call her mid-morning, so as not to appear too eager. Then he could invite her round for a takeaway and a video and they could make things up in the very best possible way. Before that, though, he had to deal with Dawn. She would not leave him alone and he had used this weekend away to have lunch with her and get her off his back for a while, telling Suzie even before the half-engineered row that he would not be back until Monday morning so that he could see Dawn on Sunday. Dawn was not really his type, nor was he hers. There was just a very strong attraction they had both felt since they were at school together. Now they met around four times a year for a short dinner and a long night of sex. He knew Dawn was seeing lots of other people but they never talked about it. But of late Dawn was getting more serious. He had seen her just the other month and now she was calling him and sending notes and even once flowers to the office, and talking of going on holiday together. He would have dinner with her and then in the evening he really would get rid of her. She would have to get up and go in any case because he had promised Michelle that he would try to get to her party and he was keen on Michelle and had high hopes of her. Michelle was the only other employee of his company. She had been with him for two weeks since Valerie left for her round-the-world hike. Michelle had shoulder-length golden blonde hair, green eyes, long legs and a fantastic figure. And she wore amazingly revealing clothes. He would sit at his desk looking across at her and think that he would give anything...

Bernard, Alice and Clara sat at the other end of the room reading. Bernard leaned back in the big armchair, filling it comfortably, with a coffee-table-sized book about a shipwreck in New Zealand open on his lap. Alice was in the other armchair reading two books at once on how to thatch a roof. Between them, Clara was curled up on the sofa with a folder of magazine and newspaper cuttings, reading about a French-Canadian coffee bar chain owner she was due to interview next week. The three were peaceful, Bernard from his seat in the corner was able to see all his family before him over the top of his book and was generally happy that they were all safe and well.

"I think it's time," said Ian, suddenly standing up and putting down his teacup, "for *mbekele shono*."

"Can you smoke it?" asked Bernard.

"It's the traditional libation to welcome the night and make friends with the Darker Spirits so they will not harm you while you sleep."

"What a great idea," said Alice. "Instead of being afraid of evil spirits, you cosy up to them and draw their sting."

"Yes, something like that," said Ian.

"So how do you do it? What is it?" said Clara.

"Basically you drink their health, as it were, and mutter a few welcoming words to them. Very pally."

"I get it," said Sam. "A sort of Women's Institute version of Devil worship. More tea, Beelzebub?"

"No, tea wouldn't work," said Ian. "Needs to be a bit stronger."

"How strong?" asked Alice.

"This is the spirit world we're talking about, I don't doubt," said Bernard.

"Exactly," said Ian. "And as we don't have any *nkini*, we'll have to make do with a drop of whisky."

He bent down and pulled a bottle from his bag.

"Speyside *nkini* should do it."

They all laughed as he filled the glasses on the tray and passed them around. Then he stood in the centre of the room.

"Which way's west?" he asked.

"Down there towards the fields," said Alice, pointing.

Ian made them all stand in a circle around him and then lifted his glass to the ceiling, facing west. He began chanting in a deep, low voice.

"Nbolo makele sholono luana,

"Watisi mbeke nananu riana

"Awewe-awewe nolansu akabi

"Awewe-awewe matutsi bileki

"Shono-tu shonu-tu

"Shona-te shona-te

"Balaleke balaki luana tekeli

"Amale amali amale BULAN"

He turned to each of them in turn and drank, indicating that the person he was facing should do the same.

Then he laughed.

"That should do the trick while I'm away. Never fails."

"Brilliant," said Clara. "You must teach me the words. And what exactly does it mean?"

"Well, it is always said by the chief elder, so it should have been Dad really, but he basically says that he will not be with them for much longer and he wants them to be looked after when he has gone to meet those he is talking to beyond the far mountains. It's a plea from Day to Night asking for Night to care for the tribe until Day returns, but it is also from Life to Death asking for Death to be kind when Life is over – that's the chief's life but also everyone's life. I love it."

"Wow," said Clara and they refilled their glasses and all had a go at saying the words with varying success.

Then Alice leaned across, whispered in Bernard's ear, turned and said.

"I have to pop out. I'll see you all for dinner."

She ran upstairs and five minutes later let herself out the back way as everyone gathered round the fire learning more about *mbekele shono*.

They were beginning to become anxious when Alice had still not appeared as they all sat around the big table in the window at their favourite Fortrose restaurant. Bernard had even ordered for her, although that was not difficult as the whole family came here expressly to enjoy their favourite langoustine, the chef's speciality. Only Bernard seemed unconcerned, simply saying that he was sure she would make it.

Then the doors to the kitchen swung open and there was Alice in full chef's uniform of buttoned white tunic, long apron and tall hat, bearing a huge silver tray with a steaming platter and a large white porcelain dish.

"Is this table 14?" she asked in flawless BBC announcer English.

It set the tone for a raucous evening after Alice had helped the waiter to serve them and joined them at the table. She explained that she had wanted to find out how to cook the langoustine dish if everyone seemed to like it so much. She had arranged to spend a lovely few hours with Mark the chef, learning the secret and in return, she had given him her recipe for a fish stew that she had learnt in a restaurant in Bangkok via a similar assault on the kitchen.

"So Mark actually let me cook what you are eating now," she concluded, "which probably explains why it isn't up to his usual standard."

"Oh better," Clara assured her.

"Far better," they all agreed in mock earnestness.

Later in the evening, Clara bumped into Alice in the Ladies.

Alice became conspiratorial.

"Not a word to Bernard, now," she said, taking hold of Clara's arm and drawing her close, "but I understand you wanted to know who Jane Laker was?"

"Yes," said Clara, surprised and eager. "Do you know, then?"

Alice gave a dark laugh.

"I know nothing at all – it makes for more peace of mind. But three words: Family Records Office."

And she was gone.

Mark the chef came to join them for a drink later after they moved into the bar at the side and sat around the blazing fire. The evening ended in whisky and laughter as Bernard suggested that Alice ought to write *The Smash And Grab Recipe Book* consisting of recipes she had hijacked by barging into restaurant kitchens uninvited.

If Jane had looked in on them now, she too, like Bernard, might have taken comfort from knowing that all was fairly well with the family if Philip could be sorted out, and that through the dark night and all that might follow, they would be protected.

"*Balaleke balaki luana tekeli,*" as Ian's tribal chief might have said.

Watch over my children till the light returns to them.

CHAPTER 10

George – A price to pay

(September 1886)

Two long weeks had passed since George had first seen the girl her friends called Becky in Langton Market, but since that moment, not a single hour had slipped by in which he had not thought of her, pictured her face, heard her laughter, inwardly rejoiced... and felt keenly the hopelessness of his situation.

Even at nights during the few fitful moments when he finally lost consciousness, he would dream of her picking up the small bronze bell and shaking it gently to make the tingling sound that had first caught his attention, had first made him look up and see her. But in those dreams, even as he gasped to relive the first moments of seeing her flashing eyes and beautiful smile when she tossed her head in laughter, her ringlets catching the sun in a shimmering halo that far outstripped in beauty any tree, flower or church window he had ever seen – even as he saw her again for the first time, the image faded, she drew away from him and vanished into the mist. He would cry out and try to follow her, but with every step he took, her image waned more quickly until she was no more. And in her place, swirling out of the mists into which she had disappeared, came the stark shape of Marjory with her starched collar, wan complexion, thin black hair pulled back in a bun from her bony skull, which looked as though the orbits had been carved by a sea monster from the face of some ocean-ravaged cliff. And always, always, that self-same sneer on her face, even when she tried to smile. There she was. Marjory, the woman he was to marry.

At first, it had seemed quite natural to him. The two of them had grown up together and roamed the fields with the other children of their age, looking for eggs and streams and mischief. George's father Thomas had known Marjory's father John since their own schooldays. The two had worked in the fields together and side by side had made the long and terrible journey to the Crimean peninsula to serve in the Anglian Light Infantry, taking part in the horrors at Sebastopol and both surviving although not without enduring horrors that neither could forget but which drew them closer to one another. Thomas walked with a heavy limp after receiving a shrapnel wound from a shell that was probably only two feet away from killing him. John lost three fingers on his left hand, hacked off by the sword of a Russian cavalry officer who charged through the front line that John was struggling to uphold. The sword swipe also removed a small part of John's left ear and a piece of his scalp. But Thomas and John were the lucky ones. Less than half the soldiers involved in that war were alive at the end of it, and those who were had suffered what no man should. None was unscathed in body or mind. John simply said that they had looked inside the mouth of hell. Other than that, they talked little about their military days.

But the bond drew them ever closer and after their return, they worked together each day on the land, glad simply to be alive. Working in among the potatoes and the cabbages rather than amid the screams of death and the gore of bodies torn open in front of their eyes or wasting away from agonising diseases. They lived in cottages just a few doors apart and of an evening, when the weather was fine, they would sit out the back, hardly speaking, smoking their pipes and thinking their thoughts, drawing comfort each from the other's presence. On Saturday nights, they would walk together down to the Red Lion just off the market square, and silently play crib or dominoes together as they enjoyed a pint or two of brown ale.

While Thomas had four children, however, John had just the one. A daughter called Marjory, whose frail and fevered mother died one bitter winter when the girl was four. Marjory had grown into a woman by the time she was 12, kept the house for her and her father, cleaned, washed and cooked the meals. She was a devout little thing, who delighted in going to chapel every Sunday, prayed morning, noon and night, and always said grace before meals in her thin but firm voice.

Perhaps in an attempt to look after his old comrade, perhaps just out of warm-heartedness, Thomas said early on that George, his eldest, and Marjory should marry one day as they were both of a similar age, Marjory just five years older. The idea brought tears to John's eyes. With no son, no other family and no wife, the dread of his declining years once he was too old to work were a source of alarm to him. If George married Marjory, at least there would be bread in the house even after John was no longer bringing it in.

And so the two talked about it for years, all through George and Marjory's school days. It brought great comfort to both the ageing soldiers and was accepted by everyone as a simple fact. George himself grew up with the knowledge and seldom gave it any thought. It seemed to him as natural as the seasons. Just as Spring followed Winter, one day he would grow into a man... one day he would marry Marjory... one day he would die. To a young boy, it all seemed so far away as to be beyond comprehension. When a four-week summer break from school seems endless, a dozen years into the future is so far over the horizon as to be invisible. And because they grew up knowing this fact, it did not change the way either viewed the other, especially in the early years.

By the time George reached puberty, he was almost relieved that this difficult part of growing up had all been sorted out for him in advance. He paid no need to the giggles and whispers of the other boys. He had no need to fret over the embarrassing intricacies of finding a mate. Certainly one day he wanted to stand alone as a man, away from his family, in his own home, with his wife and perhaps his children. He, too, wished to be cared for in his old age. And so he became grateful for the fact of the arranged marriage.

Only later, when the ceremony itself and all that it implied drew closer, did he begin to view it with alarm. It was understood that the two would marry when George attained his majority. That was now next year and a date in March had been set aside. Suddenly George looked afresh at Marjory. Suddenly she was no longer the girl from a few doors away who was destined to be his wife one day. Suddenly he was just a few months away from becoming her husband.

Now he wished he had listened to the juvenile whispers and giggles. He would look at Marjory when they met and try to imagine what it would be like when they were man and wife. Did he find her attractive? He had to admit to himself that he did not. She was plain on a good day, pinched and ugly on a bad. It was more, he felt, from her personality than her actual appearance. And soon she would be sharing his bed, or rather he would be sharing hers as the plan was that he should move in with Marjory and John to ease the overcrowding in his old home and so that the two of them could care for John as he grew older.

The worst part about the whole idea for George was that Marjory had seemed to become increasingly bossy as the day drew closer. As a child, she was always a match for any of the boys, wanting to do her share of organising in the groups they played in, having cut knees and bloodied shins like the hardiest, and generally able to look after herself. Later, as her chapel-going became more and more important to her, this bossiness showed itself in a desire that all those she came into contact with should conduct themselves with decorum and in a devout Christian manner. And as the wedding day approached, this seemed to George to take the form of picking on him, of nagging him constantly. Little that he did seemed right or good enough for

Marjory. His boots were dirty and should be left outside, his hands were unwashed, his language coarse, his table manners unbecoming, and his knowledge of the Bible poor. In short, he was constantly reminded of his mental and physical failings and urged to do something about them.

This was mixed with periods in which Marjory was kind to him. Sometimes on a Sunday evening, he would be invited around to dine with Marjory and her father. This would be preceded by a lengthy visit to the chapel, his neck rubbed sore by his starched collar. He would then be told during the meal how he had been singing the hymns out of tune and fidgeting in the pew. But after dinner, when he had helped to wash up and when John was peacefully snoring in his chair by the fire, Marjory would show a different side of herself, would smile and make plans for what would happen after they were married. Even at those times, however, although he was relieved to avoid the scolding, the shape of his life to come that was being laid out before him left his heart empty and a tightness in his chest. His main love and recreation was to roam the fields with his dogs, to throw sticks into streams for them to fetch and worry. And he loved to get out into his garden, to tend his vegetables and his fruit trees. In future, it seemed, much of this was to change.

"It will be so lovely when you no longer smell constantly of dogs," she told him with a laugh one evening. "Men who keep dogs become like them – low and base. If you want the company of an animal, we shall have a canary that will keep itself to itself and not dirty the place. It will be so lovely."

That was her constant refrain. It will be so lovely. When she spoke of them going to chapel more and more… when she talked of them walking by the river on a Sunday evening… when she enthused about him helping more at chapel… whatever dull and awful thing she laid out before him as his future, she always ended with the same phrase. It will be so lovely.

A canary, he thought bitterly. Caged and sad, not roaming free in the fields. Not free as a bird. Caged as he, it seemed, was also to be.

George, though, was all for a quiet life. He thought that he could still enjoy his work in the fields, and take his father's dogs for walks, and if he could just get through the awful bits that she was planning, he could endure anything for some hours in his garden and out in the fresh air of the fields and…

But that all changed the day that he saw Becky.

He did not even know her full name, who she was or where she came from, but he knew that while Becky was in the world, there was something else to dream about. And he knew that while Becky was in the world, he could never simply tolerate being Marjory's husband.

And that was when his torment began. What could he do? He had never been *asked* if he wanted to marry Marjory. It was simply what was going to happen. He had never agreed, never said yes. How, then, could he now say no? Apart from anything else, it would break his father's heart, not to mention Old John's. And his mother would be hurt by the upset it would cause. She just wanted everyone to be happy, and this wedding seemed to her to be making them all content.

George finished work in the fields just before noon on the Saturday two weeks after he had first seen Becky. For days now, he had planned his next move. He would go home, wash and head off to the market. He would buy the little bronze bell that had attracted Becky and he would find her and give it to her as a gift. He had no idea what would happen then, he just felt that it would somehow tell him about his future. In his dreams, she accepted his gift with a flashing smile at him. That is as far as the dream went. Just over and over again, he would hand her the bell and tell her it was a gift. She would look down, recognise it as the one she had wanted, take it from him, and fix him with a radiant smile of gratitude. How he wanted her to look at him with such a smile.

How he wanted to please her. It would be George taking control of his life, not being pushed around by everyone else, and not being a victim of the gentry. He would be changing the world into something that he, George Harvey, wanted.

He was out of breath from hurrying when he got home, and he quickly took off his working trousers and found some that were less muddy, then washed the dirt of the fields from his arms and hands, pulled on his jacket and headed off out again, leaving by the front door as he had started to do to avoid walking past Marjory's house and risk meeting her. It was a sunny day with a blue sky when he reached the market. The stalls covered the whole square, which was full of traders and shoppers milling about among the cries and shouts and bustle of a typical market day.

George quickly found the stall where he had seen the little bronze bell a fortnight earlier, a small haberdasher packed with all manner of ribbons and trinkets, buttons, clasps and bows. A small, brown wizened woman in a red headscarf knotted behind her head with wispy black hair sticking out at all angles stood beside the stall, calling out unintelligible phrases in a loud, rasping voice.

George hunted around on the table and at last found the bell he was looking for in a box among a load of pins and buckles. He grasped it in delight, held it up and heard again the tinkling sound that he remembered so well, just as he had heard it a million times in the past two weeks. Just as it had first pleased Becky.

He turned in triumph to the little old woman.

"How… how much for this bell?" he asked.

She peered at it.

"What you got there, me duck?" she asked, then stopped. "Oh, where d'you get that from? That one shouldn't even be in there. I told him to put it to one side. Give it here."

She tried to take it from George, but he closed his big hand and withdrew it.

"But… I want to buy it. How much is it?" he insisted.

"I told you. It's not for sale. Shouldn't even be out on the stall. I *told* him."

George just looked dumbfounded, so she sighed and tried to explain.

"It's promised. Someone wanted to buy it last week only they didn't have enough money, see. They said they'd come back this week, so I said I'd put it by for them. It shouldn't even be out on the stall. I told him."

George continued to hold the bell, his mouth open and a look of profound dismay on his face. It seemed to him that the fate of his entire life depended on him buying this bell.

"Come on," said the woman. "A promise is a promise and I gave my word to them. They'll likely be here any minute. Look, there's plenty of other bells in the box," she added in desperation and then coaxingly: "Why don't you have a look at one of these."

"No," said George firmly. "This is the one I want. I want to buy *this* bell."

"I don't know what's the blooming matter with everyone," said the woman to herself. "All these bells on the stall and they all want that one. What's so special about it, anyway?"

She peeled open George's hand and peered at it but could see nothing out of the ordinary to attract all this attention. At last, she looked up at him.

"Look, I'll tell you what I'll do, me duck. You come back and see me at four o'clock and if they haven't been back by then, you can have it. Now I can't say fairer than that, can I? I did promise."

And as George paused to consider what to do next, the old woman deftly snatched the bell away from him and slipped it into the pocket of her apron.

There was nothing for it, George would have to wait and hope that the mystery buyer did not return. The church clock was just striking half past one. That meant he would have to hang around for two-and-a-half hours. And what if Becky had come and gone by then? What if he saw her here and had not been able to buy his gift before she went away again? He would have to wait for another week at least to present her with the bell and to receive the beautiful smile of gratitude.

He walked up and down the market too quickly to look at any of the produce, frowning and gazing about him desperately. He did not know what to do. He went off for a walk by the river but soon returned, unable to stay away. He walked all around the market stalls and thought it *must* be almost four by now. Then he heard the clock strike two. Still two hours.

He went back towards the stall where his beloved bell was so close and yet so far away. As he turned the corner, he saw the old woman holding something up in her hand and heard the familiar tinkling sound of his bell. He was twenty yards away but could see her handing the bell over to someone who seemed to be rummaging in a purse. No! This could not be…

He rushed up to the stall, waving his arms and shouting: "NO. NO. That's *my* bell. You can't sell it to anyone else. I *must* have it. Oh please, don't you see?"

All around, this part of the market stopped and fell silent as everyone turned to look at the big man yelling about a bell.

"This is the man I told you about," said the old woman, spreading her hands wide, raising her eyebrows and giving a shrug.

Startled fearful and angry, the girl with the purse closed it with a snap and put it back in her bag.

"Well," she said indignantly, "what a *very, very* rude man. If you want a little bell badly enough to cause such an ugly scene, then you can have it and good riddance."

She turned away with some dignity back to her two friends.

"Come, Becky," she said. "You shall have something else for your birthday. Let us get away from this ruffian. Come along, Molly. Come along, Becky. How very, very rude."

Only then did George see that the girl with her back towards him was his Becky. Far from giving him a beautiful smile of gratitude for the gift of the bell as he had imagined, instead, her face was full of scorn and anger. She had wanted that bell very much indeed and it had been so very sweet of Mary to promise to buy it for her birthday. Now this shouting man had spoiled her treat. She refused even to look at him, turned haughtily, tossed her head, making her ringlets glisten in the sunshine and hurried away, disappearing into the market throng after Mary and Molly.

George was left staring after them, his mouth open in horror, his heart bleeding.

"One penny," said the little old lady at his elbow, offering him the prize.

George could barely see the money in his purse through his tears, but he fumbled among the coins and at last, found a halfpenny and two farthings, handed them over and took the little bronze bell into his shaking hand.

CHAPTER 11

Allaire

Clara hung her coat on the stand, put her bag, her coffee and her bagel wearily on her desk and sighed. She was the first one in. She was always the first one in. It gave her time to be ready with her defence. She picked up her coffee and managed to get the top off without burning herself. Good start to the week, she thought. She walked over to the window and looked out down through the rooftops to a thin sliver of the Thames about half a mile away. A small white boat sped past on the water from right to left, heading towards the open sea. She wondered where it was going, probably not all the way to the estuary. She wished that she were on the small white boat and that they were heading to France. Somewhere around Caen for lunch would be nice, she thought. She sighed and turned her back to the window, then sat on the sill and looked out over her coffee cup at the cluttered office.

Editorial as it was grandly known consisted of seven desks around the big office occupied by Peter the Editor and founder of *Allaire* magazine. Outside his big oak door was where his PA Marcia sat. Marcia was a bubbly, chatty, smart woman in her mid-thirties who was everybody's friend and kept morale in the office higher than it might otherwise have been. Over by the window was the Production Desk, presided over by Paul, the Editor's silent son, who never said a word. He had joined the magazine only a month or two earlier after finishing a journalism course at college. He laid out the pages, chose the pictures, wrote the headlines and captions and liaised with the printers. Tall with too-short black hair, he would have been quite cute if he were not so self-effacing.

Next to him sat Vincent, the Art Editor, who drew all the page schemes and created the montages and artwork for the feature pages. His hair colour changed often but the last time Clara had seen him it had been luminous orange, although his pencil-thin beard was blond. Vincent was deeply artistic with a playful streak.

Clara's desk was in the opposite corner and the other three desks were spare, used by writers and contributors as they were needed. Most of the work was commissioned by Peter and delivered directly to the office. One or two retained feature writers sometimes came into the office to write a piece or read some proofs, but otherwise, this was the London Editorial team.

The magazine occupied the whole of the top floor of an office building sitting in Shoe Lane between Holborn Viaduct and Fleet Street, most of it taken up with Advertising, Listings, Classifieds and Circulation.

Peter set up the magazine with three university friends when they left Oxford in the early days of Britain's entry to the Common Market. All the others seeped away when things became difficult in the mid-Eighties, but Peter made a reasonable living in his one-man niche market and built it up to such an extent that he could stop selling the adverts himself and employ others to do so. His masterstroke was to position the magazine well upmarket and to strike deals with several leading journals in France, Italy and Germany for printing, promotions and distribution, vastly reducing his costs and reaching a wider audience. As a result, most people in his target market of thirty-plus affluent and aspiring business people who saw Europe as their playground had heard of the magazine and liked to be seen carrying it because it gave the impression that they needed to know what was happening in Cannes or Naples before their visit there at the weekend, even if their furthest journey had been a day trip to Boulogne. Peter long dreamed of expansion into Europe and even into the US, but had never made enough money to pay for it and was reluctant to risk all on a possible failure. He therefore readily agreed to sell the magazine to the Europe-wide French publishing house *Trompette* in the early Nineties. They put more resources behind it and added French, Italian, German and Spanish editions, with offices in Paris, Rome, Bonn and Madrid, generating articles for each other to translate and use as they saw fit. Peter stayed on as Editor in Chief of the *Allaire* Group and Editor of the London Edition, and everybody was happy.

Clara became involved after she finished her National Council for the Training of Journalists qualification while she worked for her local newspaper in Langton. The *Langton Chronicle* was owned at that time by South Central Newspapers Ltd, and Clara began to learn her trade around the parish councils, magistrates courts and flower shows of Bedfordshire. But after a few years, just as she was feeling the need for a new challenge, SouthCen sold the *Langton Chronicle* and its five sister papers to the Argus & Sentinel Group, who "rationalised" its operations in the area by closing the local offices and running all the papers from Bedford, 13 miles away. Langton retained just two journalists to cover the area instead of five, and Clara was not one of the two. She began applying for other jobs feverishly, but in a crowded marketplace found no offers of work until Peter Denhartt liked a piece she had written from an interview with the Mayor of Langton that she sent in with her CV. He invited her to London, dispensed with an interview and told her instead that he could see she had talent, pure, raw talent, that she was to be his protégé and that she reminded him very much in her writing style of himself when he was younger. She started work on *Allaire* the following Monday and a month later had found a small flat to rent just off the Grays Inn Road this stopped her having to spend nearly three hours a day on packed trains. Bernard was wonderful and paid the hefty deposit for her, saying that she could let him have it back when she moved out.

Clara found Peter fascinating at first. He seemed learned, funny, educated – someone who could make things happen. Could perhaps make things happen for her.

After six months of writing short snippets for the news and gossip pages, some of which were used after much re-writing and some popped "on the spike", Clara began being given some interviews to handle, at first just a couple of questions on the phone that Peter wrote down and got her to ask, then this developed into the odd short meeting in London, again at first with questions supplied, and gradually more freedom to think for herself after carefully planning the structure of the interview with Peter in advance.

When she thought back, it sounded like the ideal way to treat a protégé, gradually bringing her on and guiding her into good habits. But the experience had left her not full of confidence as she passed each new hurdle, but rather eaten up with doubt that she would ever get anything right. No matter what she did – made phone calls, arranged meetings, planned interviews, researched subjects, wrote stories, put forward ideas – Peter pointed out with controlled exasperation how silly she had been here, what a basic mistake she had made there. He always added that she had immense talent and that she would be a star one day, but like a plant that is constantly over-pruned, Clara was finding it difficult to flourish.

"*Hic tuibus infantis suis cognoscenti,*" Peter would say, his arms and eyes raised to the ceiling in desperation, one hand clutching Clara's latest offering. "Ah, Pliny, my Pliny, you knew the trials of teaching our children. My dearest little Clara, my star of the future, how can you seriously put this forward as an offering worthy of inclusion in *Allaire*?"

He always said – or rather declaimed – the title of his magazine in the same way, almost like Uncle Bernard's favourite comedian Frankie Howerd, with all the emphasis on the last syllable.

The awful thing was that he was always, it seemed to Clara, right. She HAD missed out the man's age. She DIDN'T ask about the woman's schooldays. She SHOULD have mentioned the nude scene in the play. And no matter how pleased she had been with the rest of the piece, she was left feeling simply inadequate.

Clara pushed herself off of the window ledge, went over to her desk and turned on her computer. The last thing she had done before her holiday was to file an interview for the February edition with a Scottish painter who now lived in the South of France and was about to have an exhibition of her work in Paris. Clara wanted to re-read it. She had been pleased with it but was sure that she had made some terrible mistakes and would suffer loudly as soon as Peter got in.

She opened up the story and began to read. It seemed OK. She liked the intro and the quotes, but...

"Bloomin' heck, a new week but nobody seems to have told the trains," said Marcia, exploding into the office in a flurry of bags and coat and arms and scarf. "One hour and forty-two minutes it's taken me this morning. One hour and forty-two minutes – for a 53-minute journey."

Then she noticed Clara.

"Hello, love," she said, dumping armfuls of bags on her desk and rushing towards Clara with her arms outstretched. "Welcome back. How was your holiday? Your parents all right, are they?."

"Hello Marcia," said Clara, jumping up to return her hug. "Yes, it was lovely to get away from... you know..."

"Did you have a good rest? How's your Dad getting on? Is he OK?"

Marcia was distressed to learn of Grandma's death, although on reflection she thought that at least poor Grandma was at peace, and it was good that Clara had managed to get a break in Scotland, which must have been very peaceful and restful at this time of the year, and how lovely to see all her family again, Sam and Ian, and Uncle Bernard and Aunt Alice – how was Aunt Alice? She sounded a right one…

Marcia was a small, high-energy bundle who never stopped moving or talking. She was only a couple of inches over five foot and slender, too. She had a big mass of jet-black hair that fell past her shoulders and which she was constantly pushing back off her face with quick, darting movements of her hands and a toss of her head. Her face was small and pretty and covered in every scrap of makeup known to the cosmetics industry.

Clara learnt that Marcia's mother-in-law and parents had come for the weekend and the whole family just hadn't stopped laughing once. A real hoot, it was.

Marcia finally got down to unpacking her bags and stowing the contents into various drawers, then proceeded to open the pile of post that she spilled out onto her desk from a sack on her chair.

Clara could get back to reading her interview.

It was not half bad. She could not find the inevitable blunder anywhere. She frowned. Where WAS it?

She closed the story down and opened her e-mail, then took out the cuttings and her notes from her bag and began setting down her interview plan with the topic headings and outline questions she wanted to cover.

She glanced up at her e-mail. "Receiving message 4 of 76…" it told her. Clara groaned.

By the time message 68 of 76 was being received, she heard Peter coming out of the lift and automatically tensed with dread, pushing her pieces of paper about her desk for no reason.

"Ah, the challenge, the challenge that a new week – perchance a new era – brings to us all. Good morrow my little Classified heroines. so charming to see you all again. Hail to thee, my Circulation chickens. Ah, how I have missed you all. Come in to see me at 10.30, pray, Maurice. Ah, life never pauses in its quest for new conundrums to tempt and enlighten us. *Insperum domine quid magi fortuna est.* Good morrow, Editorial, my pride and first joy, good morrow one and – er, other."

Peter had by now arrived in the office and looked around to see only Marcia and Clara present.

"Where is my miscreant offspring and his painted strumpet?" he boomed. "Have they forgotten how to operate alarum clocks in so very short a space of one weekend? Hey? Hey?"

"Oh, they'll be here in a minute," said Marcia, bouncing up towards him and helping him off with his coat. "Did you have a good old rest like I told you to?"

"Ah, rest is for the feeble. I thrive on action and torment. Thank you, good Marcia. Thank you. And many good morrows to yourself and Clara. I trust you are both in rudest health."

"Yes, thank you, Peter," said Clara brightly. "How was Geneva?"

"Oh jewel of the Alps. Surely it will never pall."

Peter Denhartt was almost 55 going on 75. He sounded like a portly grandfather on the telephone but was actually quite slim and wiry so that people who had heard him were shocked at a first meeting until they heard him speak again. His deep, round voice sounded as though it should come from a far larger frame. He wore stout suits in worsted or twill, with a waistcoat, even in summer, and always, but always, a bow tie. Marcia said that she thought he slept in them. Today it was lime green and his suit bottle green cord. Apart from the bow tie, his moustache was the first part of him most people noticed. Pure black, it rose thickly and profusely and then drooped down both sides of his face. His hair was also black, but the word from Marcia was that its colour was bottle-assisted. "When he's been in a hurry or when he gets very hot, you can see the streaks!" she confided to Clara and Vincent one day.

Peter's eyes were slate-grey under a high, bronzed forehead, and his jaw strong and tapering beneath a small, thin nose and full lips. In all, he rather gave the impression of a prototype for a cartoon character. He was still striking and many thought him eminently handsome. But if he had one thing, it was presence. His new French paymasters loved him as an eccentric Englishman and treated him with deference even though he was their employee. They respected his flair, bowed before his persona, trusted his judgements and acceded to his every request. In fact, they were a little frightened of this *gentillhomme curieux*, who quoted obscure Latin at them, never ceased to entertain and continued to make them money.

The young Peter had been very different, quiet and studious in his Somerset boarding school. He enjoyed doing a little acting, especially playing villains where he could hide behind another character. He continued this at Oxford University in minor productions, which nonetheless engendered in him the need to carry these personae back into real life. He experimented with several before settling on the one he still wore, somewhere between Falstaff and Kenneth Williams – a kind of *Carry On Shakespeare*.

He had always loved travelling, especially in Europe, which was part of the reason why he set up his magazine, and on one trip to France, he met and fell in love with the daughter of a minor provincial nobleman, Elisabet Laguerre, small, dark and beautiful. He brought her back to live in his Hampstead home, but when their son Paul was six, she died of heart failure, taking a large part of him away with her.

Twenty-four years had passed since then and the outer shell of Peter Denhartt had not changed in the least, and since no one alive was allowed to see beyond, none could perceive the fear and loneliness of a man who saw clearly that the world had moved on, had changed without him, and who had no way of changing himself. He was what he offered to the world. If there was anything other than that, any real being behind it all, then it was a poor, frightened creature that lurked Dalek-like deep within him and feared for the future. But the show went on. And he was trapped inside its endless performance.

"Ah, my starlet, my *Accephone*, how have you passed the hours since last we met *non vi sed saepe cadende*? Away rogue hours that have kept me from my charge."

Clara stood up and received a paternal hug.

"I had a good rest, thank you, Peter," she said with a small smile.

"But her Grandma died and she had to go to Scotland and organise the funeral and all that kerfuffle," put in Marcia.

"Ah sadness creeps behind us o'er the lea and in a moment fain would feast on me. My warmest regards and commiserations *vobis parentis*. And to you my child. And to you."

He laid a large hand on her head.

"*Te benedictum, infanti, in spiritu sanctu,*"

He paused and left his hand where it was. Clara could feel the bones and gave a small shudder.

"Ah, bid me not remember my end."

Then he drew himself back to the present.

"And yet my child, our life goes on. There SHALL be cakes and ale. And even on this sad day, it is my duty to do my duty, which is, I fear, to chide you for crimes against the pen. Where is that confounded Paul? Pray when the cursed whelp arrives, do the both of you come into my sanctum."

He sighed and swept into his office, followed by Marcia clutching bundles of letters and a cup of green tea she had made him.

Clara stood hunched where he had left her, a deep dread squeezing her chest and stomach. Humiliation would be bad enough, but in front of Paul was even worse. She went back to her desk and picked up her pen, but had no heart for the interview to come.

Just then, two slim hands covered her eyes from behind and a small voice trilled: "Guess who."

"It would be more difficult, Vincent," she said, removing the hands, "if you didn't use a whole bottle of the same aftershave every morning. Bit of a giveaway."

"Aftershave? My dear, I don't shave – so barbaric. I wax. Lasts far longer and it's better for my dimples."

"Go on," said Marcia. "And how was your long weekend in Crete? Did they like your god-awful music?"

"A land of culture was bound to appreciate my combination of revolution and absurdity. Yes, they loved me. Agios Nikolaos rocks. Even more so now."

Today Vincent's hair was white, his beard blue and his glasses thin and purple. He moved over to his desk and Clara noticed that somehow Paul had also arrived unseen and was already sitting, head bowed, behind his computer screen.

"Oh, morning, Paul," said Clara. "I didn't see you come in."

Paul looked out from behind his terminal.

"Hello," he said then vanished again.

Paul was 30, tall and broad with many of the physical characteristics of his father, except that his hair was lighter brown. He tended to have his hair cut about every three months and obviously said as little to the hairdressers as he did in the office, as a result of which, they just hacked away until it was short, and he passed from the laid-back shaggy look to low-IQ criminal overnight. He had clearly just had a haircut. He dressed soberly, always in white shirts and tie, usually with a pullover that looked as though he had bought it from the remnant stall at a jumble sale, and a dark blue or brown suit, that would have fitted someone who was its shape perfectly, but unfortunately, that person was not Paul.

With parents fond of zipping around Europe, Paul had been brought up largely by a string of nannies and at a couple of boarding schools, first in Somerset – the same school and the same house that his father had been to – and then in France, just outside Paris. He then followed his father to Oxford, but to a different college, and after a year's journalism course was brought in at the end of last year as Production Editor, a role that Peter had carried out, but which he wished to relinquish to spend more time "piloting the frail craft of policy through seas of barbarous temptation" as he put it. In fact, Peter should have given up laying out and subbing the magazine several years earlier, but the general feeling was that he was keeping the job open until his son was ready to take it. Popular opinion was that the same would be true of the Editor's job at some stage.

Marcia came back out of Peter's office just as Clara was trying to settle back down to her interview questions.

"Clara, Paul – he'd like to see you both now, please."

Clara picked up her pen and pad and trooped glumly into the office, followed by Paul.

Peter sat behind a huge mahogany desk with green leather inlay. The office was more like a library with two of the walls covered in bookshelves. Behind him on the wall was a huge painting in an elaborate gilt frame of the young Peter and Elisabet, him sitting in a large armchair by a blazing log fire, looking quizzical, she standing beside him, small and meek in a plain black dress with a single string of pearls, one hand on the wing of his armchair. The remaining wall was mostly window and looked out over the rooftops of London.

"Come in, come in."

Peter waved them to the brown velvet chaise longue in front of the bookcase to the right of his desk in the far corner of the office.

When they were seated, he gathered up a handful of papers, stood up and walked slowly over towards the window, looked out for a moment, turned, looked at the papers in his hand, frowned and began, barrister-like.

"There is in this piece that you wrote before your holiday, my Clara, the kernel, the nub of a good read. Yes, I think that we can rescue it. But you fall into so many traps, still, Clara, still. All this turgid stuff about her mother. Pah! they all say that…"

"But I couldn't find anything in any cuttings about her mother trying to kill her and…"

"Exactly – and why? Why has no one bothered to print this fish-and-chippy, low-life nonsense? Least of all US! Least of all *Allaire*. Ah, Clara. So much to learn. Nobody believes a word of it and nobody cares anyway. Here we have a woman with homes in Perth and Nice. We are a magazine whose primary rallying cry is to the Hop-On-A-Plane-To-Verona brigade. To the few who do and to the thousands upon thousands who aspire to be those people. Here you have a chance to hold up an example of someone who has made the leap, an aspirational figure to warm and cheer us – and instead," he slapped the papers down onto the desk in front of him "INSTEAD you write about a grubby piece of menopausal psychobabble guaranteed to make us all choke on our croissants. *Laudate veneremus hic solo manu tuus*."

He moved back behind his desk and sat down heavily. Clara looked at the floor.

"Paul," said Peter, picking up the crumpled papers and flinging them across the desk at his son, "I've made some marks on this. A little turning around and some – ahem – excision and we'll have it on page 49. You know what to do."

Paul picked up the sheaf and turned to go. Clara stood forlornly and began to follow him out.

"And, Clara," said Peter, "when you come to interview this Gautier chappie, remember: he is French, he is Canadian, he is setting up coffee bars in France, Germany and the UK. That's a lot of countries. Do try not to tell us all about his sordid childhood."

"OK," murmured Clara, and hurried out.

"Excellent piece, though," said Peter to himself when she was out of earshot. "The girl can really get people to talk and is a fine writer."

He picked up the phone and began to dial.

Outside, Marcia, who had heard every word, took Clara over to the coffee machine in the corridor.

"Cheer up, love," she said as Clara stood staring into space by the machine.

"Look," she added brightly, "he's going to tell you himself, so don't forget to act surprised, but one of the letters he had this morning was from the Big Frogs at Trumpet."

She lowered her voice to a sharp hiss and leaned towards Clara so that her eyebrows touched Clara's ear.

"They want to beef up their office in Paris and are looking for a writer to go and do features and interviews for *all* the editions – you know, big stuff. And THEY'VE ASKED FOR YOU. They want Peter to release you."

"What?" Clara was unable to think. "What?"

"Oh, we're going to miss you, Clara, but it's too good a chance to turn down and you'll have a smashing time. Oh, I could even feel jealous."

CHAPTER 12

Philip – Day to remember

(August 1965)

P hilip got back to his room feeling elated, exuberant and thrilled. He closed the door behind him, walked to the sink, went over to the window, sat on his bed, stood up again – and all the while a double Cheshire Cat-sized smile followed him in his mirror. He stopped in front of it and studied himself. This, Ladies and Gentlemen, is Philip Harvey – *the* Philip Harvey. That's right, the very same Philip Harvey, ace salesman from Burridge, Thompson & Co Ltd, Publishers of Quality Literature, est 1896, who has just persuaded Mrs Edwina Hamilton of 135 Victoria Avenue, Brighton, to sign a contract entitling her to receive one volume of the Complete Illustrated Universal Encyclopedia, Second Edition, every month for the next twelve months at a bargain price of only £2 19/11d per month AND to pay *in advance* a further 14/11d for a stylish wooden bookcase on which to keep the treasured volumes which will build month by month into an invaluable learning aid for Mrs Edwina Hamilton's soon-to-be-clever offspring Michael, 11, and Christine, nine. His first sale! He had danced all the way back to the *Bel Air* and could not stop jigging about now.

He studied the mirror and watched himself deliver his closing speech to Mrs Edwina Hamilton all over again: "I'm sure that in years to come, you will look back on this day as a vital one, a day on which you gave your children a wonderful start in life and did something that you can really be proud of."

Such poise, such conviction. He'd done it…

After so many weeks, it was a huge relief to him to know that he could be a salesman. He had sold something. He *was* a salesman. He had talked Mrs Edwina Hamilton into parting with her cash. He felt so excited he wanted to rush out and swim around the pier. Except, of course, that he couldn't swim. But oooooh, what a *feeling*!

Ever since he had started trailing round in Mr Willoughby's wake, he had been becoming increasingly convinced that he had made a mistake. As he watched the great Willoughby with all his vast experience having doors shut in his face, Philip felt a sense of deep outrage. How dare people treat poor Mr Willoughby so badly? How dare they be so rude to him, some of them?

"Bugger off," one man in a vest had said to him.

Philip felt desperately sorry that Mr Willoughby should have to suffer such treatment.

Not that it appeared to bother Mr Willoughby in the slightest.

"Your funeral, mate," he had muttered as he left the doorstep belonging to the man in the vest. Then he added to Philip with a smile as they trudged back down the path which they had so recently trudged up: "Still with a Dad like that, the nippers didn't have much of a chance in life anyway, did they? Encyclopedias would be a bit of a waste on them as is being destined to hire out deckchairs for a living or scoop up donkey poo off the beach. Come on, let's just finish this side of the road and then we'll have a cup of tea."

In all the weeks that he accompanied Mr Willoughby, Philip had seen him make only two sales, and one of those was to an old lady who had seen an advert in the newspaper and phoned asking him to call. But Philip had grown to admire or even to wonder at the toughness of Mr Willoughby's hide. Rain or sun, smiles or scowls, Mr Willoughby was always cheerful.

"It's dead simple," he used to tell Philip. "For every 200 to 250 doors I knock on, I make a sale. On average. All I have to do is keep knocking. And if someone slams the door in my face as soon as I say hello, they've actually done me a favour. That's another door towards my next 200 to 250 without wasting any of my time. Now if every time I walked down a street all the doors slammed in my face without me needing to stop, just think how many more sales I'd make!"

When he said it like that, it seemed to make perfect sense and Philip tried to feel good about the slamming doors. But was this, he wondered, Mr Willoughby being sound and to be followed slavishly? Or was the man an idiot with his 200-250 doors rubbish, to be ignored at all costs?

Philip decided to come back to that one and meanwhile tried to pick up tips when they did get inside someone's house.

"Flatter, cajole, lie if you must, undermine, suck up to – and then if the going gets tough, you've always got nastiness and insults to fall back on," that was Mr Willoughby's stated working practice.

Philip tried to memorise as many of the phrases as possible.

"I could tell as soon as I walked in that this is a house of learning."

"Wouldn't it be awful if your children asked you a question about their homework – and you couldn't answer it?"

"Of course, like any clever parent, you want your children to get on, don't you?"

"This is the most up-to-date encyclopedia in the country. There are answers in here that nobody's even thought up the questions to yet..."

The trouble was, Philip had seen the same lines produce the desired reaction from a customer and also produce very unwanted responses along the lines of: "How dare you speak to me like that? Kindly leave my house at once."

"You have to trust your instinct and just say what comes into your head," Mr Willoughby would say.

Eventually, he could put it off no longer, and Philip was sent out on his own, with his very own case of books, forms to sign, pen, pictures, a headful of facts and patter, thumping heart, dry mouth and twisted stomach.

On the first morning, Mr Willoughby took the even numbers of Burningham Crescent, while Philip tottered up the drives to the odd numbers.

"What do you *want*?" asked a woman in curlers and dressing gown at the first house after Philip had finished his speech.

"Thank you anyway and good morning to you," said Philip, giving up on the spot rather than trying to say it all again, and scuttling back down the drive as fast as he could go.

He reached the end of the road having spoken to only three people and interested none of them, while Mr Willoughby still had a dozen homes to call at. Philip sat on his case and wanted to go home.

Next day, he was driven to the new estate going out of town on the coast road towards Rottingdean. Mr Willoughby was going to continue tramping the streets of Brighton and pick him up on the way back. And so it started. Day after day of rejections, refusals, insults and more as Philip began to wish that he were some more acceptable creature than an encyclopedia salesman – something like a shoplifter or a mass killer perhaps. Every day seemed the same as he endlessly plodded the endless streets, believing more with each passing failure that he was destined never to sell a single book.

"Any joy?" Mr Willoughby would ask him each weary evening when he got back into the car. And each evening the reply was a small, sad shake of the head.

"Don't let them get to you, dear boy, or they're the winners. Always believe that the next door is a sale."

Philip believed no such thing. He was particularly galled by the fact that Mr Willoughby, who had enjoyed so little success while he had Philip in tow, now reported overwhelming interest in book learning.

"Got a sure-fire banker this morning," he would say. "I'll go back and seal the deal tomorrow". Or "The line about some parents not loving their children was what clinched it today."

Eventually, the battle of Rottingdean was lost without a shot being fired. Mr Willoughby was heading further around the coast towards Peacehaven and Philip was given a series of addresses out to the north of Brighton to do his worst.

Now, only two weeks and three days later, he had struck. But he had needed all his wits and had to battle hard like an angler with a stubborn fish, refusing to be bested. Such craft... Such professionalism...

Mrs Edwina Hamilton at 135 Victoria Avenue had listened to his speech after inviting him to come inside out of the rain. In the end, as Philip was running out of things to say, having trotted many of his best lines out twice already, Mrs Edwina Hamilton simply said: "You just went to her next door. I saw you through the curtain. Did she buy one?"

For a second, Philip considered a small fib.

"Yes. Yes, she did," he was the tiniest fraction of a second away from saying. But he swallowed hard and instead said: "No. I'm afraid she didn't."

He was all set to pack his case and head towards 137 Victoria Avenue.

"Why didn't she, then, if it's as good as you say?"

Say the first thing that comes into your head, Mr Willoughby never grew weary of telling him. Live on your wits.

"Well, I only saw her for a few minutes and you no doubt know her a lot better than I do, but I must say that I got the distinct impression that she was so mean that she was willing to sacrifice her children's future to save a few shillings."

"*Did* you? Did you, now?" Mrs Edwina Hamilton was suddenly full of interest, so Philip rammed home the blade once more.

"Either that," he confided, "or perhaps she thought that her offspring were not blessed enough in the cranial department to make even such a small investment worthwhile. Could be one or the other really."

"Or a bit of both," said a beaming Mrs Edwina Hamilton and less than 10 minutes later she had signed her contract, which she considered worth every penny to maintain her children at the obvious intellectual advantage over her haughty neighbour that they now enjoyed.

Philip stood in front of his mirror and beamed as he played out the scene once more. Brilliant! Breath-taking! Stupendous! He couldn't wait to tell Mr Willoughby.

And he had earned his first commission, which made the day even sweeter. He did a quick calculation on a scrap of paper. Three pounds. More than THREE POUNDS. Why if he could make one sale a week, that was a HUNDRED-AND-FIFTY pounds a year. And now he had cracked it, there was no reason why he could not earn that sort of money. With the flair that he now had, he was made…

Philip wanted to celebrate. He wanted to share his news and his good fortune. It was Saturday afternoon. What could he do? He was going to burst with excitement if he didn't *do* something.

Then he had an idea. Why didn't he treat Mary, the kitchen girl, to the pictures and a fish and chip supper? Surely on this day of all days, when he was so masterful and lucky, she wouldn't say no.

For weeks, Philip had been trying to find the courage to ask Mary out, but a combination of his shyness and the further lack of self-esteem that daily failure produced in him robbed him of the necessary resolve and pluck to say anything at all to her.

Each day when Mary came into the Dining Room to collect plates, he gazed at her and she often looked back. They both smiled. But they were never alone and his misery, coupled with his lowly place in the Dining Room combined to stop him speaking anyway.

Twice, he had walked past the little grocer's shop a few streets away. She had stopped working at the *Bel Air* at weekends now and worked in the grocer's shop all day on Saturday. He knew where it was because he had heard the others talking about it. Miss Penn'orth o' Butter, they called her and asked her if that smell on her clothes was flour weevils.

Philip had found the shop and even seen Mary through the window, but had never dared to go in. Today, though, would be different. Today was a day for saying and doing the first things that came into his head, knowing that they would work. If he left it until tomorrow or the next day, he might be back in a day where such spontaneity would not succeed. No, it had to be today. In fact, it had to be now.

He put on his jacket, smoothed back his hair with his brush, checked himself out in the mirror and marched straight down the stairs, out of the front door, along Narrow Road towards the seafront, first left into Hazeldene Avenue, first left again into Ruthven Close and on the next corner he crossed the road and went straight into Bennett's the Grocers. It was a tall, dark shop in which no surface horizontal or vertical was without some sort of produce for sale. Bags and boxes of fruit and vegetables covered most of the floor and behind the dark wooden counter were rows of shelves and cupboards and drawers filled with jars, tins and more boxes. Mary was behind the counter serving an old lady who had a tiny mite of a baby in a pushchair. Mr Bennett was just coming out of the back room, twisting a brown paper bag over and over and putting it in a box on the counter.

"Now was there anything else, Mrs Jemmett," he said to the box's owner, a very short, fat lady in a brown coat and black hat.

"I'll take a bag of my usual flour, please, Mr Bennett – oh and a quarter of margarine as well, please."

"Certainly, Mrs Jemmett," he said, bustling off to find the goods.

Philip meanwhile stood patiently waiting for Mary to be free, hoping that she would finish with her customer while Mrs Jemmett was still filling her box and wondering what to do if Mr Bennett were free first.

Mary looked at him in surprise and smiled before continuing to add up a long string of figures on a piece of paper.

"That comes to one pound thirteen and sevenpence ha'penny, please Mrs Wiggins," Mary said, still looking at Philip and wondering what could be wrong.

Mrs Wiggins handed over four crumpled ten shilling notes, which Mary rang up in the big old cash register at the back of the counter. She pulled out a series of coins then turned back to Mrs Wiggins.

"Two pounds, so that's six and fourpence ha'penny change."

She counted two half-crowns, a shilling, a threepenny bit, a penny and a halfpenny into Mrs Wiggins's outstretched hand, reciting as she did so: "Two-and-six, five shillings, six shillings, and thruppence, fourpence, ha'penny. Thank you very much, Mrs Wiggins, and I hope little Anthony is soon better."

"Oh I hope so, dear," said Mrs Wiggins. "Thank you very much, dear."

And she collected up her shopping bag and expertly manoeuvred the hefty pushchair through the narrowest of gaps and out of the door, which Philip held open for her.

He quickly nipped back inside when she had gone, marched over to Mary and said: "Would you like to come to the pictures with me tonight? I'd be ever so honoured."

Oh dear, that sounded corny, he thought, his bravado ready to desert him at any moment.

"What's on?" asked Mary, startled, darting a glance at Mr Bennett, who was fortunately at the other side of the shop sorting out a bag of potatoes.

Good question, thought Philip, who hadn't a clue.

"Oh, it's a very good film," he said. "A... a love story... about people... in love... and..." He dried up completely and just stood there looking at her.

But Mary smiled again and he knew he was safe.

"That would be lovely. I'm not sure that I can. I would need to find someone to sit with Aunt Vera." She paused and frowned. "Perhaps Mrs Montgomery would pop in. Be outside the shop at half past six and I'll let you know if I can."

"Good. Right-o. By Jove," said Philip, and almost ran out of the shop.

In a daze, he headed for the beach to enjoy some fine summer air, but as he reached the seafront another thought occurred to him and he turned back and almost ran to the Odeon. *A Man For All Seasons* was showing. Was that a love story? He had no idea.

Time dragged until half past six. Philip could not eat any of his tea and as soon as he could he was back in his room polishing his shoes, brushing his hair and trying to make his suit look as presentable as possible.

At twenty-past six, he was standing outside Bennett's again, not wanting to go in. At half past six, Mary came out, smiling and said that yes she could go, but she had to make sure Aunt Vera was all right first and she couldn't stay out late.

Philip waited around the corner from Aunt Vera's, floating a couple of feet in the air, his heart twice its normal size, while Mary went in and what seemed like an age later reappeared with a black coat and a white hat on instead of her shop coat.

"It's *A Man For All Seasons*," said Philip, knowledgeably, having studied the posters at the cinema. "It's about Henry the Eighth… being in love and things."

They walked along the streets purposefully in the warm summer evening, with enough space between the two of them to make any chaperone happy, and they chatted about Henry the Eighth, although neither knew a thing about him. At the cinema, Philip paid for two Front Circles at a hefty two-and-ten each and they sat watching the B-movie about some lion cubs in Africa, which seemed to make little sense. The main feature itself finally started and although he enjoyed his ice cream tub that he had bought them from the usherette in the interval, Philip gave up on the story 15 minutes in, contenting himself with the fact that he was with Mary, sensing her presence beside him in the darkness and trying to catch and remember her scent.

It was finally over and the two of them came out into an evening that was still light.

"Thank you very much," said Mary and began walking next to him towards her home.

"Oh, you don't have to go just yet, do you?" he pleaded.

"I mustn't be late..."

"Why don't we just have a little walk down to the sea and back," he coaxed.

"Well, all right, but only as far as the pier."

They set off, still a foot apart, he with his hands in his pockets, she clutching her little black handbag in front of her.

They walked the half mile to the pier and a little way along it, hardly speaking, Philip trying desperately to find something to say, but Mary, a small smile on her face, not seeming to mind.

Then she said: "I ought to be getting back."

"All right," he said gallantly and they turned, made their way back off the pier, back along the seafront and were soon standing outside Mary's house.

"Thank you again," she said. "It really was very kind of you."

"Oh it's been a pleasure," he said. "We must do it again sometime soon. If you can get away."

"That would be nice," she said. "Good night."

"Good night."

Then with a cross between exultation and desperation, not wanting to lose the moment, he reached out his hand and was soon shaking hers. Realising this was a trifle formal, he lifted her hand to his lips and gave it a quick little kiss.

Mary smiled at him again, held the look and his hand for a long second, then turned and went into the house.

Philip the salesman went back to the Bel Air, and with a quiet smile, he went softly up to his room and lay on his bed although it was still quite early.

A sale, he thought proudly to himself, hands clasped behind his head, gazing up at the ceiling. His first sale. More than three pounds commission. And he was now "going out" with Mary.

CHAPTER 13

On the record

Clara turned another corner by the Grapes pub. Now she really was lost. She pulled out her map and looked again, then up at the street sign. Rosebery Avenue. Rosebery Avenue. So Myddelton Street had to be round here somewhere. She turned right into a street with no name and saw some market stalls ahead of her.

"Er – excuse me," she said to an old woman with a small white dog and a grubby pink shopping basket. "Could you tell me the way to Myddelton Street, please?"

"Yeh, yeh," said the old woman, and then paused and looked around her. "Midleon Street. Straight up. Here. Left. Straight up. At end of road."

She pointed with a sweep of her arm and turned to shuffle away.

"Thank you," Clara called after her and went into the street with the market stalls. Exmouth Market said an old, faded street sign.

Clara walked through the stalls selling jeans and shoes and handbags and jewellery, past the launderette and the kebab house and the amusement arcade and the video and record shop. And as the market and the street ended, she came to a crossroads, walked across Rosoman Street and found herself in Myddelton Street. Number 1. The Family Records Office.

An hour later, Clara came blinking out into the thin winter sunshine feeling quite excited and more than a little sneaky, as though she had been peering into people's drawers.

The Family Records Office was like a strange library with rows and rows of big leather-bound books in three sections: red for births, green for marriages and black for deaths.

It was a bit of trial and error because the books just gave lists of where and when people were born, married or died. Just that. All in alphabetical order by year. Three months to a volume. So you guessed the year you were looking for, searched through the appropriate volume under the right letters, tried to find a name and place match, noted down the number, filled in a slip of paper, took it to the front desk, paid what seemed like a lot of money and were handed a receipt. A couple of weeks later you received through the post a copy of the actual certificate – which may or may not be what you were looking for.

Clara had asked for a selection that she hoped would help her to understand Jane's letter. Would these certificates tell her anything? She had not spoken about any of this to Alice since their brief conversation, or to anyone else either. She laughed to herself. Probably a waste of money.

As she walked back through the market, Clara remembered the old sepia print family photos of Thomas and Jane with their babies. First Bernard in 1923, then Susan two years later, then a long gap until Philip in 1947 when Jane was past fifty. Bernard always joked that it was something to do with the ending of a war that reminded them of their youth and made them feel frisky again.

Whatever the reason, it gave the family a rather lopsided feel, especially since Bernard was married by now to Alice and they had returned from their travels a year earlier with Ian, their first son, making Uncle Philip two years younger than Nephew Ian, another source of family amusement.

When Thomas died following a short illness just after Philip's second birthday, Jane struggled on and the family "rallied round" as families do. Bernard, in particular, rose in stature. He became a kind of chieftain to the extended tribe, with Jane the matriarch in the background. While he was king, she was king-maker and he deferred to her in all serious matters.

Susan, meanwhile, had left home and gone to London to seek entertainment. She had presumably found it because she failed to come back or call or write. Clara had long since given up trying to discover what happened to her.

"She was bored living in the country," was all Bernard would say. "She went off with her friends and just stopped keeping in touch. It happens sometimes. No-one's fault. Very sad, because she was a lovely girl. But she was very headstrong."

Philip was not much more helpful.

"I don't think I ever even saw her. She was living away from home when I was born, I think, and never came back. There was some talk of her having gone abroad, and that's probably what happened. Perhaps she died abroad without being able to let us know."

Clara kept a black-and-white picture of Susan. She was very pretty even under the constraints of an awkwardly posed picture. She had long, wavy tumbling black hair – or at least, it looked black, but could equally well have been chestnut – clear skin, shining eyes and a cover-girl smile. As a girl, Clara used to make up stories to tell Sam about what happened to Susan, in which she by turns became a princess, spy, a politician and a harem slave. The last was Sam's favourite.

By the time Philip married Meg, and Bernard and Alice had young Sam, Jane was already spending a lot of her time in Ross and Cromarty and her beloved Black Isle. Finally, she moved back in the early Seventies, soon after Clara was born, saying that they all had their own families now and that she wanted to die in the lands of her ancestors.

As the years went by, she grew more and more frail, the family were all busy creating their own lives and careers, so there were fewer and fewer trips back north. And in any case, there was less and less reason to visit her, mainly because Jane did not know anyone was there when they did go, sleeping around 20 hours of each day. She was calm and settled, and Muriel took good care of her. Life went on.

Clara looked at her watch. Two o'clock. Time for her assignation with the coffee magnate Henri Gautier. She walked back towards Farringdon Road to hail a cab.

It was two days since Marcia had told her about the European job. Two days of heart-stopping excitement as she imagined herself freed from the fear of working for Peter... living a real *Allaire* lifestyle in Paris and all points south, east and west... writing for people who had *asked* for her, people who had seen some talent in her that they wanted to promote. But still Peter had said nothing. Perhaps he was waiting for the right moment. He was always the showman. Probably wanted to make a big thing of it with champagne at the end of the week, and today *was* Friday.

She had to concentrate on this interview first, though.

She couldn't *wait* to tell people.

A black cab with its orange light shining brightly came around the corner. Clara hailed it and got in.

"The Savoy Hotel, please," she said to the driver and settled back, thinking that she would soon be telling Parisian taxi drivers: "*Au Georges Cinq, s'il vous plait.*"

CHAPTER 14

George – Soul survivor

(July 1887)

"John," said Thomas contentedly as he pushed away his dinner plate, "we have seen some things and been in some places that no man should ever see or go to." He leaned back in his chair and rubbed his aching knee at the memories.

"But, John, I tell you something. For a man to end his days surrounded by his family in such contentment as this… well I think it nearly makes up for it, John."

John considered his friend's words. He lay down his knife and fork and laid a hand on his old comrade's arm, the hand blessed only with one finger and a thumb.

"You're not wrong there, Tom," he said slowly. "You're not wrong there."

He began picking his teeth with a split piece of wood as he gazed proudly around the table at his daughter Marjory, who had begun to collect the plates. How well she had turned out, he thought once more.

George's mother gave a little sigh and picked up her own plate to help, but her daughter-in-law would have none of it.

"Now you sit yourself down there, Mrs Harvey," said Marjory. "While you are a guest at our table, you shan't lift a finger on our account. George, come and lend me a hand and let your poor mother have a sit-down."

Marjory smiled at her husband, who rose, took his mother's plate and the gravy jug and followed his wife over to the draining board, where they piled all the plates and saucepans in the sink.

It being a fine, sunny late summer's day, the children had all been allowed out into the backyard, where they were busy playing hopscotch amid great shouts and whoops.

Thomas and John left the table and went over to sit in their chairs on either side of the fire, saying little, but satisfied in body and mind. Both would soon be asleep.

George's mother became fretful at her inactivity and sidled off to join George at the sink, into which he was pouring hot water ready to wash up.

"Here," she said quietly to her son, "let me do that. You go and sit down. You work hard enough all week. You should be having a rest of a Sunday."

But Marjory saw what was happening and took George's mother gently by the arm.

"Now, Mrs Harvey," she said, leading her mother-in-law back to the table, "what would you say to a nice cup of tea?"

"Well, that would be very nice," said the old lady, looking across at George, who was now scrubbing the first of the plates and setting it upside down on the draining board so that most of the water ran off back down into the sink.

"I'll put the kettle on then. I can help George with the drying up. We'll soon have it done. Then we'll have a nice cup of tea before we go to chapel."

And Marjory busied herself putting the kettle on the stove, collecting the best cups and then drying the dishes and putting them into the top cupboard of the dresser by the far wall.

When she went out of the back door for a moment to call to the children and tell them that they had to go and get clean and ready for chapel in half an hour, George's mother quietly rose and went across to her son.

"Are you all right, George?" she asked him softly. "You seem a bit quiet."

Startled, he turned around, shot a quick glance at the door, then smiled.

"Yes, Mum, I'm all right," he said, washing a handful of knives as he spoke and laying them at the top of the draining board. "Don't you worry about me."

Reassured, she sat down before Marjory returned and the peace of an orderly Sunday afternoon continued as the smells of the mutton roast wafted out of the open windows and the three settled down in the snug kitchen talking about the weather and Mrs Burnage's new baby two doors away, and the two veterans snored gently by the fire, their tea keeping warm in the pot.

A few hours later, after they returned from chapel, after George's parents had said their Thank Yous and gone home, after the stove had cooled, John had returned from sitting outside with Thomas and after a final cup of tea, he went up to bed, worn out by the long day and the walk to chapel and back.

"Good night, Marjory. Good night, George," he called back to them from the staircase as he closed the door behind him.

"Good night, father."

"Good night."

The sound of the old man's steps grew softer as he painfully climbed the creaking stairs and went into the small bedroom above the parlour. Marjory watched the staircase door intently as she listened to the sound recede. George, too, looked at the door and swallowed although his mouth was dry. Finally, they heard the bedroom door close and there was silence in the little cottage.

When she was satisfied that he had retired for the night, Marjory slowly turned in her chair and faced her husband, a smile spreading across her face.

"Now," she said at last, "we are alone."

She stood up and went across to the back door, closing it and throwing the bolt home with a firm thud and click. She paused for a moment, leaning with her back to the door, smiling to herself but looking at nothing. Her hand absent-mindedly played with the lace scarf knotted around her neck.

At last, she spoke, but softly, almost to herself. George could scarcely hear the words, but made no movement, simply stared ahead of him with wide eyes that saw nothing.

"Let us see," she began. "By my reckoning, today's count was five. I think that you avoided Anger today. There was perhaps a small flicker when you barked your shin on the bench as you and father were moving the table out for dinner, but as you were clearly in some pain and as you controlled yourself admirably after the initial outward signs of wrath, you may be pardoned for that. And of course, Lust... well," she gave a small, scornful laugh, "that is just about all you could properly be said to master."

Marjory paused again.

"But that leaves five sins to be atoned for," she went on simply.

Still, George did not speak.

"I see," said Marjory in a thin voice, not smiling any more and standing upright, away from the door. "I see, so you stubbornly refuse to accept your sins. What a weak and feeble creature man is."

Her eyes burning, she strode towards the kitchen table and leaned with her hands flat on the top, opposite George as he sat as still as a tree trunk.

"If you have any hope of being saved... if you are one day to be Redeemed by the love of the Lord Jesus Christ, who gave His life for your sake... if you are to find that Salvation that He brought to us all... then you must confront your own sins. You must be purged. You must beg for forgiveness."

There was silence again. Still, George had not moved. Marjory sat down opposite him.

"So," she continued, "let us go through your sins today. As I said, there were five that you need to beg mercy of the Lord for. And these were they. Sin the first: Pride, the most pernicious of them all. This morning when your father commented on the largeness of the marrows in the garden, I saw you looked pleased as though this was your work rather than God's.

"Sin the second: Envy. As we were walking to chapel this afternoon, you spied some ruffians running in the meadows beyond the river. You said nothing, but I who can see the evil in man's heart could tell immediately that you wished you were with them rather than being about to enter the House of the Lord.

"Sin the third: Sloth. Usually you are out of bed early and off to work, but today, on the Lord's day, when it is beholden upon everyone to rise up and praise Him, you lingered in bed, unwilling to get up for the Lord's work.

"Sin the fourth: Greed. At dinner, you helped yourself to a second piece of pudding and a large one at that, which brings me on to Sin the fifth: Gluttony. You then ate every morsel of the pudding you had seized so greedily."

Marjory paused and leaned back against the settle, breathing deeply, her eyes staring. Still, George sat motionless.

"You need to be purged, husband. For your own good, for the sake of your soul, you need to be saved."

There was silence. Then Marjory added: "On your knees."

Slowly, his eyes staring to the front, George stood up and moved towards the fire, unbuttoned and took off his shirt, laid it over the arm of the chair and knelt down facing the embers, his head bowed, leaning his massive chest on the small footstool by the hearth. Marjory walked across to the cupboard by the chimney breast, opened it, reached in and pulled out a short-handled piece of cane with five or six thin, leather thongs, each about two feet long, attached to one end. George did not look round, but just waited, the light from the fire picking out a mass of thin weals that covered his back in a random lattice pattern.

Marjory crossed and stood behind him to one side.

"Our Father..." she began.

"Our Father," said George," which art in Heaven..."

He continued to recite, softly and clearly, with hardly a catch in his voice as Marjory planted her feet firmly apart, bent her back and with the full weight of her slender but tough body brought the whip slashing down onto his back, opening up old scars where it fell and ripping out more red welts where it found some unblemished skin.

"...hallowed be thy name..." CRACK! went the whip like a musket shot in the still night. "...Thy Kingdom come on earth as it is in Heaven. Give us this day our daily bread and forgive..." CRACK! "...us our trespasses as we forgive them that trespass..." CRACK! "...against us. Lead us not into temptation, but deliver us from evil..." CRACK! "....For Thine is the Kingdom, the Power and the Glory forever and ever..." CRACK! "....Amen."

Five sins, five lashes.

"Amen," said Marjory, who was breathing heavily, her forehead glistening in the light from the fire.

Every night followed the same pattern. On weekdays, it tended to be one or two sins, perhaps because Marjory had less chance to watch her husband while he was out in the fields, perhaps because the weekend and in particular the Holy Day was special and needed to be marked out as such.

Marjory stood holding the whip out in front of her, as George raised himself up, turned around and knelt in front of her. He took the whip in both of his hands and lifted it up to his lips, kissing it five times. Then he muttered quickly: "Thank you, Lord. I am cleansed."

"Amen," said Marjory, her eyes closed in silent prayer.

George took the whip from his wife and replaced it in the cupboard by the chimney breast and closed the door. Then he picked up his shirt and without a word went upstairs in his turn, put on his dark nightshirt and got into bed.

Having finished her prayers, Marjory closed down the last of the ventilation on the fire, filled the kettle and laid it on the stove for the morning, blew out the candles and followed her husband up to bed, closing the stair door behind her.

In a few minutes, all was quiet in the small cottage on the edge of Langton. Old John in his room was snoring gently with the contentment that a full belly, a glass of ale and a strong young family to care for him brings to a simple man nearing the end of his days.

Marjory, too, was asleep, happy to have reached the conclusion of another pure day full of praise and atonement, having done what was right for her and hers.

And George lay quite still, his eyes open and moist in the darkness. In his closed fist, he gently clasped a small bronze bell. He had put paper all around the tiny ball, winding it carefully through the chain and knotting it to make sure that the bell would not make a sound and give its presence away. He took a bittersweet comfort from this tiny window on a different world that he had once glimpsed, a world of flashing smiles and beautiful eyes and chestnut ringlets and girlish laughter in the sunshine of a marketplace long ago. This was the bell whose faint tinkle had turned his head and opened his eyes, had let him gaze on a wonderful land of joy, and had briefly allowed him to imagine what it would be like to taste that joy as though it were his own. And because of this bell, he had that vision snatched away from him, never to return. It was fitting, then, that it was silenced forever. Silent as the night that lay all around the cottage where he lay beside his wife and tried to find solace in a sleep that would not come.

CHAPTER 15

Untangling the web

"Here's to Clara, Queen of Europe," said Sam, raising a glass of chilled white wine to chink Clara's glass and at the same time glancing towards the door. "It sounds absolutely brilliant, you lucky sod."

"Well, I don't actually have it yet," said Clara. "Peter still hasn't mentioned a word, so perhaps nothing will ever come of it."

"Oh, he's just trying to spin it out. Probably knows that Marcia told you about it and wants to see you squirm a little. Classic behaviour of a bully."

"Do you think so?"

"Absolutely. In any case, if the French lot have told him to jump, he'll have to in the end. They do *own* him, after all."

"Yes, they do, but... I don't know. It doesn't quite work like that. They still defer to him in a lot of ways. Look up to him. I don't know. He gets his own way a lot still."

Clara looked down at the tablecloth and played with her glass. Sam realised that if he shifted a little to his left, then he could see the door at the far end of the restaurant in the mirror over Clara's shoulder without turning round. He settled back into his seat.

"I still think you're a lucky sod," he said. "Fancy living in Paris and zipping all over Europe on expenses. What a life."

Clara laughed, then frowned.

"Oh, don't jinx it. If I wish for it too much it'll never happen and I'll be stuck so far under Peter's thumb that I'll have trouble writing so much as a full stop without thinking that I've got it upside down."

"Ah, well," said Sam, looking hard at the door as a woman and a man came in, then relaxing again.

"Oh, let's change the subject," said Clara. "I must say it's a pleasant surprise to be asked out to dinner, but you still haven't told me what it's all about. You were a bit mysterious on the phone."

Sam had not been listening.

"Sorry, what were you saying?" he asked.

"I said you were mysterious. On the ph…"

Sam suddenly sat forward and grabbed Clara's arm, frowning.

"We've known each other a long time, haven't we, Clara? And I've never asked you to do anything for me, have I? All right, a few things, but I need your help now."

"Why? What?"

"There's no time to go into it. I'll tell you later. She may be here any minute. I told her 7.45. Look, you don't know Dawn, do you? Never met her, have you?"

"Your occasional floozie? I think we met at a birthday party when we were about six, but…"

"Good. She won't recognise you."

He began talking very quickly and earnestly.

"Look, I've done something pretty awful, but only because I panicked. Very briefly. I need to get rid of her so that I can go out with Michelle, who I've just fallen in love with. I don't know what is going to happen between me and Suzie, but perhaps that's almost over as well. But Dawn is definitely getting too clinging and it's not going anywhere, but she just can't seem to get to grips with the word No, and, well, perhaps I'm not very good at saying it, either. But I can't cope with Michelle, Suzie AND Dawn, so… I… er…"

He tailed off.

"So you er what?" asked Clara, not liking the way the conversation was going.

"Well… I…"

He stopped again and looked at the door.

"Well, you what? Look, if you don't tell me, I'm going home right now."

"No, don't do that. OK. OK. Well, I said that I panicked. I phoned her this morning and told her that I was getting married..."

"Getting MARRIED..?"

"Yes... er... to you..."

Diners as far as four tables away were now straining to follow the conversation.

"Well, I had to think of something... final. Go on, play along and I'll do the same for you one day."

He looked nervously at Clara, who sat with her mouth open, trying to work out where exactly she ought to throw her wine and if she should bother to keep hold of the glass or not.

Sam punched her playfully on the arm.

"Go on," he said in his best attempt at cajoling. "It'll be a laugh."

He took one look at her face and put the cajoling away for the evening.

"Well, not a laughing matter, of course. An experience. Look, I can't go back on it now."

He looked in the mirror.

"Oh, my God. Here she is. Look, your name's Hillary..."

"Hillary?"

"It's the first name that came into my head. You're a secretary who works near me and you know the family. Uncle Bernard arranged it."

"Uncle..?"

Clara looked down at her hand and found that Sam had picked it up and was kissing it while gazing into her eyes with a dopey look. He pretended not to see Dawn, who had paused at the door and was staring around the restaurant.

Clara glanced over at her love rival.

Dawn was medium height with straight brown hair just off her shoulders. She had pale skin, a thin face and a cute nose. She wore a well-cut, cream trouser suit over a purple blouse that was straining to contain her huge chest. She spotted Sam and immediately glared at Clara.

Shaking off a waiter, she marched to where they were sitting, pulled a vacant chair from the next table and joined them.

"So this is the little tart who's trying to take you away from me, is it?" she sneered, leaning back and blowing smoke from her cigarette at Clara.

"Please," pleaded Sam, through his teeth, desperately looking around the restaurant. "Don't cause a scene."

Dawn blew smoke at him, too.

"A scene?" she said. "A SCENE? I ought to decorate the High Street with your small intestines."

She looked at Clara knowingly.

"VERY SMALL intestines," she added. Then she changed tack.

"After all you promised me..."

Tears appeared.

Theirs was now the only conversation in the restaurant. Clara looked at Sam, then at Dawn. Was this happening? She did a few calculations. Family crisis. What would Uncle Bernard do? Dawn could clearly look after herself. It HAD only been a casual affair, albeit a lengthy casual affair. Clara would do anything for Sam. He would owe her a huge favour, which might be useful one day. And it would be fun to keep the IOU and wave it around under his nose from time to time, like a Get Out Of Jail Free card at *Monopoly*. OK, she thought, let's do this.

"Listen, sister," said Clara in her best soap opera ham voice. "I don't know who you are or where you blew in from, but this is a table for two and that's the way it's going to stay. I know Sam here isn't an angel, but then neither am I. I don't care. All that's in the past now and we two are headed for the future."

Sam stared at her and squeezed her hand. Don't overdo it.

Dawn wiped her eyes and looked hard at Clara, who was now enjoying herself.

"There are very few times in your life when you know that something's right," she went on. "Sometimes you don't need to look at it too closely. Well, that's how it is with me and Sam. I'm not about to give that up for you or anyone. So why don't you just be a good girl, turn around, hail yourself a taxi and high-tail it back to all your other fancy boys."

"That simple, is it?" said Dawn, who also seemed to be enjoying the challenge.

Sam sank back into his seat and looked from one to the other in dismay. This was not how he had imagined it.

"So you think you can just waltz in off the street, turn his head for a few hours and wipe away 15 years of what we have between us?"

"Well, not on my own." Clara went for it. "But the baby will certainly help."

"The BA-BY..?" said Dawn.

"Oh, Sam, didn't you tell Dawn our lovely news?"

"I... well... no... I..." said Sam.

Dawn slumped back into her chair and gazed in front of her for a few seconds with her mouth and eyes wide open. Then, still gazing into space and focusing on nothing, she stood up and with a full swing of her straight right arm, starting well behind her back, mechanically, almost absent-mindedly, she slapped Sam's face with an almighty thwack. Then, still not looking at anything, she turned, walked slowly and steadily to the door and was gone.

There was a long silence as Sam sat with his hand to his burning cheek and the restaurant slowly got back into its rhythm. Clara took a long pull at her wine. She stared about her, frowning, as though regaining consciousness.

"Did I just do that?" she asked hesitantly.

"Bloody hell," said Sam.

They sat in silence for a few moments, then Sam took a drink and a deep breath and tried to get his balance again.

"Bloody hell," he repeated.

"I'm... er... sorry. Did I go a bit over the top?"

"Well, no. I suppose not."

He tried to laugh and lighten the tone.

"You certainly got rid of her, which was, after all, the point of it. So, thanks very much. I had no idea you..."

"Will she be all right? Hadn't you better go after her? What if she's standing outside in tears? Oh, what if she jumps under a bus? Go after her, Sam. Go and see."

"Ah, she'll be in a cab by now on her way to seek comfort with Tom Morrison or Andrew Hawks or Timothy Piper or Carl..."

"Yes, all right," cut in Clara. "Just pop outside anyway and see for me. You do owe me a few favours."

Sam went to the door, followed by most eyes in the room. Clara poured them another drink and watched him pacing up and down the pavement. He was talking on his mobile phone. Was he calling her? Or an ambulance?

Clara was relieved to see him smiling as he came back to the table.

"Is she OK? What did you say to her? You didn't tell her who I was, did you?"

"Who? Dawn? Oh, she's long gone. No, I was calling Michelle. Now you've cleared the ground, there's no problem about seeing her tonight, so I invited her to join us. She only lives a few minutes away. She'll be here in two ticks. You'll really like Michelle. She's absolutely gorgeous and..."

"Are we in some kind of bad film? I thought I was just having a quiet dinner with you, but it's turning into *The Parade Of The Seven Honeys*..."

"Seven? I should be so lucky..."

A waiter arrived and said: "Are you ready to order, sir, madam?"

"We're just waiting for a friend. Could we hold on a few minutes?"

"Certainly, sir," said the waiter with a look that made it clear that he doubted if that particular friend would be returning tonight.

"We'll have another bottle of wine, though," said Clara.

"Certainly, madam."

"I've suddenly lost my appetite," she added to Sam. "I'll stay and have a drink and then leave you two together. Christ, I feel like a deranged dating agency."

"Oh, no, do stay," said Sam, with so little conviction that they both had to laugh.

"Perhaps when Michelle walks in I should slap your face and flounce out. Your standing as a lady-killer in the restaurant would zoom up. They'd probably name this table after you."

By the time they had finished another glass, in walked Michelle, a pencil-slim and very pretty creature with long blonde hair, big green eyes and flesh that felt almost liquid when she shook hands with Clara. The hem of her tight black skirt nearly met the bottom of her scooped red T-shirt neckline, with plenty of flesh on display above and below.

"This is Michelle," Sam announced proudly to Clara as though he were introducing a work of art that had come to life. There, I told you she was stunning, was implied in his every word.

"Hello," said Michelle in a thin, high voice, looking suspiciously at Clara and darkly at Sam.

"And this," Sam added quickly, "is my cousin, Clara. We just had to sort out some business."

"Nice to meet you," said Clara. "Yes, a little family business."

Michelle relaxed.

"Oh, that's good," she said. "Families."

"In fact," said Clara, "I'm sorry to run out on you…"

"Oh, that's OK," said Sam.

"…but I'm late for my next appointment. Thanks for the drinks, Sam. Good to meet you, Michelle. Have a lovely dinner."

"Yes, we will," said Sam with a smile that touched both his ears.

"Lovely to meet you," said Michelle, looking at Sam dreamily.

"Aladdin and all the saints preserve us," sighed Clara as she climbed into a taxi outside and headed for home.

No, she thought, that most certainly ISN'T what Uncle Bernard would have done. What *would* he have done? She thought for a moment. Uncle Bernard would have sent Sam out on some errand and when he returned, Dawn would have quietly told Sam that she was leaving, no hard feelings and it been wonderful knowing him, goodbye. Uncle Bernard would have smiled calmly and then melted away. Job done.

What she had done had been pretty clumsy and amateur. She shivered. Poor Dawn. Clara hoped she was all right. She shouldn't have interfered, playing around with people's lives like that. She had no right. She wanted to get in touch with Dawn and say sorry and make it up to her. She would ask Sam for her phone number in the morning. They would be friends.

The cab sped through the dark streets, past rows of shop windows and dark figures hurrying through the showery night.

And yet, Sam HAD wanted it to end but had just not known how to do it. Left to himself, it would have just dragged on and he would have been more and more unhappy. He would have made Dawn more and more unhappy. He would have lied to Dawn, fretted about Michelle, and got into more and more of a tangle. All Clara had done was to cut through the jumble. It was a mercy killing instead of a slow, lingering, inevitable death. Now Dawn knew where she was – and where she had been for some time without admitting it to herself. Clara hoped that she really did have friends to turn to as Sam had said. No, perhaps it was for the best, even if it had been somewhat bizarre.

But what had come over her? Why had she said all that mad stuff? It was as though someone else had been talking. Someone else had taken her over for those few minutes.

She arrived home with the same two emotions battling inside her, neither able to gain a decisive victory. She had deliberately hurt someone she didn't know and had no right to harm. And she had solved a family problem and left Sam and Michelle to enjoy their life together, or at least the next few weeks of it.

Lucky girl, Michelle, she found herself thinking as she put her key in the lock. She smiled and wondered if she had really meant that.

She picked up her mail, put the kettle on, made herself a large mug of tea and settled down on her sofa, put on the lamp, switched on the TV, found a soppy film and settled down.

She looked at her two letters, one handwritten and the other more bulky and in her handwriting – the certificates she had sent away for. That was quick. She opened the hand-written note first. It was from Henri Gautier, the coffee bar hunk she had interviewed. Nice eyes, a lovely smile and an exquisitely cute bottom. He had *very much* enjoyed their lunch, he wrote, and he would *very much* like her to come to his launch party in Paris at the end of next month to celebrate the opening of his 10th European outlet. Just ring this number and Joséphine, his PA, would arrange flights, hotel and hospitality. "I am *very much* hoping that you will be able to make it and be assured that I will take personal responsibility to ensure that you enjoy your stay..." How on earth did he get her home address? she wondered. She read it twice more. She lingered on a few words. He did have very nice eyes. And beautiful hands. Not forgetting that bottom. You never know, she might even be working in Paris by then.

She sipped her tea. On TV, the heroine and the hero were standing on top of a hill kissing each other. She imagined holding Henri Gautier in her arms and kissing him on top of the Eiffel Tower at sunset with the Champ de Mars, the River Seine and all the lights of Paris spread out beneath them. She closed her eyes. Mmmm.

A few minutes later, she remembered the other letter. Ah yes, let's see. She opened it and found three folded sheets and a compliments slip. She opened the first. A birth certificate for Susan Harvey. "Born March 13 1927. Place of birth: Sandon. Father:

Gabriel Harvey. Occupation: Farm Labourer. Mother: Gwendoline Richardson." Damn. Wrong Susan Harvey. What a waste of £3.50.

The second was another birth certificate, this time for "Bernard Harvey (otherwise Laker)". Clara put down her cup and sat upright. Laker. *Otherwise* Laker. What on earth did it mean? Father: Thomas Harvey (otherwise Laker). This was getting strange. First, there was the insurance policy in Grandma's big file in the name of Jane Laker, along with the picture of Rebecca Laker. Now Uncle Bernard and Thomas Harvey, the grandfather she had never met, Grandma's husband, are both otherwise-Lakers. What did it all mean? Who were this otherwise-Laker clan who had infiltrated the family?

The next sheet was the marriage certificate for Uncle Bernard and Aunt Alice. Off we go again. "Bernard Harvey (otherwise Laker) married Alice Hughes on Saturday 7 June 1941. Witnesses: Cedric Hughes and Grace Harvey." Clara remembered that Grandad Thomas had brothers and sisters. Frederick, Ellen and Grace, she thought, so that was OK. But why wasn't Grace an otherwise-Laker?

When Clara finally fell asleep around two in the morning, she dreamed that she was coming back to her hotel after dinner in Paris with Henri, Sam and Michelle. She and Henri said goodnight to the other two and went to their room, but there was banging on the door. Dawn was trying to get in, crying and saying that she wanted to be friends. And as Clara ran away down a corridor, Henri and Dawn were chasing her and she realised that she was pregnant.

CHAPTER 16

Susan – Staying put

(July 1946)

Susan's first full day in her new London life passed in a warm glow of happiness. The morning was sunny and bright as she and Ron slipped out of his room and went for a stroll along the streets of Bethnal Green before buying a newspaper and going into a small, neat café with green gingham tablecloths for what Ron called "a slap-up breakfast".

"Real eggs," he told her giving the side of his nose a double tap with his forefinger.

"Ronaldo," said the little old lady behind the counter with a shrill cry of glee. Wiry and short with a grease-stained coarse white shop coat, she came limping out to give him a big hug. "Lovely to see you on a lovely morning," she said as she stood on tip-toe and leaned up to reach a stooping Ron's shoulders.

"Good to see you too, Mabel," he said, returning her hug.

"And this must be your cousin," said Mabel, hugging Susan in turn.

"That's right," said Ron. "She's up for the weekend."

"You're always welcome here if you're a friend of Ronaldo's," said Mabel, squeezing Susan's arm with an affectionate smile. "He looked out for us when times was hard."

They sat at a table in the window, where the sun poured in and warmed them thoroughly. Ron read his newspaper and Susan just sat and beamed – beamed at anything and everything. She beamed at Ron, at the table with its salt and pepper pots, at the window and the pavement and the odd bus that chugged and wheezed past, and at the man in the corner eating a bacon roll. And when Mabel brought out two huge white plates laden with steaming food, a large brown teapot, a small green Bakelite jug full of milk and a little white bowl of motley sugar, Susan beamed at Mabel and at her plate and at the tea as well. Ron had ordered eggs and bacon and sausages with fried bread, all of which seemed real enough, too.

Susan set to with a real hunger after using up so much energy on the dancefloor. Her headache had all but gone now and the sunshine and the strong sweet tea would take care of the remnants.

She chewed a mouthful of bacon dipped in hot, runny egg yolk and she wanted to shout and sing and jump up and down with happiness. How could the world possibly be any better than this? Having survived nearly 20 years of her life in the small, tedious confines of Langton, she had finally escaped. She was in London, she was eating breakfast in a café, not at the kitchen table, she was with her man, she had been drinking and dancing, she had got away, and overnight she had become a woman. A real woman.

She took another sip of tea and it was as hot and strong and sweet as the real world should be, as vibrant and tangy as the life she wanted to lead, as the life she was now *going* to lead.

When they had finished breakfast and Mabel had handed her a white paper bag containing a couple of bread rolls filled with cheese "to keep you going", they sauntered off into the sunshine again. Ron had some people he needed to see at a place called Spitalfields, so she took his arm and he led the way.

"Are you OK to walk, Princess?" he asked. "Only it really isn't far and it's such a nice day and it would be the devil's job to find a taxi on a Sunday morning."

Susan assured him that she was enjoying the walk. She thought that she could walk a million miles if necessary.

"Well, let me know if you start feeling tired," Ron added. "Only a princess like you should really be carried everywhere in a sedan chair with roses from the Sahara Forest strewn across your path."

He leaned across and kissed the end of her nose, patting her hand as it lay on his arm.

Susan beamed.

A little under half an hour later, Ron took them in through a green door between two shops.

"You'd best wait here," he told her in the hallway, indicating a rickety wooden chair standing in the dim and musty passageway. "I won't be long."

He leaned across and kissed her on the nose again.

"Then we'll go and do something nice."

Susan sat on the chair, still beaming, as Ron bounded up the dingy staircase two at a time. He was gone for about 20 minutes, during which time, Susan did not see a single person or hear a sound from the upper part of the building.

Finally, he reappeared, skipping down the stairs again two at a time.

"Sorry… sorry… sorry…" he called as he came back down to her. "Princess, Princess, I'm so sorry. That meeting took a lot longer than I thought. People just go on and ON sometimes and you can't shut them up."

He lifted Susan to her feet by taking her hand, pulled her towards him and kissed her on the nose once more.

"However," he added, "that was a very successful little piece of business that I have just ascertained and I am now in a filthy good mood. Let's go and have some fun."

Ron opened the door and they were back in the sunshine again. It was now warming up and the streets were dusty and beginning to bake. It would be a hot afternoon.

"I'll bet," said Ron, "That you have never been on a boat trip down the River Thames."

"I haven't," freely admitted Susan.

"Then, Princess, you shall. Like Cleopatra floating down the Amazon, you shall glide over the waters. Let us go."

He offered his arm, which Susan grabbed and they were soon climbing aboard the first of two buses that took them deep into the Isle of Dogs, past romantic-sounding places on the signposts that Ron pointed out to her on the way... Whitechapel, Stepney, Shadwell, Limehouse, Poplar, Millwall... it was like being in a strange and exotic city that was still crumbling after the war but would soon be bright and shiny again with a lick or two of paint. A wonderful, magical city. Only now it was her home.

When they finally arrived at the waterfront, they joined a small queue and were soon climbing aboard a pleasure boat with rows of seats in the front and a big wheelhouse clamped on the back with a tall, black, smoky chimney.

Off they went, the wind surprisingly cold in Susan's hair, making her laugh and snuggle closer to Ron for warmth even though the day was by now very hot.

Ron pointed out the sights along their route. Greenwich, Deptford, the docks of Millwall and Greenland to either side of the river, Rotherhithe and Wapping, then they turned a bend in the wide Thames and the mighty Tower Bridge came into view, which no sooner had they sailed under than the famous Tower of London appeared on their right.

"That's where they'll chop your head off if you're bad," Ron told her.

On they went under more and more bridges until Susan really was beginning to feel cold and Ron put his arm around her and pulled her close. Finally, they came to the Charing Cross embankment and Susan was pleased to be back on dry land again and away from that chilling river wind.

Along with the other crowds on this bright Sunday afternoon, they wandered along the embankment, gazed up at Big Ben and the Houses of Parliament then took a stroll in St James's Park and stood on the bridge looking at the ducks in the water.

Susan did not want it to end.

Ron and Susan crossed Westminster Bridge to get a better look at the Houses of Parliament and walked along the Albert Embankment. They stood against the parapet gazing into the dark swirling waters of the river. She looked across at him as the sun caught his face, his dark hair shining in the bright light, and she thought how handsome he was.

"This is just the *best* day there could possibly be," she said, squeezing his arm.

"Nothing, Princess, is too good for you," he said, gazing back into her eyes. "Now what would you like to do next? Are you warm enough? Are you thirsty? Are you hungry?"

Susan remembered the cheese rolls.

"Wait!" she said, rummaging around in her bag, then triumphantly bringing out her white paper package and showing him the cheese rolls.

"Perfect," he said. "You truly are perfect."

They stood with their arms on the embankment wall, munching cheese rolls and tossing small bits to the ducks below and the pigeons that soon came to see them, and a few crumbs to some chirpy sparrows that invited themselves to lunch too.

"Talk about feeding the five thousand!" she laughed. "If only we had two small fish to go with the bread rolls, I'm sure that we could feed all the birds in London."

"You must be a saint to make so little go so far," he said. "That's it, you're Saint Suzie…"

"Saint Susan…"

"… feeding the animals like that Francis bloke."

The meal finished and they walked on a little way towards Lambeth when Ron had a sudden thought. He turned and looked at Big Ben.

"It's three o'clock already," he said with a frown. "I hadn't realised it was so late. And your bag and things are still back at my digs. We'd best get a move on. What time's your train?"

Susan looked at him, failing to understand.

"Train? What train?" she asked.

"*Your* train, silly," he smiled, then stopped smiling. "Your train home."

"But... but I'm not *going* home... I *am* home... London... This is where I live now. With you..."

Ron almost instinctively half turned away so that Susan did not see the dark shadow that passed across his face, or his forehead screw up into deep lines, or his lips pinch tightly together as he took in this awful news. But he recovered in a second.

"Oh that's good," he said, turning back towards her with a laugh. "I thought you were going to run out on me."

They walked on in silence for a while, Susan feeling uneasy as though her new happiness could crumble at any second. But Ron's morning business *had* gone very well and he could not disguise what a good mood he was in for long. He could sort out any other problems in due course and if wriggling out of things turned out to be necessary, then it was a bit of a speciality of his, wasn't it? So Susan had moved to London for good, had she? That was why she was carrying a bag yesterday. That meant she would be sharing his bed again tonight. Ah well, he could put up with that for a while. She did have a *very* lovely body. The kind of breasts he loved. He could easily put Maude off. He wasn't doing anything early tomorrow, so why not just take what was on offer and ask questions later? He could shift her soon enough and still keep her coming back if he played his cards right.

"Let's head back anyway," he said, offering his arm again. "The sun will be going off soon and I don't want you getting chilly again. In any case, I have a few people to see and we can get some dinner in the King's Arms if you like."

Susan sighed with deep relief. Dinner in the King's Arms in the upstairs room with just her and Ronaldo sounded perfect.

"Taxi!"

This time, they rode all the way home in style and she sat back in the taxi seat, tired from her long walk, and held her Ronaldo's hand as he told her something of the life of a businessman in the east end of London Town.

CHAPTER 17

Uneasy lies the head

Alice glanced over at the clock. 3.30. She half sat up in bed and reached for the glass of water beside her on the table. She took several small nervous sips. She looked across at Bernard lying beside her and sighed. She could see the sweat glistening on his forehead in the dim glow from the nightlight on the landing. She could not see, but knew, that his hair was matted and wet too. He lay on his back, his shoulders twitching, his mouth opening in a series of strangled cries, making barely a sound. His hands were raised under the bedclothes, the fists clenching and unclenching in spasms. His legs arched one after the other as though he were attempting to run. His whole body flexed and shook.

Bernard was having the dream again.

Alice knew it well. It was not like any other dream. It was not like the peaceful, playful twitching dream of a cat or a dog, full of gentle snorts and whimpers. She remembered how they had laughed at Max their old Labrador when he used to lie on the kitchen floor in the evenings and dream he was running through the woods. Carefree and excited.

She looked at Bernard in the half-light. Bernard was not carefree. Bernard was in torment.

As always, Alice tried to make out the words he was trying to say. Strained to listen for some clue. But she could hear nothing except choked, guttural gasps.

And she felt powerless. She had tried everything she knew but nothing helped and quite often she seemed to make things worse. She had tried holding him, cuddling him, but any physical contact increased his frenzy and made him desperate. Once he had even lashed out and cut her lip quite badly. She had tried waking him but he would not come out of it and his anguish grew with every shake.

Alice sat up on the edge of the bed and swung her legs to the floor. Twenty years? Thirty years? She had been watching this dream attack her man for a long time. Not often. Perhaps two or three times a year. But it would not go away.

She had tried talking to Bernard about it, but he laughed it off and told her not to be silly. He didn't remember anything about it in the morning, he said. It was just a dream. Then he always changed the subject. But something in his look told her that he knew very well what he had been dreaming of even if he did not remember the exact details of the night before. And he always woke exhausted and fretful the next morning.

Alice pulled on her dressing gown and padded downstairs to the kitchen. She leaned back against the sink and thought. She wandered into the front room and put the television on low, flicking unseeing through the channels. Then she switched it off and sat in the darkness.

All those years. It was long enough for one man.

No. Someone else needed to take on this responsibility, whatever it was.

It was Clara's turn.

CHAPTER 18

Philip – Meg takes charge

(May 1966)

Philip sat on the train heading for Langton and let out a long, low sigh. He was glad of the break. Not just to get away from tramping around the doorsteps of Sussex, not just the egg-shell tiptoeing at the *Bel Air*. He was getting strangely used to both. What he was finding most difficult was Mary.

He managed to sell one and a half more sets of encyclopedias since that first heady success but reckoned that he was well off Mr Willoughby's 250 doorsteps per sale. He didn't like to count up but guessed that it was more like 250,000 in his case. But what he missed in sales he made up for by developing the inch-thick hide of the salesman and he could now smile like Willoughby at yet another slammed door.

With his meagre wages and those little bits of commission on sales, he still had more than enough to cover his modest needs, so what did he care if no one wanted his stupid books?

And he had learned the trick of the small table in the dining room – take a newspaper in for every meal. Gives you something to do, stops you from having to talk or listen, and provides a nice barrier both from the big table and even from Mr Humphreys right next to him.

The only time he put the paper down was when Mary came in and they spent a few minutes while she collected the plates exchanging furtive glances and quick smiles.

But that was the real problem. He saw Mary regularly now on the odd evening when she could get away for a few hours and they would occasionally go to the pictures, but more often walk on the beach or stroll along the seafront eating fish and chips out of newspaper. Philip loved those precious moments, but he was so shy that he did not know what to do, how to really make Mary his. If only she had turned to him, put her arms around his neck and kissed him all would have been well. But she did not. And nor did he. Sure they laughed, joked and chatted. In fact, they got on well and were both relaxed in each other's company and looked forward eagerly to the next meeting. But they still kept that six to nine inches apart and he had never so much as held her hand since that first night goodbye.

"Did I tell you about Christine Parks?" she would ask as they wandered along Brighton Pier, eating their ice creams.

"What's she been up to now?" asked Philip, trying to remember who she was.

"Well, she's only been seen hand-in-hand with Roger Croft..."

"Roger Croft? Er, film star? Pop singer? Prime Minister?"

"No, dopey. He's the dustman I told you about. Just come out of prison for assault. Well, Christine's mum is livid, but she daren't ban her because Christine has threatened to run away from home."

"I had no idea such things went on in a respectable place like Brighton," laughed Philip. "What does her dad think about it?"

"He died last year. I told you. Drowned trying to save a dog."

"Ah yes. Terrible thing."

And they wandered on, chatting and laughing and talking about all and everything. Everything that is except the one topic Philip wanted to talk about. Philip and Mary. And in particular, Mary kissing Philip.

He tried to bring the subject up again and again, but somehow it didn't work.

"Are you cold? Would you like my jumper?" he would ask, hoping that she would suggest that he put his arm around her shoulders. For warmth. But either she was not cold, or she would suggest that they run to that bus stop and back to warm up a bit.

He always carried an umbrella on their walks if there were even a hint of a possible shower in the newspaper weather forecast. You have to get close under one umbrella in a downpour. But the skies always stayed stubbornly fine when they were together.

In the films, he noticed that whenever two people kissed, they just went quiet and imperceptibly moved closer and closer together until their lips met and the orchestra struck up. But whenever Philip tried this, almost before he had begun to lean towards her the silence was inevitably broken by Mary offering him a toffee. "Shall we share one?" he asked once, but Mary assured him that she had plenty and the moment passed.

Even when it came to the time to part at the end of the evening, that traditional time when lovers kiss goodnight, he had not managed to write a happy ending into their script. If he tried to give her a gentle hug outside her door, she became flustered.

"Someone will see us!" she would hiss, looking up at the windows and over her shoulder down the street.

If he tried to suggest it was time to say goodbye just before they turned into her street, she looked at him in disappointment. "Are you not going to walk the last little bit with me?"

What else could he do? He had left it too late. They were like brother and sister, and you don't go throwing your arms around your sister's neck and kissing her the way he wanted to kiss Mary.

He had done all he could think of to make her free from any threat in his company. He wanted her to feel valued for herself, not sneered at or looked down on as she did every time she walked into the *Bel Air*. But by standing back, giving her space, making her feel safe, he had lost the chance to assert himself in any sexual or even just romantic way with her, he thought. At least that is how it felt to him. If he tried to make any kind of advance to her, it would have seemed as though he were undoing at a stroke all the small kindnesses that he had laid down in her path like a cloak over a puddle. He would have felt as though he were violating her every bit as much as the gentlemen around the big table.

And yet... and yet... what if she were just waiting for him to get close to her, to hug and cuddle her and make her feel loved? What if at every meeting she just wished and waited? And what if she would soon grow so tired of waiting that one day soon she would no longer be free when he asked, would no longer give him sidelong smiles in the dining room, and they would soon be no more?

And then what if he saw her walking arm-in-arm a few weeks later with some deckchair attendant or recently released violent dustman? Looking up into his eyes, standing on tip-toe to raise her sweet lips to be kissed?

It was driving Philip to despair. If he tried to kiss her, he could lose her. If he didn't, he could lose her. What should he do? There was no one he could talk to about it? Mr Willoughby? Hardly. What would Marje Proops advise? Should he write to the *Daily Mirror*'s agony aunt? It was a thought.

The train pulled into Victoria Station and he trudged off to catch the bus to King's Cross for the journey back to Langton.

"Oh it's lovely to see you again," said his mother as Philip walked in through the front door of the house in Langton that was shared by his mother Jane, brother Bernard and sister-in-law Alice, whose son Ian was away at University. "Let me take your bag. You're looking a bit tired. Hope you're getting enough to eat and enough sleep. Go up and get changed now before tea and then Bernard's invited a few people round for a sandwich and a couple of beers tonight to welcome you home."

Bernard came into the hall at the sound of his return.

"Hello, little brother," he said with a smile. "How's the world of commerce treating you?"

Bernard was 24 years older than Philip and had always been more like a half-uncle half-father to him than a brother, especially as their father Thomas died when Philip was just two-and-a-half.

Philip gave the rosiest account of his life he could manage and then slipped up to his room and lay on his bed. The very last thing he wanted was a house full of people all asking him the same questions one after another. He had been looking forward to a bit of peace, but he supposed he would get that for the rest of the week at least.

He was hungry though so he went to the bathroom, washed and changed and headed down to tea.

"Philip, this is Ivan Jenkinson who I was telling you about," said his mother. "Ivan, Philip."

Philip shook hands with a friendly-looking giant of a man, who probably played rugby and if he did was probably pretty good at it. Ivan had been a close friend of Philip's father, and when Thomas was nearing the end of his days, Ivan promised him that he would "look out for" young Philip.

"There's no need to worry on Bernard's account. He can take care of himself, that one," Jane had said after Thomas succumbed to a heart attack and left her with Bernard, then aged 26 and two-year-old Philip. "But of course, I worry about the little one. If you ever get the chance to give him the odd leg-up, or a gentle guiding hand, if you know what I mean. Thomas would have been very grateful."

Ivan promised his friend's widow that he would do anything he could. There was not much to be done while Philip was growing up, and Ivan moved away from Langton to Stevenage about 20 miles to the south, where his new company was based. But now that Philip was grown up, he had been in touch with Jane and Bernard to see if he could help at all.

"Good to meet you, Philip," said Ivan. "Bernard here tells me you're a red hot salesman. Difficult territory that. Pity really, because I'm looking for someone to come and work for me on the management side and I just can't find anyone up to the job."

"Ivan runs his own electronics firm," said Bernard. "IJP Jenkinson & Co Ltd."

"Ah," said Philip. "I've heard of them."

The last part was not completely true, but Philip did not know what else to say.

There were now about 20 people in the house and more arriving all the time. Jane and Alice had made some sandwiches and two cakes and there was plenty of tea and some bottles of beer and stout for those who wanted it. The neighbours from both sides were invited, Mrs Chubb from across the street and her mother Maud, Reverend Moneypenny the vicar, Mavis from the shop, plus a few of Thomas's old mates from the Conservative Club, including Ivan.

Still, the door knocker was being rattled and this time it was the new people from two doors away, the Garveys and their daughters Madeline and Meg. Then Horace and Margaret from the bridge club arrived and the sound of chattering and laughter filled the house.

Philip was having a surprisingly good time. He was in the kitchen talking to Bernard and his new friend Ivan, he was just starting his third bottle of stout, and he surprised himself that he was talking so much sense. Everything he said, every opinion he pronounced, seemed to him to be full of insight, far-seeing and backed by an obvious intelligence that showed a keen brain was behind it.

Here he was talking to Ivan, who had his own & Co Ltd named after him, and his big brother, who knew a lot about everything, and Philip was more than holding his own, he was the centre of the conversation. They talked of union power, employers being held to ransom, labour relations, government shortcomings, foreign policy, and the lot. And on every topic – mainly thanks to Philip's habit of taking a newspaper in with him to every meal – he had facts marshalled at his fingertips, an opinion, learned knowledge and insight. He was enjoying himself, and Ivan and Bernard were great company. Soon they were clapping each other on the back, laughing loudly and agreeing on just about every topic.

Philip even accepted a cigarette or two from Ivan. Along with drinking alcohol, this was something he rarely did. He had smoked perhaps four cigarettes in his life, hated them all and had never even bought a packet of his own. He drank hardly at all. He had had a beer in the pub with Mr Willoughby a couple of times when his mentor had made a sale and was buying. Now though, he thought he looked great. Glass in one hand and cigarette in the other, he could brandish either to help him make a point. He was in fine form.

He chatted to Mavis from the shop, Horace the bridge player, Maud from across the street, even the Reverend Moneypenny, and then to Ivan and Bernard some more, and the night was going well. He felt the star of the gathering, the focus, the reason for the invites.

Somehow, a bit later on, as the company was thinning out fast and even Ivan had left, he felt the sudden need for cold air. The kitchen had begun to sway a little like a dinghy in a storm, he was hot and sweating, he mumbled *Excuse-me* a couple of times and went outside the kitchen door and into the garden.

It was dark now and cool, but quite a warm night for May. There were a lot of thick grey clouds but also patches of clear sky lit by a thousand stars. Philip sat on a bench the other side of the apple tree beyond the back door. He half-closed his eyes and looked up, trying to pick out some constellations but could not recognise any. Then suddenly he was aware of someone standing behind him.

"Who? What?" he stammered, startled.

"It's only me. I thought you could perhaps do with this."

The shape handed him a glass filled with clear cold water.

"Oh yes. That's just perfect," he said, taking it gratefully and downing the first half at a draught. Then he looked up, peering in the darkness towards the light behind the water carrier, a light that turned this angel into a silhouette only.

"Thank you very much, er..."

"Meg," said the shape. "Mind if I join you? I could do with some air too."

"Oh, yes, please do," said Philip, quickly moving up to give her room on the bench and trying to remember who Meg was as he finally saw her face when she moved in beside him.

Meg was about the same height as Philip but seemed smaller, perhaps because she was so slim. Her hair was light brown, shoulder length and very shiny and her face was very small and well-proportioned, giving her a very beautiful smile, which was her normal expression. Her brown eyes flashed with mischief and fun. Philip was very taken by her.

"Er... I don't think we've been introduced, have we?" he asked. "I'm sure I would have remembered someone as lovely as you."

He winced inwardly at the corn.

"Ooh, is that a line from a film or the B-side of a record I haven't heard?" she laughed.

"Yeah, sorry about that. I'm not very good at this sort of thing, but you have to try, don't you?"

"I always find that people are nicer when they stop trying," she said playfully.

"Yes. Right-oh. So who..?"

"Who am I? I am Meg Garvey, younger daughter of Maurice and Rita Garvey, who have recently moved into the house two along from your family. I came here tonight after an invitation from that family to welcome home their prodigal – or fairly thrifty for all I know – son. My mother and father and elder sister Madeline decided to go home but I preferred to stay and see if I could meet said son and find out a bit more about him. Especially after catching a glimpse of him and deciding that he looked ever so slightly fab. Watching him carefully through the evening, I sensed that he was perhaps drinking slightly more than he was accustomed to and may need a little gentle looking after later on. I bided my time. When I observed him staggering out of the back door, I saw my chance. I said to myself: a glass of water may be in order, and here I am. Sir," she finished with a laugh.

"I see. I see," said Philip. "Very good. Very good. And now tell me. What do you recommend for the next stage of the prodigal's recovery?"

"We-e-ell. I have heard tell that there is a river near here, and I was just thinking that a walk alongside such a stream, followed by a reckless skinny dip might be interesting."

"Yes, yes. I see where you're coming from," said Philip, enjoying this conversation a great deal. "Well, let's go then – before anyone sees us or spots that we're missing."

"Don't worry," said Meg, "I think that almost everybody has gone now anyway."

They sneaked silently out of the gate at the far end of the garden and Philip led the way through the back alley and down towards the River Ivel that ran behind the house. Meg took his arm and pulled him close as they walked and talked nonsense until they came to the small footbridge by the mill. Here they stopped and looked down at the dark, flowing water, then up at the stars and then at each other.

How different this is from being with Mary, thought Philip as he squeezed Meg's arm when she laughed at his latest daft joke.

Then she half-turned to him, pulled him towards her by the arms, tilted her face upwards and kissed him long and gently.

The smell of the river, the scent of the early flowers, the screech of an owl, the fragrance of Meg's perfume, the darkness of the night, the loneliness of the bridge, the shimmering canopy of stars overhead… Philip wanted that moment to go on forever.

"Mmm, that was as nice as I'd imagined it would be," sighed Meg, her mouth nuzzling his neck. "I hope you don't think I'm a harlot or a brazen tramp of some sort."

"Well, I was rather hoping…"

They laughed and kissed again.

"You know, I don't think I can be bothered to skinny dip tonight," she sighed.

"Perhaps we'll save it for another day," he whispered. "I think I want to stay here forever just kissing you," he added dreamily.

"OK," said Meg, and kissed him again for a long, long time.

And several hours later, as the first glow of dawn began to creep up over the fields behind the town, Meg and Philip, arms around each other, stopping frequently in the gaps between street lamps to kiss some more, finally made it back to her house, spent no more than half an hour saying goodnight, then reluctantly parted, each through their own front door, each with a lingering look back, a pounding heart, a half smile, a sense of adventure, and very little chance of falling asleep any time soon.

CHAPTER 19

Your turn, Clara

"Hello. Clara Harvey."

The phone in her flat hardly ever rang, so who could this be? Perhaps it was Henri Gautier to say he'd just arrived in London and needed someone to show him and his bottom around. Or Peter to say he was recommending her for the job in Paris.

But no, it was Alice.

"Aunt Alice! Well, this is a surprise. Oh, is everything all right? Is everyone OK?"

"Yes, don't worry," said Alice with a laugh. "Do you really associate me with bad news only?"

"No. Just wondered though. How's it going? What can I do for you?"

"Well I won't keep you long," said Alice, her voice dropping to just above a whisper. "I was wondering if you had any luck with the Family Mystery?"

"Well, as a matter of fact, I have made a couple of discoveries. I…"

Alice cut her short.

"No. Stop. I don't want to know. It's not really my business and I'd feel I was intruding. I'm only a 'by marriage' interloper really. No, this is your ball to pick up and run with now. Look, Bernard has been managing it all for so long that he is almost worn out. He needs help. Someone to take over. It would be good to think that he would sit down with you and tell you everything, fill in all the gaps, tell you where the bodies are hidden." She gave a little laugh. "No, I didn't mean that. But, you know… Anyway, that is not going to happen. He's been keeping secrets for so long now that he's forgotten how to be open and honest. It's second nature."

"So… so what is there to know?" asked Clara slowly.

"Like I say, I don't know. I only know what I've overheard, picked up by osmosis. All I would say to you though is that the keys to all this are the runaway Susan and Jane's in-laws. That's honestly all I know."

Then as Clara tried to take it all in, Alice became even more hushed.

"Look. Please help. Help Bernard. Help me. There's no one else. Sam would be hopeless. Ian wouldn't care. It's got to be you. Good luck, Clara. Good luck, darling."

And she was gone.

Clara sat back in her armchair, holding the phone to her shoulder, and stared ahead of her. What did it all mean?

Then she dialled a number.

"Hello? Sam? Are you doing anything tonight? I need to talk to you. Can we meet for a drink?"

"OK, but can I bring Michelle with me?"

"No… I need to talk to you. I need some advice. It won't take long."

"Oh. Only Michelle's here and we just made dinner and we, er… we weren't planning to go anywhere afterwards."

"How about tomorrow?"

"Ah. Well, you see, tomorrow's Friday."

"Brilliant," said Clara.

"Yes, but Michelle and I are going away for the weekend. Getting a flight at lunchtime. To Prague…"

"You are about as much use as a papier-mâché suit of armour," Clara hissed, although she spoiled the effect of the insult by slamming the phone down between the words "a" and "papier".

The next call was far longer. Meg wanted to talk about Philip. Not because of anything that he had said or done since they got back home to Langton, but because of that incident on the plane. Meg couldn't stop thinking about it. What should she do? What could she do? Should they go to the doctor as Bernard had said? What would Clara do? Would Philip be all right?

By the time Clara had done her best to reassure her mother, had managed to soothe her quite a bit, and agreed that the doctor was a good suggestion, it was impossible to bring the conversation back to a family problem, so that was it.

Should she try Ian? "Hello, operator, could you please connect me to Endoftheworld 201537?"

Perhaps not. And anyway, as Alice had said, he wouldn't care. He was probably trying to save a baby from a bunch of stampeding elephants with a bit of string, two sharp sticks and a chant.

There was nothing for it. This really was down to her. And it called for another trip to the Family Records Office.

CHAPTER 20

St George and the damsel in distress

(March 1888)

G eorge was almost happy, at least by his own standards. He had spent the whole of yesterday working nearly as far as Longford to the south. It was an urgent job mending fences that had come down in the gales that week. George quietly volunteered to do the work all by himself and there was no one else who could really be spared in any case. He had managed to get most of it done yesterday, on the Friday but had to return on the Saturday to finish it. Only he knew that there was little more than an hour's work to be done on this second day, and he started out early to make sure he accomplished it all, telling Marjory as he left that he doubted that he would be back much before six. In fact, as he knew, it was all done and finished by a quarter to nine, so he had almost nine hours to himself, to wander along the river, sit on the stile, doze beneath the trees and do whatever he wanted. All on his own.

The day was warm, the winds and storms of the week before had abated and left behind as they so often do a gentle drying breeze and some warm spring sunshine. George took out the packet of sandwiches he had brought with him and enjoyed the first as he watched two swans float past, throwing them a crust each so that they might share the bounty of his day of freedom.

He lay back in the grass at the edge of a meadow with the path beside the river behind him where it forked, one branch heading south to Longford and the other going west towards

Broom. This was the life. Away from Marjory's eyes and tongue for a whole day with nothing to do.

He fell into a light sleep and when he came to, failed to realise for some moments where he was or for how long he had been asleep. He just knew that there was a loud noise. Horns, dogs barking, a clatter in the hedgerows. Then a scream. He jumped up and climbed onto the hedge so he could see further. It was the hunt. Probably the Oakley. Although they should not be on this common land, they were a law unto themselves. No one would question what so august a company did and if anyone complained, no magistrate would listen to a word of protest against them. They seemed to be heading to the south and were getting further away with every second. But the scream. Where had that come from? The hunters did not seem to have thought it necessary to stop and find out. They were now far away.

George thought it had come from the Longford path, so he set off in that direction, climbing the hedges and gates from time to time to see if he could see anything. He had not gone a quarter of a mile when he saw what he thought was a bundle of clothing near the hedge in the field ahead. He cleared the hedge, jumped down and raced across, hoping that no one had been hurt. Hunts killed not just foxes, he thought angrily.

As he neared the rags, he saw some movement and that it was indeed a person, dressed in a white frock with a brown cape over the top.

He reached his goal panting and bent down beside her.

"Miss… Miss… Are you hurt? What happened?"

The victim half-turned and tried to sit up but winced with the pain of the effort.

It was Becky.

"Oh thank merciful heaven that someone was here. I had thought to be in for a night in the fields for I do not think that I can stand or walk. Kind sir, my father will reward you as best we can if you will but run to Longford to let him know where I am."

It was Becky.

George stared down at her, stood up, knelt down again, his mouth refusing to work, not knowing what to do or say.

It was Becky.

"Oh my lady, do not fear. I will help in any way I can," he finally said.

From the angle that she was lying, leaning away from him on a slight slope, she had not really seen who her rescuer-to-be was, but now she looked round and saw George.

He stepped back again, expecting her to scold him for being the rude man in the market, but though she felt that she had seen him somewhere before she had no idea where and her eyes shone through her tears with gratitude, not anger.

This encouraged George.

"Where do you have any pain, my lady?" he asked.

She laughed. "I am no lady, but one of low station and yet one who has a good Christian heart and soul. My ankle, I think, hurts the most for it was twisted under me when the horse hit me."

"You were hit by a galloping horse? You are lucky to be at all sound. And the rider did not stop to help you?"

Rebecca laughed again. "Hardly, sir. The huntsman shouted something like: 'Watch where you are going, peasant!' then something even more unpleasant and was gone. But I *was* watching and he came from nowhere, over this hedge. It was but a glancing blow, but threw me to the ground."

"Well, miss, I do not like the idea of leaving you here all alone. Why it could take me an hour to find help and another to fetch it back for you. And you would be in pain and discomfort the whole time."

"I will be well, sir. Do not worry on my account. I am hardy. Why let me see if I can stand. Here, give me your arm."

George stooped on one knee and Rebecca reached up and clutched his jacket and his arm then heaved herself up on her good leg and tentatively tried to put her weight on the other ankle.

For the second time that morning, the small meadow was rent by a fearful scream from the same pair of lungs, as Rebecca collapsed in a heap from the pain.

"Well, that will not be much use," she panted, sitting back down on the grass.

"I cannot leave you here, though. What if the hunt returns the way it came and tramples you as you lie here? I should never be able to live with myself."

"Oh, do you think they might? But what else can we do?"

"Well, miss. I am quite a strong man and I am sure that I could carry you back to your house. If… if that is not taking a liberty with you."

Rebecca looked straight ahead. It would not be proper for a woman to be carried along by a stranger, even such a pleasant and handsome stranger as this one. But the thought of the hunt returning and trampling her, of hearing it coming closer and closer and being unable to remove herself from its path, not even knowing which way to try to move for the best, terrified her.

"Perhaps," she said finally, "perhaps you could begin to carry me and as soon as we meet another person on the path, you can leave me safely with that person and go to seek help at my father's house."

"Yes," said George eagerly, thankfully – and secretly praying that the road would stay deserted.

He hoisted her gently into his strong arms and put her bag on top of her. Becky put her arms around his neck and looked up at his tanned face. She, too, hoped that no other walkers would spoil this brave rescue.

And so they set off, George sticking to the path, bracing his knees and trying for all his might not to jar or rock his most precious charge.

"Where were you heading, miss, when this accident befell you?"

"I was just taking a shortcut through the field. But please, call me Becky, sir. And what must I call you? Sir seems somehow ungrateful."

"I am George."

"You are my hero and saviour, George. You are my Saint George."

She laughed and George laughed too. She was light enough and he felt he could carry her to Africa and back without a care. He was exhilarated. He could not believe that Becky had gone from being angry with him to being grateful to him in an instant. From calling him rude to saying that he was her saviour. It was too much to take in. He still carried her bell with him everywhere and he wanted to take it out of his pocket and give it to her, but then realised that it could remind her who he was and ruin everything.

Becky was relaxed now. The pain had subsided a little and by resting her injured foot on top of her good leg she managed to take most of the pressure off it.

"Are you sure that I am not too heavy, George? Would you like to rest a while and then perhaps I could try to walk again?"

"No, Becky, you hardly weigh an ounce and I have a peasant's strength that will suffice."

She had called him by his name, and he had said Becky for the first time ever in his life. On they walked and talked about Langton and its market, about her friends and his work, about the weather and the path they were on. Could life ever be as sweet as this moment?

About halfway to Longford, Becky grew tired from being gently rocked in this cradle of George's massive arms. She rested her head on his chest and was soon asleep, her hair brushing his mouth and cheek, filling his nostrils with her wonderful scent. Yes, life could be even better and had just become so. George crossed into a field rather than walk on the path. No stranger was going to deny him this joy. As he approached Longford, Becky was still asleep. He realised that he did not know where her house was. No matter, if he just took this turning instead of that, he could add another field to their journey and avoid the moment he dreaded when he would have to relinquish her and end this unbearable sweetness.

Eventually, she roused, looked around startled, realised where she was, that she was safe, and looked up and smiled at George.

"Oh, I am so sorry, George. I am taking advantage of your kindness. It is too much."

"I could walk another hundred miles like this," said George and would have loved nothing more than to try. "But where is your house? Where are we going now?"

Becky looked around.

"We are almost there. Do you see the white wall at the end of this lane? Our cottage is just beyond it and you shall have some tea and cake for your trouble."

When they reached the cottage, Becky's mother was in the garden pulling up weeds. She looked alarmed to see her daughter trussed up in the arms of a strange man.

"Rebecca! Rebecca? Rebecca!" she shouted. "What has happened to you?"

Becky introduced George and quickly told her story of what had befallen her and how George had come to the rescue. Becky's mother took them into the cottage and George laid Becky on a chair in the front parlour as instructed while her mother arranged a footstool.

"And now, mother," said Becky, "we owe George a big debt of gratitude. If he had not been there I think I would have lain in the field all night long. I cannot walk or even stand. Please make him some tea and give him some cake at least to mend his strength."

Becky's mother did not know what to do first. She wanted more than anything to fuss around her daughter and bind up the ankle, but Becky insisted that she would not be ministered to until George had been taken care of. So while George, bursting with pride and happiness, washed himself at the kitchen sink and was settled into the best chair and brought tea and a large slice of seed cake, Becky looked on and beamed and chatted, grateful beyond words at being safely back in her home and seeing George rewarded.

Then Becky's father returned home and after a look of disquiet and suspicion at seeing George in his house, he heard the full story from Becky and her mother, often both talking at once, and he became relieved and grateful.

"George," he said at last, "I don't know how to thank-ee for what th'as done and for the help th'as given my daughter. Sir, th'art one of the family now and always welcome at our hearth and I hope that we shall see thee often."

And he stood up, crossed over to George and solemnly shook his hand.

When George finally made his way back into Langton, it was a little after six as he had foretold. He was expecting to be feeling relaxed after a peaceful day in the fields by himself. Instead, he just kept thinking about Becky. Everything from the first time he saw her and the tinkling bell, to the smell and touch of her hair on his face, the weight of her body against his, her smile and her kind words of gratitude. Those thoughts, those memories, those sensations would stay with him forever.

But now, he was going back home to Marjory. To his wife. To his own, real life.

Which was more cruel? To be parted from Becky because she was angry with him over a misunderstanding and would probably never speak to him again? Or to be the object of her gratitude and affection, to be looked at with smiles and flashing eyes, but to be parted forever by the hideous fact that he was married to Marjory?

Both were more than he could bear, but the second, his new estate, had threats that made it even more impossible than the first. He could now perhaps see Becky again, could drop in as he had been earnestly instructed by all three of them in the little cottage at his parting, but he could be no more than a friend of the family – a friend who would perhaps one day be introduced to the man Becky was to marry.

His mind tumbling in a turmoil of joy and despair, of elation and misery, he pushed open the door and went into his house.

CHAPTER 21

Lord Peter unlocked

Clara looked up from the computer screen and saw that the clock said six thirty.

"Damn," she said to herself. "I've left it too late."

She had planned another trip to the Family Records Office but had become so engrossed in writing and rewriting and revising the rewrites and rewriting the revisions of her interview with Henri Gautier that the time had slipped away and she had missed it. It would have to wait another day.

She looked around and realised that she was all alone in the office and probably on the whole floor, which looked in darkness across the corridor. Marcia had long gone. Tonight was her yoga class and she always slipped away a few minutes early on Thursdays. Paul had gone too, almost certainly without a goodbye, and Vincent was off this week. He will be furious when he finds out that his holiday coincided with Peter taking a trip to France. She smiled.

Ah well, may as well head for home now, thought Clara, switching off her computer, putting on her coat, turning off the lights and heading for the door. It's macaroni cheese from the fridge washed down with soap opera for me tonight. She had almost reached the lift when behind her she heard a phone ringing and instinctively rushed straight back. It was the phone on Marcia's desk, but who could be calling at this hour?

"Hello, *Allaire*. Clara speaking. How may I help you?"

"So I have found not the mother hen, but the fairest chick of the brood, toiling on alone at the nest coalface whilst all the rest have fled."

"Hello, Peter. How's Paris? And why aren't you in a posh restaurant at this hour instead of phoning home?"

"But that is just the problem, my dear. The restaurant awaits, to be sure, but the client has temporarily disremembered its whereabouts and misrecollected the telephonic code that might have connected him to his supposed dining companion. I can say with Thoraxitus: 'veni, vidi, desiderabat'."

"Right," said Clara. "So how can I help you with whatever you need?"

"My dear girl, you can twine the two broken ends of the riddle into a melding place that is currently obscured from view."

"And how precisely..?"

"I need you to look up a telephone number for me."

"Ah. I can do that. Whose number? I'll get the phone book."

"Stay, child. Not so fast. The answer to this quest lies not in the arms of the Anglophile dialaphorous heritage but in the realms of my electric haven."

"I'm sorry?"

"You need to seek it within my computer."

"Of course. But won't there be a password?"

"And that same will I impart to you when you are seated somewhat incongruously at my desk and have sparked the contraption into life."

Clara switched the call through to Peter's phone, hurried through into the office, switched on the lights and then the computer, picked up his phone and waited for the opening screen. Finally, it appeared:

Name: Lord Peter Of Allaire
Password: ...

"Right. Ready when you are."

"Password, my child."

"That's right. What is it?" asked Clara.

"It is what it is. Password. The technical people told me that I should alter it but I forgot how to do so and somehow never attained the heights of asking them to call back and demonstrate. Frightful people. I will change it upon my return."

"OK."

Clara typed in Password and the machine sprang into being.

"That worked. Now where?"

"Into my electronic Mercury, god of messengers."

Clara clicked on the email icon when she finally found it on a desktop that was full of a thousand documents and folders.

Up came the next screen:

Name: Lord Peter Of Allaire

Password: …

"Is the password Password here too?"

"Of course not. That would be perilous. It is – do you have a pencil?"

"I can type it straight in."

"Very well then. It is MarcusAurelius. All one word, capital M to begin and capital A in the middle. I am informed that this is important."

"Could you spell it please?"

"Child, you must have read his Meditations and if you have not you should do so. One of the finest pieces of philosophy every set on parchment."

Peter spelled it slowly and Clara was through the final gate. Up came the email. 2,478 unread messages, it told her.

"Right. We're in. Now where?"

"Please search for Quentin Philomastre."

Again Peter spelled it.

"He sent me a message some week or two weeks ago advising of the time and place to meet tonight, and also appended his telephone number in case it was needed. I was sure that Marcia printed it out for me but nowhere can I find it, so she cannot have done so."

"OK. Let's see. A... quick... search. Yes here we are. The restaurant is Le Rossignol, which he says is just off the Avenue Paul Doumer. And the phone number he gives is 01 23 87 51 26."

"...875126. My child, you have rescued me from an edacious evening. *Quod habitum manducans, quis lancet huic* was never more true. I go and it is done. Sleep well and write better until we meet again. Many thanks to your nobleness."

And he hung up.

Phew, thought Clara and began to switch the computer off so that she could go home. She did not get far. Wait a minute, she thought. The office is empty, I have access to Peter's computer, email and anything else that I can find. My fingerprints are quite properly on the keyboard. Way-hey, tally-ho, last one to find some embarrassing secrets is a scaredy cat.

It was half an hour later that Cara turned out the office lights for the second time and walked towards the lift again. Her face if there had been anyone around to try to make it out in the gloom, was white, her eyes wide and round.

She was angry. Furious. Right there on the desktop, in the middle of the desktop, she had found a document called "Clara reply". It was Peter's response to *Trompette*'s request for her to move to Paris. She was not, according to his Lordship Peter of Allaire, "remotely ready for such a transfer to the heady heights of self-motivation and creativity but needs nurturing some more until the stray shoots are pruned and the plant is whole and rounded and would benefit from a richer soil".

What a total and utter bas-... she thought and closed the computer angrily.

It was only after she got home and began to stop seething quite so much with the second glass of wine that she realised what she had done. There she was in the holiest of holies, able to peek into whatever dim recesses she liked, possibly finding all sorts of things at the very least to hold Peter up to ridicule in the office – and seeing that one letter had made her so angry that she had closed the computer down and come home. What a mug. And Peter had said he was going to change his passwords so that was probably her one and only chance. Idiot.

CHAPTER 22

Philip – Better never than late

(June 1966)

All the talk around the big table at breakfast was about next month's World Cup in England and Mr Lazenby was sure that the key for the home team would be the two wingers Ian Callaghan of Liverpool and John Connelly from Manchester United, "They will supply the ammunition for Jimmy Greaves to shoot the goals," he declaimed. Everyone agreed that this was a sound analysis and a very exciting prospect.

Philip sat behind his newspaper but did not read a word of it. He was thinking of Meg and when he could see her and kiss her again. It was two days since their walk on the bridge and he still had scarcely touched the ground. They had hardly been able to see each other since that wonderful Saturday night because he was leaving Langton the next day on the mid-morning train so that he could be back in time for an early night before work on the Monday, but she did manage to slip away and walk him to the station when he left.

He remembered their conversation.

"When can I see you again..?" they had both said at the same time and laughed.

"Perhaps you could come down to Brighton for a visit?" he suggested.

"Mmm. Bit of a long way for a day trip," said Meg.

"Yes. I suppose so," said Philip glumly.

"No, I mean it would have to be for the weekend," she pulled the arm she was holding closer to her and laid her head on his shoulder as they walked.

He tried to work out what she meant. She could hardly stay at the *Bel Air*. She could book into a guest house for a night or two. Or they *both* could. Mr and Mrs Smith. Is that what she meant? Surely not?

"That would be grand," he said. "Brighton's lovely. There's so much to do. There's a pier, boat rides and you can even go paddling if it's warm."

"We promised ourselves a skinny dip too," she laughed.

Philip wanted to hug her but had his suitcase in one hand and his other arm was being grasped tightly by Meg, so it wasn't an option.

"I'll have to find another excuse to visit home again soon too," he said.

"Or," she added archly, "didn't you say that very nice man from Stevenage had practically offered you a job? You could live at home and see me whenever you wanted."

"What a lovely, lovely thought," said Philip dreamily.

His daydream was suddenly interrupted as Mary came into the dining room and looked anxiously across at him. She collected the bowls from the big table, ignored the shouts of: "Let's swap shirts at the end of breakfast, love!" and: "I could do with a massage – I'm feeling a little stiff…" and the howls of laughter they produced. When she came to Philip's table, Mary put her hand into her apron pocket and pulled out a crumpled piece of paper that she dropped into his lap as she picked up his bowl. Then she was gone.

Philip had to hurry to catch his lift with Mr Willoughby and so did not read the note until he found it stuffed in his pocket at lunchtime as he was eating his sandwiches on a park bench. He unfolded it and read: "Please, please let's meet tonight. Usual place at eight? I have to talk to you. Mary".

Whatever can that be about, he wondered.

He had decided to take a week's holiday in August and spend it at home. It was all cleared with Mr Willoughby that morning. He would write to Meg tonight and suggest the dates, then they could start planning what they would do with all that lovely time together. And he was hoping that Meg could come down to visit him for a weekend in the meantime. And who knew what would happen then?

He chewed his ham sandwich – carefully made for him using the best bits of the boiled joint that morning in the kitchen by Mary – and he thought of Meg. He wanted to see her so much. The rest of his lunchtime was spent dreaming of all the things they would do either down here or up in Langton. And he came up with a list of 101 places they could visit and things they could do on days out together.

These lovely images were still filling his head as he finished his dinner that night, folded his newspaper and went up to his room, where he was looking forward to spending the evening writing a long letter to Meg. Then he felt in his pocket for a handkerchief and found Mary's crumpled note. What a nuisance, he thought. I'd better go though, I'm late already. I won't stay long and I'll write the letter when I get back.

He picked up his jacket, didn't bother with the umbrella and hurried down the stairs, out into the street and off to the seafront, to the quiet bench where he used to meet Mary. As he turned the corner, he saw her standing beside it and craning her neck to see if he was coming.

"I'm sorry I'm late. I, er… I had some things I had to finish. For work. How are you?"

In fact, he could see how Mary was from her tear-stained face. He became concerned.

"Hey, what is it? Has someone died? It's OK."

Instinctively he put his arms around her to comfort her, and she buried her head in his neck and sobbed. She felt about the same size as Meg but somehow frailer.

"What is it? What's the matter? What's happened?" he said softly, holding her close for the first time in their lives.

"Oh Philip. I had an awful weekend. I felt so lost without you," she spoke quickly with hardly a breath, letting out everything that had built up since she last saw him on Thursday evening. "I couldn't believe how horrible it was. If you'd been here I would probably only have been able to see you for a couple of hours, but it was just the fact that you weren't there that made it so bad. I started thinking what it would be like if you weren't here at all and I realised how lost I would be. Then I started to imagine that one day you'd never come back and oh…"

Mary was sobbing too much to speak.

"Hey, come on," said Philip quietly, trying to find the words that would make her better. "I'm back. I'm here now. Everything's OK."

He held her close against his chest and gently brushed her hair back off her face with his hand.

"I don't know why I suddenly felt like this," she said, relaxing a little under his touch. "I think I must have been taking you for granted. You were just always there. I don't know, I felt somehow safe with you around. You were the one person who was kind to me and when you went away I saw how much I had grown to rely on you and how awful it would be if I had to go into that dining room twice a day and you were not there to give me the strength to get through it. If you weren't there to give me a little smile, some encouragement, to be on my side. I realised that I needed you more than just as a friend."

She breathed deeply, forced herself to calm down and smiled up at him through her tears.

"Oh, Philip, it was horrible going to the *Bel Air* when you weren't there. Even more horrible than it always used to be before you arrived. Oh, don't go away again."

Now she had her two arms around him as they held each other in a tight embrace.

"Would you like to go for a little walk and you can tell me how much better you're feeling now I'm back?" he said coaxingly, making her laugh.

"Yes, I would. Let's just walk along the beach and look at the sea. Only," she added quickly with a smile, "don't let go of me. I like it. I like it more this way."

Philip's mind was in turmoil. This was the last thing that he was expecting, or even that he wanted now. And yet he had to admit to himself, that *he* liked it more this way too.

They walked along, his arm around her shoulder, her head leaning on his chest, her arm around his waist and their free hands clasped together in front of them. As they walked he could feel the pressure of the whole side of her body moving gently against his, he could smell her fragrant hair and hear her soft breath.

It was a lovely evening and the seafront was busy, but they saw no one else. The sun was dipping down behind them over the pier as they walked, painting the sea red and making the whole world in front of them seem translucent and ethereal. Philip let out a sigh and, hardly thinking what he was doing, kissed the top of Mary's head. As if it were a signal, she stopped walking, rolled towards him, lifted her face and found his mouth with hers. They stood in silence, kissing softly for what must have been a full three minutes.

"Oh, that's so much nicer than just being friends," she whispered dreamily as they continued to cling tightly to each other. "We should have done that a long time ago," she added with a small laugh.

"Yes," agreed Philip. "Yes, we really should. A long time ago."

CHAPTER 23

The raw and the (over)cooked

"Au Gare du Nord, s'il vous plait," said Clara to the taxi driver. "Is that right?" she thought for the hundredth time today. Oh, hang it all. It's over now in any case.

She sat back in the taxi and watched the shops and cafés and people of Paris swish past the window. Just think, I could soon be working here, finishing my day at a little bistro off the Champs-Élysées, popping into the shops in the Carrousel du Louvre, or strolling along the banks of the Seine with Marcel Hunk or ice-cool but red-hot-Émile Stud. Mmmm.

Steady, girl, you haven't even got the job yet. Although the interview had gone well, she thought.

Chic magazine was located just off the Boulevard Beaumarchais, a wide and leafy avenue in the swanky (at least to Clara) 11th Arrondissement. Its pages covered mainly fashion but increasingly lifestyle and that is why they were looking to beef up the staff, advertising for three feature writers to join the team. The advert appeared in *Allaire* the week after Clara found out that Peter had scuppered her dream job with *Trompette*. There's karma, then, she thought. *Allaire* ruins my chance to get a job in Paris and then offers me a second chance to do just that. Wouldn't it be sweet?

So Clara applied, not without a feeling of hopelessness, it must be said. When someone has been telling you for a long time that you are not good enough, it takes a lot to believe that you might be after all.

Then there was the language bit. Clara had done French A-level and could sort of speak it. She could read French with no trouble and more than got by at speaking it when she went there on holiday. But having it as her working language and doing interviews in French, well, that was something else. A long way from ordering steak, frites with a bouteille de vin rouge.

She was sure that if she lived in the country and spoke nothing but, then she would be fluent in a week or two, but going for an interview without doing that was daunting. So she got her disappointment in first and told herself that when the inevitable rejection letter came back, she would not be too surprised.

In fact, she got a very nice reply from Agnès Moulesième, the *Éditrice de Fonctionnalités* or Features Editor, saying that she particularly liked the latest, as yet unpublished, piece on Henri Gautier, which she felt had a lot more flair and insight than some of her earlier published work. On the strength of that, she would very much like to meet Clara for an interview. If Clara would suggest a date in the next two weeks, Agnès would arrange her travel.

So let me get this straight, thought Clara, her self-confidence levels rising towards the smug mark, Agnès likes the piece on Henri as I wrote it, but not the cuttings that Peter had "improved". Well, well, well. How interesting.

"Tous les anciens articles publiés dans Allaire sont passés par les mains de l'éditeur, et il a vraiment beaucoup changé," Clara said in her best pre-rehearsed French as she sat on a couch in Agnès's office about 10 days later.. *"Je suis très content que vous préfériez le dernier."*

Without actually mentioning Peter by name, Clara managed to drop on him from a height and made it clear that the pieces that she had written that had not appealed to Agnès had gone through the hands of the editor and come out the other side in a very different guise. Agnès laughed and said that she had had similar experiences in the past and could sympathise.

Agnès Moulesième was tall, stylish and stunning. She looked as though she got out of bed each morning with her hair and make-up perfect. Her black hair was swept back from her face revealing perfect skin and cobalt blue eyes that sparkled and pierced at the same time. Her clothes would not have looked out of place on the film set of *Breakfast At Tiffany's*.

She welcomed Clara into her busy office and chatted away, sometimes too fast for Clara to grasp, but by smiling at what appeared to be the right places and responding to the bits that she did understand, Clara felt that she was above water.

Agnès explained what *Chic* was trying to do and how it wanted to expand, then where Clara would fit into this. She also said that it would be fine if Clara wanted to write in English, to begin with as they would be translating everything into Italian and German too, so French could easily be added.

She asked Clara a lot about herself, her background, her hopes and fears, and when after an hour, she paused and sat back with a half-smile on her face, Clara braced herself for bad news. Instead, Agnès announced that she was hungry and had a table for two booked at a small restaurant just down the street.

"And I think that you have spoken enough French for one day, so why don't we switch to English now?"

Her English was flawless. "I spent two years at school in Cambridge," she revealed. "It helps."

Lunch was far more relaxing for Clara, who really warmed to Agnès and asked lots of questions about what it was like to live and work in Paris, the social life, the entertainment, the people, and the shopping. In the end, she did not want to go home but wanted to start work tomorrow in this adventure park of a city.

As the taxi reached the station, she sighed. Agnès had promised to get back in touch with her in a week or two "when we have seen all the other applicants". That doesn't sound good, does it?

It was just after 9.30 when Clara reached her flat, weary, excited at what might be, but resigned to that not happening.

195

CHAPTER 24

Susan – Fate's guiding hand

(August 1946)

"Ciao, bella. What'sa on the agenda today, *la mia ragazza più bella del mondo*?"

Susan liked Mario calling her that as he had earlier explained that it meant "my most beautiful girl in the world".

"Good morning to you too. Well, we should be able to collect some overdues from Constantine plus the rest of what's owed by the Harrisons. They are both coming around to our way of thinking and there's a visit to each booked for today. Should bring in a tidy sum. Then you're meeting Mr Watson from the council over that restoration building works grant at two. Want me to book you a table or a room somewhere?"

"Nah, that's OK, *bambino*. I know where I take him. Somewhere quiet where we can – heh, heh – relax, you know."

Susan knew exactly the club Mario used. "Right-oh. Then I'll rearrange the rest of the day and put off anybody who's sniffing around."

"Ah, *perfetto*. What would I do without you? And don't forget that we are dancing tonight. It's Friday and you promised. If all goes well, we should have some celebrating to do."

Susan laughed. "Oh, I wouldn't miss it for the world. Now you'd better get off. The boys will be here for instructions soon and you don't want to get your hands dirty with that side of the business, now do you?"

"I leave all of that to you, *la mia donna angelo*. See you at about seven."

"I'll be here, Mario. I'll be here."

And he was gone.

Susan got up and put the kettle on to make a cup of coffee. She was satisfied. She was practically running Mario's business for him. And just as she had always known that it would, the world was beginning to discover her. She was well on the path to something special.

Still, she did owe her break to Ronaldo in a way, she supposed.

In her first week at her new home, he arranged for her to work behind the saloon bar at the King's Arms. There were usually all of 20 customers in the whole week in that bar, most patrons preferring to save their pennies by drinking in the cheaper public bar. The landlord did not need another barmaid but could hardly say no to Ronaldo and his cousin, and so it came to pass. Not only did she work five lunchtimes and four evenings a week, but she also had her own room in the garret at the top of the building. Ronaldo explained that he often had to go to look after his poor ailing mother in Gillingham and it would not do for her to be seen in his room when he was not there. He would be thrown out, cousin or no cousin.

"No, this way, Princess, whenever I'm there you can come to join me but if I have to go and care for mother, then you can have your own little nest to wait for me in. You do understand, don't you, Princess."

Susan was beginning to understand Ronaldo quite well, but she let it pass. It finally made her free from Langton. Independent. Standing on her own two feet.

She would not tolerate it for any longer than she needed, but it was certainly better than catching a train back north from King's Cross.

It began well enough. There was hardly anything to do on her days and nights behind the bar. She had a free meal of stew or hotpot on the house, and she took away a few shillings in her pocket at the end of each evening. *And* she had her own room – her *own room* – her *own room in London*. How good did that sound?

And on the nights when Ronaldo was around, there was often dancing, there were gin and oranges, which she could now drink at the correct speed to keep her upright, and there was the pleasure of Ronaldo's bed at the end of a long day. She was having fun, she told herself.

Gradually she began to help Ronaldo out during the days and evenings too. He told her what he needed to be organised and Susan would do it, arrange things, bring in the right people to be in the right places at the right times to make sure that everything ran, smoothly. It only took her a few hours a week, but Ronaldo seemed pleased with how it was going.

But already she was beginning to look for the next step up on her path to greatness.

That step came out of nowhere one Wednesday evening when she was sitting at a table in the saloon bar reading the evening paper – as was her custom rather than stand forlornly behind the bar all evening. Suddenly the door swung open and a man she had never seen before walked in.

"Hey, lovely lady," he said. "I am looking for Ronaldo. I wonder if you have seen him?"

The man was tall, swarthy and good-looking. Around five foot eleven, slim with broad shoulders and a dark complexion. Unlike Ronaldo, who pretended to be Italian without any of the ammunition, Mario was as English as they come, but had actually lived in Italy when he was young for around five years. It was after his parents split up and neither wanted him, so he was sent to live just outside Rome with an aunt who didn't speak a word of English, but agreed to take him. Now Mario could speak both English and Italian fluently and so could pass himself off as whichever he chose to fit the moment. In fact, now the war was over, he usually added an Italian accent to his English to complete the dashing picture.

"Er, no, sir. I have seen no Ronaldo this evening. I am waiting for a friend."

"Then perhaps you would not mind if I waited alongside you, in case *il mio amico* Ronaldo should appear."

"Why please do. It will help to while away the time."

"I would offer to buy you a drink, *bella donna*, but there seems to be no one to serve us."

"Ah leave that to me. The landlord is a friend of mine and is happy to let me pop behind the bar when necessary. What would you like?"

"I don't suppose a glass of *chianti* is possible, so a half of stout will do just fine," said Mario. "And for yourself."

"Well, a gin and orange if that is acceptable to you, sir."

"Pour them out," said Mario, and Susan was soon busy behind the bar, setting the drinks in front of Mario at the table and putting his money into the box behind the bar.

"So do I detect a slight and very attractive accent in your speech, sir?" she asked as she joined Mario at the table and they clinked glasses.

He told her the practised story of his childhood in Corsica ("the birthplace of Napoleon") and his struggles to find a haven for himself in London that culminated in his far-reaching business empire. A business, he said, that was all about supply and demand.

"And you, fair lady. What brings you here?"

So Susan told him her life story. How she had been abandoned by a lord of the realm as a child and left to grow up in rural England, and then found her way to London to seek what fame and fortune might throw at her.

"You know," said Mario, inching his barstool closer to hers, "I think that we have *molto* in common, fair lady. But I do not even know your name."

"Susan, kind sir. And I do not know yours."

"I am Mario, *signorina*. And I think that we are the same. Forgotten outcasts in a cruel world, who are thrown together, like what they see and want to get to know each other better. I tell you, I have seen many women in this wide world, but never one so beautiful as you. What do you do every day?"

"Oh not much," said Susan, heart pounding. Here, she sensed, was fate taking her once more by the hand and propelling her towards her destiny. So this was the famous Mario, was it? She had heard Ronaldo talking about him a lot. He had started out as Ronaldo's boss and was still a far bigger "operator" than her Ron. Was this a chance that fate had thrown into her path? Was this the next step on her road to greatness? Perhaps. If she played it right.

"Actually, Mario, I cannot lie to you."

"Lie to me? How is this?"

"I know Ronaldo – in fact, I work with him, for him. And I know that he is not coming in here tonight. He was called away suddenly to see his sick mother."

"See his sick mother?" snorted Mario. "He will need a good strong shovel then."

He paused, frowned and looked again at Susan.

"Did you say that you work for Ronaldo? Can it be then, that I am speaking not to just any old Susan but to *the* famous Susan?"

Famous, eh? thought Susan. Here we go, fate. Take it away.

"Well, not too famous yet, but who knows? One day..."

Mario held up his hand.

"You do not need to be modest, Susan. I hear all about you. Ronaldo speaks fine things of you. I know that without you, he would be not so much as he is today."

"Well, I do manage to look after a lot of the details for him."

"And now you will do the same for me, *bellissima*? I need someone with looks and a brain to assist me in my business life. I have much to do and there is only me. I can look after the supply part of things, no trouble, but I need someone who can manage me and keep track on, shall we say, the demanding. Might you like to give me a help?"

As he spoke, he reached across and laid his hand on hers.

So Ronaldo had thought she was only fit to be a barmaid, had he? Idiot.

"Mario," said Susan. "I think fate has decided that we are both going to be important people in each other's lives."

Mario agreed: "I too have a notion that tonight is just the beginning. I can feel it in my bones. We are going places, you and I."

CHAPTER 25

Womanhunt

O h, it was no good, there was nothing. Clara had been here at the Family Records Office for almost an hour and a half and had looked through about a thousand books over a 55-year timespan. Bernard was born in 1923 and Susan a few years later, so if she died somewhere after the age of 20, that would be from around 1945 until today. Each book covers three months. Clara had looked through every year in the black death books for a Susan Harvey or a Susan Laker dying. Nothing. That's a lot of books.

Ah, I can hear you saying, but what if she had got married at that time? Glad you asked. Clara had also looked all through the marriage records for the same period, three months per book, to see if a Susan Harvey or Susan Laker had got married. Equally fruitless.

It was as though the woman had vanished from the planet. Or she was still alive somewhere. If Bernard was about 78, Susan would be 74 or 75. Possible. And she could still be engaged to someone. Can't rush these things.

Clara remembered what her Dad had told her: "There was some talk of her having gone abroad, and that's probably what happened. She must have died abroad without being able to let us know."

Perhaps that was it. In any case, if Susan were one of the keys to this family mystery, as Alice had told her, then there appeared to be no lock that she would fit. And come to think of it, no key either, Clara thought gloomily.

Ah well, she had made a few finds. Jane's in-laws, Alice had suggested. So Clara had sent for Jane's husband Thomas's birth certificate, which should have his parents on it, and for Rebecca and George's marriage certificate. Would that clear anything up? Who knows.

Now I'm going home to watch a film, eat pizza and drink some very red wine.

CHAPTER 26

George – Home comfort

(June 1888)

"Another cake, St George?" asked Becky.

"I couldn't touch one more crumb," said George, lying back in the grass and closing his eyes.

"No, nor I neither," she said, putting the last of the picnic back into her basket and spreading the blanket out so that she could lie down near him.

They were on a bend beside the River Ivel as it flowed northward from Longford to Langton and beyond, at a spot not far from where Becky had been struck by the horse and almost midway between their two homes. George had fashioned a hideout of twigs and undergrowth to make it invisible from the path, sheltered from light showers, and yet open to a view of the river. It was enclosed on three sides by dense bramble and thorn thickets, but George had found that by moving one branch to the side, it was easily possible to slip through and close the "door" after you. In the past few weeks, the two had spent as much time as they could here. It was not much, never any more than an hour or two a week, but it was precious.

The first time they met after the rescue had been difficult to contrive. George had begun organising things so that he might work on this part of the estate between the town and the village more and more in the hope of seeing Becky again. And when there was no work there, he pretended to Marjory on Saturdays that he had been called away on extra duties.

He did not want to go to Becky's house as he would not know what to say or what reason to give for his unannounced visit. Perhaps later. He also still feared meeting a suitor of Becky's.

She for her part was curious to meet again the handsome man who had rescued her, and wondered why he did not visit them as he had promised when he left. When she walked to Langton, which she now did rather more often, she made sure that she was alone and always arranged to meet her friends in Langton, each time saying that she may not be able to join them, that she did not know at what time she would be free and that in case she could not come they should go ahead without her and do whatever was planned. Then if she did chance upon George, she could spend some time with him.

Both had all but given up hope of seeing the other when one fine Saturday, George climbed over the stile and there was Becky walking towards him, wearing the same white frock and brown cloak as she was when the Oakley Hunt struck her down.

"George!"

"Becky!"

They ran towards each other as fast as they could, then stopped dead a yard apart, not knowing what to do or say.

Then they both started talking at once, about anything, nothing, the river, the trees. They strolled towards Langton, stopped half a mile before getting there and made their way back towards Longford, then took the turning towards Broom. It was a fine day, with a few clouds in a mainly clear blue sky, a gentle breeze, and shadows under the trees. On they walked, back and forth, until it was time for both to leave.

"How can we arrange to meet again?" he asked. "We cannot leave it to chance again."

"No, I have been looking out for you so often in vain. What if we say that we will try to meet on Saturdays at a little after noon? If one or other of us cannot come, then that is bad luck, and we go on to the next week. But at least we will have a plan, a hope."

"I like your plan," said George, and they parted all smiles, without even a kiss, but with pounding hearts and uplifted souls.

Since then they had met three or four times. If Becky did not come, George was beset with gloom, but her presence made up for any past disappointment.

The first time she did not arrive, George took his chance to begin their shelter, an idea he had been forming for some weeks. He began constructing the main frame that would hide them away. He finished it during his lunchtimes in the week, so that the next time she arrived they did not have to spend their whole time walking, but could relax in their own "home", somewhere they could wait for each other on their appointed days. After that Becky began to bring a small basket of food with her and they really were in their own world.

It was here that George had finally presented Becky with her bell.

"Now you mustn't be cross with me, for everything I have done has been for you and to try to make you happy. All I ever wanted was for you to smile at me. There was a day at Langton Market, which I hope you have forgotten, when a man bought something that one of your friends wanted to give you for your birthday…"

A look of remembrance came into Becky's eyes.

"Why yes, a very rude man who snatched it away that I might not have it."

Of course, she thought, this is why I felt that I had seen him before when he came into the meadow after my accident. She decided to tease him a little.

"Oh if I ever see that man again, I will strike him and tell him what I think of him. My simple treasure, my simple pleasure, and he snatched it away without a second's thought."

"No, no. Do not say so, Becky, for that man was me."

"You? You?" she stood up, hands on her hips, brows tight-knitted, an angry look on her face.

"Oh Becky, do not look at me this way. Let me explain…"

"Explain? Why to think that I have since smiled upon you and said kind words. I am going home and do not wish ever to see you again."

"Becky, no. Let me tell you the truth. I did not know it was you. I did not see you."

He was on his knees, his arms raised towards her, imploring.

"I was trying to buy the small bell as a gift for you. You had liked it before when I first saw you, and I wanted nothing more than to present it to you and see you smile at me and say thank you. Oh Becky, that is all."

She sat down and looked at him.

"In that case, sir, You will most certainly still possess the bell – for I very much hope that you have not given it to another. That indeed would double your crime and your guilt."

George fumbled in his pocket and brought out the bell, taking the paper from around the tiny ball and handing it over.

Becky took it, looked at it in wonder, held it up and shook it gently. The bronze bell made its tiny tinkling sound for the first time in almost two years. George thrilled to see Becky smile at the tiny chime just as she had on that first afternoon that he saw her.

"You kept it. You kept it for me. Oh, George, it's as lovely as I remember," she said, gazing at it. "And you saved it all this time?"

"Do not be angry with me. Please, Becky, I beg you. I could not bear it."

Becky smiled the smile that George had so often imagined. "Thank you so much. It is lovely."

She leaned across and gave him a small hug. "I am very wicked to tease you so. Pray forgive me. I could never be so angry with you no matter what you had done."

"Then you forgive me?"

"I have nothing to forgive you for, George. This is a wonderful gift, it was a lovely thought to buy it for me. It is even much nicer to receive it from you in our own 'home' here than it would have been as a birthday gift from Mary. It is henceforth my most treasured possession in the world."

George was too happy to speak. He had nothing to say.

He lay back under their shelter beneath the plane trees and thought that he could now die a happy man. This was everything he had dreamed of. Nothing could be as sweet as this moment.

He was wrong, for Becky came and lay down beside him and he folded her in his arms and held her close.

On his way back to Langton, George was torn between the same extremes of joy and despair. Unbounded happiness that all he had ever wanted since he first saw Becky had now come to pass. They had delicious moments to share, she smiled at him, she carried her bell wherever she went, and he was in love with this strong yet delicate, funny, loving woman.

Then came the reality of going back to Marjory at the end of every day he spent with Becky, of their woeful married life together, the torment and baseness, the grim and terrible hours alone in their house. Oh curse her, he thought. Why did I ever let myself marry her? Why is she alive? If a man can control his own destiny as Becky has shown me, why cannot I control mine? Why am I a slave to the world and what it demands of me?

And then another thought came to him, more dreadful than all of the rest. In his exuberance to meet Becky, he had not even told her that he was married.

CHAPTER 27

The art of l'impossible

Sam had asked to see Clara and they arranged to meet for drinks after work.

"This is not another charade where you want me to pretend to be Annie Oakley or Florence Nightingale and warn off some floozie, is it?" Clara wanted to know on the phone.

"No. Nothing like that this time," he promised.

Even when they were sitting in the back garden of the pub with their drinks, Clara was still suspicious.

"You're sure I'm not going to be sent packing as soon as Michelle snaps her fingers?"

"Afraid not. In any case, if Michelle snaps her fingers now it will be at someone else," he said gloomily.

"Oh, I'm sorry."

"No, it's not a problem. I was definitely thinking of chucking her anyway, but she, er... she got in first. She quit her job and upped and left. Apparently, she's gone to Spain with a surfer."

"Ah, so are we in crying-on-the-shoulder mode tonight, then? Do we need a cuddle?"

"Hell no. Look, you speak French, don't you?"

"*Un tout petit peu,*" Clara agreed.

"Whatever. Well then, I need to learn it."

"You're a bit old for GCSEs, aren't you?"

"No, I don't want to pass exams. I want to be able to talk to Claudette."

"Claudette?"

"Claudette."

"Well we can carry on just saying her name to each other all night if you like, or you can tell me a little more about her."

"She's Claudette..."

"Yes, I gathered that bit. And..?"

"She's beautiful and gorgeous and lovely. She makes Michelle look like a... a... I don't know. Like something not very nice. You can fill in the blank."

"And she can't speak English?"

"Well, she can sort of, but it's hard going. You don't always know what she means. She called me a 'sweet doom' the other day."

"Not a bad description. Perhaps 'sweet' is going a bit far."

"Yes but you see, there's a business deal up for grabs and I need to be able to understand what she's saying."

"So in business terms, you want to get into bed with her?"

"And then some. She's loaded."

"I'm getting lost in the metaphor here. Are we talking money or chests?"

"Well, both really. She's got a treasure chest all right. But leaving her obvious attractions to one side for the moment, her dad is worth about two Bank of Englands and a Footsie, and he wants to set her up in business as soon as she comes up with a venture that he approves of."

"And that's where you come in?"

"Too right. Business Plans R Us, that's me. I can't decide whether to go back to the seaweed health kick tablets or open a franchise of spa boutique hotels for couples only or produce mini flying cameras that people can pilot themselves by remote control. But I sure do want to get my hands on Papa Claudette's readies. It's the only thing that's held me back up to now. I'm a great ideas man..."

Clara gave a small cough and left it at that.

"...but I've never had the cash to make them work. And that has meant bringing in other people who thought they knew better and watching them wreck it all. Story of my life. Now though, I could really be my own master."

"And you think that all you need to do is to learn French in a day or two, gabble away to Claudette and her dad, and the world opens all its chequebooks for you?"

"Well, sort of, yes. So will you teach me?"

"Sam, do you have any idea how long it takes to become fluent in a language? Fluent enough to talk business with a native?"

Sam smiled reassuringly and held up his hands.

"It's OK, I've thought this through. Claudette has gone back to see her folks, so I have a completely clear week and I don't mind grafting, as you know."

"Let's have another drink and I'll explain *les oiseaux et les abeilles* to you." She stood up and headed for the bar.

Sam called after her: "That's *the scissors are happy*, right? I can *do* this…"

CHAPTER 28

Susan – A week of delights

(October 1947)

What a week that was, thought Susan to herself as she climbed the 148 steps to her room just before noon on the Sunday. She reached the door, opened it and strolled into Her Room. In fact, it was not much bigger than the room she used to sleep in at Langton, except that she had been sharing that one with the baby Ian, and sometimes other people who came to stay. Here, she was gloriously all alone.

She kicked off her shoes, took off her sweaty clothes, had a quick all-over wash at the sink, and climbed into bed. Gloriously naked. She was not working in the pub any more. The thought of it. She, Susan Harvey, destined for big things, pouring glasses of beer in a back street alehouse. She did not have to be at the office until around 10 the next morning so that she could organise the week before Mario arrived just after 11. That meant that she could actually get some sleep. She did the calculation. Twenty hours' sleep. Heaven.

She stretched out luxuriously.

The past week *had* been rather hectic. She thought back, trying to remember. Monday she had seen Ronaldo for the first time in a while. He was working much more on his own these days, just helping Mario out with the bigger jobs. And he was spending a lot of his time in Gillingham with his ailing mother. It kept him busy. At least that's what he said. Susan had her doubts, especially after that day a couple of weeks back when he had cancelled their arrangement to meet in the King's Arms at the last minute when he got a message to say that his mother had taken a turn for the worse and he had no choice but to go to her. Of course, Princess understood.

She found it rather harder to understand later that night when she went to the dancehall for a drink with Brenda, one of the barmaids at the King's Arms. There on the floor with a blousy blonde was Ronaldo. Susan was surprised to find that she was not even angry. She found it funny. She had grown tired of Ronaldo since meeting Mario and could take him or leave him. Now having this clear evidence meant that she had something over him. Something to save. Just in case. She made sure that Ronaldo did not see her. She felt free.

Anyway, his mother must have been fine and the blousy blonde unavailable – or perhaps Ronaldo had fixed it for the blousy blonde to look after his mother for a night – because on Monday, he had been charm itself. They enjoyed a fine dinner and a drink or two in their cosy upstairs room at the King's Arms, went for a stroll, and before she knew what was happening, she was leaving Ronaldo's room and heading for the office on Tuesday morning. Ronaldo *was* fun to sleep with, she thought.

What did she do Tuesday? Ah yes, that was the quiet night. She went round to Brenda's flat and they read magazines, listened to the radio and giggled all evening. Brenda was so much better than Annie, thought Susan. She knew about things, had lived all her life in London, could look after herself, and made Susan laugh. She could mimic the customers who came into the King's Arms and you'd think it *was* them in the room. Susan stayed quite late because she was enjoying herself.

Wednesday was a little naughty. She had left her bag at Ronaldo's flat, by mistake or on purpose, and she called him to see if she could pop around and pick it up.

"Let me just make one phone call to see how my mother is," he told her. "And if she is well enough, then Princess I am all yours."

Two minutes later he rang back to say his mother thought she could manage without him for one night. They skipped all pretence, had a very early, very light dinner, with only two or three drinks, and were soon climbing into Ronaldo's wonderful bed and attacking each other with wild frenzy.

Thursday? Yes, on Thursday, Henry took her out to dinner "in town", as he put it. Henry St John, was a toff, a proper toff. He spoke like a lord or a judge, with a deep voice that made you melt, and lovely manners. Henry was a level above anyone else Susan had ever known. He was what he called a "business associate" of Mario's, coming to see them about once a month, or rather more just lately as he and Mario were plotting something "on a rather grander scale than usual", Henry told her.

Henry came into the office on Thursday and lingered when Mario left. He paid Susan a lot of attention, complimented her on how well she ran Mario's business, and then asked her to accompany him to dinner as he had "a proposal to put to her".

He took her by taxi through the rush hour streets to "his club", where lackeys in uniforms bowed and scraped to him. As he and Susan enjoyed drinks and dinner, Henry explained his intentions.

"There are not many people with the *nous* to keep their heads when all about are floundering," he said in his rich, seductive voice. "When I meet such a person, I instinctively recognise the fact and want to draw them closer to me. So it is with you, Susan, so it is with you."

This is fate again, thought Susan. I found Ronaldo through my own adventure. I found Mario through Ronaldo and he recognised something in me. And now I've found Henry through Mario and he too can see that I am not just a silly girl but am born to be... to be... *something*. Who will I meet through Henry? she wondered. Probably a prince or a king. I am on my way, just as I knew it would be.

Henry was a little older than Mario but upright, proper, graceful and rather strict. When he said something you just did it. There was no argument. He was the master. Tall, probably over six foot, slim, with a mass of very well-cut dark hair, and eyes so dark brown that they were almost black. He always wore a suit and tie, with silver cufflinks and a handkerchief that matched the shirt in his top pocket. He was... amazing. Like nothing else in Susan's life so far. And here he was telling Susan that she had something, that she was special.

True she could not understand every single word he said, but she could follow enough to understand that Henry wanted Susan to be his "associate" because she had beauty and brains.

It was a wonderful evening and Susan did not realise how late it was getting. Henry was very easy to be with. At the end of the meal, he stood up, looked at his pocket watch and said: "Well, how charming an evening we have had. And now it is time for carriages."

By this he meant another taxi and Susan thrilled slightly, wondering where he was going to take her now and what it would be like. What *he* would be like. He had been a perfect gentleman so far and not so much as brushed her hand, but it was late, the wine had made her ever so slightly woozy and she waited expectantly.

A message came to say that the taxi had arrived, and Henry took Susan's arm and walked her down the stairs and out to the front. He opened the taxi door, helped Susan into it – then *closed* the door behind her, and leaned in through the window.

"The taxi is paid for to wherever you are going. It is on my account, so you have no need to worry. I very much hope that you have had as pleasant an evening as I have, my dear Susan. Now I want you to think carefully about all that I have said, for I meant every word and I do not go back on my promises. You and I will be a fearsome team. If you can do for me what you are doing for Mario, we will sweep the property world off its feet and clean up London, my dear. Sleep well. Drive on!"

And she was gone. Excited and stunned, Susan basked in the latest stage of her adventure and could barely wait for it to begin again. She was also, it is true, not a little disappointed at the sudden ending. She wanted to be taken further by Henry that evening, and she would have followed him to his rooms, flat or hotel without a moment's pause. But perhaps this was the way gentlemen did things. Not like Ronaldo. And there was plenty of time. She would see him again. He had promised.

No wonder she was tired. And then it was the weekend. Friday she went dancing with Brenda and her sister, Christine, and the three of them had a wonderful time. Some sailors bought them drinks all night and danced with them in a whirl of fun until Brenda said it was time to go, and extricated them neatly from the sailors' clutches. The three wandered off into the night, still giggling and hooting as the moon shone brightly down on them.

Susan fell into a deep sleep without completing the catalogue of her wild week.

Had she stayed awake, she would have remembered going out for a picnic with Brenda and her sister on the Saturday afternoon, going dancing with Mario in the evening and the two of them falling asleep in Mario's room somewhere, wherever it was, at some hour she did not know. She would have had some difficulty if asked directly whether or not she had slept with Mario that evening too. It was a bit of a blur. She didn't think so, although she may have done. They had certainly made up for it this morning though, she recalled with a tingle when she woke.

But what a week, what a hoot, and tomorrow was Monday, when it started all over again.

And so her life continued in a whirl of organising, convincing and threatening by day and dances, drinks and beds by night. It was a whirl that she quickly grew to love every moment of.

The only blemish on her otherwise perfect new life came from a little nagging voice inside that kept saying that her time of the month was about a week late. It was normally fairly regular, but she supposed that she had been living differently these past weeks so her body was just taking a bit of time to catch up.

As she sat in the office one morning, though, she realised that if she were pregnant, she would not be a hundred per cent sure who the father was.

She pushed the thought away, turned back to her desk, and immersed herself in her work. The work that everyone said she excelled at, and which was about to propel her towards the fame and fortune that destiny had decreed.

CHAPTER 29

Census sensibility

f Sam had a second brain cell, he'd be dangerous, thought Clara as she kicked off her shoes and dipped her feet into the bowl of warm soapy water she had prepared. On the other hand, if I had one brain cell I might learn never to listen to him again.

Clara had spent the morning of her day off following Sam's advice and looking up who was living where on the census. Or at least that had been the plan.

After she persuaded him that it would take him several years to learn French and that most French people spoke passable American anyway and it would be easier for him to learn Claudette-speak, she turned the conversation to her problems and asked his advice on where to get the information she needed.

"Well, someone I used to know…"

"You mean someone you used to sleep with…"

"Well, OK, as it happens, but… anyway… this person wanted to find out who her father was and it wasn't easy because she could only narrow it down to four different possibilities. Well, during her research – that I helped her with so she would be pleased with me and owe me a favour – during her research, I told her to look at something called The Census."

"Yes?" said Clara.

"That's it," said Sam, clearly thinking that he had contributed enough already. "I have no idea what it is, but she gave it a go. Didn't work, but it might have done. And in the time between her gratitude at my suggestion and her disappointment at its lack of success, we spent a very pleasant weekend in Carlisle."

"Dear god. You have measured out your life in hotel rooms."

"Come again?"

"Never mind. But I wonder if you could be right?"

"So you're grateful, then, my dearest darling Clara? Fancy a weekend in Carlisle?"

For just under a split second, Clara imagined what that would be like and the quick mental picture was not unappealing, but then she snapped back to reality.

"Only if I can go on my own," she said.

"I've always had a soft spot for you."

"What? Your brain?"

"You know you want to. But hey-ho, you don't know what you're missing. Anyway, it proves that I do have good ideas sometimes."

"Oh yes. I remember the last. 'Let's have rusks for breakfast,' you said. Four, I think you were. You peaked too early."

"Ratbag."

"But surprise to end all surprises, you actually might be onto something. Just one thing. How does one consult The Census? I've no idea."

"Ah, I know this. Kew. It's at a place in Kew. You walk in, tell them what you want and they let you look it up in books. Or on microfilm. Or in a paper bag of some kind. Or..."

And so Clara, without doing the research necessary to save herself from one of Sam's ideas, had taken a tube train to Kew Gardens, which is about a hundred stops from the centre of London, had traipsed for miles, walked in and out of several different buildings and had finally been advised by a puzzled clerk at a desk where Clara should not have been, that you can consult the Census online in many big libraries.

Mentally sticking pins in the tender places of a wax model of Sam, Clara trudged back to the tube.

She did finally not only make it, but also find what she was looking for at the Guildhall Library. In 1891, George and Rebecca Harvey were living at 25 Sultan Street in Broom just outside Langton with their children Thomas and Grace. Interesting.

While she was at it, she popped over to the Family Records Office and ordered Thomas and Grace's birth certificates. Would they help? Who knew?

It was almost closing time at the Office by now and she had left home before 10 that morning, so she crawled back on the tube and limped wearily home.

CHAPTER 30

Philip – taking the plunge

(July 1966)

Philip had been dreading telling Mary that he would not be able to see her this weekend. They had been getting on so well since their first kisses and he was almost sorry that he would not be able to see her from Thursday until Sunday evening. But Meg was coming down to Brighton for the weekend, just like she had promised. And they had booked into the Wellbourne Guest House, down towards Hove.

They were to be Mr and Mrs Harvey and their confirmed accommodation was one twin bedded room with a garden view. He had looked at the letter a hundred times and it grew no less exciting. He was a little disturbed by the "twin-bedded room" bit. He did not really understand what it meant. Did it mean that they had two beds in one room, or a bed each in two rooms? If it was two rooms, would it be obvious if one of them went into the other's? Would they be sent back, separated, shamed, pointed at over breakfast? Or would there be two beds in one room, in which case, they were free to do what they wanted in private? Meg had suggested one room in her letter (and put a small x in brackets after it, which must mean something). But what if at the end of the day, she would just climb into her bed and scream the house down if he did not slink away to his?

And should he buy any... you know... from the chemist? And if so how many? He had no idea. And what if he did buy them and it wasn't that sort of weekend that Meg was planning and then she found them in his bag?

Philip was so torn between ecstatic excitement and desperate fear of getting it all wrong that he did not know what to do or to expect.

Either way, he had to free himself from Mary for the weekend, and he now knew that this would not be easy.

He saw her briefly on the Wednesday and they shared an early evening stroll along the seafront. He suggested walking down towards Hove so that he could try to spot the Wellbourne Guest House, but for all his neck craning, he failed to see it.

Mary walked along with her arm around his waist and her head on his shoulder, as was now her habit. He laid a gentle arm around her shoulder and her hair smelled good. She chatted happily about her day, her Aunt Vera, and the picnic that she was planning for the weekend. She was not working on Saturday because it was her turn to take a day off. It came around about every eight weeks and she was looking forward to it. She could rustle up a basket of goodies and they could go anywhere Philip liked, put a blanket on the ground and make it their pretend home for the afternoon.

"If we ignore everybody else, we can just lie down, hug, kiss, laugh, snooze and eat. Or rather not snooze, because I don't want to waste a moment of it. Won't it be just divine? I know a really lovely park we can go to with some willow trees beside a pond. I walk there on my own sometimes. It's very shady and hardly anybody goes there. Except for the ducks, but they are very friendly. We can have our picnic under the trees and there will be nobody but us two."

Philip let her prattle on. She was happy and what was the sense of making her unhappy by saying that he could not go? Let her enjoy herself today, he thought. There was plenty of time to postpone it. Only by a week. They could have their picnic the following Saturday and all would be well. He would mention it later on the way back.

They did not make it all the way to Hove because Mary kept wanting to stop and kiss him. It was very nice, but it did stop him saying what he intended to say. Then it was time for her to go and he didn't get a chance.

"See you on Saturday," she laughed as she ran off after their long goodbye kiss tucked into a dark niche that they had found near the end of her road where two high walls met in a shadowy corner.

Mary could not get away on Thursday as she had hoped, so Philip had to find a way of letting her know that he could not see her on Friday and that the picnic on Saturday was off. He thought the best way was a note – just as she had dropped her note into his lap before.

He thought for a few moments about what he should say. Best to keep it brief. How about this:

Mary. So sorry, but have to work this weekend. Special project. Will be back Sunday evening. Philip

Well that was about all there was to say, wasn't it? No point in dragging it out. He wrote it out carefully on a sheet of paper, added a small x at the end after his name to be even nicer to her and then climbed into bed, his mind in a whirl of what the near future might hold. He thought about kissing Meg on the bridge by the river, then thought about lying down beside her in an actual bed in their own room and kissing her, and his mind leaped and turned somersaults. Was it possible? Could it really happen? In just two days' time? He took a while to fall asleep.

Philip was all set to pass his note to Mary at breakfast on the Thursday morning but she looked so happy when she came into the dining room that he did not want to spoil her day for her. That would not be a kind thing to do, he reasoned. She gave him a small wave and a big smile, and when no one was looking she even blew him a quick kiss. I'll give her the note tomorrow so that she can have a happy day today and only one less happy day tomorrow instead of two. Then he went back to wondering what Meg would be wearing when she got off the train and ran towards him, and what it would be like to hold her in his arms naked. Was that really going to happen? Tomorrow?

That afternoon, Philip sold a set of encyclopedias. It was easy. He knocked on the door, a man answered, Philip gave his spiel about the benefits of buying the books and the man said: "Yes, that sounds like a good idea. Come in."

Half an hour later, the deal was done.

Philip took it as a sign. The gods were smiling on him.

The next morning, he slipped his note to Mary, who also smiled on him, put it to her lips and kissed it, before dropping it into her apron pocket and running lightly out of the room. So the last hurdle that stood between him and Meg was sorted. She would arrive on the 6.28 train from London, he would meet her with his case and they would take the bus on the short hop to Hove. And then... he did not have a clue, but he knew that it could change his life. Meg lying naked in his naked arms... Oh, more than anything in the world.

"Thank you very much, Mr Harvey, sir. Here is your room key..."

Key, thought Philip in ecstasy. Key. Not keys. Oh, it would be soon.

"...and your room is number 15 up those stairs and down the corridor to your right. Dinner is from 7.30 with last orders at 9, and breakfast between 8 and 10. If you need to stay out after 11 at night, please ask here at reception for a front door key."

Stay out after 11? Are you mad? thought Philip.

"Thank you," he said as casually as he could manage, picked up the key and their two small cases, and followed Meg up the stairs, studying the flick of her hips as she walked, and her long slender legs as they emerged from her very short skirt.

They found their room, Philip unlocked the door and they walked in.

"Oh," said Meg in a disappointed voice. "Twin beds. I was rather hoping for a double. I've never slept in a double before."

"Nor have I," said Philip.

"But then," added Meg, "I've never slept in a bed with a man in it before either."

"Nor have I," said Philip.

"That's less surprising," laughed Meg. "Now shall we go for a pot of tea in the dining room, or a walk on the beach, or…"

She stood in front of him and reached her arms up to twine around his neck.

"Or shall we pretend that we're standing on that river bridge back in Langton," she kissed him as she had done that night, "… and pretend that that," she nodded towards the nearest bed, "…is the river, and we can at long, long last have what we promised ourselves. A skinny dip."

Now they were standing at the foot of the bed, arms locked around each other, kissing as though for the first time, their minds thinking three steps ahead. Without taking her mouth from his, Meg began to unbutton Philip's shirt, giving him the licence to do the same to her blouse.

When the kitchen stopped serving dinner at 9 pm, Philip was lying on his back with Meg draped heavily over him as the Brighton sunset bathed the room. I just want this to go on for ever and ever, he thought, enjoying feeling the pressure of Meg's body on top of his. I cannot believe how beautiful this feels. Meg Garvey, you are the most wonderful creature in the world and I want this forever. He realised that he had said that last thought aloud. Eyes still closed, Meg turned towards him, kissed him slowly and gently, sighed deeply and fell fast asleep in his arms.

"I want you to know, Mr Harvey," Meg said at breakfast the next morning, "that I do not make a habit of running off to guest houses in secret with strange men."

"I am *not* strange," Philip said, eyes playfully wide.

He poured some more tomato sauce on his plate and mopped it up with his fried bread. After having no dinner at all last night, he could have eaten three breakfasts and was having a good shot at it.

"The first time I saw you, standing in Bernard's kitchen, pretending you could smoke cigarettes," Meg continued, "I just knew. I don't know why, but I knew two things."

"Go on," laughed Philip. "Name them."

"Well, first I knew that you needed looking after. I didn't know how or why, but I just knew. Oh, I don't mean anything mundane like making you dinner and darning your smalls. I mean looking after *you*, taking care of your... your mind. It was a very strange feeling. But it just came to me right away, right at that first sighting."

"It was a lovely feeling," said Philip. "I like the idea a lot. And the second?"

"The second was that we would be together always. I've only been on dates with two other boys and I hated both of them. They were so... so small, so full of themselves, so worthless and so unfathomably confident. I didn't see either of them for a second time. But with you, I knew it would be different. I knew we would get married one day."

Hungry as he was, Philip paused and diverted some of his attention away from the toast he was buttering. He looked at Meg, mouth open.

"So you see coming here with you and doing... doing what we did last night, doesn't mean that I'm some kind of a tramp. It means that we are a married-couple-in-waiting and that's what those sorts of people are allowed to do."

Could this weekend possibly get any better? thought Philip. He did not know what to say. But that last thought might work.

"Could this weekend possibly get any better?" he asked, then finished buttering his toast and began to load it with an inch-thick covering of marmalade.

"Well that depends, I suppose," laughed Meg, "on what you have planned for today. You talked about walking on the beach and the pier and paddling in the sea, with probably a few dodgems and a bit of candy floss thrown in. It's going to be a lot of exercise."

Philip thought: if we go down to that end of town, we could bump into Mary and that would be embarrassing. Far better to stay at this end, or even stay in the guest house.

"Well," said Philip, "I suppose that we'll have to go out for a bit while they do up the room, but it's probably best not to go too far."

He looked over Meg's shoulder and out of the window.

"I'm sure it looks like rain and you don't want to catch a chill. I think perhaps we should have a quiet day in today to get our strength up for dinner tonight."

"We could always go swimming," said Meg with an arch smile.

"Swimming?" said Philip. "It would be a lot of fuss and the sea's probably a bit cold even at this time of year..."

"No, not in the sea. You know, like we did yesterday. Another skinny dip..."

"Oh yes," said Philip. "Oh yes. That would be very lovely. Very lovely indeed. And this afternoon, I think I may need a little looking after. Just to give you some practice, you know."

Philip awoke in the early afternoon and stayed perfectly still. Meg lay beside him, breathing softly in the warm afternoon air as gusts of sea breeze flicked the net curtains through the open window and played around them in the quiet room. He turned softly and looked across at her lovely face beside him on the pillow. He wanted it to be this way forever. But their lives were so far apart. He could not bear the thought that tomorrow afternoon, Meg would board a train for London, go back to Langton and leave him here hundreds of miles away in Brighton all alone. He would not perhaps see her for several weeks, perhaps longer, perhaps more than a month or two months. All he wanted now was to come home to her every night, to run and hold her when his work was done, to have dinner together, just the two of them and then to spend the nights just like this, asleep in each other's arms.

They did seem destined to be together. Meg had as good as proposed to him this morning at breakfast. 'I knew we would get married one day,' she had said. And: 'we are a married-couple-in-waiting."

Meg, the beautiful, special, sexy, fantastic, gorgeous Meg, wanted to be his wife. Meg was not only lovely but she thought of everything. *She* had been to the chemist and arrived with a plain paper bag crammed full. Meg, who to kiss was to sip champagne and to hold was to touch the stars, Meg wanted to spend her life with him. She said she just knew – and he did too.

Oh, why had he come to work here in Brighton in the first place? Why had he ever left Langton? He realised that he needed to return. So the way forward for him was obvious.

Without disturbing the sleeping Meg, he slipped out of bed, pulled on a pair of pyjama bottoms and sat down at the small writing-cum-dressing table in the window. He silently opened a couple of drawers until he found some writing paper and a pen, put his address and the date at the top, screwed up his face as he thought and then began to write:

"Dear Mr Jenkinson,

"You may remember me from a party at my brother's house in Langton a few weeks ago..."

When he finished, he re-read it three more times, screwed up the early drafts and threw them in the waste bin under the table, carefully folded the letter in three and put it in one of the envelopes on the desk. Then he rummaged in his jacket pocket on the back of the chair, took out his wallet and found the piece of paper he was looking for. He slowly copied the address onto the envelope, put the letter inside, and held it up in front of him just looking at it with a smile.

He was so engrossed that he did not notice that Meg had slipped out of bed and run to stand behind him and throw her arms around his neck.

"What are you doing, my secretive one?" she asked, kissing him several times on the neck and ear.

"Mmm," said Philip with a shiver of pleasure at the touch of her naked body against his back. "This," he said, holding up the envelope, "is my return ticket to Langton, I hope. I wrote it just the way you told me to and it sounded very good, I thought."

She read the name and address on the front.

"That would make it far easier for you to see me than when you're living here," she said. "Much better all round."

Philip picked Meg up, carried her back to the bed, lay her gently down and sat beside her.

"And if it works," he continued, "then nothing can keep us apart so..."

He slid off the bed and dropped down onto one knee beside it.

"...Meg Garvey, would you do me the honour of making me the happiest of men by becoming my wife?"

She pulled him towards her, kissed him slowly then said with a sigh: "I thought you'd never ask. Yes, my dearest darling Philip. Yes, I will. Now come here..."

They almost missed dinner for the second night running.

CHAPTER 31

Paul takes a risk

The following week, Peter was away again. This was becoming a habit that Clara liked a lot. And Vincent was pleased that he was working this week and did not miss out.

"Marcia," he pleaded, "would you be a honey and make sure that our holidays never clash again? This place is so much nicer when the old goat isn't here, don't you think? We can all breathe and smile and all those other things humans do when the bossy old grown-ups aren't around."

"Hey, that's my cherished boss you're talking about," said Marcia in mock horror. "I know what you mean though."

"Make the most of it, chums," warned Clara. "He'll be back on Monday and it's press week, so we'll pay for this holiday."

"True," said Vincent. "Perhaps I should throw a sickie next week. You don't need me, do you? Just use old pages, swap in new words and pictures and you'll be fine."

"Is that all you do?" asked Clara sweetly.

"I'll never admit it, but pretty much, yes."

"Hey, we should all go out for a drink after work tonight to celebrate," said Clara.

"Sounds lovely," said Marcia. "But tonight is my art class and I can't miss that. I've only just started and it's very hard."

"Do you get to hold the brushes and splash about with the paints?" asked Vincent. "Or are you a nude model? Still life but only just?"

"Nude model? Not sure that if anyone saw me in the nude they'd be inspired to paint me."

"Oh I don't know," said Vincent. "I think you'd come up lovely with a couple of coats of gloss. How would you like magnolia?"

"How would you like a clip round the ear?"

"Anyway," said Clara, "how about you, Vincent? Are you up for a drink or is it basket weaving for beginners tonight?"

"You are a basket case, after all," laughed Marcia.

"I'd love to join you for a drink but I'm afraid I can't stay long. A friend of mine is putting on a fashion show and I promised to go over and help him design the set tonight."

"We-ll," mused Clara, "we could always sneak off a bit early while there's no one looking. Could you join us for a quick one, Marcia, before you're off to the painting lark?"

"Well I suppose one wouldn't hurt," she said.

"That's settled then. A little before six o'clock at the Red Lion," said Clara and they all went back to their desks and started to work.

Almost a minute later, a small voice from over by the window said: "I'm free tonight."

They all turned. Paul had spoken. They had forgotten that he was there.

"Oh Paul, of course," said Clara, mortified that she had not included him in the first place. "That would be lovely. Six o'clock it is."

Perhaps because of the overbearing presence of Peter in the office, such a commonplace event as after-hours drinks had never happened before while any of them had been working at *Allaire*. They were all so relieved to get out of the firing line as soon as the hooter went in their heads, that socialising was never considered.

But Clara wanted a distraction tonight. Last night as she got home, she found an envelope with a handwritten address on it next to a couple of bills. It was from Agnès.

"My dear Clara," it read. "It was so nice to meet you, and I thank you so much for coming over to visit. I did enjoy talking to you and learning all about you. Now I have some good and some bad news to tell you, so let's do the good first. I was very impressed with you, your (unadulterated) work and your ideas. And I very much want to offer you a job with us. Now, sadly, the bad news. Our development and expansion has been put on hold by the board and nothing is going to move for at least six months. At least. That is not to say that our plans will come to nothing, far from it, but for now, my hands are tied up and there is nothing I can do. I realise that this is not the news you wanted to hear, and it is also not the news that I wanted to give, but keep all of your fingers crossed and I hope that we can meet again soon when this comes to pass. Keep me in your address book and do not forget, your bonne amie, Agnès."

Blast, thought Clara. That's almost worse than being turned down. To get that close and have the chance taken away by the bean counters. I know how Sam feels now. Or at least part of what goes on deep inside that rather strange head of his.

So, in need of cheering up, Clara led her three comrades down in the lift at just after 5.30 and along the 100 yards to the Red Lion, where she bought the first round. It was a warm night so they joined the growing crowd outside the pub on the pavement and watched the stream of commuters heading off in different directions towards Blackfriars and St Paul's and Chancery Lane stations.

Marcia told them all about her art class, which turned out to have been a birthday present from her husband Richard.

"I've only been to two so far, but I'm quite enjoying it – although I don't think I'm very good."

"I'm sure you are," said Clara. "What have you done so far?"

"Well, last week we had to draw an apple."

"I went to art classes once," said Vincent. "But they threw me out."

"Threw you out?" asked Clara. "Why did they do that?"

"I drew a blank," said Vincent.

"Idiot," snorted Marcia.

"So how did your apple come out?" said Clara. "Did it look good enough to eat?"

"Well, yes it did, I suppose, in a way. But it actually looked more like a potato if I'm honest."

"And what's on the menu tonight?" asked Vincent. "A bowl of roses that looks like a radish? Or the ceiling of the Sistine Chapel pretending to be a cucumber."

"Leave her alone, you bully," said Clara, thumping him playfully in the chest. "I think it's a wonderful thing to do."

"Thank you, Clara. It's nice to have one adult in the office. And what about you, then? What's your fashion set going to look like? The back end of a bus, I should think."

Vincent became almost conspiratorial and drew Marcia close to him. "Apparently... How can I describe it? Well, you like animals. Have you ever seen a cat walk?" Vincent asked her.

"Of course I have. Lots of times. We've got one."

"Well, the word is that it's going to look a bit like that."

"What? Oh... You daft fool. What's he like?"

"He likes this South American beer," said Vincent. "and he would very much like to have another, but unfortunately he needs to go. Marcus is a worrier and if I don't get there to be a calming influence, he will begin to imagine all sorts of bad things are about to happen. So I am afraid that I will have to leave you. We really must do this again, if only to find out what Marcia has etched this week."

"I'll etch you if you don't watch out," said Marcia. "But I'll walk you to your station first. I need to be there in plenty of time to relax before it all starts."

"Chancery Lane here we come," said Vincent. "Would you like me to carry you so you can start relaxing straight away?"

"I'd like to throw you under a train and paint that. Goodbye, Clara. Goodbye, Paul. See you both tomorrow."

"And if she has red under her fingernails, let's hope it's just paint and not my blood. See you tomorrow."

And they were off, wandering down the road, arm-in-arm, still both trying to get one over on the other.

Clara was left with Paul and thought that this would be the end of the evening.

"Are you rushing off to evening classes too?" she asked, wondering what he might learn. How to be a mime artist, she thought. Must remember to tell Vincent and Marcia that in the morning.

"Um, I'm not in a tearing hurry. Unless you want to get away?" said Paul.

"No, no," said Clara. "I've got nothing to head off to."

"Can I get you another drink, then?"

"Yes, please. Just the house red will do fine, thanks."

Paul went inside and Clara wondered what was coming next. This hadn't been what she had planned. She thought she would have a relaxed laugh with Marcia and Vincent and now she was stuck with something out of a Harold Pinter play. Or Samuel Beckett. Yes, that's it. *Waiting For Godot*, and she had got Lucky. She had got Lucky! Ooh, Marcia and Vincent were missing all these gems.

Paul came back and handed Clara her drink.

"Cheers," she said, wondering how to follow that.

"It feels weird being out of the office with you three," said Paul after a short pause. "Almost like being free somehow."

"Free? How do you mean?"

"Well without father being there."

"No, it can't be easy working for your dad."

She wanted to add that it couldn't be easy being his son in the first place but thought that might be going a bit far.

"It's not that easy being his son at all," said Paul, with a small laugh. "He's not the easiest."

"Does he give you a hard time too?"

"Well, not as much as he does you. I hate to see him bullying you the way he does, but he's so... I don't know... difficult. Overbearing."

"Ha. Yes, he is a bit. Is he like that at home too?"

"Pretty much."

Clara noticed that Paul was almost relaxing. He was leaning back against the pub wall, and rocking his chair gently back and forth.

"So is that why," said Clara, thinking that she may as well get to the point, "is that why you don't come out of your shell much?"

"Yes. I developed it as a defence mechanism really and I suppose it's taken me over. If I say anything he jumps on me. At least if I'm quiet and do what I'm told, I don't have him laughing and shouting at me. I'm sorry, I must come across as a complete clod."

"No, no, no," said Clara, a little too quickly. "You are quite hard to get to know though."

"I don't really notice I'm doing it any more, but once you start down that road, you know, keeping quiet all the time, it's very hard to stop. I wish I could be more like you three. More like you."

"Perhaps you could start slowly. You know, the odd word here and there."

"Oh, I don't know. When I listen to you all talking I can never think of anything to say. And by the time I think of something you've moved on and are talking about something else. And if I suddenly piped up and said something stupid, you'd all stare at me and I'd just shrivel up. I probably wouldn't have the nerve anyway."

"Well, you have a good chance to practise this week, with Peter being away."

He smiled. "I'm a bit out of touch." He looked at Clara. "Will you... will you help me? It feels like bungee jumping and I'm not sure I could do it on my own."

"Help you? What can I do?"

"I'm sorry. I don't know really. I would like very much to be just, just one of the crowd. You all say clever things. I wish I could too. Could you just try to include me in conversations and I'll try to join in? Because I'm so stuck in this mute persona, everyone forgets that I'm there at all. Like when you were arranging these drinks and you only asked the other two. Look I know it's my fault, but if I try, will you help me?"

"That sounds like a fair bargain. So come on then, let's give it a try. Paul, tell me about you. What do you like doing, reading, watching? What makes you laugh?"

"Ooh, that's a bit of a mouthful so early in the trial. Can't we start by talking about an apple?"

She laughed. "You see, you *can* do it. I tell you what, let's simplify it a bit. What is it like at home? When it's just the two of you?"

"Oh, we have a great time together. A few beers, watch the football game on TV, tell a few jokes and have some of the boys over for a barbecue. You know, the things all dads and sons do."

"Really?"

"No, not really. None of that. If you think I'm quiet in the office, you should see me at home." He laughed. "No, I tend to stay in my room. I have my computer with some games on there. I read quite a lot. Get plenty of early nights."

"It, er… it sounds a bit like house arrest."

"Yes. Yes, that's not a bad description."

There was a pause, Paul looking down into his glass. Then he looked at Clara and said slowly but with determination.

"But do you know what? I've just about had enough of it. I don't want to be like this and I'd do anything to get out of it."

"Good for you."

"Today, when I said that I was free – when I actually spoke up and invited myself out for a drink with you all – you don't know what a big achievement that was for me. You don't know what a massive step it was, how I almost didn't dare, how close I came to sitting there and saying nothing and then having to watch you all go off to the pub while I slunk home on my own. But here I am. Look at me."

Clara was looking at him. For the first time properly. When he spoke, his voice was quite rich and sort of deep, though nothing like as pompous as Peter's. And when he smiled and looked animated, he wasn't at all bad looking. The hair and clothes were a real problem, but that could be fixed.

"You're doing just great, Paul," she said, laying a hand on his arm. "It can't be easy when you've been trapped like that for so long. You stick with it and I'll help you in any way I can."

"Only don't say anything to Marcia and Vincent," he pleaded. "I don't want to become some kind of charity object that you all have to be nice to. But if I try, I just want to be included. Slowly, mind..."

"I think I understand. Perhaps we could come up with some scripts where I start talking about something to the whole office, feed you a line, you know exactly what you're going to say, and you go for it. I can certainly help with that. And it can be our secret. No one else will know what we're doing."

"Oh, would you? I'd like that so much. Not having to think up something to say on the spot but still being able to join in. It would be like bungee jumping with a safety net."

He paused, took a drink, then a very deep breath and then looked up.

"And now, here goes nothing," he said. "Or everything. Clara, would you like to go out to dinner with me tonight?"

He looked worried, but Clara just smiled and said: "Paul, I would like that very much indeed."

CHAPTER 32

Susan – No problem

(August 1948)

S usan smiled as she sat on the train that chuffed slowly and noisily into King's Cross. A couple of hours earlier, it had chugged through Langton station, but she kept her face hidden by a newspaper and as she peeked out from behind it, she saw that the platform was empty. No one got off and no one got on. Perfect.

Susan remembered her day trip to London with Annie all that time ago, when, so full of excitement and trepidation, she had travelled this same journey, climbing onto the train from this very platform in the hope of changing her life forever. That had certainly happened. Must be two or three years ago now and it seemed an age. Although in terms of her life, so much had altered in those two years that she might as well be a different person.

And this time, although she was again travelling in secret, she had not come just from Langton but all the way from the Black Isle. All in all, things had worked out pretty well, she thought. Considering that when she first found out that she really was pregnant, she was distraught and thought her world had ended. But just look at her now. She had managed to organise everything so that she could just pick up where she left off as though nothing had happened. She congratulated herself. Didn't it only go to prove that nothing was going to stand in her way? Her destiny was not to be so easily denied.

Of course, she owed a great debt to Bernard, the best brother in the world. Without him on her side, heaven knows *what* she would have done.

When she told Ronaldo that he was the father, he barely missed a beat, whatever he was thinking inside.

"Oh, Princess, that's not a problem," he said, rushing over to her and giving her a big hug, burying her face in his neck so that at least she could not see his expression while he cooed: "There, there. It's all going to be all right, Princess."

It gave him time to think. How could I have been so stupid? he thought. Didn't we always take precautions? Well perhaps not once or twice, when the need was, well, urgent. How unlucky can you get? Now how could he get rid of her? His mother might have a long-term illness that would take him out of the way, but he'd have to come back at some point so that didn't really solve anything.

No, it looked as though this would be best solved by Princess paying a little visit to Mrs Heggerty. She had helped him out once before, no trouble. And she wasn't too expensive. And fairly safe by all accounts.

And so it was arranged. Susan was numb with terror at the thought of being a mother and losing everything that she and destiny had worked so hard to set up. Ronaldo said this was what London women did and she was now a London woman, so she went along with it.

Susan recalled with a shudder her visit to Mrs Heggerty's house, a rambling old building just by the river in Poplar. It was a chill, rainy evening and Susan knocked on the door and waited, miserable and scared. Mrs Heggerty herself came to the door, a small, thin woman with dark hair and glasses.

"Is it Susan?" she said, ushering her into the dry but dank hallway. "I've been expecting you, my dear. Ronaldo said you'd be coming. How is he these days? Haven't seen him for a while."

She led Susan into a brightly lit room with a dingy sofa along one wall, some cupboards along another, a door in the far wall, a large window with the curtains fully closed although it was only about four in the afternoon, and a high bed in the centre with a tall anglepoise lamp standing on a small chest at the foot. Mrs Heggerty carried on chatting as Susan stood and stared, her heart feeling nothing but horror for what was about to happen to her.

"Oh I've done this loads of times and there's never been a problem. Well.. no… never a problem. There's nothing to be afraid of. It's all going to be all right, my dear. You'll soon be on your way, right as ninepence."

She indicated the door in the far wall.

"Now if you'd like to pop into that toilet and strip off your bottom clothes, then come and lie on the bed."

Susan went into the tiny toilet and just stood there. The thought of lying on the bed, opening her legs and letting this woman carve away at her was terrifying. But what was the alternative?

"Are you all right, dear?" Mrs Heggerty called through the door at last. "Can I get you anything? There's nothing to worry about. I'll put the kettle on."

Susan still stood in the toilet, not daring to move, hardly daring to breathe. She was desperately unhappy.

Then… No, she thought. No, I can't do this. I can't. Anything's better than this.

She opened the door and with a quick: "I have to go," flung over her shoulder at Mrs Heggerty, she was out into the hallway and then back into the spitting, comforting rain and heading for home.

"Oh, Princess," said Ronaldo when she told him. "It would have all been over by now. Over and back to normal. I'm surprised at you, Princess. Surprised and a little disappointed. Look, I'll speak to Mrs Heggerty and we'll try again. I can come with you if you like. So you're not frightened. I'll hold your hand."

And I'll make sure she stays this time, he thought to himself.

Mario was comforting too.

"I'm going to be a daddy?" he said with a big grin. "Well, well, well. That's wonderful news. Just wonderful. When will you leave your job, do you know yet? Only I'm going to have to find someone else, obviously. If you're going to be a mummy, then I still need another Susan in here to run things, don't I?"

So she really *was* going to lose everything that fate had provided for her. Mario confirmed it and it came as a bitter shock. Someone else would be here doing her job and she would be pushing a pram around the streets and changing nappies, while Ronaldo and Mario and Henry got on with life without her. Probably taking Mario's new Susan out for dinner instead. She may as well have stayed in Langton and pushed a pram around there. What was she going to do?

Bernard. Bernard, she thought. He would know what to do. He always knew what to do.

"Mario," she said next day when the work was done and they were just about to close up and lock the doors. "Mario, I need to speak to you."

"Certainly, *bambino* – or should I say *madre* now?" He laughed, then noticed that Susan was not joining in. "Let's go to the pub and you can tell me all about it."

They walked over to the Royal Oak and sat in the quiet bar with their drinks.

"Now, what is it, my precious one?"

"Mario, I've had an idea. Well, half an idea, but I just know that somehow it will sort things out. I can work for another couple of months and that will take us to about the end of spring, and then nothing much happens for several months anyway, right?"

"That's right. It all goes quiet until things pick up again in the autumn. It's just the business we are in."

"OK, then I will go away for a bit and somehow, I don't know how, but somehow, I will be back in time for the autumn just to carry on as normal."

She put her hand on his arm and looked earnestly into his eyes.

"Mario, you don't need to replace me. I'm not going to give all of this up, not everything I've worked for. I'm just not."

"Well, I don't want to lose you, *mia cara*. There is no one who could be as good and as beautiful as you. If you can find a way to be my own helper in spite of this, then I will let you. Take as much time as you need, only let me know that you will be back or I have no choice. You know..."

"I know. I will be back, Mario. I promise you. I will be back."

"Well, why don't we finish this drink and go to the pictures tonight? I don't know what's on, but as long as it makes you cry at the end, we'll both be happy."

"Yes, Mario." said Susan. "We'll both be happy."

And now here she was. She had said she would come back, and as she stepped off the train and made her way along the King's Cross platform towards the buses out in the already dark night, she *was* back. She had had a very difficult few months but she had done it.

That first meeting with Bernard had been the toughest.

"Oh Bernard, I don't know what I'm going to do. I've been such a fool. I believed what people told me. I should have listened to you. But please help me. Please help me. I have no one else to turn to."

Her tear-stained face showed the depth of her feelings and Bernard was moved despite his shock. Susan had arrived unannounced with a small suitcase. It was the first time he had seen his sister for nearly two years, since she had gone on her day trip to London and then vanished. Not a letter, not a Christmas card, not a word. Now here she was, full of contrition and pregnant. It was a lot to take in.

Bernard thought of their mother and father, and how he was going to tell them. What would their reaction be? And how would Alice take it when she found out?

Bernard looked across his front room at Susan, sitting slumped on the sofa, her face in her hands, sobbing quietly. One thing was sure and that was that Susan could not do this on her own. He would have to help. He would have to manage things.

He went and sat beside his sister and put his arms around her.

"It's OK. It's OK. It will all sort itself out. You're only having a baby, you've not murdered anyone or robbed a bank. No one is going to send you to jail. You're not the first woman to be in this position and it's not the end of the world. Not by a long shot. You'll smile and laugh again, my darling, dopey Susan. And it *is* good to see you after so long. I'm not even cross with you. Alice will be home soon, young Ian will be awake for his tea and bath in a bit, and there's one of my famous stews bubbling away on the stove. I'll put some dumplings in it so it goes around, and we'll have a lovely dinner and get down to some planning."

Susan brightened and looked up at him.

"When you talk like that anything seems possible, darling Bernard. You really are the best brother in the whole world," she said and began crying again.

This is going well, so far, she thought. I knew it would. Bernard is just so good in a crisis. Always was. Can't help himself.

"And now," said Bernard, "how about I run you a nice hot bath and you settle into the spare room. The bed's always made up, just in case, so there's nothing to do."

"That would be lovely, Bernard. Just what I need. Thank you so much. You make me feel so much better."

Once Ian had been introduced to Susan, had jumped all over her, got tired, had his bath, had his tea and gone to bed, the three of them did actually spend quite a pleasant evening together. Bernard's stew tasted as good as it smelled, he opened the last bottle of wine that he and Alice had brought back from France the summer before, and Susan told them the story she had made up about what she had been doing in London. She had decided that the simplest way out of complicated answers was to invent a secret that meant she could not say too much. No one can give away a secret, so all questions are easily batted away.

"Look, I'm sorry but I can't say too much about what I'm doing in London," she told them as they ate. "It's the Official Secrets Act and I could go to prison for about 14 years if I give anything away. I've been trying to make some money, my fortune if you like, so that I can come back and live here with you all and we can all be comfortable. It's been going well, with the odd setback on the way of course, but on the whole, as well as could be expected. Or better. But now this and I don't know what to do. I've taken some leave but I could lose everything I've worked for. All those risks I've taken would be wasted."

Her eyes began welling up again.

"Don't worry about that tonight," said Bernard quickly. "I have the seeds of the beginning of a plan going round in my head. I'll keep it secret too for now. But leave it with me for a day or two."

"Come on, Susan," said Alice. "Bernard has slaved away making us dinner, so let's clear away and make him some coffee. It is good to see you again. We've missed you."

About a week later, Bernard, Alice, Ian and Susan boarded an early morning train at Langton station and much later as it grew dark around them, arrived by taxi at Jane and Thomas's cottage in the Black Isle. Bernard and Susan's parents were taking a break there as they had started doing at this time of year, and welcomed them with hugs and mince and tatties.

Jane was thrilled to see Susan again, almost banishing the pain of their separation. Bernard had prepared the ground, had written to her and spoken several times on the phone at the post office. He had told her how sorry Susan was, how mixed up, how unhappy and tearful, and how much she wanted to see her mother and father again.

"It will be… very strange," said Jane. "When do you arrive?"

"On Friday evening," said Bernard. "I'm looking forward to seeing the place again."

"Yes, it's beautiful at this time of year. And so many memories."

Both Jane and Susan had been looking forward to meeting again but were desperately worried about it. In the end, as the three climbed out of the taxi, after a short pause, they flew into each other's arms and were inseparable for the next few days. Thomas was very quiet but smiled at Jane's happiness and decided not to say most of the things that he wanted to say to his daughter.

Life settled down. The weather was awful with torrential rain almost every hour of every day and night, so the five hardly ventured out at all.

The best part, remembered Susan as she stood at the bus stop waiting to head back to her old new life, was having time to relax, not feeling that she had to be on her guard the whole time to prevent a gift from destiny passing her by because she happened to be looking the other way. She had a time-out.

The bus arrived and she climbed on board and went upstairs. Almost there. Almost ready for the next stage. She knew from the snatched phone calls she had managed to have with both Mario and Henry that all was well, she had missed hardly anything, and the business was about to rachet up another few gears on the way to a very interesting life ahead.

As the bus pulled away from King's Cross station and rattled off down Pentonville Road, she recalled the birth with a shudder. What an awful day. A woman with such a strong accent that Susan could barely understand her gave orders, soothed, shouted, coaxed and finally stood up with a wrinkly dark pink baby. It was such a relief that the terrible pains had stopped, that Susan was almost pleased to see it, although blaming it for the worst time of her life.

Who does it look like? she wondered as they made her hold it. Not Ronaldo really? Wrong shaped face. Perhaps Mario? She wished it could have been Henry, but that was out of the question. Still a perfect gentleman.

At least it seemed to be a good baby and slept a lot. Jane and Alice enjoyed fussing around it, feeding it, bathing it and changing it, so Susan willingly let them. She was very tired but feigned even more exhaustion so that she might be left alone to recover more speedily.

They all wanted to know what name Susan would give it. How should she know? Ronaldo? Mario? She laughed to herself. In the end, she told them it was to be called Philip, the first name that she could think of after reading in the paper about Princess Elizabeth's impending wedding to that handsome Greek man called Philip. That would do.

Susan was feeling a lot better within a matter of days, so the following Tuesday when the rain stopped at last, Bernard, Alice, Ian and Jane wanted to take the baby, Philip, on his first walk around the Black Isle while Thomas took his morning nap, Susan readily agreed, saying that she felt well enough to manage on her own if they could set her up with a pot of tea and some biscuits.

They had barely gone half a mile before Susan was out of the door, her small suitcase in her hand, heading for the town. She caught the bus to Inverness and was on a London-bound train before the rest of the family had reached Munlochy Bay. By the time they got back home they found only Thomas in the house, Susan was heading toward the border and back out of their lives again.

As she climbed the stairs wearily to her room, Susan was glad that she had sorted out her problem, glad that Bernard had come good again, glad that she had seen her mother and father once more, glad to have had a rest in the Black Isle, glad that Philip was surrounded by a loving family... but above all, glad to be back where she belonged.

CHAPTER 33

Riddle answered, riddle posed

Well, who would have guessed that? Paul is a really nice guy, good-looking and very funny when he comes out in the open. She was going to have to be careful how she handled this. She was hardly going to point at him open-mouthed and tell Marcia and Vincent that there was actually a person in there. It would need to be taken slowly.

They had been to a small Italian restaurant that she knew and Paul had been surprisingly good company. They liked some of the same books and TV programmes, and both loved France, where Paul had spent several years during his childhood with his mother's family in Besançon. He told her all about the place and she told him what the Black Isle was like. They also plotted some scripts that would help Paul start to talk in the office more.

Clara would never have believed it. She had actually spent an evening with Paul and had a great laugh. *Allaire* was going to be very different from now on. Probably far more interesting.

Clara got home, feeling ever so slightly light-headed, to find another fat envelope on the doormat. What have we here? she thought.

She made herself a big cup of hot chocolate and settled down to open it.

There were three certificates and the first she opened was Grace Harvey, born 1891, Mother Rebecca Harvey, Father George Harvey. OK.

Next came Thomas, Jane's husband-to-be. Born 1888. Hello. Thomas *Laker* said the birth certificate. Mother Rebecca Laker, father left blank. Oh. Interesting.

One more, this must be George and Rebecca's wedding certificate. Dated 1890. Rebecca Laker, spinster, married George Harvey, widower. WIDOWER?

Clara found a scrap of paper and a pen and tried to put it all in some sort of order. So George and Rebecca married in 1890 when Rebecca already had Thomas, a two-year-old son without a father. Grace Harvey was born a year later.

Hmm, doesn't take a genius to work out who Thomas's father was, does it? But what happened to George's first wife?

Whatever it was, she already knew from the census that Rebecca and George Harvey lived with Thomas and Grace. Clara thought and then seemed to see back into the foggy past. Hardly surprising, the young boy became known as Thomas Harvey, but when it came to official documents – insurance and the like – they had to tell the truth, so he was the first of the Harvey (Otherwise Laker) clan. It was all falling into place.

But what else was there to find out? And would she ever be able to do it?

CHAPTER 34

Philip – Careless whisper

(August 1966)

P hilip braced himself for the slap or scream that never came. Mary had finally stopped crying and was breathing normally again. They sat on their bench on the Sunday evening after Meg had left Brighton on the late afternoon train. It had been as hard as Philip thought to say goodbye after such a weekend together.

"Parting like this will just make it so much sweeter when we don't have to any more," Meg had said as she leaned down out of the open train window, with her arms around Philip's neck as he stood on the platform below.

"I'm going to miss you so much." There were real tears in Philip's eyes as he gazed up at her. "I don't know what I'm going to do without you."

"Well here's one thing. I'm going to write you a letter with the number of the phone box by Langton station on it. Then we can arrange times when you can ring it and we can talk at least. How about next Friday at 6 o'clock for the first? Give us time to sort things out."

"What a lovely idea. You're a genius."

"That's what I mean by looking after you. And me, come to think of it. And I won't forget to post your letter to Mr Jenkinson as soon as I get back. It will get there quicker that way. You must let me know the minute you hear from him."

The guard blew his whistle and the final doors slammed shut. Philip gave Meg a last kiss and stood back onto the platform as the train slowly wheezed into motion, pulling her away from him and gradually quickening as it snaked out of the station and rounded the bend at the far end so that the kisses they were blowing each other could no longer reach their destination.

Philip picked up his own case and wearily, sadly, slowly made his way back towards the town, his mind a mixture of elation at what had happened between them and stomach-wringing emptiness that Meg was gone.

He walked all the way back to the *Bel Air* with the conflicting emotions tearing him first one way and then the other. In the end, though, the overriding feeling was elation at the images and sensations that Meg had left him with. When he thought back to his feeling on Thursday when he did not even know if they would share the same room, to now, when he had so much to look back on and so much to look forward to, he could scarcely believe that it had all happened so quickly. And he was even engaged to be married. He smiled.

He remembered that he had told Mary he would be back on Sunday and hoped that she would not be free so he would not have to go out. All he wanted was a sit-down, an early dinner and some sleep before it all started again tomorrow. But when he finally walked into his room, his foot touched a folded sheet of paper that had been pushed under the door.

"A shame you had to work. I can be at our bench at 7 o'clock if you are back. Mary x"

Poor Mary, he thought. I hope she was better this weekend than the last time I went away. I had better go and see her.

So he washed and changed before dinner and set off in plenty of time. He was sitting on the bench looking out to sea and picturing Meg's face in every wave, tree and flower when he heard footsteps running up behind him. He jumped up just in time as Mary landed in his arms and hugged him.

"Oh, Mary, it's good to see you. I'm so sorry I had to work, but it was a last-minute thi…"

Mary stopped him talking with a long, lingering kiss, then buried her face in his neck and sighed: "Oh I missed you so much. It's so good to have you back."

They sat down together on the bench, his arm slung around her shoulder.

"We can have our picnic next weekend perhaps," he told her soothingly.

"If we can. I'll have to work next Saturday."

"We'll organise something," he promised.

They sat in silence for a short while, and then Philip slowly became aware that Mary was sobbing.

"Hey, hey, come on," he said softly. "It's all right. I'm back now. Don't cry."

"Oh I told myself to be brave and I have been all weekend. I can't fall to pieces every time you're not in the room, can I? I have been good. Only now the relief that you're back is a bit too much for me. I'm sorry. I'll be all right in a moment."

She smiled up at him through her tears, then her body heaved with more sobs.

"Oh, come on now, Meg," he said, immediately realised, and tensed for a reaction. He waited but it never came. After a few moments, he dared to breathe again. Had he really got away with it?

But he quickly saw the peril he was in. What if he did it again? And what if he called Meg Mary? That would be a *real* disaster. He must think of a way to stop it happening. He must give himself time to think before he said anything from now on. He must, what? Count to 10. That's it. He gave it a little practice.

1-2-3-4-5-6-7-8-9-10, he counted but then realised that all he had done was count, just think the numbers and not think of what he was going to say next. It was too many numbers.

"Would you like to go for a little walk?" asked Mary.

1-2-3 1-2-3 1-2-3 10, thought Philip, at the same time preparing his answer and checking that it would not cause any problems.

"Philip? Would you like to go for a walk?" she repeated.

This was no good. He had taken too long, he must speed up. He must practise counting so that he could do it without thinking about the numbers at all. It was something to work on.

"Yes, that would be very nice..." he answered, "...darling," he added. Good idea that, he thought. Call them both darling and I can't go wrong. He smiled at his own cleverness.

The two got up and walked arm-in-arm along the seafront, unhurriedly, both with their own thoughts.

"I'm glad you're back," murmured Mary. "It's so much better when you're here."

1-2-3 1-2-3 1-2-3 10, thought Philip, tapping his leg gently with his free hand on the beat of each three and on the 10. Four beats. If he practised that enough it would become second nature and he would be free to think about what he was going to say, not about counting. Tap tap tap tap in a moderate rhythm.

"It's great to be back," he first thought and then said.

And so the two wandered on, holding each other tightly, sharing the intimacy of their closeness until it was time to go to their dark alcove and share some long, lingering goodnight kisses.

"See you at breakfast," said Mary, and skipped away, thankful that Philip had returned.

Philip headed back towards his room.

"I wonder if Meg is home yet?" he thought.

CHAPTER 35

Paul to the rescue

"No, no, no, no, no, no, no, no no. No. Not at all. Just no. *Lictus tugent posset est.*"

Clara stared straight at Peter, but she was thinking of Agnès and she was not going to be put down again.

"And what," she said in a level voice, "is wrong with it?"

Peter was reading her interview with her coffee magnate Henri Gautier – the one that Agnès thought was so good that she wanted to offer her a job on the strength of it. Of that very piece. Only Peter found something displeasing about it.

"Oh *tempora fugit in diem obliquus.* Life is too short to discuss everything that is marred in these few short pages. I will dwell only on the major crimes…"

Clara did not sit down and cower into her chair as she usually did but remained standing in front of his desk, feet apart, staring directly at him.

"Well then? I'm waiting."

"Oh, the tone. We are not matey with these icons whom we hold up for public scrutiny. We are mirrors, interlocuters, inquisitors. How do they do what they do? Where did their success come from? How may it be copied? Not this turgid spiel about how he sits on his chair and whether or not his head is to one side when he speaks."

Clara breathed deeply.

"Observations of how a person comports themselves give an insight into their character. Many writers use the technique from Evelyn Waugh to F. Scott Fitzgerald, Steinbeck to Jane Austen, and probably a few dead Romans and Greeks for all I know."

Peter put down the sheaf of papers he was holding and looked hard at Clara.

"Not one of them works for me, Miss Harvey," said Peter. "And if you wish to continue to do so it might be an idea to remember that I built this magazine that pays your salary up from nothing, crafted it into what it is today, and honed its *nihil sed aestheticum* to its current heights. And I did it by being right about this kind of thing. That will be all. Paul. Paul. Come in here."

Paul came to the door and looked at Clara, who turned and marched out past him. He gave her a sly wink of comradeship as they crossed.

"I have made some marks on this... this..." Peter said to him and threw the interview across the desk at him. A few sheets fell on the floor and Paul bent to pick them up.

"There will no doubt be more corrections on the proof," added Peter in a voice loud enough for everyone in the office to hear, "when I have had time to ponder further."

Paul went back to his desk and began typing. When he finished there was a ping on Clara's computer. She opened her email and read the new arrival. It was from Paul.

"I apologise on behalf of my family. I've read your piece and really liked it and you said that your Agnès in Paris liked it too. So that's 3-1. Don't let him get to you. Or as he'd probably say: *nolle batarde carborundum* (don't let the bastard grind you down). Shall we go out for a drink tonight to cheer each other up?"

Clara laughed out loud, then started typing too.

Soon Paul heard a ping and read: "I was sitting here wondering if I should either quit or kill him with his bust of Emperor Nero or whatever that thing on his desk is. A drink is a far better idea than being either jobless or in custody though, so yes, that would be a lovely idea. Six at the Red Lion?" Ping.

"No," wrote Paul, "let's get a bit further away. How about Covent Garden? Then we can grab dinner too." Ping.

"Perfect," pinged Clara.

As Paul kissed Clara on both cheeks some hours later and closed the door of her taxi behind her, she felt much better than she had expected to after her performance in Peter's office. Paul's advice had been to see her current circumstances as temporary, to avoid stand-up fights and let it all wash over her. Paul told her how good he thought she was and that she should carry on applying for other jobs where her talent would be recognised, but take the *Allaire* shilling in the meantime.

"I do so hope that you will find another job very soon, but..." He went quiet.

"But what?" asked Clara.

"But that office without you in it would be an even more hideous place."

"He really is a sweetie," thought Clara as she wriggled back into her taxi seat to get comfortable and headed out into the dark London night. "I wonder what it's like to kiss him?"

CHAPTER 36

George – Hide your love away

(July 1888)

George was glad that he had some trees to chop down today. Two young oaks that had established themselves in the corner of a wheat field and were getting too big. He took his axe and began raining mighty blows on the trunk of the first. The anger inside him needed this release.

He remembered the first time he had ever seen Becky, back on Langton market square. He vividly recalled how he felt, that the world was an unjust place but that if a man wanted to, he could shape his own destiny. George had failed to do that and so the unjust world had done it for him. Now he was trapped. One life, one bad life was standing in his way.

If a king wants something, like power over another country, George thought bitterly, why he just takes an army and invades it. He cares not a jot how many people in that country he kills. He scarce cares any more that thousands of his fellow countrymen must also die to appease his lust for power. If that king wins his battles thanks to the death of his own soldiers, he is called a hero, a conqueror. While widows mourn on both sides and children grow up without fathers and often without food, the king lives in finery, in riches, in splendour. He is given or he takes even more than he already has. There is no justice in the world.

Thwack! George hit the first tree, the larger of the two, so hard that this single blow did it a power of damage.

And all the while, the church tells the impoverished peasants, who live in tiny, cold, damp hovels with nothing to eat from one day to the next, the church tells them that all is fine. There is a better world coming. Leave the rich to their plunder and stay in your poverty, for that is God's will. That suits the rich, doesn't it? They must love that message.

Crash! Splinters flew everywhere and the whole ground shook.

That is the only way the poor put up with living near to rich people, seeing their houses, seeing how well-fed and fat they are, their fine clothes, their carriages, and their servants running around after them. While we, the poor, abide in our misery. And then we are expected to bow and scrape to them. It is not enough that they have more of everything than us. We must call them Lord and Lady.

Splinter! the first tree gave way and fell to the earth. George wiped the sweat from his forehead with a handkerchief and turned to his second victim. He measured it up and saw where he would strike.

I am not an educated man and know little but one thing I know is that there is no such thing as rich, there is only richer. If everyone had fifty pounds, nobody would live in mansions and palaces and no one would starve. You can only be rich if you have *more* than the next man. If everybody in the world had fifty pounds, the man who had a thousand could do what he wanted.

Chop! George all but broke the axe with this last stroke and the sapling stood no chance, giving way and splintering the length of its trunk.

George sat down on the first tree, but his rage had abated not at all.

And what can I do? Becky showed me how the world was, but now Becky smiles at me and I am still in chains. Before I even set eyes on her, I had agreed to marry Marjory. My parents wanted me to do it for their ends and I did not refuse. Do I not count for anything? Why did I not say?

Marjory, Marjory. How he hated that name. How he wished that he had never seen her, that she had never existed. Why oh why could Old John not have had a son rather than a daughter? A son to look after him in his age. Then he would not have needed me. None of this would have happened. I would be free.

Smash! George jumped up and hit the base of the second tree to flatten it. He chopped the trunks quickly into large logs and dragged them into a pile at the side of the field. That was enough for today. They would be collected by cart on Monday and taken back to the farm. He picked up his coat, swung the axe over his shoulder and began making his way to the hideaway. If he was lucky, Becky would be able to slip away for a few hours. It would be as wonderful as ever to see her, but what was the point? He could not be with her properly because of Marjory. They could never openly be together, walk arm-in-arm through the streets of Langton, sit together on the green or wander up and down the market of an afternoon – he could do none of this. Because of Marjory.

And inevitably, in the end, Becky would grow tired of these fleeting trysts, of meeting him in hiding for a few hours. She would stop being free as often to see him, she would drift away, and she would find someone new, someone, without all of George's complications. She would marry another man. Because of Marjory. How he despised Marjory. Her very being made him seethe with rage.

And yet, he still meekly gave in to her thrashings. In the name of God. To save his soul. Well, perhaps he had had enough of the pain and the humiliation. He could never take his shirt off in the fields no matter how hot it was because his back was such a mess. Perhaps he had had enough. Perhaps tonight he would say no. Oh, how he would like to strike Marjory in two as he had done the oaks.

But even that would not answer his needs. Oh, Marjory would be no more, but George would be hauled to the gallows, not led to Becky's side. There was no way out of this hideous trap.

He reached their hideaway, went in, laid down his axe and took off his coat, hanging it on a tree as usual. Then he sat down and waited, clouded in dark and bitter thoughts.

About half a mile down the path, treading briskly with a basket in hand, Becky herself was thinking happy thoughts as she hurried towards the bend in the river where she hoped that her George was waiting for her. She had been wondering how she could persuade him to come to see her parents again instead of always meeting in secret like this. Whenever she suggested it, George just said he could not today and spoke of other things. Was he too shy? He had got on well with them when they had met at her house that day after he carried her home. And her father had invited him to come again. Why would he not do so? Becky wanted to walk out with him properly. With her George. She wanted to be his and he hers. He was the sweetest, kindest man, very handsome and strong. She was determined to change his mind.

"George," she called softly as she rounded the final bend and slipped into the undergrowth lifting the branch and squeezing through the gap that did not seem to be there in the tangle of briars and nettles, but which both of them knew how to pull open. "George."

"Becky. You came. Oh come in, come in."

Becky ran to his arms and they kissed a long hello.

"Here, let me spread out your blanket. Tis a warm day, take off your shawl and come sit beside me in the shade."

"I have brought some apples, some cake and a jug of cider. Twas all that I could find, but it will keep us refreshed. Oh George, how has your work been this week?"

"Same as always. Long and hard," he laughed. "But every second that I think of you, it makes each ton weigh but an ounce and turns all work into a children's plaything. And what of my Becky? Is your mother well again?"

"She is. She was out and about yesterday. I had thought I would not be able to come today if she needed looking after, but here I am."

She sat up and reached into her basket to pull out the cider. "Here, this will make all well. It is pressed from our finest apples, from the trees behind our cottage."

She passed the jug across and George took a long swig.

"Beautiful," he agreed, wiping the top with a cloth and handing it back to Becky. She drank thirstily too.

Then they made a picnic of the seed cake that Becky had made specially and an apple each as they chatted about the weather and the harvest and the birds in the trees. George thought how easy and wonderful it was to be with Becky. How natural it felt and how he could be himself. He looked at her and watched as she cleared the rest of their meal back into her basket. She was just *so* beautiful, he thought.

Becky herself forgot how little time they had left together today, forgot how long the next week would be until she could be with her George again, almost forgot that she wanted to persuade him to come back and see her parents. She just wanted this sweet, sweet moment to last forever.

They both took another drink of cider and she pushed the cork back into the bottle and set it down on the ground next to them.

George lay on his back and Becky lay beside him as she loved to do, his arm around her shoulder, her head on his chest, feeling the mighty rise and fall as he breathed.

"I had a dream this week," said George quietly. "I dreamed that you went away and married another."

"Oh I will never do that," said Becky. "I will never leave my George. How could I? You must not think such things."

"Oh hold me, Becky. Hold me. I need you so."

"And I need you, my George. So do not fret."

With scarce a word more, they lay together, earnestly, each holding the other in a close embrace until their mouths met again and both knew that they could deny themselves no more.

As the river slipped almost silently past on this sultry afternoon, they finally accepted the passion that had been growing inside them. George forgot his rage, Becky forgot her fears and all that mattered was giving in to each other with mouth, lips, body and heart.

CHAPTER 37

Lord Peter uncovered

Clara took Paul's advice and said nothing at each of Peter's new rebukes, merely obeying instructions, continuing to look out for other jobs and keeping copies of her original work to submit with any future job applications.

"The thing about bullies," Paul said as they came back from the coffee shop one lunchtime, "is that if they don't get a reaction, there's nothing in it for them, so in the end they just stop."

"Have you been reading one of those airport management training books?" Clara laughed. "Or is that from *Psychobabble For Idiots*?"

"Hey, I'm still vulnerable, remember? You don't want to tip me over the edge and be responsible for a wobbling lower lip, now do you?"

"No," agreed Clara. "That would be terrible. And I suppose you're right. Standing up to him hardly worked anyway, did it? I think he only left about a dozen of my original words in that piece. And four of those were coffee."

Peter had not even noticed but there had been a major shift in his staff over the past few weeks. Paul had started to talk. Only to the other three and definitely only when Peter was not around. If his father were there, Paul retreated into his former persona, sat at his desk, head down, and working in silence.

But when Peter was not there, Paul had gradually become one of the crowd. Softly-softly at first. Clara and Paul had managed it well between them, working on the exchanges in advance.

It started on the morning after their first dinner together and went exactly as planned. Clara was stuck for a word and threw it out to the office.

"Oh, what do you call someone who's afraid of open spaces?" asked Clara when only the four of them were there. "I know but I just can't think of the word. Oooooh. It's so annoying."

"A minimalist who's lost his nerve?" suggested Vincent.

"Fool," said Clara. "Come on Marcia, you know a lot of words."

"Yes, but not big ones like you lot," laughed Marcia. "Fear of open spaces? I dunno. Space sickness?"

"Nice try," said Clara.

"Do you mean agoraphobic?" said Paul, matter-of-factly, continuing to work.

"That's it. That's the one. Thanks, Paul."

And without glancing up, making a fuss or seeming to think that this was odd or even worthy of comment, Clara carried on typing, leaving Marcia and Vincent to exchange wide-eyed stares.

Clara and Paul continued to build on this over the next few days and weeks until Paul was joining in many conversations in the office and even instigating some of them. He would ask if anyone saw a TV programme last night, or comment on something a politician had said, or on a news story.

Fairly soon, Marcia and Vincent stopped gawping at each other and accepted the new Paul.

"I don't know how to thank you enough," he said to Clara one evening as they were walking out of the office.

"Hey, I haven't done anything. This has all come from you. You're being very brave. When I think of the dark place you came from and how terrified you said you were. You've conquered it all. It can't have been easy."

"Well, I've started to conquer it. It's still terrifying, just not quite as terrifying as before. But I couldn't have done any of it without you. It was your plan to start slowly and step it up. And you're not a bad actor either."

"Well I'm not acting now and I'm not taking any of the credit for this. I'm proud of you."

"You must at least let me buy you dinner to say thank you."

"Most certainly not," said Clara.

"Oh…"

"If you remember, you bought me dinner last time. Even with my shocking maths, I can tell that it's my turn to pay."

"Even better. I get to spend some time with you and it doesn't cost me anything."

"Not so fast. I only said I'd buy the dinner. I want a bottle of champagne somewhere rather nice first."

"You're on. Tonight?"

"It will have to be Monday, I'm afraid. I've got to go away for the weekend to my Dad's birthday party. And I just remembered that I left my latest masterpiece in the office and I really need to take it home and check some facts tonight before I hand it in to the headmaster in the morning and wait for my 30 lashes."

"I'll throw myself between you and the whip," he said.

"You know I do believe you would too," she laughed, then kissed him on both cheeks.

"See you in the morning. I'll work out where we get the champagne and you can sort out the rest."

"Deal," he said and disappeared down the busy street.

I know just the place, thought Clara, as she walked briskly back to the office. When she got there it was all in darkness and she had to flick some switches to see where she was going.

She found the pages that she had printed out and stuffed them into her handbag, then turned to go.

But then she noticed that Peter's office door was open.

"No, I shouldn't. It wouldn't be right," she told herself but stayed where she was and failed to walk towards the lift or turn the lights off. She lingered. "He'll have changed his passwords by now anyway, so it's not worth it. Although it will eat away at me if I don't at least try…"

Then she brightened. The only thing to do was to demonstrate to herself that Peter really had changed his passwords and snooping was entirely out of the question. Then she could go home. That way it would not bug her forever and a day. Good thinking.

Clara sat at Peter's desk and clicked his computer into life. Soon up came the opening screen:

Name: Lord Peter Of Allaire

Password: …

He'll have changed it the next day or got Marcia to do it, she thought as she typed in Password.

But no, the desktop appeared. He'll have changed the email though.

Again she was faced with:

Name: Lord Peter Of Allaire

Password: …

MarcusOrelius, she typed. Incorrect password, she was told. Damn. So near and yet… Oh but wait. Is that how you spell it? Wasn't it 'All one word, capital M to begin and capital A in the middle'? She tried again. MarcusAurelius.

Oh, bloody bingo. She was in. She couldn't believe it. Now let's see.

There was nothing from *Trompette*. She searched in vain for the email that said: "Oh come off it Peter, you clown. Clara's a genius. We can all see that, so why can't you? She starts here in Paris on Monday."

Nothing.

But what she did find after reading around 100 emails, would need some very careful thought. It was gob-smacking. Incredible. Unbelievable. She printed out some six or seven emails and put the paper carefully into her bag, then forwarded those emails to her home account, went into Peter's Sent box and deleted them all. Then she switched everything off and headed towards home in something of a daze.

What she now knew could lead to Lord Peter Of Allaire fulfilling his dream and beginning to move in royal circles at last, though not exactly as he would have wished it. Clara was almost certain that if the authorities ever found out what she had just discovered, Lord P would soon be residing for quite a while as a guest at Her Majesty's Pleasure.

CHAPTER 38

Philip – Escape clause

(August 1966)

"Come on, pick up the phone," thought Philip. He looked at his watch. It was five to seven and they had said seven tonight. He hung up and paced around. He had walked away from the centre and up towards a park and some houses well away from the sea. He didn't want to be spotted by anyone he might know.

He looked at his watch again. Four minutes to seven. If I walk once around this park, that should take about four minutes, he said to himself. It's only quite small and it will look less suspicious. He started walking. He was dying to tell Meg his news, dreading telling Mary. But that could wait. Let's do the happy bit first.

He was about halfway around the park, mulling over these thoughts when he realised that he had taken three minutes and it was now one minute to seven. He ran directly across the park instead of keeping to the edge, jumped over the fence and made it to the phone box just in time. He pulled open the door, dialled the number, and held the coins in his hand ready to insert. He heard the ringtone and before it rang a second time, the phone was lifted and he heard Meg's voice.

"Hullo…"

"Darling," said Philip. "Darling I have some wonderful news."

"What? What? What?" said Meg eagerly.

"I got a reply from Mr Jenkinson, you know, the man who…"

"Yes, yes, I know. What did he say? Tell me quickly."

"Well he wants me to come and work for him, he wants me to do a six-month trial and he wants me to start as soon as I can. Isn't that wonderful? I'll be moving back to Langton and will have a proper job with proper wages."

"Oh Philip, that's unbelievable. I'm so pleased for you. And I'm even more pleased for me. I've missed you so much."

"And I've missed you, too, darling. This must be the longest two weeks ever."

"So when will you be moving back?"

"Well I have to give two weeks' notice, which I will do tomorrow, and then I should be free to leave about a week on Friday, or the Monday after at the latest."

"Oh, that still seems an age away…"

"Yes, but Mrs Harvey, this will be our last separation ever."

"So you still want to change my name to yours? I thought you might have had a rethink after all this time."

"Well," said Philip, "it's not much of a change, is it? Garvey to Harvey – it's only one letter. Hardly worth making a fuss about."

They prattled on for 10 more minutes until by the time they had got to the "Oh I wish I could kiss you" stage, Philip was running out of 10 pence pieces, and the man outside the phone box, who had been pacing up and down for the last five minutes, looked as though he were about to drag Philip out and throw him under the first car that passed.

"I have to go, darling. No more money. When shall I call you again?"

"How about tomorrow at 7 o'clock again? And bring some more change with you – I want a long chat."

"OK, darling. Goodnight. Goodnight."

"Goodnight, my love."

Philip hung up, dodged the comments from the man outside, and headed back. He already knew that Mary could not get away tonight, so he was free. He made his way back to his room, poured a glass of water, sat on his bed and read the letter from

Ivan Jenkinson for the hundredth time. It was his ticket to freedom, his passport out of here, his escape tunnel from the *Bel Air* and the encyclopedias, and tramping the streets with Mr Willoughby and knocking on door after door after door. And it was his passport to a new life with Meg, with Mrs Meg Harvey, and perhaps one day soon, their own little house.

If all went well, he would have two more weeks to work, two more weekends and then he would be gone.

He swallowed. So at some point, he would have to tell Mary. But how? She would be upset. Oh, he hadn't meant it to turn out like this. If only she had kissed him before he went on his weekend to Langton and met Meg, none of this muddle would have happened. He probably wouldn't even have gone home, he would have stayed to be with Mary. He would never have met Meg. Mary would have been enough for him. He would probably have ended up living with her one day. They would have been happy and he wouldn't keep making her cry. But now whatever he did he would be in the wrong. He did not want to hurt Mary. Oh if only he could be with *both* of them. He should make sure that he and Mary have a nice weekend to finish with, so they both have good things to remember each other by.

But he could work all of that out tomorrow. For tonight, his thoughts were all for Meg and kisses and skinny-dips. Please let me dream about skinny-dips, he thought as he climbed into bed that night and turned off the light.

CHAPTER 39

Four options

"Happy birthday, Philip," said Bernard, raising his glass of champagne. "Happy birthday, little brother. And many more of them."

"Happy birthday, Philip... Dad... Uncle," joined in a chorus of voices, clinking their glasses.

"Now, who's hungry? The food is ready. Let battle commence."

Bernard had long ago built a huge barbecue in his garden, with a grill as big as half a table tennis table held in place over a three-sided brick and stone alcove with a double pit below, the top half holding a whole bag of charcoal at once and the bottom glowing with dropped red-hot ashes.

On it, he had brought to perfection and all at the same time a huge selection of skewers, burgers, sausages, steak, sweetcorn, chicken, lamb and anything else he and Alice had found in the freezer. There was, in truth, enough to feed twice as many as the eight people assembled to celebrate Philip's birthday.

"Barbeque food is always nice cold if there's anything left," they agreed.

It all looked and smelled perfect. And together with the salads and potatoes and tomatoes that Alice, Ian and Meg had prepared, there was a feast to enjoy.

The gathering comprised all the remaining family: Alice, Bernard, Philip, Meg, Ian, Sam, Clara, plus Claudette – who was still a part of Sam's life while he worked on winning over her papa. They had assembled at Bernard and Alice's house just outside Godalming in Surrey on the Saturday lunchtime after Philip's actual birthday on the previous Thursday.

It was a lovely summer's day and everyone was in a good mood. They were all staying overnight in Bernard's house, except for Sam and Claudette, who were getting a cab back for an early morning call with some potential partners in Dubai. The cake was waiting with too many candles to count all ready to be lit. It was going to be a good night.

Clara was enjoying seeing everyone again, had exchanged a few meaningful glances with Alice and threatening ones with Sam, was pleased to see her father looking so well and relaxed and her mother so obviously happy, and all was right with the world.

She was sure to be able at some stage to talk to Alice some more, and to Bernard about her findings. And she equally needed to talk to her Uncle about Peter and what on earth she should do now.

"Dad's looking good – have you stopped worrying about him now?" Clara asked Meg, as they sat under an umbrella and enjoyed the food.

"Oh I don't think I'll ever stop worrying," smiled Meg. "But he has been more like his old self lately. It's easier when it's just the two of us really. I know how to keep his mind on the things he likes to do and off the things that upset him – even if I don't know what those upsetting thoughts are."

Clara fished to see what she might know: "Perhaps there are dark secrets in his past that only he knows about?"

She watched her mother closely as she said this, but Meg just took a sip of wine and laughed.

"Oh, I don't suppose so. Well, every family has its secrets, I shouldn't wonder. This chicken is delicious, isn't it? I must ask Alice for the marinade recipe. I suppose she stole it from a chef in some exotic restaurant somewhere."

So she doesn't know anything, thought Clara, or she's a good actor, but she decided not to push it any further.

"I think I heard Alice say it was Ian on chicken duty. It is good though. Shall I get you some more? And I'll grab us a refill on the way back."

It was not until about 11.30 that night that Clara managed to get Bernard on his own. After the lunchtime barbecue and the long afternoon walk along the banks of the River Wey, plus the two-hour stop-off in a pub garden on the return journey, everyone was in good spirits. She had a long talk to her father and he was calm and happy, which was a relief. Sam and Claudette had slipped away at around 10. They seemed to be getting on very well, but were not, as the French say, *les yeux dans les yeux*. They were not holding hands, Clara didn't once see them kiss, and unlike with his normal girlfriends, Sam was not spending the whole time about a centimetre away from her and fixing her with a soppy expression. She's different, thought Clara. Seems to have him well under control. Wonder how Dawn's getting on?

Even Ian was in good spirits. It was only a weekend visit and he was off back to Peru in a couple of days, so he could put up with this family of worriers-about-nothing for a short time.

Only Alice was hard to read. She was very attentive to Bernard, gave Clara some sideways smiles, but seemed to be avoiding a one-to-one where Clara could ask for more clues. Perhaps she didn't have any.

One by one, the houseguests disappeared to bed. Finally, only Bernard, Alice and Clara were left, sipping cocoa on the patio and listening to the wind rustling in the trees.

Then Alice got up and said goodnight to them both, and Bernard turned to Clara. "Alice says you want a chat. Why don't we go out into the garden? It's a lovely night and I don't think there are too many wolves around in Surrey."

"That sounds like a very good idea. It does look very cool out there."

Bernard led the way, stopping only to pick up a loitering half-empty bottle of wine and a couple of glasses from the table in the kitchen.

"How did Alice know I wanted to talk to you?" asked Clara as they sat on the large swing seat at the end of the garden. "I didn't say anything to her."

"That woman knows everything," laughed Bernard. "Either that or she meant that she wanted you to talk to me. Who knows? Don't you then?"

"I always want to talk to you, Uncle Bernard," said Clara, tucking her feet up under her on the cushion and leaving Bernard to swing the chair gently back and forth. "But as it happens, there is one thing..."

"Fire away then."

As he poured them a glass of wine, Clara started her story about Peter's emails. The ones that detailed a VAT black hole of some £250,000 that had been accounted into oblivion and fallen between *Allaire's* UK audit, *Trompette's* French accounts and a European-wide scheme that Clara did not begin to understand but which the emails admitted was illegal. Clara had brought some of her print-outs and showed them to Bernard. He sat and read the whole thread.

"We must be clear that if what we are doing is found out, then the consequences are far-reaching," read an email to Peter from Cecil Warnock of Warnock, Teddington and Laskey, *Allaire's* accountancy firm. "This is highly irregular, and although it is very unlikely that it will ever be discovered because of the way the waters are muddied between here and France, with blind alleys over Europe, it is my duty to warn you as a long-term colleague and I think a friend that we are running serious risks. Please delete this email and all copies once you have read it."

When he had finished, Bernard looked up at Clara and let out a long low whistle.

"This is serious stuff," he said. "And this email is dated 18 months ago, so if it's still going on then the total will have gone on rising."

"So what are they actually doing?" asked Clara.

"Well I'm not an accountant so I don't understand all of it but it seems to be about what they are declaring where as costs, revenue and tax. They seem to be mixing it all up so that losses are somehow duplicated to show in both countries while revenue is shared and some of it is not declared at all. The figure they say is saved is a quarter of a million."

"And is this *Trompette* forcing the scheme on Peter?

"Quite the reverse, it seems. Look, here's the bit where the accountant says that Peter must be careful what he says to 'the French lot'. Peter's reply is staggering too."

"Read it out," said Clara.

" 'Oh there is no need for anxiety. Nice customs curtsey to great kings.' Unbelievable. It's Shakespeare. Henry V."

"And he doesn't seem to have deleted any of it as instructed."

"No. You often find that people who come from a background of privilege think that they are above the laws that govern the rest of us. What do they call it? DAM, I think. Doesn't Apply to Me."

"And he screwed up my Paris job. I told you that bit already, well this is how I found out. But now what should I do?"

Bernard took a long sip of his drink, swilled it around in his mouth and swallowed slowly as he thought.

"Well," he said at last, "I'd say you have four options."

"Go on," said Clara. "Which four?"

"One," said Bernard, "is do nothing. Two is to have a quiet word with him and to tell him to be careful about what he leaves lying around on his computer. Three is to tell the police. And four is blackmailing him."

"OK. And which of the four would you recommend? This is where it gets tough. The way I see it, two, the quiet word, is the worst. He would just delete it all, hold it against me forever and be even more unbearable if that's possible. One, do nothing, is an option I suppose but it sticks in my throat to let him get away with robbing the country of so much money."

"That leaves three and four," said Bernard. "Now it's interesting."

"Well I wouldn't know how to blackmail him, and anyway, wouldn't that make me a criminal too, so no better than him? I suppose that leaves three, tell the police."

"Become a whistle-blower?" said Bernard, raising his eyebrows. "Thing is, they tend to get a hard time in this country. Remember Sarah Tisdall?"

"Er... Remind me..."

"Sarah Tisdall was a clerk in the Foreign Office who leaked some documents to the *Guardian* newspaper in the early Eighties about when American Cruise nuclear missiles were coming to the UK and how the government planned to sell the scheme to the commons. It was very controversial. Instead of everyone applauding her bravery, the government demanded that the *Guardian* revealed where the documents came from. After a couple of court hearings, what do you think the newspaper did? Nobly refuse to reveal its source in the traditional way even if it means the editor spending a few nights in jail? No, they handed over the documents, which were traced to Sarah and she was jailed. Shameful but there you go."

"So you think it might somehow rebound on me?"

"You never know." He put on a phoney barrister voice: " 'And how did you come by this information, Miss Harvey? Do you really expect the court to believe that Mr Denhartt, would leave such explosive material unprotected on his computer and then give an office junior his password? No, Miss Harvey, isn't it the case that when you were quite rightly passed over for a plum job that you were unsuited to, you decided to take revenge by planting these scurrilous lies on Mr Denhartt's computer and then sending them to the police in the hope of seeing an innocent man go to prison?'"

"Blimey. So you think I could be the one for the high jump? Well put like that, three doesn't sound so good. Doesn't that mean that we've ruled them all out? Remind me what they were again?"

"One nothing, two quiet word, three police and four blackmail."

"And if you were me?"

"I think I might say Yes when my dear old Uncle Bernard offered to fetch me a whisky nightcap."

"Yes," said Clara. "And you can tell me when you come back."

Bernard quickly returned with the drinks.

"All right then," he said as he poured a splash of water into their glasses and sat back, swinging the seat gently with his legs. "I'd do one, two and four," he said.

"You can't do nothing and do something, Uncle," Clara pointed out.

"Ah, I didn't say in which order I would do them. Or if I would do them all at once. It would go something like this. I'd start off by doing nothing. There's no rush. You have a big trump card in your hand, there's no need to lay it down in the first round. Bide your time."

"OK, good so far."

"Peter is mean to you so deserves a whack. We now know that he's also a crook, a cheat and a fraudster. That's a couple more whacks he's due. If I were you I'd wait until the time is right for you and then tell him what you know. He'll be completely trapped so you just need to work out what your demands are. It's kind of half two and a half four."

"Yes, I see."

"So first you need to work out what you want to gain from this because when you make your demands he will be in no position to turn you down. So you have to be really sure that you know what you want. It's like a fairy giving you three wishes and you ask for a glass of water, a bag of crisps and some nuts. Then you realise that you could have got a whole lot more out of the deal but it's too late."

"OK. I think I get the idea. Like a cobra, you can only strike once, so make it a killer blow."

"That's it exactly. Time it wrong and you get your fangs in the dirt."

"OK. We'd better stop now before we turn me into a gangster screenplay. Thanks, though. Very helpful to set it all out."

"It's what families are for," said Bernard.

CHAPTER 40

George –Trapped

(July 1888)

"Becky, I cannot lie to you any more," said George one Saturday a few weeks after their first lovemaking. He lay in their hideaway, his head on her breast as they remained entwined and sated in the late afternoon breeze.

"Lie to me, my love? Why you never need to do that. I am your own Becky and nothing that you can do or say or think can possibly upset me."

He raised himself on an elbow and looked earnestly into her eyes.

"Becky my darling, you must not think any ill of me until you have heard all of my story. I do not know what to do, my love. I fear your anger most of all."

She sat up and pulled her bodice around her.

"You are frightening me, George. Pray stop saying these things."

Becky had been planning to invite George to her house that evening to meet her parents again. She had hinted to her mother that morning that she may be seeing George this afternoon and that she would like to ask him to walk her home. Both her mother and father had been eager for it to happen.

"Tha' man as brought you home when you fell?" asked her father. "Oh yes, I would be glad to meet him again."

"A very nice man," added her mother, who had been secretly worried that her daughter was not walking out with anyone and did not seem interested in any of the young men of the village.

Becky knew how she was going to invite him, but now George was about to tell her something that he feared would make her angry. What could it be?

"George? Do tell me quickly."

He held her hand and kissed it.

"Becky you are all the world to me and my only wish is to be with you always…"

"And I with you. What then..?"

"My dearest. It is not my fault. I had no say in it happening, but my parents expected me, forced me, and led me to it. Oh, Becky, I am married."

"Married?" She stood up, putting her dishevelled clothes back in order. "Married? Oh, then we cannot be together?"

"Becky please do hear me out before you grow angry, for I want none of it but only you."

And George told the story of the old comrades, John and Thomas, of how they planned this from the time George was no more than six, how there was no reason for him not to grant their wishes as he had not then met Becky, how it made their parents' dreams and secured their future, and how now that George had found his one true love, he was trapped.

Becky sat in silence when he finally finished. So this is why we meet in secret. This is why George had never been back to see her parents. Married. What an ugly, ugly word, a word to dash all of her hopes and dreams and life.

"My Becky, what can I do?"

"What can we do?" she said slowly, sitting down again.

They stayed silent for some time, Becky looking straight ahead of her, George watching her anxiously. At least she was still here, he thought. At least she did not simply walk away from him. Was there some hope yet?

"We could… we could run away together," she said at last.

"Oh Becky, to be with you all the time would be sweetness itself. But where would we go?"

"Anywhere. Somewhere. You are strong and can work. I can cook and clean and mend and know my letters. We can find something."

"Oh my darling, I can think of nothing I want more. But what of our parents? What would happen to your mother and father?"

"They would die of sadness," said Becky slowly.

"As would mine too."

This is the end, then, thought Becky to herself. There is no way out. I am trapped so close to my happiness.

"Oh George," she said at last. "What are we to do?"

He held her close, her head on his shoulder.

"I do not know, Becky. I do not know. But there has to be a way. I cannot live without you now."

And he added, slowly but firmly. "I will find a way."

CHAPTER 41

Who wants to know?

Clara picked up the fat envelope from the doormat as she arrived home from her weekend away. It was from the Family Records Office, some more certificates that she had sent away for during a visit about a week before Philip's birthday barbecue.

She turned the envelope over and over in her hands.

"Now what?" she thought. Part of her wanted to tear it open and devour the knowledge that was inside it, perhaps the answers to some more questions, perhaps the vital clues that would make everything slot into place.

But the other part remembered what Bernard had said to her in his garden at the end of their nightcap when she had tried once more to probe him about family secrets.

"You always have to ask yourself, Clara, why you want to know things that may very well turn your world upside down without giving you any tangible benefit in return. What is the good of lifting the stone to see what is underneath? It is never going to be a butterfly or an orchid, but may very well be a slug or a snake. Ask yourself if you are happy now and if those around you are happy. That is something that you *can* affect, where you can make a difference to the people you love. Discovering their secrets is unlikely to do the same."

Clara did not know what to say so Bernard continued.

"You ask me why I don't tell you everything, and yet I repeat, what benefit is served by your no longer being ignorant of facts that bring you no gain, but only uncertainty? Once you know, you know, forever – but is the world a better place than it was yesterday?

"And you must remember that there are others who do not know what you know, so now you have a choice. Do you tell them all what you know? Even if it hurts them? Or do you keep it to yourself? If you do that, you need to learn to become a good liar. You must never let it slip, and must never say the wrong word to the wrong person. You must remember who knows and who does not know at all times. And if you know three secrets there will be some people who know some but not all of what you know. You must speak the truth to some while lying to the others. And what about when you meet them together? Some know one thing and some another. It becomes impossible."

He took a drink and sighed, running his fingers through his hair.

"If there were a way that I could cease to know some of the things that I do know – if I could wipe the board, burn the paper, go back to ignorance – oh, do you think I wouldn't grab that chance and drain the cup of forgetfulness? I would. I would not hesitate for a second. You think that I am simply refusing to tell you some things that I keep from you for your own peace of mind. And there are other things that you still do not know, that I profoundly hope that you will *never* know.

"And I know all. I have kept much to myself. No one on earth knows all that I know, so I am the keeper of the restful nights. Alice says that I should tell you everything, that I should somehow hand on to you the keys to the secrets, and bow out, let you take the strain. But I tell her that some secrets will die with me, no one will ever discover them and no one will be any the richer or poorer. I have told secrets and watched them all but destroy the person I told. And I can never right that wrong. I would not wish on you what I have put up with for so long. Think very carefully before you open that door, Clara."

She put the envelope down on the low table in front of the television and went into the kitchen to heat up a frozen pizza and pour a half pint of Médoc into her favourite big wine glass. She ate the pizza at the table in the kitchen, washed and dried the plate, dish and knife, wiped down the surfaces, emptied the rest of the wine into her glass and went back into the lounge, letting herself fall back onto the sofa, picking up the remote and switching the TV on.

Bernard was right, she thought. What was the point of finding out things that could not do her any good? She should throw the envelope into the bin and not go any further.

She paused and took a drink, then slowly began singing an old song to herself, one of her favourites, one that Uncle Bernard used to play on car journeys. Then she started to hum the tune softly:

Da dadada dada da da dadada dada da da da da da da da

Da da da da da da dada da dada da dada da da da da da dada da

She took another big sip of wine and laid her glass carefully on the table in front of her, then sang a little more quickly:

Da dada dada da dadadadadadada da da da da da da da da dada

Da dada dada dada da da da da dada dada da da da da da dada da da

Clara switched off the TV, threw the remote away onto the couch beside her and began to sing the chorus more loudly. She couldn't even remember the words but sang the song anyway.

And he was blind from all the light

Out loose like a moose in all the sunshine in the night

Blind from all the light

Mama used to tell me not to stare straight at the sun

She picked up the fat envelope, tore it open and pulled out the contents as she finished the chorus loud and strong:

Oh but mama that's where all the fun is…

CHAPTER 42

Susan – Sucker wanted

(January 1949)

"We need someone, an outsider, a trustworthy outsider who has no obvious ties to the business," Mario said to Henry and Susan. "He can earn some big money for doing very, very little with almost no risk at all. Just take delivery of the consignment, look after it until the trail has gone cold, and then hand it over to us again. No questions, no worries, here's your cut."

"My circle of acquaintance is extensive," said Henry, "but there is none among them who I would trust enough not to betray us unwittingly or otherwise, or to seek to gain some extra advantage by playing their own hand and conflicting ours."

"Yeah, I'm the same." Mario rubbed his chin and looked out of the window. "I only know other crooks too." He laughed. "There must be *someone* though. I do mean big money. We can afford to pay handsomely for a little silence without affecting our cut too drastically."

Susan sat quietly, her heart beating a little faster than usual. They couldn't let this golden chance slip for the want of a stooge to play pass-the-parcel for a while.

"Would it matter," she asked casually, "if this person did not live in London?"

"Nah," said Mario. "Far from it."

"Almost anywhere in mainland Britain," added Henry. "In fact, London would not be so good. Too close to prying eyes. The further away the better really. As long as we can reach it with a van or two within a day or two. Do you have someone in mind? They would need some secure storage space where no one too curious would dream of investigating."

"And how much money would this person stand to make? What are we talking about?"

"We're talking about a grand or two or more. Depending on how generous we feel when it's done and what price we get," said Mario.

Henry looked at her and smiled. "Do you know how long it would take even the average top-money coal miner to earn that? Something like five years."

And so a little over two weeks later, Susan sat in the smoke-filled bar of the Old Oak Tavern in Holborn and waited. She kept looking nervously towards the door, but each time it swung open and let a gust of cold air into the crowded bar, she quickly looked away again and continued pretending to read her newspaper.

Finally, it opened and a familiar face looked in, and walked over to stand in front of her.

"Hello, Bernard," said Susan.

"Hello again," he replied somewhat coldly. "I wasn't expecting to find you here. You have a habit of vanishing into the clouds when no one is looking."

"What are you drinking?" she asked.

"I'll have a pint of mild if you're paying. You owe me one or two."

"I know I do," she said, standing up and picking up her handbag. "And as I told you, that's what all of this is about."

She went to the bar and was soon back with Bernard's beer.

"You see..." she began, but Bernard held up his hand and stopped her.

"Not yet. First I want to know why you walked out on us again. Why you walked out on your son when he was just barely a week old and left us to pick up the pieces for you."

Susan offered Bernard a cigarette and said nothing while he lit hers and his own. "I'm not proud of what I did," she said blowing a long stream of smoke up towards the ceiling. "I, er... I didn't have a choice. I told you that I was doing some dangerous work for the government. I was mixed up with some people who don't ask questions if you get in their way. I can't say any more, but if I hadn't gone back to London when I did, Philip still wouldn't have had a mother, if you take my drift."

Bernard looked at her suspiciously but said nothing.

"That's in the past now and as you can see, I'm still here. Now I want to start putting things right, giving something back to my family, looking after the ones I love, and taking the first step to making you proud of me, of coming back to live with you all again, of taking care of all your wants and needs – yes, even being a mother if it's not too late."

She looked him straight in the eye. "But I'm going to need your help, not a lecture of where I've gone wrong and what I've done badly in my life, or who I've let down. I know all that."

This is not what Bernard had been expecting. He thought he would see Susan once more in floods of tears, possibly even pregnant again. He could think of no other reason why she would want to see him. The letter had been brief, saying little more than that she needed to see him urgently and giving a time and a place for the rendezvous. Bernard was angry but worried about Susan and not a little intrigued. Alice agreed that he had to go.

But Susan knew exactly what she was going to say this time. She had practised it with Henry, first in his room over breakfast, and then they had even tried it out for real, as it were. Susan went to a quiet pub on a Sunday lunchtime and Henry played Bernard, storming into the empty bar full of anger and accusations. Susan handled herself well apart from a couple of small blunders when she departed from the script, even calling him Henry once.

They laughed about it when they returned to Henry's spacious rooms, and spent several hours calming Susan's stage fright with more and more rehearsals until Henry was happy that she was word-perfect no matter what Bernard threw at her. She took her reward greedily.

"So what *do* you want?" asked Bernard.

"I want you to do me a favour. Not an especially big favour really, but one that will change your life and mine. And not just our lives, but Alice's, the baby's, your parents', your children's. You'll never need to work again. Our family will be looked after. That's what you want, isn't it? That's all you've ever wanted, Bernard. Well, now I'm offering it to you. I can't believe that you will not be interested."

Bernard sat back and took a drink to give himself time to think.

"If it's not much of a favour, why does it pay so well? And how much are we talking about?"

"Five grand. Perhaps more. A lot more than you get for your books and lectures in any case."

Bernard did a sum in his head. Five thousand pounds? That was more than he earned in 15 years. They could stop his parents' cottage from falling down, pay off all their debts, pay for so many things...

"If there is a lot of money on offer for doing not very much, then it has to be crooked," he said at last. "And if you move in the circles you have described, presumably I could equally find myself a target as well. I would need to take some big risks."

"We're not amateurs, Bernard," she said. "You have been chosen carefully because there is absolutely no way anyone could trace this back to you. You are an ordinary citizen without any links to anyone else. If someone did want to find you out there, where would they start? There's no risk unless you do something stupid."

"So what does it involve? What would I have to do?"

About an hour later, Susan stood up to leave. Mission accomplished. Bernard did not want to help but had agreed to do it for Susan and Philip.

Just before she walked away, he caught her by the arm.

"You haven't asked me once how your son is. Or even where he is."

"Oh... of course... how bad of me. How is he?"

"He's thriving. A healthy boy. He has been adopted by your mother and father, who are bringing him up as their own. Not too many questions are asked in a place like the Black Isle. They've moved back there, for a while at least. People there just think that Mum had a child late in life. It happens."

"I'm glad. I'm glad it worked out well. Thank you, Bernard," she said. "I'll be in touch. Nearer the time."

And she was gone.

Bernard gave her a 30 second start, then finished his drink and left the pub, spotting her along the road that was not too crowded at this hour and following her at a distance. She boarded a no 149 bus that said it was going to Mile End. London buses being London buses, there was a second right behind it. Bernard jumped on that and ran upstairs to sit in a space at the front so that he could watch where Susan got off. "Single to Mile End please," he told the conductor.

CHAPTER 43

The waiting game

C lara had not seen Sam for a while. Not since he wanted to learn French in half an hour. He had presumably been busy with Claudette. And his new business venture. And Claudette. And trying to get some money out of her old man. And Claudette.

So it was something of a surprise to get an email from him asking if she fancied a drink that evening. For all his faults, she liked Sam and they always had a laugh when they met. In fact, there was a time when she was seriously considering giving him a try as a boyfriend. She didn't want to marry him or anything, not just because he was her cousin, and definitely did not want to have children with him – Sam would be the worst father anyone could imagine, she thought. Just, you know, give him a test drive.

She had thought better of it, though, and seeing his performance around his girlfriends since, she realised that she had had a pretty fortunate escape there.

But when Sam asked to meet, it usually meant that Sam had a problem. Like how to get rid of Dawn, for example.

"Are there strings attached?" she emailed back. "Should I bring any costumes or face paints?"

"Well if a chap can't invite his dearest darling cousin out for a drink without raising suspicion, it's a sad day for humanity," he replied.

They agreed to meet on one of the big riverboat bar-restaurants on the Thames and took their drinks out onto the deck, where it was a warm and sunny evening.

"So despite your protestations, I know you well enough by now to lump a fat wager on the fact that you need some help," she said. "Would I be right?"

"You really do have a suspicious mind," he said.

"Yeah, well, is it any wonder? I still haven't got over the Dawn dinner."

"I wish I had that on video…"

"How is Dawn, by the way? You never did tell me. Have you seen her or heard from her since that night? Is she OK?"

"Dawn is just fine as I predicted. And as a matter of fact, I have heard from her. She invited me to her wedding."

"Wedding? So if she can't have you she'll go off and marry the first chap the agency sends round, eh?"

"Timothy Piper. We were all at the same school together. Loathsome creature."

"There's a joke in there somewhere about *Piper At The Gates Of Dawn*, but it's probably filthy."

"Oh, he got past those gates a long time ago. While we were still at school I think," snorted Sam.

"So are you going? To her wedding?"

"You must be joking. That's all in the past. And he *really* is objectionable. A banker. In every sense of the word."

Clara looked puzzled but moved on.

"Sounds a bit like someone's jealous. Almost as if you regret having your plaything snatched away. We could go together and I could stuff a pillow up my jumper if you like."

"The invite specified 'No plus one'. Apparently, seating is limited and you know they have just *so* many friends to accommodate, dahling."

"You'll send her a wedding present, though?"

"Already have. She'll get the joke, but Timmy Toodles won't." He laughed scornfully.

"Er, wedding presents are not supposed to be jokes. They're meant to be useful things like toasters or teapots or meat cleavers."

"Not a bad shout that last one…"

"So what *did* you send?"

"A set of three matching trays."

"Matching trays? Very rock and roll."

"In different sizes…"

"Different sizes, eh? That'll take pride of place when they go on display then. But how's that a joke?"

"Hahaha. They all have a picture of a double-decker bus on them."

"I'm guessing there's a hidden meaning here that I'm not sure I want to know about. Might double-decker be a euphemism for Dawn's… er, spacious upper deck?"

"Partly. But it was also a bit of an in-joke between us. I used to call her Double Decker Dawn because…"

"Please don't leave me with an image that I can never forget."

"…because she always wanted to go on top. Geddit?"

"And there it is. Oh, how I wish that you'd kept that a secret. Now every time I see a double-decker bus, I'll be forced to imagine… Urrrgh…"

"I do too. She was very good at it though, I'll give her that…"

"Stop! Different subject. Tell me there really was a reason to meet tonight and then we can talk about that instead."

"Well, there is one thing that I could use your advice about."

"Believe me, I have never been so glad to hear you say that. I'll collect my winnings later. Pour me another drink and go for it."

Sam picked up the bottle and splashed some more wine into their glasses.

"Well, it's Claudette…"

"Do you only *ever* think about women? Is there any room at all in your head for anyone that you haven't slept with?"

"Ah that's just it, you see."

"What's just what?"

"I haven't actually slept with Claudette yet and it's been... what? two, three months? Feels like years. I haven't even had a rummage up her jumper. I haven't so much as kissed her or held her hand. In fact, I haven't laid the end of my fingernail on her... on her... anything."

"Well I would have said that it sounds like you are finally treating a woman with some respect, but that phrase 'a rummage up her jumper' suggests you still have a little way to go."

"But it's so... I don't know, unnatural. It's not normal."

"And at the risk of getting another image that I'd need a brain scrub to remove, what is 'normal' with your girlfriends? Or normal for you at any rate."

Sam laughed.

"My record is 37 minutes."

"You had a stop-watch on it?"

"No, New Year's Eve party. We were both well gone. I met her doing the rounds of kisses as the clock struck midnight and we just carried on kissing each other and ignored everybody else. Then I couldn't help noticing as we locked the spare bedroom door, threw the coats off the bed onto the floor and dived under the covers that the bedside clock said 00:37. Some going, eh?"

He beamed proudly.

"I bet she still boasts about it too. But I don't mean drunken one-night stands..."

"It wasn't a one-night stand. It lasted nearly three weeks. Her name was... let me think, I know this... Wendy. Or Christine. Or was it Lillian? Anyway..."

"But when you have a serious girlfriend? If you can in any way grasp how those two words might go together in the same sentence. Don't you woo for a week or two first at least?"

"Not if I can help it. If the attraction's there, it's impossible. If not the first night, then usually the first weekend, surely? I bet you're the same."

"Let's leave me out of this, shall we? So why is Claudette different? Do you want to cherish her a bit first?"

"No, I don't. Last bloody thing on my mind. It's her rule. We go out all the time, see films, have drinks or dinner, go to concerts, work together nearly every day in a small office, just us two, and have a good laugh. She's great to be with, but she won't let me anywhere near her until she says the time is being right."

"The language problem must have eased though. She has clearly learned the English for 'Get your filthy hands off me'."

"Well, kind of. Except when she first said all this, it was: 'Not until I am already. I will say the go.' Of course, I didn't have the faintest idea what she was talking about, so I carried on as normal. This led to a bit of a misunderstanding until I grasped that, well, grasping was out. And she's promised that the Promised Land time *will* come. Only meanwhile I'm left high and dry."

"Oh joy," said Clara, clapping with delight. "Please let me come out on a date with the two of you just to watch. I'd give a lot to see you squirm. Do you have to sit on your hands?"

"It's not funny," said Sam with his best sad face on. "The thing is, do you think I should carry on waiting or is she just stringing me along? Should I dump her and move on?"

"Do you like her? I mean really like her, not just want to go to bed with her?"

"Hell yes, or I'd have got out long ago."

"Then I think that you should wait. It sounds as though your Claudette is trying to make sure that your relationship lasts more than nearly three weeks. She wants to make it special when it does happen, special for both of you. It probably means that she really likes you."

Sam brightened.

"Do you think so? And how long do you, er… suppose she's going to, you know, make me wait?"

"Oh not long," said Clara, but she thought: I hope it's at least another couple of years.

Then Sam brightened.

"Hey, Clara. I've had an idea. I don't suppose you're free tonight, are you? We've known each other a long time and we've hardly ever touched each other. I've always liked you a lot and thought how beautiful you are..."

"Oh but Sam, my darling, you are only twenty years into the forty you have to wait." She smiled sweetly. "And then, of course, you can take me to bed."

CHAPTER 44

George – Becky has some news

(August 1888)

There has to be a way, thought George as he headed towards the hideaway. There must be a way. Becky is becoming unhappier by the day. Perhaps we really *should* run away. We could catch a bus south towards London, or to Kent. Get some work in the hop picking. If we went at the right time of year, around September, there would be plenty. And Becky is right. I *am* strong. I would be strong for her.

Or we could go north. To the midlands. Or to East Anglia. They must need work in the fields too. We could make a go of it. Start again. And we would be together. A fresh start. Free. Together. This would be a man of poor birth changing his life, not just accepting. Doing what he wanted to do, just like kings do. Only without the deaths and the widows and the orphans and the hunger. Nor would we have committed any crime so no one would come looking for us.

Ah yes, but what of our families?

This is where he got to time after time. How could he imagine himself happy with Becky while his mother and Becky's mother, were waking up one morning to find them gone? They would be truly heartbroken. Not just to have lost us, but to have lost the very beings who would look after them when they were too old, too frail to do it for themselves. Starving widows and orphans all over again.

The rich had no such worries. They could go on collecting their rents or having them collected for them even if they were too feeble to get out of bed. Not like his parents and Becky's parents. And they called this a just country to live in. Curses…

No, there was nothing else for it. Marjory must leave. If only there was some way to make that happen. Then he could stay here in Langton with Becky. He could be with her. They could be together, live together, and perhaps even one day marry. If only Marjory were not here. He screamed inside at the frustration of it all.

Then he gave a small, grim smile.

At least he had one small victory over her. It had happened one night when Old John had gone up to bed and Marjory began reciting his sins for the day. George had committed four sins and was to have four lashes. To save his soul. Gluttony, greed, pride and envy. Those were his sins.

"You need to be purged, husband. For your own good, for the sake of your soul, you need to be saved," said Marjory, then added: "On your knees."

But instead of Marjory getting up and walking across to the cupboard by the chimney breast to fetch the vicious cane, while George took off his shirt and leaned across the footstool by the fire, tonight it was George who rose, crossed to the cupboard, fetched the short-handled piece of cane with the five or six thin, leather thongs attached to it, turned back to Marjory and held it out to her. She made a move to take it from him, but then staring straight into her eyes, he took it back, away from her clutching hands and with a single movement broke it in two across his knee. He held the two pieces and looked at them. The straps still bore dark smears of his dried blood. George took a step towards the hearth and threw the two pieces into the fire, where they at once flared up in an arc of flames.

"There will be no whipping tonight," he said. "And there will be no whipping ever again. Do you understand?"

Marjory looked at him with wide frightened eyes.

"But George. If we do not purge your sins, your soul is in grave jeopardy," she whispered. "I do it for love of you."

He brought his face close to hers and said with a voice full of menace: "Not tonight. And not ever again."

Then he walked firmly towards the door and without a backwards glance went out of the room and up to bed.

He lay in bed without a throbbing back for the first time that he could remember. But what good did it do him? Marjory was still there. Marjory was still alive. He was still trapped.

He reached the hideaway and as he moved the branches to let himself in, he heard a gentle call from inside: "George."

"Here I am, my sweet. Oh, it is so good to see…"

Rebecca dived into his arms, full of gasps and sobs.

"Oh, George. I am so happy and yet so very, very frightened."

"What is it, my darling Becky? Whatever is it?"

"Oh, George. There can no longer be any doubt. I am going to have our baby."

CHAPTER 45

Lord Peter undone

"Gather around, all of my followers, *mei secatores*, for I have tidings to impart."

Three faces in the office looked surprised at being called unexpectedly into Peter's office on a Thursday morning when the next press day was almost three weeks away. The fourth face, Clara's, looked surprised too and exchanged puzzled looks with Marcia, Paul and Vincent as they shuffled through the big door and made themselves comfortable on the chaise longue and the wooden chair beside it. Marcia dragged her own chair through the door to make four.

Clara's surprise, though, was feigned. She knew not only why Peter had called them in, but also what he was about to say. It had all been arranged between them around the mahogany desk the evening before.

As the last traces of daylight had disappeared outside the windows and the lift doors had closed on the sales team for the last time that night. Clara seemed to be busily typing at her workstation, knowing that Peter had some correspondence to finish because he had told everyone earlier that he was to have a *nuper nocte scerilorum*. And that he was in for a late night.

Once Clara was sure there was no one else on the floor, and she heard Peter packing up his briefcase – she did not want to disturb him while he was working – she poked her head around his door and said matter-of-factly: "Oh Peter, could I have a quick word before you leave?"

He looked up and frowned, obviously having been under the impression that he was alone in the office, and not appearing to be too pleased to find that he was mistaken.

"Will it wait? Is it about your piece on the wine importer? If so I fear that there is so much to be done that we would be here until lunchtime tomorrow. Pray, let us set aside some daylight hours for the task and…"

"No, it's not about that," Clara cut him short, came into the office and closed the door behind her.

Peter began to look alarmed. Surely she was not about to take her clothes off and make a pass at him, was she? He had heard about such things. Women trying to achieve the upper hand.

"Look I am not your type," he said nervously, "and you are most assuredly not mine. And I will have no truck with office liaisons. They only ever end badly when…"

"And it certainly isn't about THAT."

"Then what..?" he faltered.

Clara pulled up the chair opposite Peter's desk, sat down, put her elbows on his desk and stared him straight in the eye.

"I'll come straight to the point," she said. "I know everything."

She sat back and let it sink in.

"Everything? I don't know what you mean."

"Oh yes, you do. I know everything about the fraud, the accounting scheme that you have set up with Warnock, the losses declared twice, the profits lost somewhere between here and France and the rest of Europe, the warnings you were given about the illegality, and the way you brushed them off. That kind of everything. I have it all safely tucked away, emails and all. Everything. Just everything."

Peter opened his mouth, then closed it again. His hand shook slightly as he brushed his hair back off his forehead. Clara remained silent.

"So what are you going to do?" he asked at last, quietly. Clara thought how different he was now from his usual shouty self. He looked small, old and frail. She could almost feel quite sorry for him.

"Well, it seems to me," she said slowly, "that I have four options."

"Four?"

"Four. One, I can do nothing. Two, I can have a quiet word with you about what you leave lying around on your computer. Three, I can tell the police. And four, I can blackmail you. I can't think of any others, can you?"

"No, that seems to cover it. I like one and two," he said, trying to lighten the tone of a conversation he was not enjoying.

"Yes, I can see why they would appeal to you. Not very much in it for me, though, is there? Not in one and two, really?"

"Not very much in three for you either. Even if I went to prison, where would that leave you? Who is going to want to employ someone who is prepared to betray them after all they have done for her, after they have helped her career, put her on..."

"I'm going to have to stop you there before I get angry. I was just starting to feel sorry for you. Don't ruin it for yourself."

"Going to the police might rebound on you, all the same."

"Yes, like Sarah Tisdall."

"Sarah who?"

"It doesn't matter. Well, that just leaves four then. Blackmail. Such an ugly word."

"Is that the plan? Used banknotes in a holdall? Threats dropped through my letterbox? Notes made with letters cut from newspapers? All a bit clichéd, don't you think?"

"Oh, I'm not interested in money. And it's not even revenge that I'm after. Just justice."

"Justice? I'm not sure I follow."

"Among the other things that I know, is how you turned down the offer from *Trompette* for me to go and work in Paris. Spiteful that."

He gave a small, scornful laugh.

"My dear, if I had let you go there you would have been torn to shreds, would have been a total failure, and would have come crawling back to me within a month, begging for your old job back and for me to continue to mould and shape you. No, that was quite out of the ques…"

"We'll disagree on that point." Once again Clara stopped him short. This had never happened before in their one-sided relationship. "You see, in spite of all the bullying that I have suffered here, I actually have quite a good opinion of my abilities. And that is why I relish the chance to work for someone else, someone who will not batter me and ridicule me whatever I do."

Clara almost snarled the last sentence, glaring directly at Peter. The worm had not only turned but had pulled out a gun.

There was a silence, Peter clearly wondering what was coming next or what he should say.

"I see that you have given this a good deal of thought," he said at last. "I suppose then that you will have a suggestion that you are about to make."

"Suggestion is not really a strong enough word," said Clara slowly. "Remember that we are still technically discussing option four."

"The blackmail? Ultimatum, then."

"Is that the first Latin you've tried to use in this conversation?" laughed Clara. "What does that tell you?"

"Please get to the point."

"All right then. Two things. I don't want to work with you as my boss any more. And you have to un-accountant the wrong you have done and pay all the money you owe. That's my price to keep quiet. And you're getting off lightly."

"You don't want to work for me. So one of us has to leave. You no doubt have a preference."

"It's too late for my preference. That would have been my perfect job in Paris. You robbed me of that and it would seem a little strange if you suddenly had a change of heart. They've probably filled the vacancy by now anyway. No that will have to wait."

"So? What else then?"

"Well if I can't leave just yet..."

"You want me to go? Where? I can't do anything else. This has been my life's work, building it all up from scratch. Where will I go?"

"Oh spare me the violins," said Clara. "Remember, this is a way to make sure that where you go is *not* to jail. I don't really care what you do. You can retire. Become Editor-in-Chief working from home. Be a roving reporter, submitting features for consideration. Whatever you like. That's your problem. I just don't want you working here, as my boss. Suggest something to *Trompette*. They'll go for it. And don't try to be clever. I want the letter AND the spirit of this delivered."

"We would need a new editor here. Is that what you're angling for?"

"No. I don't want that. I just want to do my job un-bullied and to stand or fall by what I produce."

Peter looked out of the window. He gave a small laugh.

"What you are suggesting is something that I have been considering myself and was planning to do anyway. In a year or two."

"No. Now. Right now. To be announced tomorrow."

"You haven't heard the rest of my plan."

"I'm listening."

"The new editor in my future scenario was going to be," he paused and watched her reaction, "Paul."

"Paul?" Clara was surprised and delighted but did not want to give too much away. "Paul? I wasn't expecting that," she said.

"Oh, I grant you that he is very shy. I know that. But the boy does have talent. I would keep an eye on him, be there to help – to help, not to bully," he added quickly. "I would let him have his head. And you cannot deny that he would give you a far easier ride than I have."

"That could be acceptable, but you are to have absolutely *no* involvement. No keeping an eye on. Nothing. Paul can stand or fall by his own talent too, and if he succeeds, then none of the credit goes to you."

"As you wish."

She mused and thought: "This will make the office a very different place."

"And so as I drift into the shadows of circumspection, we will have a new editor, a new Achilles to drive us forward into the era that lies ahead. After much deliberation, I can today announce that this editor will be..." he paused... "Paul. With immediate effect. That is all."

Everyone's head turned towards the new boss on the chaise longue.

"Speech," Vincent almost shouted, but then realised that now Paul was no longer the office recluse it wouldn't be funny any more.

CHAPTER 46

Philip –The wrong goodbye

(August 1967)

This was it, then, the big final weekend with Mary. Philip had finished working his notice with Burridge, Thompson & Co Ltd, Publishers of Quality Literature, est 1896. He had said goodbye to Mr Willoughby over a pint or two at the end of their last day together on Friday. It was not without a little sadness, either. He couldn't remember when it happened, but now that he was leaving he realised that he had a certain fondness for Mr Willoughby. They had shared many a mile in Mr Willoughby's car, many a lunchtime sandwich, and many a rainy street together.

"I'm going to miss you, young Philip," Willoughby told him over their third pint. "You have been a good partner."

"I've enjoyed it too, Mr Willoughby," said Philip. "All those doors in the rain, it builds a certain comradeship."

"That, young Philip, is a very good word. That is what it is. Comradeship. Shall we have another?"

They did and Philip was not at his brightest on Saturday morning as he smiled at Mary over breakfast. He was seeing her tonight and again tomorrow and then he would be on the early train to London and to Meg on Monday morning. He wanted these last two meetings with Mary to be special. Something that she could remember, could treasure. After this, they would probably never see each other again and he wanted to remember her too. They had shared some very pleasant times together and he was very fond of her. He would miss kissing her. They may as well have two lovely days together if possible and then he would explain on Sunday as he left that he was forced to go back to Langton, that he had lost his job, that he would try to come to visit when he could and he hoped that she would have a wonderful life. That should be comforting to her. If he told her tonight it would deprive them both of two final days of happiness. He didn't want Mary to be unhappy but he could barely wait to get on that train on Monday. Meg would meet him off it and their whole wonderful life together would begin.

Philip packed his suitcase with his few possessions that Saturday afternoon, leaving out just the clothes and bits and pieces he would need for the rest of the weekend. He had a sleep in the afternoon on his bed to rid him of the final traces of the Willoughby farewell. If only feeling better about leaving Mary were so easy.

They were due to meet at their bench at 6.30, quite early for them and now that things were sorted, Philip was looking forward to seeing her. She was always soft and welcoming towards him and her kisses were still as sweet.

He put on his good jacket as there was a slight chill in the air, and went down to the bench in plenty of time. When Mary arrived, she looked stunning. She was wearing a dress that he had not seen before. It was low-cut, showed off her delightful cleavage and her figure as he had hardly imagined it. Rather than looking like a young girl, she looked like a young woman tonight.

"Darling, you look lovely," he said truthfully, rising and taking her hands in his, then leaning forward to give her a hello kiss. "And I have a surprise for you."

"A surprise?" she asked excitedly. "What is it?"

"Tonight, my darling, you and I are not going to eat fish and chips from a newspaper parcel as we walk along the seafront. Tonight, we are going to dine at… Marcello's."

"Marcello's? No, you don't mean it? You *do* mean it, don't you? Oh, Philip – I'm glad I put on my posh frock."

"Oh and so am I. You look just divine. But I do indeed mean it. Tonight is our night."

Philip wanted so much for this farewell to be special. Marcello's was the finest restaurant in Brighton and they had hardly dared to so much as walk past it before. But tonight, they were dining at Marcello's. True the only booking Philip could get was for 7 o'clock. "...and we must have the table back by 8," he was told when he rang to make the reservation. But that's an hour, laughed Philip to himself. We'd need to order about 10 courses to make it last any longer than that.

And so at exactly 7 pm, Philip and Mary approached the imposing façade of Marcello's, just off the seafront. A man in uniform swung the heavy door open for them and ushered them inside.

"Can I help you sir?" asked a woman who looked as though she were worth about nine million dollars.

"Er... we have a reservation for 7 o'clock. A table for two. Name of Harvey."

The vision looked them up and down suspiciously but found them on her list.

"Ah yes. Please come this way."

She led them to the back of the restaurant, down a flight of stairs into a windowless room with about six other tables, two of which were occupied.

When they were seated, she offered them a menu each and a leather-bound book.

"Your waiter will be with you shortly," she said, gave a brief bow of her head and was gone.

Philip studied the menu, and especially the prices, and wondered if a fish supper would not be more romantic after all. It was a lot more than he had expected, but... this was after all Mary's night and he was ready to do anything for her.

Mary looked at the menu.

"Philip, look at these prices. It can't be right."

"Darling, ignore the prices. Let us have the best night ever. What would you like? Why look here. There is a crab salad for starter and I know how much you like crab."

They managed to find some food that they both understood and could pronounce and gave their order. Then Philip turned to the leather-bound wine list and went momentarily dizzy. The cheapest wine was £7 a bottle. He could not be seen to order that, so went for the Médoc at £7.50. They would have to drink slowly.

While they waited for the food to arrive, Philip took Mary's hand across the table and gazed into her eyes. In this light, with her new dress and her hair shimmering, she really did look very beautiful. He had barely noticed how attractive she was before but she definitely had something. She had always been kind to him, right from their first meeting in the *Bel Air* dining room, and now he wanted to repay her.

"Darling, this is our night. I want it to be special. Really special," he told her.

Mary smiled and gazed back at him. She wanted to kiss him right now very much but thought that it would be frowned upon here. Later. Later she would kiss him lots. And she had a surprise for him too. A wonderful surprise.

And so with a few mistakes, lots of smiles and a couple of shocks, they dined together in the finest restaurant in Brighton, enjoyed some superb food, drank a whole bottle of fine wine, held hands under the table, gazed into each other's eyes, and both thought that all was well with the world.

When the bill came, Philip choked quietly. It was as much as he earned in a week and a good week at that. But luckily he had closed his account at his Brighton bank that morning and withdrawn all of his money, so he had enough to cover it, and even a little to spare for the rest of the weekend and his journey back to Langton on Monday.

As they left Marcello's, Philip put his arm around Mary and when they had turned two corners, he pulled her towards him and kissed her with gusto. She really did look something tonight, he thought, the best she had ever looked.

"How was your dinner?" he asked. "Mine was lovely. Shall we take a stroll along the front? just to walk off the food a little?"

"That's a very good idea," she said, snuggling up to him. "Philip, that was the best dinner that I have ever, ever eaten. Thank you so much. It must have cost you half a fortune."

"Oh you are worth it, darling," he said, kissing her again.

"And now," she announced, "I have a surprise for you."

"A surprise," asked Philip with a laugh, thinking that she might have some toffees.

"A surprise. One you will definitely not be expecting. Let's walk a little further and then I will tell you."

They walked down to the pier, stood at the railing gazing out at the sea, then fell into each other's arms in the still night air, and kissed slowly and sensuously.

It was just starting to get chilly, so Philip asked: "And what is your surprise?" kissing her on the nose and thinking how well the evening was going.

"Well," she said, turning towards him, pulling him down for another kiss and taking her time. "You see, my Aunt Vera has gone away. She is at her sister's in Eastbourne for the weekend. She goes there about once a year. I told them I had to work and couldn't go. The house is empty. Completely empty. So you can come in and... well... kiss me goodnight properly."

Philip felt the thrill run through his body. After the wine and the closeness of the evening, the walk along the front, the touch of her body against him, and the feel of her lips on his, he could scarcely take in this news.

Mary kissed him seductively and whispered: "Follow me."

She led him back towards her home, but instead of going into the street where she lived, or towards their dark kissing niche, she took his hand and ducked down a side street, through a small alleyway and up to a tall wooden gate.

"Nearly there, don't worry," she laughed in a whisper and fished around at the base of the gate until she found a key, stood up, silently unlocked the gate, led him through and locked it again behind them and replaced the key. Then they skipped to the back of the house and again she reached under a pot to find another key, unlocked the back door and relocked it behind them. She switched on the lights and the two of them were in a large airy kitchen that smelled of paint, onions and embrocation.

"Cup of tea?" she asked. "Or would you like something a little stronger?"

With that, Mary took his face in both of her hands and began kissing him with even more vivacity than she usually did on the seafront. Then, still holding his hand, she backed away, looked at him and said: "We have this house to ourselves. There will be no one else here until Monday afternoon. Shall I show you where I sleep?"

Mary's bed smelled just like Mary, Philip thought when he woke up in it the next morning. He had barely realised where he was when Mary rolled over on top of him and began kissing him again.

"Oh Philip, that was the best night of my life. No one has ever taken me seriously, but you do. With you, I feel a person. With you I feel a woman, not a silly little girl, something to laugh at and make fun of. Oh Philip, hold me tight and don't ever let me go."

Mary's flesh felt so good against his skin, that Philip found it hard to think straight. This was not how he had planned this weekend, but when he looked at her, tasted her lips, felt her naked body beneath his touch, he lost all of his control. He just wanted her. What else could he do? Here was a very pretty young woman, kissing him, offering herself to him, wanting him. It would have taken the willpower of a saint to say no. And he could not say no.

Mary's body did not feel the same as Meg's. Altogether more fragile, almost liquid under his touch. He could hardly believe that he had made love to two beautiful young women in the space of less than a month. On that level, he felt just pure heady excitement. The complexity that he would now have to deal with was something that scared him, but while Mary's body was enlaced with his, her arms around him, her mouth on his, her whole self open to him... at that moment, he was not in control. He could not say No.

It was almost noon when they decided that they really needed something to sustain them apart from each other and went down to the kitchen to see the special shopping Mary had done for them.

If Saturday was glorious, then Sunday was equally blissful. The house was quiet and still, so they could do as they pleased. And that meant staying in Mary's bed, laughing and kissing and enjoying the sort of intimacy they had long craved on the beach and on their walks.

Philip was disturbed by thoughts of Meg, but kept telling himself that this had to come to an end by Monday morning so what harm could one more day of pleasure do to anyone? Mary was happy, he was happy, and Meg would never know about it. Why cause problems? Why not just enjoy Mary's lovely body and give her the pleasure that she was obviously deriving from this beautiful goodbye?

For her part, Mary felt only relief. She had planned this for several weeks, knowing that Aunt Vera would soon be away and wanting to use the time and the empty house to cement her relationship with Philip. She had always felt that he was the only person on earth who was on her side, but now she was determined to make Philip feel that she was on his side. She wanted him to enjoy her, to depend on her, to need her as much as she needed him. By making them close in this way, she was sure that he would feel the same, that they would become one entity, that he would stop going away from her and leaving her defenceless and alone.

And she felt the strength that came when they were together. No matter how bad her day had been, who had mocked and scorned her, how beaten down she felt, sitting on the bench beside Philip, looking out to sea, holding his hand, walking by his side and kissing him, made everything good again. That feeling, that comfort, that sensation – that was what she wanted to make *him* feel too. She wanted to give him everything she had, all of herself, mind and body so that he could share the liberation that he gave to her.

Last night had been the start of that. Now she had him to herself all day today and tonight too. After that, she did not know. A year was too long to wait for Aunt Vera to go to Eastbourne again, so they would have to find another way of meeting like this, in private, just the two of them, behind closed doors, all night long.

Mary was sure that Philip would find a way. He protected her. He would protect their love and let it grow and flourish. She felt too happy for words as she fried some bacon and cut some thick slices of bread, buttered them and set the still-sizzling bacon onto the butter to melt into it. Then she stirred the pot of tea, and put it all on a tray with cups and milk, and watched Philip carry it up the stairs to her bedroom.

Philip had been pondering the best time to tell Mary that he was leaving in the morning, and the best way to say it, the right words to use to make her feel good about herself. She was so happy now and already talking about him staying with her for another night, that he was unwilling to spoil her pleasure. Now they had a massive tray of sweet-smelling food to share. The badness could wait, he thought. Bacon sandwiches, tea and Mary was a very enticing combination.

Mary looked at Philip's expression as he put the tray on the bed, and she handed him a plate with two thick dripping bacon sandwiches to share, poured them some tea and set it on the bedside table, slipped off her dressing gown and climbed naked and inviting into bed beside him. This had been a good idea, she thought. It was working. Philip was now her man.

Try as he might, there just had not been the right time to say what he needed to say. Whenever he was about to try, Mary kissed him or said how happy she was, or asked him what he wanted her to do for him. It had been impossible. The only way was to write it down for her, he thought, when their nights of bliss finally came to an end and Mary had to run off to work early. She left him in her bed and explained to him how to let himself out so that no one would see him go and where to put the keys. Leaving Philip behind in her bed was symbolic for her. In her bed. That was where he now belonged, where their love had become real, a physical entity. If only he could be there when she returned home. Perhaps one day. One day. She hummed softly to herself as she tripped lightly down the dark streets to the *Bel Air*.

Meanwhile, Philip was hunting for some paper, which he found downstairs in a drawer in the parlour. He sat at the kitchen table and began writing.

"My darling Mary," he began and stopped for a very long time. What could he say? He just did not know. Oh well, the important thing was that he wrote his letter, picked up his case and went to the station and home to Meg.

313

"My darling Mary, This has been a wonderful weekend with you, but I have just had some very bad news. I have learned that I have lost my job, and without any money, I have no choice but to return home. By the time you read this, I will already be on my way. I do not know what the future holds. I will do everything I can to come back to visit you, but if I cannot, we both have some wonderful memories of each other to treasure forever. This has been a perfect weekend on which to finish if that is to be our fate. You are a very beautiful woman. Look after yourself and always know that I will think of my darling Mary and that I will forever be, Your Philip x"

He was very pleased with his effort. It was much better than anything that he could have said. It gave Mary tenderness, love, some hope for the future, reassurance, kind words, and praise. She could, he thought, keep it and treasure it for years to come. In any case, she was young and pretty, there would be no shortage of other men who would want her. She would be fine.

He folded the letter in half, wrote Mary on it, propped it up on her bedside table, where she would see it when she returned, pulled the bed straight and walked out of the room, with just a glance behind to remind him of a very, very pleasant weekend. It was done.

Philip did not go into breakfast, he slipped quietly up the stairs of the *Bel Air*, picked up his case and put in the rest of his belongings and left his key in the lock outside his door as arranged. Then he listened as he had that first day – when he had not dared to go down the stairs in case he was seen.

He smiled to himself. That all seemed so very long ago now. Almost a whole lifetime away. Philip could hardly remember what he was like or how he felt back then. He was a different person today. He had changed and developed and grown, he thought. And now he was a man. A real man. This entire chapter of his life here had started so badly but was now ending so well. Now he was leaving and Meg awaited.

Not caring if anyone heard or saw him, he strode down the stairs with his chest puffed out.

Mary was disappointed not to see Philip at breakfast but smiled to herself. It meant that he was still in her bed, and had probably fallen asleep again. She pictured the scene and wished with all of her heart that she could be there with him right now. Then she got on with her day, happier than she had been for a very, very long time.

CHAPTER 47

Love's night is noon

"We're nearly there. Second right at the next roundabout and it's about two miles into the town and up the hill," said Clara, folding up the map that she hadn't needed anyway and throwing it onto the back seat of the hire car.

"Good," said Paul. "It's been a long day and I could do with some food and drink."

"And – as I can't help noticing that you really should have said – to paying me some proper attention."

"That's what I need the food and drink for. Er, refuelling. Definitely not Dutch courage," he added quickly.

Clara slapped him on the arm and looked out of the car window at the passing scenery. It was good to be back on the Black Isle again. They had flown up that morning, picked up a hire car at Inverness Airport and had a drive out to Cromarty at the far end of the Black Isle. Now they were heading back towards Grandma's cottage.

Clara still could not believe that her whole world had been stood on its head so quickly. Four or five weeks ago, she was being bullied by her boss and the quiet boy of the office was a complete unknown. Now she had overthrown the tyrant and he was gone. And the quiet boy, who was no longer quiet, had become her boss. And her lover.

Paul was officially due to take up his new post as editor in a week, the latest press day being yesterday and the team had made a very good start on next month's edition. Paul had a week's holiday booked, which he had planned to spend largely in his room: reading, trying out a new game and learning some software he had just got his hands on. Instead, he told his father, he was going hill walking in the Cotswolds. Quite a departure for him, but he said he needed to clear his head and had a lot to think about before he started his new challenge.

Clara also booked a week off at the last minute as a girlfriend of hers had two tickets to a music festival and had just broken up with her boyfriend, so didn't want to waste the ticket. Paul had granted her last-minute holiday request and hoped she had a good time at the festival. It was all very sudden, but manageable.

They had not made any of these plans earlier that week when they began the evening with their usual bottle of champagne, which had already become a bit of a tradition with them. Start the evening with champagne at a secluded wine bar just off the Strand, and then head for a quiet restaurant. One paid for the champagne, the other the dinner, by turns.

Only this night, Clara suggested that she cook for Paul after the champagne. Nothing fancy. Pasta, chicken and sauce. A bit more relaxing, she suggested.

They had reached the stage of brief, tantalising goodnight kisses, which at least answered Clara's earlier question. Paul kissed deliciously.

Tonight, they left the wine bar and waited for a taxi, as they had done three or four times before at this spot, ready to head off to a restaurant. This time, almost without realising it, they found that they had linked arms as they stood on the kerb. It all seemed very natural.

Back at the flat, Clara whipped up Meg's chicken in white sauce, boiled far too much fusilli, as Paul struggled with Clara's almost useless corkscrew. They chatted and laughed over dinner, collapsed on the sofa with the rest of the wine afterwards, laughed some more and were soon kissing frantically.

It was early the next morning, as the first rays of light began sending faint tinges of white across the dark horizon of rooftops, that, both completely exhausted, they dreamily came up with the idea of a holiday and began planning how they could get away with spending a whole week together.

There were quite a few pages "in the bottom drawer" that both of them liked a lot but that Peter had spiked for reasons they did not agree with. They had some more rejected features and a new crop of material that could be drawn up by Vincent while they were away, and that would mean that when they came back almost half the magazine would be in good shape – a far better position than usual at that stage of the monthly cycle.

"And when we do get back, you are not going to know what has hit you," laughed Paul, turning his head on the pillow and kissing Clara gently. "Work? You'll soon be wishing father was back in charge."

"That's quite a challenge you've set yourself there, my son. But I'm afraid it's just wishful thinking on your part since I now have total control over you. You are in my power, see? A plaything to do with as I please."

"That sounds delightful. When can you start?"

"I may need a cup of tea and a small nap first if that's OK with you."

"Sure is. I'll have a cup too, while you're making it. I'll skip the nap though. I don't want to take my eyes off you."

"Well, you'll have to while you make the tea unless you can see round corners. Go..." she said, pushing him gently but firmly out of her bed.

"Can I see my contract? I don't remember anything about being bossed around in my KPIs."

"It's being rewritten. In fact, I'm making it up as I go along. Tea!"

They were late for work that morning, arriving from different directions until they felt ready to tell their secret. Paul organised the next edition, then called Clara, Vincent, and Marcia into his office and they all gave their thoughts on the leftover pages, he got the flat plan from advertising to show which ads went where, drew up a list of pages for Vincent to resurrect, and another list of roughs that he would give him that night before he left for his holiday. Walking in the Cotswolds.

In the kitchen, Clara told Marcia all about her friend's tickets, that Paul had agreed to her sudden holiday request, and how much she was looking forward to the festival.

"That's lovely," said Marcia. "But it's OK, your secret is safe with me. Who could I tell anyway? Only Vincent, and he's probably guessed too."

"Secret?" asked Clara, wide-eyed and innocent. "Guessed? What *are* you talking about, Marcia?"

"Clara Harvey, it is very clear that you and Paul are very close to being, if not already, an item. And I'm very happy for you."

"Marcia! How on earth did you know? Not that I'm admitting anything, of course. I mean: how did you jump to that ridiculous conclusion?"

"There are lots of ways of looking at another person, but when two people both look at each other the way you two are both looking at each other this morning, when they think they are playing it cool and not giving anything away but in fact may as well both be wearing T-shirts that say WE DID IT, when both arrive late for work, two minutes apart, one with the same shirt he wore yesterday, both with coffee from a different shop, even though they both go past a totally different coffee outlet on their way between their usual routes in and the office, well, let's just say, that one and one seem to add up to about a dozen. Wouldn't you think?"

"Are you training to be a private eye, Marcia?"

"You've stopped denying it, then. What's he like? He's really opened up lately. And he looks great with his new haircut."

"Oh Marcia, he's just lovely. I'm feeling 10 feet tall."

"You deserve it, Clara, you really do. After all you've been through here. It's somehow fitting. Now – as that festival you allegedly have tickets for finished last weekend, where are the two of you *actually* going?"

They were going to Grandma's cottage on the Black Isle. No decision had even been made on what if anything was going to happen to it, so Clara knew it would be empty. And she knew where the key was kept – or where Muriel lived in the unlikely event of the key being moved – or where the best hotel on the Black Isle was and that it was never full at this time of year in the even more unlikely event that Muriel would not give them the key or could not be found.

They parked around the back of the cottage and Clara found the key in its normal place.

"You know," she told Paul. "I must have been to this cottage a hundred times but I've never slept with anyone here."

"Your record's in no danger," he laughed and kissed her. "Who's planning to sleep?"

CHAPTER 48

Susan – special delivery

(April 1949)

I t had been an intense few days but it looked good. Everything had worked very smoothly and the consignment was now safely at its new home in the Black Isle, where it would lie low until it was not being looked for by anyone too curious any more.

The network of vans that Susan had organised was perfect. Each one had picked up the four large crates, driven them no more than 100 miles, most of them far less and dropped them off, ready for the next van or vans to pick up. No single driver knew anything other than he had a routine short hop to make. Nothing connected the consignment from its starting point in Bristol to its final destination on the Black Isle. There was no overall picture for anyone to look at, nothing to arouse suspicion, just a series of local deliveries. The only real difficulty had been the first stage. The driver who loaded the crates at Bristol docks had a delivery address in London. Susan managed to speak to him on the phone when he arrived and tell him that there had been a change of plan and he need only take the crates to Swindon, where they would be picked up by a driver who was making another drop to London.

The new paperwork would be waiting for him when he got back to base. All sorted. The Bristol driver was not at all suspicious and Susan easily answered all his questions and gave him the new address. Mario was waiting at Swindon in a lock-up garage that they had rented for the week. As soon as the drop was made, the next driver was summoned, loaded and sent on his way to Oxford before the first driver had got back to Bristol and the alarm was raised. By the time they had sent someone back to the lock-up, there was no one to be found, and no crates either. From then on it went like a clockwork trainset. Bristol, Swindon, Oxford, Northampton, Peterborough, Grantham, Newark, Doncaster, Leeds, York, Thirsk, Darlington, Durham, Newcastle, Alnwick, Berwick, Edinburgh, Perth, Aviemore and the Black Isle cottage. They took a chance by letting each driver meet the next on his own at the new driver's depot, but that was far safer than having every driver catch sight of Mario, or having one of Mario's men know the exact route. Only once did they have a problem, when the drivers from Perth to Aviemore were delayed and when they reached their destination there was no one there. Fortunately, they slept in their vans and passed on their precious cargo the next morning.

Bernard was to confirm the safe arrival by placing a pre-arranged small ad in the London Evening News. Susan bought the paper every day and anxiously tore it open at the classified ads page. For day after day there was nothing, then suddenly there it was: *To Harvey and Susan, a boy. Safely delivered on April 14.* She dashed straight round to Mario and they hugged each other in glee, then called Henry to tell him.

So now they just had to wait. Meanwhile, they could enjoy a quiet celebration or two. The three of them had a riotous night in the Star on the day that the ad appeared, whooping it up from opening time until they were thrown out and all tottered off their separate ways.

The next evening, Susan and Mario had what he called a "slap-up dinner" at an elegant (by Bethnal Green standards) restaurant, where they wined and dined and made plans of how they were going to spend their share of this fortune when the job was done.

"Of course," said Mario, "this was all my idea and my contacts to set it up in the first place, was it not? By rights, I should be taking half and leaving the rest for you two to share. Don't you think?"

"No I don't," said Susan. "We all did our bit and it wouldn't have worked if one of us had messed up. And there will be plenty for everyone. No funny ideas."

"Of course not, but it makes you think, *mia caro*. The more ways you slice a cake, the smaller everyone's piece is. If I have half and you a quarter that's three-quarters of the stash between us. We would be loaded. By the way, how much does Bernard think he's getting?"

"What we agreed. I said it would be somewhere between one and five grand. Like we said."

"Five? Oh, that's a bit steep, don't you think?"

"Well, a bit. I think he'd be happy with less."

"Of course, two grand is between one and five, isn't it, sugar?"

"Yes, but..."

"And so is one, technically."

"Oh, Mario, stop it."

"But it's a straightforward sum, *bellissima*. If we give Bernard a grand, that's another four grand to share between us three. A lot more to put into your bottom drawer."

He patted her leg under the table.

"Well, yes, but..."

"And if we don't give him anything..."

"Oh, that's not fair!"

"He's done it now, he can't undo it, can he? It's like that Pied Piper. Once all the rats were gone, he wasn't in nearly such a strong bargaining position, you see. And once the consignment is handed back over to us... *A thousand guilders, come, take fifty.* Hahaha. I love that story."

"Have you read the ending yet? I don't want to spoil it for you, but... Anyway, this is my brother we're talking about."

"Look, all is fair in love and business. And if you're unhappy, you can always give him some of yours. You'll have plenty, my little love bunny. And anyway, there's something else that I need to talk to you about, but it can wait. Tonight, we celebrate."

And celebrate they did. And they were still celebrating as the sun came up next morning, only by now the venue had changed from the pub to Mario's bedroom, and their disputes over money had changed into an altogether more harmonious sound, whose cadence rose and fell with the coming of dawn.

The next day it was Henry's turn to celebrate and this time he took Susan to a quiet but very respectable restaurant near St James's Park, where the talk was about the future.

"I have told you before how much I need what you can give," said Henry, playing with her hand on the restaurant table and looking directly into her eyes. "I know what you do for Mario. I know that without you he would not be in the situation that he is enjoying today. I know that without you, this whole project would simply not have happened. Organising the route from Bristol to Scotland was very, very special. Now I am ready for the next stage. I have given you some outlines of what I intend and now – now that we are on the brink of possessing the wherewithal to accomplish our dreams – now is the time to share those dreams with you."

Henry picked up her hand and put it to his lips without ever stopping the flow of words.

"Property, my Susan. Property will be the currency that will see us ascend to greatness and splendour. This is how it works. If you have the money, you buy a property. You now have an asset but no debt. Depending on the size of it you either convert it into offices or to homes. You then rent it out for more than it costs you to repay what you outlay for the refurbishment. With what remains and continues to flood in as rent, you buy another property and do the same again. Before long, you have a portfolio of property and you keep repeating the process."

He kissed her palm and the inside of her wrist as he spoke.

"Now at this time around London, there is a lot of damaged property on valuable sites, going for ha'pence because no one has the money to buy and develop it. But we shall have the money, my sweet. And so we accelerate our acquisition and our development and our capture of tenants who pay us money every week, every month to make us grow more. Oh, certainly some of this property needs work done on it. But there are grants aplenty to help us honest folk to restore the city to its former splendour. It will just fall into our laps. And not a penny of it needs to be repaid. And if we need workmen, why there is a surfeit of returned soldiers and sailors without jobs, but with the muscle to do our bidding. And on it goes."

Henry poured them some more wine and clinked his glass against hers as he toasted the future.

"Oh Susan, do you not see? Once we have an abundance of initial capital, I can source the properties, get a good price, and find the grants to redevelop them for no outlay of our own. You can bring in the labour, organise the tenants, keep track of all angles of this multi-faceted enterprise, and ensure that where money is owed to us, then that money is forthcoming. This is the nub of it. This is where we work as a team. This is where we grow rich beyond anything you could ever imagine. Now we so nearly have our first capital, there is no stopping us. Do you not see?"

Henry was still painting vivid pictures of the future that was within their grasp all the way back in their taxi, all the way up the stairs to his rooms, and even when he slipped off Susan's dress, lay her down on his feather bed, and held her close to him in a mutual ecstasy of insatiable greed.

As they had to, the celebrations finally came to an end and the three were left with a period of waiting and hoping that nothing could go wrong to spoil their plans and their dreams.

Susan was worried about Mario's suggestion that Bernard should be squeezed out of the picture. She mentioned it to Henry one morning, but he waved her fears aside.

"There is more than enough here for all of us, no matter what Mario pretends," he said.

But Mario was becoming twitchy. He was saying things that Susan neither fully understood nor liked the sound of.

"I'm hearing that this will only go quiet if there's someone to carry the can," Mario said one day. "If they can lay their hands on someone to blame, then it takes all of the pressure off them. It's just one deal among hundreds for them. They were robbed and someone has paid the price. They do not lose face. As long as they can point to someone who was taught a lesson for crossing them, well it makes others think twice and their position is safe. Even if they lose a bit of money by their standards it is feed for chickens. Give them a loser and all will be well – the whole thing will fade away quietly. But if not then they will be impossible to shake off. Give me some time to think about this. What I do know is that I'm not going to let the whole thing slip through my hands for the want of a sucker."

While Susan was mulling all of this over in her room one evening, there was a knock at the door. All the time she had been here no one had ever knocked on her door. She looked at her alarm clock. Just after nine-thirty. Surely they don't need an emergency barmaid now, do they? I'm sorry but they are going to be disappointed if they think I'll step in. I need some sleep.

She opened the door and there on the landing, bending slightly because of the low ceiling, was Bernard.

CHAPTER 49

Whisky sour

"**M**rs Harvey, that is the best trifle I have ever tasted. You must give Clara the recipe," said Paul, pushing away his bowl after a second helping and sipping his glass of Chablis.

"Oh do call me Meg," said Meg. "It's good to be appreciated. These oafs just eat whatever's put in front of them and grunt a bit."

"Oy, both of you," said Clara. "First, even if I did have the recipe, which as it happens I do, what makes you think that it is *my* job to make *you* trifle, Lord Paul of Allaire? And secondly, Dad and I are not oafs, although I grant you that we do grunt after meals from time to time."

"No, sweetest heart," said Paul, "I meant that if you have the recipe *I* can make it for *you*."

"Almost nicely back-tracked. If only I believed a word of it. Now get to the fridge and open the next bottle before what's left in my glass evaporates."

They exchanged a quick glance that said: "Thanks for telling me what to say. It went down well."

"And you delivered it perfectly – all that practice on the train paid off."

Clara could scarcely believe that things had gone so smoothly. She and Paul had arrived unannounced on their way back from their week of bliss in the Black Isle, Clara had introduced Paul to her parents as her new friend who works with her, and they had immediately hit it off.

Paul had been dreading it. All the way south, he had fretted.

"You know what dads are like," he said. "Especially girls' dads. What if he challenges me to a duel? Pistols at dawn or whatever the weapon of choice is these days. I don't know. Strimmers. Or chainsaws…"

"Paul, you're in what passes for your prime and my dad's nearly a pensioner. If you can't handle him, then you're not the man I took you for and I may have to reconsider my sleeping arrangements."

"Oh and if I *do* run him through with a rapier, you'll be all smiles and say: never mind. Is that how it works?"

"Certainly not. If you kill my dad I'll never speak to you again."

"And if he kills me?"

"You'll never speak to me again. Look, I think you're worrying too much. If you'd ever met my dad, you'd know that he's not the fighting kind."

Paul sipped his coffee and leaned back. The two were quiet for a while as the train clinked and rattled over the rails. Paul smiled.

"You know, that was one of the best weeks of my life."

"You liked the Black Isle?"

"Is that where we were? I liked that cottage, and making love in your crow's nest under the stars…"

"Another first. Shame about the midges."

"…and in the kitchen, and on the stairs, and in front of the fire, and…"

"OK, OK, I get the picture."

"And the walk on the beach…"

"One walk in a whole week. Normally I would go on seven…"

"And dinner in the restaurant…"

"That was beautiful," agreed Clara.

She snuggled up to him on the train seat. It *had* been a lovely week. She couldn't remember the last time she had been to bed with a man. Oh, wait. Yes, she could. She shuddered. This was so very different, though. Paul had become a completely altered human being. OK, she had helped in a way. The haircut she suggested suited him so much better and made him look the 30 he was, not the 50 he had been posing as. And the new clothes he was wearing were now those of a young man and not some he seemed to have borrowed from his father's wardrobe in a hurry in the dark.

Clara was happy to take some credit, and more than happy with his gratitude. But she had to keep on reminding him that the transformation had chiefly been down to him. Whatever she had suggested would have counted for nothing if he had not taken it and run with it. And the new Paul had brought them instantly closer. Every time they came up with a plan together and it worked, it was the two of them helping Paul progress. And from fretting about every word he had to say, Paul was soon suggesting phrases to Clara, and even making things up on the spot. Of course, there were setbacks. Like the time he went too far welcoming a contributor to the office to discuss a piece she had written about speed dating in Luxembourg. "Why don't you come and sit over here by me and we can see what comes up..." wasn't in the script, and she thought he was hitting on her. Clara smoothed things over and Paul agreed not to try that line again. But gradually the change was made and in a few weeks what would have been unthinkable for Paul was becoming natural. And when he stopped fretting and trying, he was even good at it and funny.

They changed trains at Peterborough and finally reached Langton a little after 4 pm on the Sunday afternoon. They walked to Clara's parents' house and she let them in. Even her professed calm wobbled slightly as the door swung open.

"Mum! Dad! It's me, Clara. Anyone home?"

Meg took to Paul immediately. Philip was as quiet as normal, but full of smiles and clearly not wanting a duel.

They had a cup of tea in the garden as Clara told them about the secret holiday and what they had got up to in the Black Isle – or at least, the walk and the restaurant.

Meg rustled up a quick dinner, making the beef she had been cooking for two stretch to four plates with the help of a very large Yorkshire pudding. Dinner went well and the three of them chatted away as if they'd known each other for years, with Philip looking relaxed and happily joining in the conversation from time to time.

Clara was a little concerned about what would happen when it came to organising the quarters for the night.

"Well I'm turning in now," said Meg when the last of the dinner had been finished and cleared away. "Lovely to meet you, Paul, and you must come again. I've made up a bed for you in the spare room and I'm sure you'll be comfortable, but I can get you an extra pillow if you want one."

Clara and Paul looked at each other but said nothing, Clara working out that it was but three steps across the landing from the spare room to hers. But Philip suddenly sprang to life.

"Meg, these are two young people. You don't suppose they had separate rooms at Mum's do you? Remember what we were like at that age? Oh, darling, I do! And times have moved on since then. Let's have a nice whisky nightcap and then all get to bed. Paul, you've just come from the Black Isle. Do you like a drop of scotch?"

"I do, Mr Harvey. Very much. What's your favourite?"

"Well, I've a bottle of 12-year-old Talisker that's burning a hole in my drinks cabinet. I've been looking for an excuse to open it – and it looks as though I've found one."

"Oooooh, that's one of my favourites," said Paul.

It was more than Philip had said all evening in one go, but he was clearly in a good mood. Meg and Clara looked at each other and smiled. They were glad he was relaxed and if Paul's company did this to him, then let him come more often.

Meg caught up with Clara in the kitchen.

"He seems a very nice boy," she said as they collected glasses and Clara filled a jug with cold water.

"Oh Mum, he is. I'm trying to make myself see that it could all end as quickly as it has started, but I'm really happy."

"He's polite, interesting and funny – and your father likes him too."

"Yes, but we'd better get these glasses into them or they'll both go off us."

It was close to midnight when Meg announced that she really could not stay awake any longer as Philip finished a long story about selling encyclopedias in Brighton that had them all laughing.

"Are you staying up for one more, darling?" she asked.

"Oh yes. Don't go, don't go, don't go," said Philip. "I just remembered a story I was going to tell you. Paul, pour us all another large one, please."

"Not for me," said Clara. "I'm done. Shall we go up, Mum?"

"Wait," said Philip. "I had something to tell you all. To tell you. Bernard's not here, is he? Only I don't think he knows that I know that he doesn't know I know. Or not. Or whatever. It's hard to remember what I do know, in fact – what he told me and what I worked out for myself and what I dreamed or made up. Just a tiny bit more water in there please, Paul. Hard to tell them apart, don't you find? Awfully hard."

He laughed, looked puzzled, then drank a little more.

"Come on, darling, let's go to bed," said Meg gently.

"And I can't ever remember what I know that I'm not supposed to know and who else knows it, so that means that I never know if I can say anything to anyone. But I do know. I know more than I know I know, you know. And whenever I think about it I get this very sad feeling. It's too late to do anything about it now, of course. But it's a hard thing to bear. And there's something that I did, but I can't always remember any more. Bernard told me off once but didn't tell me why. Or I don't think he did, or I can't remember what he said if he said it. But I think from his tone in what he did say that it was very, very bad indeed and now there's nothing I can do. I just have to bear it. It's so very hard, don't you think? Do you have any bad secrets, Paul? No, no, no, no, no of course not. That's the best way."

He drained his glass in one and stared straight ahead.

"Meg, feel a bit sleepy. Meg, take me to bed. Or bring me a glass of water outside and we'll go for a walk by the river. Hahaha. Stand on the bridge. Look at the stars. Go to the guest house. Then everything will be all right. I can't sort these things out like Bernard can. I never know what to say. I…"

Meg had got him to his feet by now and was easing him towards the door.

"It's all right, Philip. Everything's all right. Goodnight, Clara. Goodnight, Paul. Don't mind Philip, he's a bit tired. It's been a long day and such a lot of excitement. Philip is not used to drinking this much. Sleep well. Goodnight. Goodnight."

And they were gone.

In the silence, Clara looked at Paul.

"You know, I think I will have a drop more of that whisky, please," she said.

CHAPTER 50

George – Silent witness

(September 1888)

Marjory was determined. Since his rebellion, George had hardly spoken to her and not at all when they were alone together. His only words were those of subservience when Old John or his parents were present. Something was happening and she had to find out what.

For a long time now he had been going out to work every Saturday morning. But unlike when he first started, he did not return at lunchtime. Now he did not come back until 6 o'clock or later, sometimes even closer to 8 o'clock. And he always looked troubled. What was he doing? Where was he going? There was only one way to find out and Marjory was ready to do it.

She feared for his soul. She saw him every day committing sins in the eyes of the Lord, sins that she could save him from if he would let her. But he would not let her now. Pride had seen him rebel. And that meant that he was in mortal danger. How could she convince him to let her look after his soul so that he would enjoy the next world? So that they could be together forever?

All that she had ever wanted was to care for him. To cook his meals and clean his house, yes but what did that amount to? Dusting and mending. Any peasant could accomplish that for him. No, she wanted to save him forever and the only way was to constantly watch over him, to care not for his body but for his eternal, everlasting soul. Some evil spirit was surely influencing him. And she was desperate, desperate to track it down so that she might save him.

Marjory loved George. She had loved him as a small boy, playing in the fields with the other imps, and when it became clear from the things her mother said that the two of them were destined to be together, she bent her whole life into caring for him. She would save her last sweet for him, always pick him to be on her side in games, attack and try to hurt anyone, even a boy far bigger than her, who tried to do George down as they played. She did not think that George even noticed, but she did it anyway because he was hers. She was spoken for.

But when she began to understand the way God shaped their lives, she grew fearful for George. He was breaking the Commandments, flouting God's rules, and putting himself in peril. Marjory could hardly sleep with worry. She wanted to be with George for all eternity, but what if his actions, his thoughtlessness made him prey to the darker side? Without even realising that he was doing anything wrong, George was endangering his very soul. And she, Marjory, was the only one who could save him.

For a long while, after they married, George allowed her to intervene and to safeguard him. It did not seem to stop him committing the sins, but at least he could go to his rest each night with a clean soul, purged of all wrongdoing. And Marjory found that she enjoyed saving him. The physical action of damaging the wrong in George, of driving out the evil blood, gave her more pleasure than she had expected. It was not an ordeal that she had to force herself to endure, but something that she looked forward to each night.

Marjory had explained what she was compelled to do on their first night together as man and wife. She went carefully through the threats that he faced, and how she could help and save him. George seemed to understand, or at least allowed her to intercede on his behalf. At last, she thought, I do not have to sit back and watch my beloved face a danger that he does not even begin to understand. Greater love hath no woman than to save the very soul of her husband.

And yet, although he submitted to his penance and absolved himself each evening, he did not seem to understand his faults, for he committed them again and again with each new day. It was almost as though he were defying her, defying his Lord.

Now he had refused his daily salvation and was once more in grave danger. What was she to do? And he was acting very strangely. He would go off for whole days at a time without more than a word of explanation, and return, surly, sullen and silent.

She *had* to know what was happening to him, which demon had control over him, and where the power now lay. She could see only one way of finding this out and bringing him safely back into the fold that would ensure his soul's survival. She, Marjory, would have to put herself in harm's way. She would have to follow him, perhaps come face to face with the spirit that was taking him away from the righteous path, and do what she could to battle that demon and win him back. Her love for her husband would have to conquer all. Her fear, her doubt, her terror.

She was exhilarated by the very thought.

So when George left home the next Saturday morning, saying in a few words that he had a lot to do that day and would not be home early, Marjory put on her shawl. Not the shawl that she wore to chapel or to go into town, but a plain and dowdy shawl that he would not immediately recognise if he saw her at a distance. And she followed him from afar. This was made easier by the fact that George never once looked behind him or turned back to glance the way he had come. He marched on resolutely, determined.

First, he went to the pastures between Langton and Broom and set about moving some fence posts to accommodate a new field layout. This took more than three hours and Marjory grew weary standing behind a hedge and watching her husband at work.

But when the church clock chimed noon, just as she was beginning to think that he really had nothing to hide and was telling the truth about his work, he suddenly stood up, gathered together his tools and strode off towards Longford.

Marjory could barely keep up and was running to make sure that she could still see him in the distance when he rounded a corner and seemed to disappear into some thick undergrowth at a bend in the river.

Marjory stopped, put her hands on her knees and panted hard until she finally began to get her breath back.

She carried on along the path but could see where it stretched off in the distance toward Longford in a long straight sweep. If George had taken that path then she would still see him. He had not had time to reach the end some half a mile or more away, but he was nowhere to be seen. He had simply vanished. No, he must still be on this bend in the river. Unless a demon had helped him to disappear and reappear who knew where.

She walked back and forth along the river path, but he was not there. He must have somehow infiltrated into that seemingly impassable and dense clump of brambles. What should she do? There was just no way through.

She walked past it twice more but could see no answer. Then she noticed a small patch of grass between the river and the far side of the brambles. If she could climb around there, she would perhaps be able to see into the immense thicket from the other side. It looked almost impossible, but the stakes were high and she must show fortitude. Her husband's very soul was at stake here, and if she balked at a few cuts to her legs, what kind of wife would she be? Marjory tensed her jaw and began to creep around the edge of the briars, in the slender gap between dense foliage and the swirling river.

More than once, she almost lost her footing and thought that she would tumble into the water, but by grabbing hold of the thorn bushes until her hands bled and her arms were lacerated by the sharp spikes, she managed to stay upright, keep her balance and inch her way around the edge of the jungle.

She thought she heard a sound from within, from just inside the bushes, but when she paused, there was nothing more to be heard. Just past this next outcrop of thorns, the river seemed to bend back on itself and from there she might be able to see into the interior. It was so hard, her hands and arms were hurting and speckled with blood where she had been forced to hold the thorns themselves to stay upright, but her plight made her overjoyed. My crown of thorns, she thought. I am overcoming this terrible ordeal to save my husband. This can only be good and can only help his cause when we come to plead for his soul.

She reached the limit of the next cascade of thorns, struggled painfully around it, and saw a clearing inside the mass of briars themselves and there in the very centre was George, sitting on the ground with his head in his hands.

Without thinking, she let out a cry and George immediately looked up and saw her there, hanging on grimly to the briars. They were no more than 10 feet apart.

Marjory looked at him in amazement. What was he doing there? How did he get in there without so much as a scratch to his flesh? What trickery was this? What evil power had set him down within this cage of thorns?

For a long moment, they stood and stared at each other, then Marjory tried to say: "I am here to help you, my darling George."

But she only got as far as "I am" when the bramble that she was holding gave way, her foot slipped on the wet grass and although she tried desperately to grab another handful of thorns, she fell slowly backwards and into a deep swirling pool on the bend of the river.

Marjory? thought George. Marjory? How did she get here? She is in the river. She cannot swim.

Encumbered by her long, thick skirt, her petticoats and her shawl, Marjory flailed her arms and looked up at George. He is strong, she thought, reassured. He will save me. I am safe. She waited for her husband to tear off his coat and leap into the swirling water to pluck her from danger to the bank. But George just stared at her.

"Get me out!" she pleaded. "Please!" Her mouth and nose were full of water, and she coughed and choked as her lungs tried to get rid of the foul-tasting liquid.

George stood on the bank and watched. He could swim only poorly himself but he could perhaps have torn down a long branch and reached it out to her to save her.

But he did not move.

Their eyes met, hers in increasing panic, his in flat silence, as her head went under in the deep water, and her skirts became entangled in the thick reeds below the surface.

Marjory clawed her way back into the air, but she was growing weaker.

"Help!" she gasped and tried to repeat the plea but failed. Too much water.

George thought: I do not think that I can reach Marjory, but if I did succeed in pulling her out everything would be just as it is now. It would be me finally saying yes to our marriage, a marriage where my agreement was never asked. He knew that he could not try to save her. So he did not move a single muscle, just looked into Marjory's eyes as she fought to try to look back in helpless fear, not understanding what was happening.

Again she thrashed her way to the surface, beating her arms on the water with little result.

She tried to shout: "Please!" but her lungs were full of water by now and felt as though they would burst as she tried desperately to breathe in some air. She had no strength left. She went under the water again and grew weaker and weaker until there was no fight left in her body. Her wild arms slowed and then stopped altogether and she was left floating face down just under the surface of the water, still tethered by the reeds around her ankles, inert.

For a long time, George stood and watched in silence. He saw his wife's body bobbing gently in the current. He swallowed hard.

He had no idea what was going to happen to him, to Becky, or to anything around him.

Slowly, he turned, opened the hideaway briars, and then trudged homewards.

Half an hour later, Becky approached. "George," she cried in a small voice. "George, it's me."

Becky made her way into the hideaway, but George was not there. She waited for an hour, sitting in silence and hardly moving, hardly breathing. Then she realised that he was not going to come today. She would have to wait another week to see him.

With a heaving heart, she parted the brambles, slipped through the gap, and headed back home toward Longford, just as the body of Marjory freed itself from the reeds and went bobbing down the river in the other direction towards Langton.

CHAPTER 51

Cause of death

C lara still got a thrill of excitement when she opened an envelope with FRO on the front. Family Records Office. What secrets would she uncover now? She was especially looking forward to this one. It could be a biggie.

She had already received George's first wedding certificate from 1887 when he was 21. He married Marjory Gwyneth Hobson, who was five years older than him.

Clara knew that the marriage could not have lasted long as it was only just over three years later that George the widower married Rebecca Laker.

That made it easier to track down Marjory's death certificate. Somewhere between 1887 and 1890. Only 12 black books to look through. And there it was. Piece of cake – she was getting good at this.

Now it had arrived. As Clara let her and Paul into her flat, her foot touched the envelope and she picked it up. But when the door closed behind her, Paul slid the shopping bags containing tonight's dinner across the hallway and grabbed Clara from behind around the waist.

"I've been wanting to do this to you all day," he said, kissing her neck. "Just gazing at you in the office, looking so gorgeous, and not being able to grab you and hold you is the sweetest unbearable torment..."

Clara was torn between on the one hand wanting to let Paul carry on without putting up the slightest resistance, in fact even helping a bit here and there, and on the other giving in to a second burning desire, this time to find out how Marjory met her end.

It was a very short struggle and Paul won by a landslide.

Much later, she awoke in bed as he called her gently from the doorway.

"Supper is served, my lady," he said, coming into the room and holding up her dressing gown for her to slip into.

"Delicious," she murmured.

"You most certainly are. And I hope the dinner will be too."

Even a novice chef like Paul could not go far wrong with grilled steak, baked beans and oven chips. They were both ravenous by now and enjoyed the feast while talking about the piece they wanted to make into a two-page spread the next day.

"You know," said Clara. "We really do need to make a rule here or we'll go quietly bananas."

"What, eat first when we get home?"

"Um, no. I don't mind waiting a bit for my food when there's a good reason." She smiled and leaned across to kiss him. "No, I mean that we really need to ban talking about work when we're not there."

"Fair point. Otherwise, we'll be *Allaire* slaves 24 hours a day."

"Exactly. The magazine came out OK before when we only talked about it at the office. So that is the new rule. Rule number 21 I think."

"I hear and obey."

"And another thing… Oh, Marjory," Clara remembered.

"Actually, I'm Paul, not Marjory. Unless you've just invented rule number 22."

"No. Marjory. I need to find out what she died of."

"I didn't even know she was dead. When did that happen?"

"About 1888."

"Bit late to do anything about it now then, isn't it?"

"I knew you weren't listening. Marjory was George's first wife. When George married Rebecca three years after he married Marjory, he was a widower, so how did Marjory die?"

"Can't we just wait for the film to come out?"

"Where did I put the envelope? It was on the mat when we came in and you, er… distracted me.

"Yes, I'm so sorry. Hell of a battle you put up though. It took all of four seconds before you were the one taking the lead. I've never seen clothes come off so fast. You'd make a lousy stripper."

"Do be a love. Shut up and go and look on the doormat to see if it's still there."

It was. Paul found the envelope under a shopping bag, came back and handed it over. Clara ripped the top off, tore out the certificate and read.

"Bloody hell. Marjory Gwyneth Harvey. Cause of death: drowning. Verdict: misadventure."

"Ah," said Paul. "So George bumped her off. Held her under in the bath and was free to marry his fancy woman."

"You don't think so, do you?"

"1888? Yeah, they were all getting up to that kind of thing then. People married and the first one to get fed up did away with the other one and tried again with a younger mate."

"Hmm," said Clara. "I think I have just come up with rule number 22…"

CHAPTER 52

Susan – Fall guy

(May 1949)

"**B**ernard?" gasped Susan. "What? How did you..? No one saw you, did they? Don't just stand there, you'd better come in."

She stood back and Bernard brushed past her into the tiny room.

When she had shaken off the initial shock, Susan became very angry.

"What in the devil's name are you doing here? Don't you realise that this could ruin everything? If anyone has followed you to me then they have a link to the consignment and we could lose everything. And I mean everything. You fool. You bloody, bloody fool. You can't stay here. You need to go and quickly."

"Not so fast," said Bernard. "I'm here because I want some answers and I'm not going until I get them."

"How did you find me then?"

"That doesn't matter now. What matters is..."

"It *does* matter. You really don't get it, do you? This isn't playing. This is dangerous."

"I know," said Bernard calmly. "That's why I'm here." He pulled a large handgun out of his pocket and spun it around on his finger. "I took the liberty of peeking into one of the crates and found this. Why didn't you tell me this was about gun-running? And ammunition too."

He took a handful of bullets from his pocket and threw them on the bed.

"This isn't earning a bob or two, this is breaking the law big time. How dare you get me involved in something like this?"

Susan smiled. "Oh Bernard, stop making me laugh. What did you think was in the crates? Corn Flakes? Teddy bears? Do you really think we'd have gone to so much trouble if it wasn't dangerous? Do you really think you'd be making so much money out of it if was legal? Oh, don't be such a naïve baby."

"Well, I want nothing to do with it." Bernard threw the gun on the bed and sat down on the wooden chair beside the washbasin. "I'm out."

"Hahaha. Out. It's not that easy, I'm afraid. Your hands are dirty. Receiving stolen goods, aiding and abetting, and handling illegal arms. How would a 10-year prison sentence look on your precious CV?"

"I'll risk that. Will you? I'm going to tell the police what I've found, how it got there, how I thought I was just helping my sister out with an agricultural load. Then it will be my word against yours and Mario's or whatever his name is. I'll take my chance."

"You think that you'll be allowed to get away with that? These people are professionals. They know how to treat squealers. You won't know what's hit you."

"Are you threatening me?"

"I'm just trying to open your eyes. This isn't a parish council meeting or one of your university committees. This is serious. Life and death."

"That's why if anything happens to me, Alice knows what to do."

"They'll soon find out where Alice is, you fool."

"Perhaps. But they don't know where she is now. I don't even know. I've thought things through too."

Bernard was lying about this, but it sounded good. The sort of thing people said in films.

"And what are you proposing?"

"You collect your goods tomorrow and take them away. Leave it any longer and they won't be there."

Susan looked at him.

"Why do you want to spoil everything? This deal will set up the whole family for…"

"I don't care. We're doing just fine. I should never have let us get mixed up in this."

Susan snorted, then sat on the bed and said nothing for a long moment.

"I can't authorise anything like that," she said at last. "I'll need to talk to people. See what they say. They are not going to be happy."

"Yes, well I'm not happy either. Why don't you let me talk to them?"

"You'll need to give me a few minutes to organise things," said Susan. "Stay here and don't go outside whatever happens. I'll be as quick as I can."

Susan slipped on her cardigan and went out of the door, not even looking at Bernard as she left. She went down to the street outside and into the phone box on the corner, fetched some pennies from her purse and dialled.

"Hello? Hello, Henry. We have a problem."

A few minutes later, Susan was back in her room.

"Mario's coming round," she said. "And he's in a mood."

"But he's coming to listen, I hope, not just to shout and try to bully me. That would be wasting his time."

"He can speak for himself," said Susan. "While we're waiting, you never did tell me how you found me here."

"Didn't I?" said Bernard, and left it at that.

The two sat in silence for what must have been about 20 minutes before some heavy footsteps could be heard coming up the stairs. There was no knock but the door opened.

"Mario," said Susan. "This is Bernard."

"And I hear that someone has developed cold feet," said Henry, coming through the door, shaking hands with Bernard and smiling at him affably, then sitting down beside Susan on the bed. "What seems to be the problem?"

"The problem," said Bernard simply, "is that I have found out what is in your precious consignment and I don't want anything to do with it. I want it off my property tomorrow or I tell the police. Couldn't be simpler."

"Oh, it's very simple now, Bernard," smiled Henry. "You entered into a deal with us knowing exactly what you were involved in. We discussed it fully, you, me and Susan. I remember some of the helpful suggestions you made. It was your idea to use the Scotland hideout, isn't that right, Susan?"

"That's right, Mario," said Susan quietly. "We were going to stash it just outside London, But Bernard's idea of Scotland was much better."

"So you see," said Henry, "if you think that you can walk away, drop us in it, stay squeaky clean and the police will just give you a gold star and say no more about it, then you are very, very mistaken. Now let's all sleep on this and then carry on as we were, shall we? No harm done. All friends again."

Bernard gave a small laugh.

"Either you are not listening to me or you don't understand English very well. I want out. I'm done with this. It was a mistake. This is not what I want or what my family wants. You don't need me. Just take the stuff away and be done with it."

"We're not moving it an inch," said Henry calmly. "Now I don't want to play hardball with you, but I will if necessary. And you don't want to see that…"

They all froze as more footsteps could be heard coming slowly up the stairs. Susan looked at Henry in alarm. No one ever came to her room and now she was about to have a third guest of the evening. It was all getting a bit cramped.

The steps reached the top landing and this time there *was* a knock at the door.

Susan looked at Henry. He slipped quietly behind the door and nodded to Susan to open it.

"Hey, *bambina*, I was passing and thought you might be lonely, so I was coming to see if you would like to have a little walk with me." He noticed Bernard sitting in the corner and his smile vanished. "Ah, but I see you have company. Forgive me..." He looked at Bernard with a scowl, then smiled at Susan, then turned to go.

Without thinking, Susan caught his arm to stop him. "Mario. No, don't go," she began.

"Mario?" said, Bernard. "How many Marios are there?"

"There is only one Mario," said Mario.

"Then what about the Mario behind the door?" asked Bernard.

Henry stepped out. "I... we... were just sorting something out. There's only one Mario."

Mario looked from Bernard to Henry and back again, his expression not yet angry, just crestfallen and amazed. Then he turned to Susan. "You are a busy lady, I see," he said. "I will not get in your way. Goodnight."

Again he turned to go and again Susan caught his arm.

"Mario," she said quietly. "This is Bernard. My brother."

"Bernard?" Now Mario *was* angry. "What is he doing here for the love of *il Papa*? He makes a link between him and us, between the cargo in Scotland and us. This is crazy."

Now he was shouting. Henry took him to one side just out of the doorway.

"I can handle this, Mario," he said. "It's a little more complicated now, but I can do it. Why don't you take Susan for a walk like you said and I'll have a quiet word with Bernard?"

"No. I am staying. Perhaps he has played right into our hands."

Unseen by anyone inside the room, Mario drew a forefinger slowly across his throat and raised his eyebrows at Henry.

"Oh don't be a fool," hissed Henry. "There's no need for that. You'd have the cops crawling all over his place in Scotland. You'd never get away with it."

"That's if they ever find the body," said Mario. "We just need to produce evidence that someone has paid the price. Keep the suppliers off our backs. These things are easily managed. I don't suppose anyone knows he is here?"

"No, Mario," said Henry, grabbing him by the lapels. "That's not the way."

"Well, have you got a better way? Because I can't see one."

"Boys, boys. Keep your voices down," said Susan, poking her head out of the door and looking down the staircase with concern. We need to keep our heads cool or we risk losing everything."

"You," said Mario to Henry. "Come downstairs where we can talk properly without everyone listening to us. And you," he added to Susan, "keep your brother here until we come back."

"But..."

"Just do as I say," snapped Mario, then smiled at her. "Be a good girl and let me take care of everything."

The pub was closed and silent by now with hardly anyone left inside it, and the only people left knew that they should keep out of the way when Mario was angry. Mario and Henry went down to the Function Room on the floor below and Susan looked at Bernard. They could not make out what the pair were saying but it was obvious that they were having a serious argument.

Bernard began to wish he had not come, or even better that he had said no to Susan from the start in the Holborn pub. What had he been thinking? Only she had made it seem so straightforward, so neat, so simple. So rewarding.

Susan realised that her whole future depended on the outcome of the discussion in the room below. She strained to hear, but could not make out any words. One of them thumped a table with a loud crash.

Susan stood up from the bed.

"Stay here," she hissed to Bernard, and she too went down the stairs.

Now it was Bernard's turn to listen and wonder. Perhaps he should just sneak past them all, down to the ground floor, out and run away, just get the hell out of this nightmare world that he wanted nothing to do with. Or he could go and tell them that he had changed his mind, that they could leave the cases where they were and he would not breathe a word.

He opened the door and there seemed to be a fight going on now with a chair crashing against a wall. Then Susan screamed. That was it, Bernard ran down the stairs two at a time, leaving Susan's cramped room still and empty once again.

Below, the sounds of arguing continued, then scuffling and more shouting, a cry of pain. And then a shot. Then silence.

CHAPTER 53

Parcel passed

After all this time, Bernard could still hear the sound of that shot. Just a single spitting crack with scarcely an echo, followed by deep, deep quiet.

He strolled along the wide walkway towards the front of the massive liner and gazed out at the sea, which reflected the near full moon broken up by the waves into a thousand fragments of silver on the surface far below him. He put both elbows on the rail and stared down at its reflection. They had sailed from Southampton, around France and Spain, through the Mediterranean, down the Suez Canal, along the Red Sea and had now emerged into the Indian Ocean, heading for the north coast of Australia en route to Wellington, New Zealand. Around 40 days at sea. One way.

Alice had fixed it up, they had said goodbye, and come and see us, and had promised to write and call often.

To Ian, it was no big deal. On the rare occasions he could get away, visiting his parents in New Zealand or the UK was all the same to him. For example, he reasoned, New Zealand and London were about equidistant from Peru.

Sam was equally relaxed. He had managed to extract enough money from Claudette's father to go for his dream. He had released the power of life-giving, anti-ageing, invigorating, rejuvenating seaweed tablets. Atlantis Capsules, they were called and the advertising – without actually saying it in so many words – gave the impression that taking just one a day would make you feel as though you were young again. The actual words said that users would "feel as though you have been cleansed and washed by the tides of an ethereal, youthful ocean". They can't touch you for that sort of vague waffle, can they, those advertising watchdog nit-pickers? Production had begun and the first orders were placed. "Next time I see you," Sam had promised them on that last night, "I will arrive on my private jet, lighting my Havana cigar with a fistful of rolled up £50 notes."

"You'll be the biggest thing to come out of the water since the monster from the green lagoon," laughed Alice. "Good luck to you."

Meg was a little more worried. Coping with Philip on her own was not usually a problem, but she liked to know that Bernard was always just a phone call away and would come at once, take over and fix things up for them. Without him, she felt less safe.

"You have Clara now," Bernard told her. "I am growing old and doddery, Meg. Your daughter is a very, very bright young woman. She can do everything that I could, and will get better and better at it as my powers would surely decline."

Bernard and Philip shared a late-night whisky on the day before the big adventure began. When the two of them were alone, Bernard turned to him and said: "All that matters now is Meg. Look after her and you will come to no harm. I'm proud of the way that you are doing just that. Now keep going. She is a fine woman."

"She is," agreed Philip after a pause. "She surely is. I do try, only sometimes that feeling comes flooding back to me and I can't cope. It's a terrible thing to carry with you, Bernard. I don't even always know what it is, but I always know I did something bad. I should have done something that I didn't."

"I know. I know. But you have tried to make up for it by making Meg happy. That is all that matters."

"Thanks to you. I don't even understand what happened when this thing happened, but I just know that somehow you saved my life."

"Well, now Clara is in charge. It's time I handed over and there could not be a finer person to take the reins. She is a real star, your daughter, and she hasn't even reached her peak yet."

"I'm so proud of her."

Bernard was now at the front of the upper deck and looking down at the massive swimming pool below, deserted and shimmering in the early evening semi-darkness.

So now it was over, he thought. Now all that he had to do was enjoy some quiet days and some adventures with Alice in their new home overlooking the sea down in the south of the south island. It looked blissful. They had toured the country twice and this was the haven they had fallen for.

All a long way from the Black Isle, and the back streets of east London. Perhaps one day he could forget some of the things he had seen and done. But he would never forget the sound of that single shot.

He still remembered running down the stairs after hearing a chair crash against a wall and Susan scream. He rushed into the room and there at the far end, Mario and Henry were fighting, or rather grappling, clutching each other like small-scale sumo wrestlers, pushing back and forth without either gaining the advantage. Too close and entangled even to throw a punch. Mario was a much bigger man, but Henry was wiry and a lot stronger than he looked.

Susan was standing behind them, telling them to stop and talk instead of this. Both ignored her. Bernard wondered if he should join in. But on which side? Should he just try to pull them apart?

Slowly Mario seemed to be getting the upper hand, and then he threw a vicious low blow that doubled Henry over in agony and sent him to the floor, clutching his groin, unable to defend himself. At this point, there was a glint of steel as Mario drew a long blade out of his pocket.

"No!" screamed Susan and tried to wrestle him away, but he swiped the back of his free hand into her face and sent her sprawling against the far wall.

Mario walked slowly up to Henry and kicked him hard in the head, then leaned over and raised the blade.

Then the shot rang out. Mario dropped the knife, fell to his knees and slumped forward over the prostrate form of Henry. It was all over in a second, and for Mario, it was all over.

Bernard turned back the way he had come towards the large entrance door that led to the body of the ship. Alice should soon be ready for pre-dinner drinks.

There were still things that he had not told her. Things that she did not need to know, things that she did not want to know. He had always intended to come clean but it had somehow never happened. One of them always dodged it.

"When he tried to say: 'Shall I tell you exactly what happened that night?' it came out as: 'It was all a long time ago. There's nothing we can do about it. Let it lie.' "

Should he tell her now as a post-script to their old life? Full stop. End. Turn the page for a new chapter.

Just then he heard footsteps behind him and turned to see Alice looking at her loveliest in a black off-the-shoulder dress, her dark hair swept back and held by a shining comb at one side of her face.

"I thought I might find you out here," she said, coming up and adjusting his bow tie, then kissing him and wiping away the lipstick with a tissue.

"You look fabulous," he said, slipping an arm around her waist. "Do you fancy once around the ship, gin and tonics at the bar and then another tour of the menu that never grows old?"

"That, sir, sounds good to me."

They began to walk along the deck towards the stern this time, with the moon now dead in front sending a path of light towards them.

"I've been thinking," began Bernard. "Would the best way to draw a line under our old life before we turn the page and begin our new life, be for me to tell you everything, all my secrets? Share and bury? Then move on?" He stopped and turned to look at her. "There is a lot that you don't know. I'm keeping secrets from you and I don't like doing that."

Alice looked directly into his eyes.

"You still don't get it, do you? We are not *about* to turn the page and begin our new life. We have already turned it. This *is* our new life. We *have* moved on. Whatever you wanted to tell me is all in the past now. That is why we had to go, to leave it all behind. And that is what we have done. You are not in charge any more, Clara is, remember? If there are any secrets to be told, then it's up to her to find someone to tell them to – someone who wants to listen, if such a person exists."

"But I never even told you where all of our money came from. The money to renovate the cottage in the Black Isle, to fund your extravagant lifestyle. You don't think I got all of that from my university scratchings, do you."

Alice reached out her hand and put her upright forefinger firmly across Bernard's lips.

"Can you hear that noise?" she asked.

Bernard looked around him. "Noise? What noise? All I can hear is the ships' engines, and the waves splashing."

"No, no. There it is again. Ah, yes. I know what it is. It's a large gin and tonic with a slice of lime and a big scoop of crushed ice. And I think – yes, it's calling my name."

He laughed. "Ah right, yes, I hear it now. I think I can even hear a second seductively murmuring: 'Bernard! Bernard!' "

"We'd best go in, then. We don't want to keep them waiting, now do we? And the toast is: To the future."

She kissed him warmly and led him gently along the deck, through the big swing door and up the steps to the brightly lit bar.

CHAPTER 54

Philip – Something new, something old

(May 1968)

P hilip's wedding day had been everything he could have wished. His life had just gone on getting better since he had arrived back at Langton. He was crazily, madly, dottily in love with Meg and every minute that he spent with her seemed to him to have been better than the one that went before it. She was beautiful, playful, sensible, arch, organised, sexy, funny, interesting, seductive, warm… just everything that a man could wish for. Whether they were having dinner, talking about a book or something political, watching a television programme, whether they were walking along a beach, talking to family or neighbours, lying in bed reading the newspapers or sitting in their garden – whatever it was that they were doing, Philip just could not imagine anything in the world that he would *rather* be doing instead at that moment.

How had he got so lucky? There did not seem to be a cloud in his sky.

His six-month trial at IJP Jenkinson & Co Ltd in Stevenage had gone so well that he had been offered and had accepted a permanent staff job after just four months. His responsibility was to oversee projects as they came to the business, to make sure that the right people were available at the right time to fulfil each task, to make sure that the client was happy with what the company was producing and to bring the whole to a conclusion that meant the work was done on time, the client was pleased and IJP

Jenkinson & Co Ltd were paid for their trouble. Philip could have been born for the job. He found it easy to juggle all the balls in the air at once, to switch people from one task to another as needed without jeopardising either project and to keep track of everything he was doing. He made lists. Endless, endless lists. Overlapping lists. And he ticked each item off as it was completed. It worked for him and for IJP Jenkinson & Co Ltd. He was now Mr Philip Harvey, Deputy Projects Manager. And he was more proud than he could say to see all those gleaming words at the foot of every one of his letters and memos.

His wages, brought him about three times as much as he was earning on the streets of Brighton and its environs. And no one slammed doors in his face any more. He even shared a secretary, Elizabeth, with the Deputy Technical Manager. Not that he needed to ask her to do anything much. A few letters a week. He preferred to rattle out memos himself on the old office typewriter.

"I'm very pleased with your progress," Ivan told him when he signed his full contract. "I knew that any lad of Thomas's was going to be a good 'un. And that first time I met you confirmed it to me. You haven't disappointed, Philip. Now all you have to do is keep it up and get even better."

He liked Ivan. He was a warm, solid character, who expected much from his staff and somehow seemed to get it.

And Philip saw Meg every day. Living two doors apart made it easy. And sharing a house with Bernard and Alice, who liked to travel, and their son Ian, who had not only flown the nest but most of the time had flown the hemisphere too, and his mother Jane, who was now in her mid-eighties and spent most of her time up in the Black Isle, all meant that Philip was on his own in the house for well over six months of the year. But not for long. Usually less than 10 minutes after he walked through the door, so did Meg.

The first time was when Philip had only been back for a couple of weeks and Bernard and Alice embarked on a coast-to-coast trip across the USA by railroad, starting at Boston and finishing at San

Francisco. That took them a lot of nights. A lot of lovely long nights for Meg to come to dinner and stay for breakfast. When Meg's mother mildly objected and said that Meg was only 19 and wasn't that a bit young to be practically living with a man out of wedlock, even in these permissive times? Meg just said: "Oh, but Mum, we *are* engaged. That makes a difference, surely?"

It did. Meg's mother was overjoyed and could put up no further objections.

"Oh, there's something I forgot to tell you," said Meg casually to Philip as they washed up their dinner plates that evening.

"Let me guess," said Philip. "You're planning to be even lovelier by the weekend. Well, that's a tough task you've set yourself. The very best of luck, because I just don't see anything that you can improve on."

"True, true," said Meg. "But meanwhile if my mother says congratulations to you in the next day or two, don't give her one of your blank looks with your mouth hanging open, will you? Try to look as though you can speak a little English."

"You had better give me a clue as to what she is congratulating me for."

"We-e-e-ell, I *may* just have given her the impression that we are – *cough* – engaged to be married."

"Oh, did you now? How presumptuous. You haven't even asked me yet."

"Didn't we propose to each other a while ago in Brighton?" asked Meg.

"Doesn't count. We were already pretending to be Mr and Mrs Harvey that weekend. But no, we have to go through it all again to make it official. Come on."

He took Meg's hand, got down on one knee, and pulled her down too so that they were both on one knee in the middle of the kitchen floor.

"Come on, then. One… two… three…"

"Will you marry me?" they chorused.

Both jumped to their feet.

"Oh yes," they both answered, then twirled each other around in a long, lingering embrace that become slower and slower as the kissing took over.

An hour later, as they lay on their backs in the hot bedroom, Meg said: "Hey, where's my engagement ring, then?"

"Yes, and where's mine?" asked Philip.

"You don't get one. You just buy *me* one. Haven't you read the small print?"

"Oh, well we'd better go shopping tomorrow. Can't disappoint your mother, can we?"

Naming the day took a little longer. They did not want to get married and live apart, nor did they want to share their home with four other people, even if those people were absent for much of the time. They looked around.

A couple of months later, they went to see a three-roomed flat that had come up for rent just off Langton market square, down towards the river. Their river. They had to put down a hefty deposit but Bernard gave them the money and a bit more besides.

"You can pay me back when you can. Or not. Let's see," he said.

They could afford the rent easily from Philip's new wages. Now they were all set. They picked a Saturday in springtime for the Big Day. It meant waiting for another few months, but they needed that time to make all the arrangements. Meg did most of it, with a lot of help and guidance from her mother, Bernard and Alice, and with Philip doing whatever the other four told him.

Everything was set, with a honeymoon in Spain to follow, a whole week in the sun at a lovely hotel near the beach with its own pool that looked sparkling and sun-drenched in the brochure.

"Oh darling, I can't wait," said Philip.

Meg sighed. "Neither can I. It is going to be a magical day."

It was about 10.30 in the morning on the Thursday before the wedding Saturday and Alice was alone in the house when there was a ring at the doorbell.

"Oh, I've just sat down with a cup of tea," she complained to herself. "What is it now? Flowers? Seating plans? Wedding presents? Suits? Dresses? Jehovah's Witnesses?"

"I'm coming," she called aloud as she got wearily to her feet and crossed the hallway to the front door.

On the step was a young woman, slender and pretty, with long blonde hair and a beige raincoat over a navy print dress. She was very heavily pregnant.

"I'm sorry," she said to Alice. "I'm looking for Philip Harvey. I was told that he lived here, but I'm so sorry if I'm mistaken and I won't bother you any more."

"You'd better come in, love. Are you OK?"

"Yes, I think so."

Alice took her coat and showed her into the front room.

"Make yourself comfortable and I'll get you a cup of tea,… My name is Alice, by the way, and you are?"

"Mary. Mary Brown."

Over a cup of tea, Mary managed to tell Alice her story. How she was in love with Philip and they had wonderful times together in Brighton, but then he lost his job and had to leave suddenly, almost without saying goodbye. He had said that he would come to visit her but he had not been back yet and had not written. After he had gone, she found that she was pregnant. She had lost her job at the guest house where she worked because of it and only had a little money from a few hours a week working in a grocery store. She did not know where Philip lived, but she had heard him talking about a place called Langton so she looked it up in the library. She desperately wanted him to come back again because he was the only person in the world who had ever been kind to her. Then last week her Aunt Vera, who she lived with, died. The only other family she had was Aunt Vera's sister-in-law Emily in Eastbourne, but when Emily saw Mary's condition at the funeral, she called her a "hussy" and made it clear that she wanted nothing to do with her.

"I had to leave Aunt Vera's house because I couldn't afford the rent and I didn't know where to go. I walked up and down Brighton but it was starting to hurt my side. Then I thought that if I could find Philip, he would be nice to me again, would be my friend, and would be on my side. Like before. I just had enough money saved up to try to get to Langton. I came to London by bus, then it took ages walking up and down but in the end, I found the coach up to Langton. I didn't want to ask people in the street for Philip looking like this, so I looked in the phone book for Harvey. There were four and I've tried two of the others with no luck. They were all over the place and took a lot of walking to find them and it was hurting me more and more to move. I have one more chance if this is wrong too. And if I can't find Philip, then I just don't know what else to do or where to go. Does Philip live here?"

Alice moved beside her and put her arms around her.

"That's a horribly sad story, Mary. Let's see what we can do. After all that walking, you need a rest. How would you like a nice bath? Come on, I'll run it for you and you can have a relaxing soak. Always makes me feel better."

"I'd like that, but I don't want to put you to any trouble."

"No trouble at all. I've been pregnant and I know it helped me."

"But does Philip live here? You have been so kind, but you must tell me."

"He does. Yes he does," said Alice. What else could she say?

"Oh thank God. Oh, I'm safe. Philip will look after me. He always has." She burst into tears of sadness and joy.

When Mary was safely in the tub, Alice rushed down to the hallway and picked up the telephone. She dialled a number, got it wrong in her haste and tried again.

"Bernard Harvey," said a voice.

"Bernard, it's Alice. Bernard, you have to come home right now."

By the time Bernard got home and heard Mary's story, it was already gone three o'clock. Philip would be home at about 6.30 and Meg would arrive at the same time. They could not let the two of them walk in and find Mary sitting there waiting. But nor could they send her away.

"What on earth can we do, Bernard?" asked Alice as they left Mary resting on the front room sofa and said they were going into the kitchen to start on dinner. For about the first time, since she had known him, Bernard was at a complete loss.

"We could set her up in the Crown Hotel, but that hardly solves anything," he said. "It buys us a bit of time, but time for what? Philip has done this and he should be the one to sort it out, but this is Meg's wedding week. We can't just dump it on them and ruin everything for her."

Bernard paced up and down. It was now 3.30 and they would soon run out of time.

"Alice, please help," came a faint cry from the front room and the pair raced back to Mary.

"What is it, love?" asked Alice. "Are you OK?"

"The pain in my side has come back. It's really hurting to move or breathe."

Bernard looked at Alice. "I'll call an ambulance, you stay with Mary," he said.

An hour or so later, Bernard and Alice were in a corridor at Bedford General Hospital as Mary was being treated in a closed-off room.

"At least it got us – and Mary – out of the house and out of Meg's way," said Alice.

"He deserves to be horse-whipped," hissed Bernard.

"The poor girl," said Alice, her eyes full of tears. "Oh, it breaks my heart."

"I know," said Bernard, putting his arm around her. "At least she's in good hands now."

It was a little over three hours later when a Dr Sangakarra came out and took them into a private room.

"Are you Miss Brown's relatives?" he asked.

"Well yes, we are," said Bernard. "How is she, doctor?"

"She is sedated now, but she has some fairly serious complications and some internal bleeding. We will know more in the morning. The baby is fine, its heart is sound. The mother, well... You should go and get some rest now. There's nothing more that you can do tonight. We will know more in the morning."

"Thank you, doctor."

Back in the car, Bernard looked at Alice.

"Philip and Meg will be sat at home now without a care in the world. How are we going to go back there and pretend nothing has happened?"

"But we must," said Alice. "None of this is Meg's fault. We can't ruin her life."

"No, you're right. The wedding is in 36 hours. Let's put on the show of our lives, get them married, pack them off on honeymoon and then we have a week to come up with a plan."

"Well my plan tonight," said Alice grimly, "is to feign a headache and smuggle a big glass of wine up to bed."

"Make it a bottle and I'll join you," said Bernard, as he started the engine and swung the car around, out of the hospital car park and back on the road towards Langton.

They visited the hospital the next morning too, but Mary was still being kept asleep and they could not see her. They asked to see Dr Sangakarra and filled him in about their son's wedding the next day but made him promise to call them if there were any developments and assured him that they would be back on Saturday evening when the Big Day was over.

"I do," said Meg.

"You may kiss the bride," said the vicar.

And Philip did, thrilling to the touch of his wife's – his *wife's* – lips on his for the first time. His panic was over now. All he had to do was smile a lot, have his picture taken endlessly, make a short speech, that was in his pocket and that he was reasonably happy with, and then go dancing and drinking champagne for a bit until it was time to jump into the car and head off to Luton Airport and their flight to the Costa Brava sun.

Outside the church, a smiling Bernard came up and shook his hand, then hugged Meg and kissed her on both cheeks. "You look absolutely radiant," he told her. Alice too looked radiant and smiled at everybody. The photographer finally finished and they all went on the 100-yard walk to the Langton Memorial Hall where the reception was to be held. They got there and the tables were laid for a wedding breakfast for 85 guests, with seating plans all drawn up by Meg and Alice, keeping the right mix on each table. The food was very good, and the wine and beer flowed. Bernard, as best man brought the house down with his speech, revealing some secrets about Philip that no one knew, mainly because not all of them were true.

"...and that is when Philip discovered that not *every* cloud has a silver lining..."

He proposed a toast and sat down to wild applause. Philip stood up nervously and thanked everyone from the bottom of his heart, said all the right things, praised Meg, thanked Bernard for being such a good best man, Jane for looking after him when he was "young and foolish", Meg's parents for producing such a wonderful human being, Ivan for giving him the chance to return to Langton. Everyone was in high spirits and the toasts were joined enthusiastically. Then the tables were cleared away and from a bench in the corner, a man with hair down way past his shoulders began to play music. Philip and Meg shared the first dance – *You Were Made For Me* by Freddie And The Dreamers – drank some more champagne and soon it was time for them to leave to catch their flight. Everything was already loaded in the car. "Yes, I've got the tickets *and* the passports," Philip assured his mother. Ivan had led some of his employees on a clandestine trip to the back of the hall to decorate the car with a few tin cans tied to the bumper and *JUST MARRED* written in spray foam on the back windscreen (junior electrician Harry Moffat's spelling had never been too good). And then the bride and groom were gone and the crowd got back to some more serious roistering.

The car stopped around the corner briefly while the driver hopped out to remove the tin cans and toss them into a rubbish bin.

In the car, Philip turned to Meg.

"I don't think I could possibly be happier, darling," he said. "How was your day?"

"Just divine, my lord and master, just divine."

"You did look rather lovely in your frock."

"Gown, you peasant."

"Oh yes? You're a bit lippy for someone who's just been given away, aren't you?"

"Yeah, not even sold. I must be really worthless."

"Oh, I'm sure I'll find a use for you. Draught excluder perhaps."

"I'd prefer bed-warmer."

Then they sped off again into the growing darkness, down through Longford towards Luton Airport and off to a blissful week in the Spanish sun with their whole lives ahead of them and not a care in the world.

Back in Langton, Bernard and Alice – who had restricted themselves to two small glasses of champagne over which they had lingered – slipped away soon after the happy couple and drove back towards Bedford. They did not say much on the way, but Alice had wet eyes for the whole 13 miles. Their false smiles and bonhomie had left both of them exhausted. They knew what no one else in Langton or on the road towards Luton knew. That morning they had received a telephone call from Dr Sangakarra. He apologised profusely for having to give such news over the telephone, but Bernard had asked him to call, and he thought that they should know. A healthy baby had been born a week or two early at a little after 10.15 this morning by caesarean section. Unfortunately, they had been unable to save the mother. Mary died without ever seeing her son.

Now Bernard and Alice, as the baby's closest available living relatives, were off to visit that son and to start to work out what was going to happen to him.

CHAPTER 55

The job interview

A few weeks before Bernard and Alice left the country, Clara had opened yet another fat envelope that she found on her doormat. She unfolded the paper inside and read it. "What?" she said aloud. "WHAT?"

She studied the paper again, from close up. That's definitely what it said. She had just opened Philip's birth certificate. She wondered why she had bothered to get it, but was running out of things to send for. Of course, it would say Mother: Jane Harvey. Father: Thomas Harvey (Laker). But it didn't. Instead, it read:

Philip Ronald Harvey (Laker). Born: February 3 1947. Mother: Susan Harvey (Laker), spinster. Father: -.

Clara's hands were trembling as she tried to piece it all together. Her father's mother was not Grandma Jane after all, but the mysterious Susan who ran away. That meant that Bernard was Philip's *uncle,* not his brother. So her Uncle Bernard was in fact, what? Her *great*-uncle? Her whole family tree, everything she had known all her life about the people she grew up with was coming apart in front of her.

What else did it mean?

Grandma was really *Great*-Grandma and her real grandmother was Susan. Goodness only knew who her real grandfather was. And what about Sam and Ian? If Bernard were Philip's uncle, then Sam and Ian were not Philip's nephews, but his cousins. And they were not her cousins, but... but what? Second cousins? No idea.

Clara came close to panicking. She wished that she did not know any of this, but now that she knew it, she could not un-know it. And what could she do with it? Who could she talk to?

She remembered the picture she kept of Susan, and tried to remember her face. Dark hair and dark eyes. Pretty. A knowing smile on her lips. Susan Harvey. Otherwise Laker. Grandma...

Clara realised that she needed to have a serious talk with Bernard before he got on that ship. Alone. On her terms and without any bluster or avoiding the issue. What did he know? And what would he tell her?

She ran over in her mind the growing list of puzzles, answers and mysteries that were piling up in her family in-tray:

George and the Otherwise Lakers

Marjory

Philip and his mother Susan

Philip's ramblings about the bad thing he had done

And then there was Muriel's revelation while they were at Grandma's cottage.

She and Paul were sitting out in the garden one morning having a very late breakfast when they heard a voice behind them.

"Well, this *is* a surprise. Clara, how lovely to see you. We weren't expecting you. And you've brought a friend. How wonderful. I thought it was Sam at first."

"Muriel, good to see you too. I was going to pop down and say hello later but you've beaten us to it. Muriel, this is Paul. We work together. We thought we'd take advantage of this beautiful cottage before anything happens to it and someone decides to sell up."

"Hello, Paul. Lovely to meet you." Muriel did her best curtsey. "Oh, they're not planning to sell it, are they? That would be such a pity. Lose all those links to the past."

"Well no decisions have been made," said Clara. "I don't think they will but you really can never tell. I agree with you. I would vote to keep it if we can afford it. I'd certainly miss coming here. Muriel, do come and join us."

"Oh, I won't stop. I have a few errands to run..."

"Nonsense. Paul, why don't you get Muriel a cup of tea and bring those biscuits out."

"Yes, ma'am. Muriel, please come and sit down here. I won't be a second."

In fact, Muriel stayed for more than an hour and told them stories of the old days, of when Jane and Thomas first lived here in the cottage. And she told of the two long visits by Bernard and Alice.

"How long were those visits, Muriel?" asked Clara.

"Oh, let me think. Let me think. It was all a long time ago. Let me see. The first would have been just after the war, a year or so after. I didn't know they were here at first. Ian was with them but he was just a toddler. And before we knew anything, Jane had given birth to another baby – to your father, Philip. Oh he was a lovely boy and they made a very sweet family. I didn't even know she was expecting, well she was such a slim lady you could not have told really. And we didn't see much of them for a while. It was very wet around that time and no one went out too much."

"Really? I suppose a lot of people gave birth at home in those days?" asked Clara.

"Oh, yes, especially round here. The midwife, Mrs MacDonald would come round on her bicycle and that was it."

"And you said *two* long visits?"

"The other one was more recent. Probably towards the end of the Sixties, I would think. Thank you," said Muriel, taking the biscuit that Paul offered her. "It was strange. A bit like the other time. We didn't know anyone was here, although it was a bit hotter. Then Alice had a baby boy? Must have been Sam, I suppose. Yes, that's it. Little rascal, he was. Some of the tricks he got up to."

"So Bernard and Alice arrived, and this time you didn't realise that Alice was pregnant?"

"Well, you often don't. Not around here. People are not busybodies the way they are in towns. Folk can come and go and no one is standing on a street corner checking them in and out with a clipboard. We're not a nosy bunch, you know." She laughed.

When Muriel had gone, Clara just stared into the middle distance with a frown on her face. What did it all mean?

She had to temporarily put such thoughts to one side as she realised that Paul had pulled her up gently by the hand and without a word being said, was already leading her down the garden path, back into the cottage and up the narrow stairs. Ah well. It will keep, she thought dreamily.

It was one more mystery to add to the list, though. One more question to ask Bernard. She got her chance suddenly without having to beg for it. Her office phone rang in the middle of a quiet afternoon and it was Bernard.

"Can you talk? I'm not interrupting anything, am I?"

"Well, I was just about to make myself some tea, but talking to you is every bit as good."

"And no messy teabags to clear up," he laughed. "Are you doing anything tonight?"

"Not especially," she said. The plan had been to have an early night with Paul, but that was now the lovely plan almost every night, so a slightly later early night would not hurt. "Why, what's on?"

"Well, Alice is away seeing some friends and I thought it might be a chance to catch up with my favourite niece before I go on my travels."

"Don't you mean *great*-niece," Clara thought but stopped herself and went instead with: "Hey, I'm your *only* niece. That's no compliment at all."

"Still true, though. I was going to buy you dinner."

"Favourite nieces don't come cheap."

"I wasn't thinking burger joint. How about that place in Notting Hill that we went to for Alice's birthday last year."

Wow, thought Clara, that is certainly not cheap.

369

"Sounds divine. I'd better get changed out of my boiler suit and wellies, I suppose."

"See you there for a drink at the bar at 7.30?"

"Lovely. Thanks, Uncle Bernard. See you there."

Clara typed out all of her questions, printed the list and popped the paper into her handbag. She might never get such a good chance again and didn't want to forget anything.

"Isn't this the place that Aunt Alice got her Eton Mess recipe from?" asked Clara as she sat on her high barstool and took a drink of the best Sancerre she had ever tasted.

"You know, I think it was. Nearly got us thrown out for barging into the kitchen unannounced, but she managed to talk her way out of it. She still makes the best Eton Mess ever."

"Yes, she does. I might have it tonight. Just to compare, you know."

Bernard was looking tanned and well, but if anything a touch worn and tired around the edges. Something about his eyes suggested that he had not been enjoying the full eight hours every night of late.

"So how's life with you, young Clara?" he asked brightly enough. "That evil boss of yours still beating you with clubs and defrauding HMRC?"

"Shhh... that's a secret," laughed Clara. "No, your pep talk worked like a dream." She put on a deep barristery voice. " 'Well it seems to me that I have four options, wouldn't you say, Peter?' Long story short, I got him to agree that he would rather leave his job and wander around Europe pretending to be human than leave it escorted by the boys in blue and taken off to be measured for a nice suit with arrows all over it."

"He went quietly, eh?"

370

"Surprisingly. And he left his son in charge."

"What the one who never says anything? What was his name? Patrick? Peter?"

"Paul. And he turns out to be such a nice guy – now that I have, shall we say, tweaked him here and there – that I have fallen madly, hopelessly in love with him and we are officially a bona fide lovey-dovey couple."

"Well, well, well. Congratulations, Clara. I wish you all the best. Sounds as though it all worked out well after our last little chat."

"Beautifully. Really beautifully, thank you. I should be paying for this meal, only…" she looked around her with a mock-scared face, "…I think I might have to take out a second mortgage just to cover the wine."

"No, this one's on me," reassured Bernard. "And," he added, looking directly at her with a half smile, "this time it's *me* who needs *you* to do *me* a favour."

"A favour, eh? That might cost you a starter *and* a dessert."

The waiter hovered up from nowhere to tell them that their table was ready if they would like to follow him. He took their glasses onto a silver tray and walked to the back of the restaurant to an airy table by a window which overlooked a small heavily flowered garden and some trees beyond.

"So what is this favour that little me can possibly do for big grown-up you?" asked Clara when they had ordered. "Seriously I can't begin to think of how you might need me for anything. You're so… so in charge…so capable… of anything."

He sat back while the waiter topped up their glasses with another eighth of a centimetre of wine each.

"Families," he said slowly at last, "are like companies. They don't run themselves. They need people in charge, making decisions and doing what's best. Unlike companies though it's not just a question of making a lot of money and if anyone gets in the way, that's too bad. Just 'let some people go' as the euphemism says. Families aren't like that. You have to take everyone along with you, take them all into account and do what's best for every single member if you can. You can't lose a couple even if you want to and they deserve it. They're all there for keeps. Then there are conflicts. What's right for one member might not be what's best for another. So then what do you do? And there are secrets. What one person knows another doesn't, and the second person may be harmed if they *did* know. And once you are locked into keeping secrets, you are in trouble. We talked a bit about this once before, didn't we?"

"We did," said Clara, "but go on."

"Well, it's the same with keeping secrets in peoples' 'best interests'. Gets tricky. And what if you make a wrong call? Who knows if a decision you made could blow up in your face? Or in someone else's face?"

Bernard grabbed the bottle and poured them each a proper glassful, then as the waiter started hurrying over, he held it up, empty, with a smile, raised eyebrows and a nod to indicate that another might be a good idea.

Clara said nothing. She did not want to stop Bernard from revealing whatever he was about to reveal. The questions could wait.

"So I suppose what I'm saying is that it's not an easy job and that in the end, it takes it out of you. And that in the end, you need to hand over the torch to someone younger. To, say, a favourite niece."

"Or do you mean," asked Clara, "to a favourite *great*-niece?"

Bernard looked up with wide eyes.

"Ah, you know that much at least."

"I know some but not all. I know enough to know the questions I need to ask to know more."

"And after all I've said, you still want to know more?" he asked gently.

"I don't know. Part of me wants not to know what I already know, but that's not an option. I'm left with a three-quarters finished crossword puzzle. The last few clues are driving me nuts."

"Ah yes: I am in blood stepped in so far that should I wade no more, returning were as tedious as go o'er. As they say."

"Blood? You haven't been going around stabbing kings, have you, MacBernard?"

"Not really. Sometimes feels like it. Anyway, this is like a job interview in reverse. The starting point is that I want to give you the job. Now I need to convince you to take it. I am getting on for 70, I'm growing tired, and I need to retire. And Alice is right, if I stay in this country, surrounded by you all, I'll never bow out. The buck will always find its way to me. New Zealand, now, that's a different haka of fish."

A gaggle of waiters approached with the main course and elaborately served up some splendid fillet steak and sea bass that both smelled divine.

"So is this the point at which you ask me what I see myself doing in five years' time?" asked Clara when they had gone. "Or shall we go straight to: 'Do you have anything you'd like to ask me?'"

"And do you?"

"Oh boy, how long have you got? I think we'd better order breakfast as well."

"Perhaps we should start with what you *do* already know," said Bernard. "It could save a lot of time."

"All right," said Clara. "This steak is fantastic, by the way. It just melts when you bite it. Anyway. Let's start with what I know from the birth, marriage and death certificates I've been sending away for..."

"I see," said Bernard. "You're a real pro, Clara. Job's yours. Can we have the bill please?"

"Not so fast. Right, where shall we start? You, your dad Thomas, your sister Susan, and your 'brother' Philip are all officially Otherwise Lakers. By rights, Sam, Ian and I should be too, but it seems to have been dropped by the time we came along."

She told him her supposition that between Thomas being born fatherless to Rebecca Laker and the rest coming along,

Rebecca had actually later married Thomas's father, to whit, George.

"I can't prove that at this late stage," laughed Bernard, "but that's the conclusion I came to as well."

"Ah but did you know what happened to George's *first* wife?"

"His first wife? I didn't even know he had one."

"Ah, well then, Sherlock, here's another mystery that we'll never solve. George's first wife was called Marjory and just before Thomas was born, she drowned."

"Wow. That's a real turn-up. Drowned, eh? And what no criminal charges?"

"Coroner's verdict was misadventure. Tad suspicious though."

"Just a bit. You don't think that George and Rebecca did away with her, do you?"

"Who knows? I hope it was just an accident. Guess we'll never know."

"Not a bad start though. I wasn't expecting to learn much new tonight, but that's a stonker. But not really a problem or burden for us to bear now after more than a hundred years."

"True," agreed Clara, "but I included it to be thorough. And it is a rather important moment in the family tree. If Marjory hadn't died, then you and I would not even exist. George would not have married Rebecca, Thomas would not have been born, would not have married Jane, would not have had you and Susan, there would be no Philip, and without you and Philip, there would be no Ian and Sam and me. We owe everything to that little word Misadventure."

"When you put it like that, it is rather key," agreed Bernard.

"Now it gets more tricky, though." Clara paused, took a long breath and then went on. "My Dad is *not* your brother but your nephew. His parents were not Grandma and Thomas but the mysterious Susan and *another* unnamed father. I don't have a guess this time. Do you want to start there? Oh, and Muriel on the Black Isle told me about some very interesting and lengthy visits that you and Alice paid to Grandma's cottage just before Sam and Philip were born. Very mysterious. Nobody knew that Jane or Alice were pregnant, no one saw them around and then POP two babies appeared."

"You do know a lot more than I thought," said Bernard. "I'm so impressed."

"And... and there's some more that I don't know if I should mention it."

"Mention away. We're in slate-clean-wiping territory now. No secrets left."

"OK. Well, I saw Mum and Dad recently and we sat up drinking whisky after dinner. Paul was there on an introductory visit and they got on well..."

"Always a relief," laughed Bernard.

"Anyway, after the umpteenth drink, Dad started talking. He came out with the most amazing stuff as though he were saying that he had an egg for breakfast. I don't know what he meant but he kept saying that he had done something really bad and you told him off for it and it was hard to live with."

"You see," said Bernard. "This is where it starts getting tricky, where it starts unravelling. Philip is now paying the price for a lifetime of guilt. And I'm paying the price for telling him too much that I now wish I hadn't. He couldn't handle it. *Crime And Punishment*. He is showing signs of a strained mind, shall we say. Not an entirely reliable witness."

"But you're not denying point blank what he says."

"As with many things that happened a long time ago, truth gets twisted until no one can say with any certainty what really happened and what didn't."

"That's prevaricating, isn't it?"

"Perhaps. Perhaps it is. Look, the fact remains that I cannot tell you everything but that doesn't matter. Your job now is to safeguard the future. The past can take care of itself in the end. It will die with me and Philip and then it's as cold as George and Rebecca. No one alive knows a thing. All safe. But there will be issues in the future, and that's where you need to come in. That's when, if there's a problem that threatens the family, Clara Harvey comes swooping out of a starry sky and tidies it up before stripping off the green paint and climbing back into her phone box."

"Um, I think you're getting your superheroes mixed up a little there," laughed Clara.

"Probably," said Bernard, "but this superhero is not going to be around any more. So if Philip has a problem he cannot cope with or Sam has an identity crisis or if anything else unforeseen crops up, this family needs someone to sort things out. And it's not me. It's you. I cannot answer all of your questions. I can only ask you to trust me on some things that it really is better for you not to know, and to take it from here without trying to force my hand."

"But I thought we were in slate-clean-wiping territory? No secrets, you said."

"Some secrets will always remain. Even if you complete your crossword you will never know why the compiler picked that particular word for 14 across."

"So you won't tell me everything?"

"Clara, have you told your mum about Philip? What would she make of it? She has grown up with a picture of how the world around her works. Are you going to destroy that for her? What good would it do? You are the future, not the past. Why try to solve everything when it would just hurt people?"

"I know what you mean. It's been going round and round in my head since I knew. They have a right to know but I don't have a right to tell them."

"Correct. Let me tell you a story," said Bernard. "I knew something that you still do not know about Philip and I kept it from him for some very good reasons, mainly to protect Meg. But as time passed, it kept eating away at me. Did I have any right to keep such a big secret from him? It was his life. Surely he had a right to know? In the end, I felt I had to, so I told him. Some of it at least. Do you know, your father has never been the same man since? It was too big for him to take in. He went from a happy, loving husband and father to a guilt-riddled, nervous, frightened, broken shell of what he was. It's the worst thing I ever did to him. If I'd just kept that secret, Philip would have been well. Instead, I've hurt him and Meg – even though she doesn't know what I told him. And all for nothing. It's the worst thing I've ever done and I swore then and there that I would never be reckless with secrets again. And I didn't even tell him the whole story. Thank goodness."

He shook his head sadly and went on.

"People have a right not to be lied to if they ask, but if they are perfectly happy as they are and they *don't* ask, because they have no idea that there is even a question *to be* asked, what right do you have to slap them in the face with something that could do them untold damage? And that is why I cannot, will not answer some of your questions," said Bernard and took a long drink from his glass.

"You mean, because I know some things but can't tell the truth, I am now really just like you?"

There was a pause as they both stared straight ahead.

"Just like me."

"I'm no better than you. I *am* you."

"Welcome to the club. There are only two members," said Bernard, laying a hand gently on her arm.

"Yes," said Clara. "And one of them has just resigned."

377

POSTSCRIPT:

Ghosts' reunion

"**I** do," said Clara.

"You may kiss the bride," said the vicar.

Clara and Paul were standing on exactly the same two worn flagstones where Philip and Meg had stood to make their vows some 30 years earlier. The same stones again where Rebecca and George had pledged their lives to each other more than a century before. St Andrew's Church in Langton had seen a very large number of young men being told by a cohort of vicars down the years that they could now kiss their brides.

It was the last thing that either George or Rebecca had expected they would ever be able to do – to stand in this church and be accepted as an officially married couple. When they used to meet in their hideaway, they thought that their choice was either to hide away or to run away – with all the uncertainty and pain left behind that such an action would entail.

When Marjory's body was found early on the Sunday morning, caught up in some reeds by the weir in Langton, where the river had taken it after George had reported his wife missing the evening before, the town was shocked and the police baffled. There was not a mark of violence on Marjory's body, except for some nasty scratches on her hands and arms and legs, but there were brambles and thorn bushes all along that stretch of the River Ivel, so that did not provide any clues. Neither police nor magistrates could find a motive or a culprit. George was questioned but his grief was plain for all to see and no hint of suspicion was levelled at him. He had been working some miles away, moving a large number of fence posts. He had been seen there by several walkers and horse riders, and the work he said he was doing had certainly been done.

The equally puzzled coroner recorded a verdict of Misadventure, and the mystery was put to sleep. George was consoled by all but took his fate with stoicism. He was always a quiet man and although inwardly his thoughts were a turmoil of joy, fear and guilt, outwardly he bore his grief with equal dignity.

Not so Old John. His sadness at losing his only child could find no solace. Although he and George made the best of their life together, and George's parents invited him into their home for all of their meals, he soon became a husk of himself and that winter a chest infection carried him off. He had no more resistance.

George and Rebecca kept their joy to themselves. They knew that they had to respect the laws of decency and not be seen together too soon, but when their son Thomas was born, George did begin to call on Becky's parents, where he was welcomed. The old couple were filled with shame at their daughter's fall, but the baby Thomas was such a darling that he comforted them all and soon had them laughing again at his gurgles and his smiles. And they began to suspect and even hope that they knew who the real father was, although their daughter had always refused to say.

"George dotes on that baby," said Becky's mother one day.

"He does, mother. He most certainly does," agreed Becky's father. "Dost thou think that Becky's saviour has become Becky's secret admirer?"

"I would not be surprised, father. I think that in some lights the shape of the baby's and the man's noses look somewhat the same."

"Well," said Becky's father. "It is not as we'd ha wished it to happen, but she could do a lot worse for herself."

"Ay, that she could."

Gradually George and Becky with little Thomas began to be seen together around Langton, soon walking out quite openly, and within 18 months of Marjory's drowning, their banns were read at St Andrew's.

"I can scarce believe that we are soon going to be together, my own darling Becky," George said one day as they strolled arm-in-arm through Langton Market just as he had always wished but never dared to hope that they one day would. Becky's mother was taking care of the young Thomas, so they were a carefree young couple with nothing to keep them apart.

"Nor I, my love. Nor I," said Becky. "It has hardly been a straight road and I would not have wished for such an awful accident to befall that poor woman, but that is all the past now and today I could not be happier."

"Shall I buy you a gift at the market to celebrate?" he asked. "What would you have?"

"Why I always took a shine to those trinkets on the stall with the black canvas canopy. Shall we go and take a look?" She smiled at him archly, understanding his thoughts.

They went over and Becky picked about among the boxes and bags of ornaments, bric-a-brac, pottery and toys. George backed off a little and stood on the very spot where he had stood when he first saw Becky more than three years earlier. He remembered vividly how he had known that day that a man is in charge of his own fate if he has the will to take it in his hands. That is not exactly how it worked out for him. Or had it? Fate had to intervene and do its own work. But he had stood by instead of trying to avert its purpose. Had he been wrong about his thoughts on that first day then? He did not know. But he did know that when Becky looked up and saw him standing there gazing at her, the world had turned on its head for them.

Now she smiled and beckoned him over.

"Look, George. Look at this small bronze bell. Why I think it is the very twin of my dearest treasure that a very sweet man once gave me."

"I think an even sweeter man should buy this one for you then. I hope it is not spoken for by some gaggle of ruffian girls."

"You are still the rudest man in Langton as ever you were," she laughed.

It was not spoken for, so George bought the bell, handed it over to Becky and she lifted it up and made the same sweet tinkling sound that had resounded down the years. Becky repaid him with a smile and a kiss. In all his dreams of that moment, he had received only the smile. The kiss was more than he had ever dared to hope.

"I can't begin to tell why," said George, "but life is so much simpler now."

"It must be because you did a good thing and rescued me when I most needed a friend."

"So it must," smiled George, turning his head away so that Becky would not see the dark shadow which briefly clouded his eyes.

He had never told Becky what happened on the day that Marjory tried to look into their hideaway. What purpose would it serve? It would only upset her and possibly ruin their life together and their children's lives for generations to come. He would have to keep that knowledge locked in his own heart and hope that it would slowly fade and not fester there.

George often thought about the flash of insight he had that first day when a veil seemed to be lifted from his eyes. In the end, he concluded, that moment *had* changed him.

Before that day, the old George would just have accepted his lot and got on with what fate had given him, not daring to think that he, a puny, poor peasant, could change anything. That old George would never have built the hideaway, never tried his all to meet Becky again, and so Marjory would not have risked her life to find him out. He would still be living unhappily with her.

But his first sight of Becky told him that there was life in this life that a man could seize. It was not just do as you are bid and wait for the afterlife. He had dared to hope.

And so George and Becky made their vows and became man and wife. Behind them at the back of the church by the little porch where parishioners shuffled in, was the large stone font, which had also seen its share of history. Here over the course of the next six years, Grace, Ellen and Frederick Harvey were all one at a time welcomed into the world as Becky and George looked proudly on, with young Thomas standing beside them. Later, Thomas too was baptised, now that he was part of the Harvey family, even though he would secretly carry the Laker badge for the rest of his life. He had not been christened as a baby, because, although Becky was planning to marry the widower George, Thomas was not recognised as having a father and it was not felt right at the time. But now they were a whole family, living together in the cottage where Marjory grew up, just by George's old home. His old parents were thrilled at his new happiness.

"George smiles now," said his mother. "I never thought to see him smile again."

"I don't think that he was ever happy with Marjory," mused George's father. "It was perhaps a mistake to force them on each other."

"Well at least we are a happy family now," said George's mother.

At last, she thought to herself. At last.

Susan never stood on those flagstones to be kissed as a bride, but she had been there many times for christenings, weddings and the odd funeral. And she did drive by the church one day when the fancy took her to see the old town of her birth once more.

"There, that is the hovel where I grew up. Slow down. Stop a minute." She pointed out the house as they drove into Langton from London on a Tour Of My Murky Past, as she called it. "Can you believe that this is where I breathed my first air. This small town wasteland."

Henry brought the Bentley to a halt and they both gazed at the tiny, weather-beaten cottage. Then he drove on with a smile. Susan had been itching to revisit Langton for some time, having told him all about her childhood and how she came to London seeking work and met Ronaldo, though skipping most of the details of that early encounter.

"I think," said Henry, that the three buildings we sold in Westminster this week would buy this whole town."

"And all the people in it," laughed Susan. "Ugh! Not that anyone would want them."

Susan was not concerned that anyone in Langton would recognise her. She looked nothing like the former waif that ran away on the train that morning with Annie. For a start, Susan was no longer a brunette with straight, badly cut hair, but a voluptuous blonde with a high hairdo that cost plenty. Her clothes too were not makeshift and mend any longer, but came from the finest West End fashion houses, imported from Paris and Italy.

Everything that she had hoped and dreamed had come to pass as it was foretold so many times by Susan herself. Their property empire worked exactly as Henry had described it, flourishing from the earliest post-war boom and then steadily growing. Money makes money was not their official slogan, but might as well have been. They were legitimate, respected, a part of the establishment. Henry had even begun the process of standing as a Member of Parliament, and Susan served on several prestigious charity boards that boosted her standing in society.

Henry had been as good as his promises in every way. After Mario was shot, he sprang effortlessly into action. First, he sent Bernard packing and told him that all would be well and no one would be arrested just as long as he kept to his part of the original bargain.

"You are in this too deeply now," Henry told him calmly. "The upside for you is that we now have one fewer hand reaching out for a share of the money, so that means that your cut goes up. What could be better? But if you cross us, then I swear that you will go to the gallows for this murder. There are two witnesses here and we can find a few more if we need them. They will all testify that they saw you shoot Mario dead in cold blood as he sat on a chair pleading for his life. So it's not much of a choice for you, is it? Now get out and I never want to see you around here again. Understand?"

Bernard nodded silently, turned and after a quick mute glance at Susan he was gone.

But Henry still had some work to do. He had a dead body and a murder weapon on his hands. He dealt with the weapon first, taking the gun from Susan, who was still holding it and had not moved from the spot. Henry spent some time wiping it all over carefully with a soft handkerchief, wrapping it in a thick wodge of paper and stuffing it into a big envelope that he found in a desk in the corner of the room, then sealing it with line after line of sticky tape. He went down to the back of the pub and up to a car that was waiting. Opening the passenger door, he put his package on the empty seat and said to the driver: "Michael, take that to Waterloo Station in the morning, check it into the Left Luggage office and bring me the ticket."

"OK boss," confirmed the driver.

Henry went back into the pub. I'll deal with that at my leisure, he thought.

"Are you OK, Susan," he asked when he got back. She had not moved from the spot.

"I think so," she said.

"You saved my life. Thank you. I won't forget what you did. If you hadn't it would have been you and Mario standing here now wondering how to dispose of my body."

"I couldn't let him kill you in cold blood, darling," she said. She was glad she had the idea of taking the gun down with her and of loading it on the stairs and slipping it into her pocket, just in case. She had a feeling that the row on the floor below could turn ugly. And when she saw Mario pull out the blade it was an instant, simple choice. If Mario survived and Henry died, she would be a well-off small-time crook in the east end of London, still looking for the main chance. But if Henry came out of it alive, she would be a property queen in the swanky west end of London. So either let Mario kill Henry. Or stop him. It was the choice of a moment. Stagnate or move on upwards. Her whole destiny was before her. It was obvious what she must do and she was glad she had. But what now?

"What are we going to do?" she asked Henry.

"Two things we have to do. Let them know that Mario tried to double-cross everyone and keep the goods and the money for himself, but that he was ambushed and shot. And that only he knew where the stuff is. That bit's easy. I'll sort that tomorrow."

He went behind the bar and fished out a couple of glasses. "Scotch?" he asked. "You look as though you could do with a drink."

"Yes. Please," she said softly. "And Mario?"

Henry poured two good slugs and brought the glasses over to where Susan still stood.

"Here."

He took a drink and winced from the cuts inside his mouth, then swallowed. Susan sipped hers slowly.

"What about Mario?" she repeated.

"I can't decide whether to let the cops in and we all plead dumb or whether to disappear him. Trouble with calling the police is that they tend to spot things that we may have missed. And they will probably want to know why I have cuts and bruises. Doesn't look good. I think on the whole the disappearing game is favourite."

And so, if ever a particular railway bridge over a major road in the east end of London is one day demolished and the concrete that makes up its main support is ever bulldozed to rubble – which would take quite a lot of smashing, given that it is reinforced with a lattice network of inch-thick steel rods, bound up and lashed together with steel wire – if that ever happens, the mystery of what became of Martin Johnson, or Mario Giacomelli as he was known, might be solved. Yet such a demolition is unlikely to occur within the next 50 years, by which time few living souls will remember Mario Giacomelli or even know that he went missing, and if anyone did, the chances of a concrete-riddled rotted corpse yielding up too many secrets is small.

It had all worked out for the best, thought Henry as he drove on through Langton, down to the market square.

"What now, my darling?" he asked Susan, who was staring around her, wide-eyed and mouth open. Secretly she was hoping to meet Annie again. She had a dream of seeing a dowdy creature pushing a pram along the road and of making the Bentley stop beside her, winding down the window, telling Annie who she was and reminding her of what she had said on that first trip to London. "I know something good will happen."

But Annie was nowhere to be seen.

"I cannot believe that I used to live in this rat hole with these rat people," said Susan. "Oh darling, you do see why I had to leave, don't you?"

"Well if you hadn't, I would not be here now," he said. "I might be the one encased in some heavy-duty concrete by now. And if you hadn't left this place and we'd never met, that would have deprived me of some of the finest days and hours and exquisite moments of my entire life."

"You say all of the sweetest things, Henry, darling," she said, patting his arm. "Drive on round to the right now. I just want to see my old school and then we can get out of this stinkpit and go somewhere nicer. Where are you taking me now? You never did tell me?"

"We have a reservation at the finest hotel in Cambridge. We check in and then I will personally carry you aboard a stylish punt and propel you in seemingly effortless majestic luxury along the backs down the heavenly Cam while we sip champagne and nibble something or other that the hotel is preparing for us, after which we will repair to our hotel suite and try to find some way of passing the hours until it is time for us to enjoy the most exquisite dinner. How does that sound, my darling?"

"Why just divine," she laughed. "And I think that I might be able to help you with the passing the hours until dinner part of your project. I have a plan that is every bit as enjoyable as it is filthy."

Susan stretching herself as the Bentley passed St Andrew's Church and the Community Hall and headed up towards her old school and then north towards Cambridge.

Everything that she had dreamed from that first trip to London with Annie had come to pass. From a grubby farmyard wretch, she had become one of the most prestigious women in London. Propelled by her destiny, she had climbed step after step from barmaid to society darling, property magnate, Mrs Susan St John (in name if not in fact), half of St John Partners (pronounced *sin-jun* to rhyme with bacon), the reputable development company that straddled the capital and was about to launch its proven business acumen in six other English towns and cities, one every six months for the next three years. Henry had joked that when they were married she should shorten her surname since Susan Sin suited her much better, and he so much enjoyed living in Sin.

A little over a year after the shooting, Bernard received a phone call to say that the consignment was to be collected at midnight on the last day of the next month. He must be there to hand it over and when it was checked and found to be all in order, he would be given an envelope that contained £10,000. Did he have any questions? He had no questions.

Bernard made the trip to the Black Isle and at exactly midnight on the last day of the month, two large but unremarkable vans drove quietly round to the back of the cottage and four men got out. They did not bother to knock but went round to the shed at the back and found Bernard waiting for them. They exchanged a glance but said nothing. Then one of them, Henry, went alone into the shed where Bernard indicated. He carefully pulled away the plastic sheets that had been covering the cases, examining each crate one by one, taking everything out, counting it twice, ticking it off a list and replacing it. Then he took one more gun out of his pocket, slipped it into the case that was one short and re-sealed all of the crates. It took almost an hour. In another 20 minutes, the other three men had loaded the crates into the vans and then got in themselves. Henry, who had watched the operation carefully, came back to Bernard. If they recognised each other they gave no sign of it.

"All seems in order," said Henry and handed Bernard a fat envelope. It was sealed.

He turned, climbed into the leading van and the two vehicles silently pulled away and were gone into the night.

Bernard counted the money. There was even more than he had been promised as Susan had slipped an extra present in when she counted it out. For the baby, she thought to herself. Bernard realised that his life had just changed. He had all the repairs and improvements they had planned to Grandma Jane's cottage done and paid cash with a fraction of it, bought his own house outright, and invested the rest. There was about to be a post-war boom and within five years, the money Bernard put away was worth twenty times as much. It continued to grow. His family would never have money worries again.

Before Henry and Susan took a right turn off the A1 at Sandy to head eastwards to Cambridge, this was the same route that Bernard and Alice had driven towards Bedford Hospital a few days after Philip's wedding. They found the baby boy sleeping soundly and seeming content and well as they peered through the screen from the hospital corridor.

"Oh he's a darling," said Alice. "The poor little mite." And she wiped her eyes again on her sopping wet hanky.

"These are unusual circumstances," the hospital official said as they sat in a small room to "work out the details".

"They are," said Bernard. "But I think you will agree that what is most important now is the welfare of the child."

"Oh, indeed it is. But we must be sure that we know exactly what that welfare entails."

He consulted a sheaf of notes. "Apparently, Miss Brown has no living relatives, not even it seems the father of this child. She did, however, make a verbal plea on several occasions while she was being treated here."

"Oh?" said Bernard. "What did she say?"

"She expressed a desire that a Philip Harvey should be told where she was. He would come at once and 'fix' everything, she insisted. She maintained that he is the father and he would save her once he knew about the baby. Do you know Philip Harvey or his whereabouts?"

"Yes we do," said Alice with a sigh. "He is our son."

"I see. Well, perhaps you would be so good as to ask him to come and visit us so that we can effect a transfer."

"It's not that easy, I'm afraid," said Bernard.

"Not that easy?"

"He left yesterday for Spain."

"For Spain?"

"On his honeymoon."

"I see. And when will he be back."

"In a week. Look, I have a suggestion or two to make."

Bernard did what Bernard always did and an hour later, he and Alice were signing some papers that gave them temporary custody of the baby, as its only known grandparents, pending a full adoption inquiry at a date to be confirmed. The boy would probably be discharged from the hospital in the morning unless there were any complications, and they would be free to pick him up as soon as they could after that.

It was dark when Bernard and Alice were back in the car and heading once more for Langton.

"I can't bear the thought of that tiny baby being all alone in a great big hospital without a mother or father to comfort him," said Alice.

"With any luck, this will be his last night there," Bernard reassured her, "and he probably won't remember it when he grows up. Do you remember your first day on earth?"

"Ha. Not in detail," said Alice. "But where is he going to go? I can't imagine Philip will want a newborn baby plonked on him when he gets back from honeymoon all set to start a new life with his bride."

"Philip deserves everything he gets," snorted Bernard. "But Meg doesn't."

"What are we going to do?"

"There is one option, darling," said Bernard, smiling across at Alice.

"Are you thinking what I think you're thinking?" she asked.

"That depends entirely on what you think I'm thinking, I suppose."

Alice was quiet for a mile or two.

"I'm 45. Isn't that a bit old to adopt?"

"My mother was 53 when she had Philip," he reminded her. "It runs in the family."

"You mean, we could try that trick again?"

"It's a thought."

"It's quite a nice thought," she said slowly. "We get to look after that wonderful baby without all the contractions, the baby gets a loving home and family, Meg gets her life to live as she planned, and Philip – what about Philip?"

"I can't decide about Philip," said Bernard. "I can't decide whether to keep it a secret from him too, so he never knows and can't put his foot in it and blurt it out to Meg one day, or..."

"Or what?"

"...or to nail him to the top of a telegraph pole by his gonads."

"Bernard!"

"Well, you did ask."

"Perhaps keeping the secret would be more conciliatory for us all. Should we though?" she added after a moment. "Doesn't he have the right to know that he's a father."

"Do you have a right to ruin his – and Meg's – life?"

"Not easy. But we have a little time to think about it," said Alice, then after a moment added: "You remember when we went to Mary's funeral?"

Bernard did. They were the only two mourners as the poor girl was laid to rest in Langton cemetery with a simple headstone that gave nothing much away.

"The poor girl," said Bernard. "She deserved more than life gave her."

"She did," said Alice. "And I promised myself there and then, that if we couldn't help her, then I would do everything to see that her son had a good life. I don't know what more we could have done for her, but it just feels as though we let her down. I feel that I let her down. We weren't even with her when she died."

"We wouldn't have been allowed anyway," said Bernard softly, laying a gentle hand on her shoulder.

"Perhaps not, but this mite has no one in the world. And if... well, if no one wants him, then *I* want him. Make it happen, Bernard. Tell me you'll make it happen."

And so next day, Bernard and Alice took some papers and documents to the hospital, signed some more papers, picked up the baby boy, and headed this time not to Langton but to Scotland. They deliberately arrived at the cottage after dark and stayed for three months, during which time, Alice and Bernard gradually began to appear in the village with a new baby. Soon afterwards, official adoption papers arrived in the post. Everyone who saw Alice with the baby congratulated her, thinking that she looked well and that being a mother again even at her age clearly suited her. They asked what the bonny bairn's name was.

"Sam," said Alice proudly. "Samuel Thomas Harvey."

Samuel Thomas Harvey pushed away his laptop and sighed. Sales were not quite as good as he had hoped. In fact, they were a lot worse and yet – he did a quick sum – even at this level and with scarcely any marketing yet, the venture would still produce more than enough for him to live comfortably on. He would not order the private jet just yet, but he was not going to be penniless by a long way.

"Ow is it looking up, chéri?" said Claudette, coming up and sitting at the table beside him in the tiny windowless office that they had rented.

"See for yourself," he opened up the screen and let her study the spreadsheet that he had just been sent.

She read it carefully for a while. "But that's very good. It's better than I expected."

"Not as good as I wanted," said Sam, "but I suppose it's not a bad start. If we can just get the next three products on stream, that will give us a much bigger impact on the market."

Clamshell powder that "made your skin feel rejuvenated", Sea salt brine effusion "to give your hair that ocean freshness", and Ginger and Turmeric pills "to add a spice of youthfulness to your whole being" were all close to production, enhancing the Atlantis brand and giving it a real chance when the TV advertising kicked in.

"We have it all ready to go now. It just needs a final push," said Sam.

"OK then. It is now," said Claudette, turning to face him.

"What is now?"

She got up from the chair and went over to the door, turned the key in the lock, and then came back towards him.

"OK, you have proved your worthy as a business and a doing partnerman. You have been a noronable gentlerman. My father will be happy and will back us up even more. So OK."

"You mean?"

"I am a woman of the word and I promised it," said Claudette. "I told you from at the beginning that I wanted to waiting to make sure that you were not just behind my money..."

"*After* my money," corrected Sam.

"As you like it. You have waited on me like a good boy. We have had some lovely together times and never even done the kissing. You have behaved very good. Now you are no need waiting more. And I, I am not any more needing to be the waiting."

She took hold of his tie and lifted him to his feet, took it off and then pulled him gently towards the sofa in the corner of the room by one of his shirt buttons.

"So now OK. I have been looking upward to this moment and I am sure that you have too."

"Oh yes indeed," said Sam in a small, breathless voice.

"Dinner can waiting." said Claudette, turning her golden sweatshirt inside out as she peeled it off over her head and began to unbutton her trousers. "Right here, right now, please..."

Sam made a small gurgling noise in the back of his throat and obeyed.

Clara had given up searching for family secrets. In fact, the last certificate that she had sent away for had been thrown in the bin unopened. It was only Sam's birth certificate and so unlikely to produce any bombshells, she reasoned.

Had she opened it, she would have found that Sam's "parents" Bernard and Alice, were in fact his adopted parents. That is all that the birth certificate would have given away, so she would not have discovered that his father was Philip or that Sam was not her cousin after all but her (half-) brother. Given that she and Sam had pulled back at the last minute on more than one occasion, it was probably as well to keep that fact from her. It meant she was spared some sharp panic attacks and a whole series of juicy nightmares.

In fact, Clara had enough to do to manage her own life now. Things had moved quickly since Peter left. *Trompette* looked at the revised figures that the accountants had supplied and decided that it was time to "disinvest" in *Allaire*. They were moving away from magazines and into online betting, which seemed far more profitable. The four members of editorial in London and the entire sales and advertising team were therefore put on immediate notice that in one month the magazine would close and they would all be out of work.

"Council of war," said Paul. "Red Lion at six."

By the time Paul, Marcia and Vincent had found a table and sat down to commiserate with each other, they were looking glum as they waited moodily for Clara to arrive.

"I suppose I shall have to go back to male modelling," sighed Vincent.

"Making little men out of balsa wood doesn't seem much of a career," said Marcia.

"And what will you do, Marcia?" asked Paul. "Painting?"

"I hear the Forth Bridge needs a new coat," said Vincent.

Just then there was a clatter at the door and Clara appeared through it and ran to the table.

"Well," she said as she sat down in the spare seat and took a gulp of her wine, "I've just spoken to Agnès – you remember Agnès, the woman in France from *Chic* magazine who thought that Peter was a prize chump and liked me – well, her outfit was trying to expand into what *Allaire* does but thought it was going to be too expensive and so cancelled the whole project. She has told me since that there was not a big enough hole in the market while we existed as competition. Well, I called her earlier to see if she had heard of *Trompette's* decision and if it changed anything for her and for them, and she didn't know, they hadn't heard and she said that was very interesting, so I told her that she could probably buy the name and goodwill of *Allaire* for a few centimes and then combine the title with their *Chic* magazine and – hey presto, no more competition, just combined resources and circulations and readerships and advertising and all sorts.

"So she just called me back as I was leaving and they have been in touch with *Trompette*, because she knows their managing director quite well – she was at university with her. And she thinks that my idea might fly. It's still a bit of a long shot, but it's the best news I've heard for days and if they do go for it and buy *Allaire*, we could end up being the English arm of *Chic, incorporating Allaire* or *Allaire and Chic* or whatever they call it, but I think that it could be very exciting, don't you?"

Clara took another drink and slumped back into her seat.

"Just run that past me again, would you?" said Vincent.

"Idiot," said Marcia. "That sounds wonderful – I think..."

"Does it have a chance, though? You've met Agnès," asked Paul.

"Well, she seems to think so. We can only wait..."

"We could turn it round a bit," said Vincent thoughtfully. "We could make it more medical, perhaps giving advice to people who get ill from too much zipping about on jets, and we could call it..."

"I think this is going to end in a punchline that will force me to hurt you," said Marcia.

"...we could call it *Aire Chic*. Ouch."

"I warned you. Now wait quietly like the rest of us."

They were still waiting. As Clara walked to her reception with Paul, the project had moved forward and was now at the legal contract stage, but neither side could see any major obstacles.

"I do hope it comes off," said Clara.

"Yes, I know what you mean. So do I. I've been looking at it and wondering the best way to go about it," said Paul.

"What are you talking about? Go about what?"

"Getting your wedding dress off. Isn't that what you meant? It looks complicated with all those ribbons and stuff, but I'm up for the challenge."

Clara hit him on the arm.

"You're not ripping this dress off if that's what you think. I want to take away something from today. If I go off you, at least I'll have a nice dress for next time."

Meg and Philip came up behind them.

"Did you say you've gone off him?" asked Meg. "You might have done it last week, and we could have saved a bit of money."

"No, he's still just about acceptable, but he's on a warning," said Clara.

"This is what my life will be like now, I suppose," said Paul. "Our first dance tonight is going to be *Under My Thumb*. So I'm told…"

Philip listened to the happy buzz of their conversation.

"Do you remember, Meg," he said, "when we were walking arm-in-arm along this very path from that church to that hall, only it was you wearing the wedding dress?"

"I do," said Meg.

"That's exactly what you said that day," said Philip. "Can't you be a bit more original?"

"Well I could marry someone else, I suppose. Is that original enough? Are you doing anything next Saturday, Paul?"

"I don't think I'll have learned to make tea or boil eggs exactly the way Cleopatra here likes them by then, so I'll probably still be practising," said Paul. "How about the Saturday after?"

"If that is all you think you need to practise, you have a shock coming," said Clara.

Philip laughed and turned to Meg. "Your boiled eggs aren't bad these days, but then we've had a lifetime to practise, haven't we? And we've had a fabulous time working on it too."

He seems his old self again, thought Meg happily. It's like a shadow has been lifted somehow. I don't even know what the shadow was, and I don't care. I just don't ever want it back. And the four went happily towards the rest of the day's festivities.

Philip thought that he might, at last, be able to shake off the sad undertone that still seeped through every feeling that he had. Since Bernard had gone there was nothing to remind him any more. He had forgotten for a long time what exactly it was behind the feeling of guilt. It was just a dull ache that came back every time he got near to or saw Bernard. But lately, he had remembered why he felt that he had done something wrong. Mary. He had said in his note to her when he left Brighton that he would try to go and visit her, but he never had. That must be it. That must be why he felt this way. He wondered what she was doing at that moment. He tried to picture her all these years later. She must be, what? in her mid-fifties by now. Probably had grandchildren. Was probably sitting in a nice house in Brighton with her husband, probably a doctor or a dentist, her children around her, looking after her. She was lovely, was Mary, he remembered.

He thought back to their kisses on the seafront, of walking along the pier with his arm around her, of their delightful nights in Aunt Vera's house. Beautiful memories. Beautiful memories for both of them. He would like to see her again but knew that was impossible. But, he thought, she is bound to be happy. Someone as nice as Mary would certainly find a nice man, who was nice to her. She was possibly even remembering those nice times they had together right now, just as he was. Perhaps she was seeing one of her children getting married today too. All was well. No need for him to worry. He hoped so. Somehow now that he had confronted it, the feeling of guilt and pain was lifting. He was so relieved. He could smile and laugh with Meg as before. His wonderful Meg. He should do everything he could to make her happy as Bernard had told him to long ago.

He saw Sam up ahead with Claudette on his arm, gazing into each other's eyes. They made a lovely couple, thought Philip. And they seemed to be making a go of their business. Who'd have thought that one of Sam's ideas would actually work? And did Clara say that they were getting married too? Well, well.

Everything was slotting into place. Everything always seemed to slot into place with families if you gave it long enough.

Shortly before they had to leave, Paul had a dance with Claudette, and Clara took to the floor with Sam. It was a romantic slow number.

"So things seem to have worked out OK for you and Claudette."

"Yes. Oh yes. Oh very yes indeed," said Sam.

"You realise that you are starting to talk like her, don't you?"

"What are you meaning?"

"But she was worth waiting for?"

"I can't believe I'm saying this, but she was. It made everything so very... I don't even know a word for it... *yabba-dabba-doo's* probably somewhere near."

"You see, I told you. A bit of wooing first makes everything better."

"It so absolutely does. And it's not only that. She's got all the moves. She's amazing. She does this thing where..."

Even wearing a fairly tight wedding dress Clara could still lift her knee just high enough to make Sam forget what he was about to say.

"Remember what I told you?" she whispered. "Some things are private. Just between the two of you."

"I'll try to remember," he said a little hoarsely. "I can't see very well at the moment. My eyes are watering."

"Never mind. Are you inviting Dawn to the wedding?"

"Do you think I should? I wonder if she'd come?"

"You could send her an invite that said 'Dawn minus one' "

"Oh yes. Oh, that's brilliant. I'll do it..."

"And when is the sad day when all the women in Britain wear black because Our Sam has been taken out of circulation?"

"I dunno but I think you've just taken the circulation out of me. They've gone all numb."

"Would you like some more?"

"No, no, don't trouble yourself. I'll be quiet. Claudette hasn't decided on the day yet. She says she'll let me know."

"So, er... does Claudette make all the decisions?"

"Every last one. And do you know? I don't mind at all. Claudette is very much my boss and I wouldn't have it any other way. I even told her I loved her after she proposed."

"And what did she say?"

" 'You are going to be marrying at me?' I think."

"No, what did she say when you said you loved her?"

"She said that I was a sweet doom. I still don't know what she means." He smiled as if remembering something. "And then she took hold of me by the... Ow!"

Clara wielded a mean knee when it came to stopping herself hearing what she would sooner not hear.

As the bride and groom left the reception a little later, arm-in-arm, Clara felt that she had come a long way. They were surrounded by a crowd of well-wishers as they walked slowly back towards the church where their car was waiting to whisk them off to a hotel near Heathrow for the night and then to their honeymoon villa in Provence in the morning. She looked around her and felt that she was surrounded by family ghosts. She could picture George and Rebecca with Thomas Otherwise Laker over there by the trees where they would have stood on their important days. They looked so happy as they gazed into each other's eyes and laughed at Thomas's antics. She saw Jane the matriarch walking unsteadily on Philip's arm after the funeral of that same Thomas, her own dear Thomas. Philip, Jane's son, who was really her grandson. They too came out into the bright sun. And where was the mysterious Susan? She was over the other side of the churchyard, looking a little bored and wanting to get away from this place even then. And there was a teenage Sam laughing as he talked to the prettiest bridesmaid and leaned across to whisper something in her ear, making her giggle and blush.

It seemed that Clara's whole family was present there all the time, for all time, all at the same time, down through the ages. Or almost her whole family.

Bernard and Alice had gone. Bernard had gone, taking his mysteries with him. Clara was Bernard now. The keeper of the secrets, the righter of wrongs, the fixer. Clara knew some of the things that time had hidden but not others, and she knew too that she would never know the rest because she would never again seek them out. She would never know the secret of 14 across. Let sleeping families lie. Lie to each other. Lie to hide. Lie to protect. This was Clara's story, and Clara was no longer about the past. Clara was now about the future.

And so she and Paul, and Sam and Claudette headed off towards their future lives together. And they all lived happily…

TO BE CONTINUED

Copyright

PAT DEVEREAUX
PUBLISHING WORKS
patdevereaux@mac.com

Printed in Great Britain
by Amazon

30504353R00235